**Praise for the Novels
of Juliet Blackwell**

Secondhand Spirits

"An excellent blend of mystery, paranormal, and light humor, creating a cozy that is a must-read for anyone with an interest in literature with paranormal elements."
—*The Romance Readers Connection*

"It's a fun story, with romance possibilities with a couple hunky men, terrific vintage clothing, and the enchanting Oscar. But there is so much more to this book. It has serious depth." —*The Herald News* (MA)

"Lily Ivory is a twenty-first-century Samantha Stevens, minus the nose w̶i̶g̶g̶l̶i̶n̶g̶. The story combines fun and seriousness for an e̶ Times

"Juliet Blackwell with the opening of th views

**The Art Lover's Mysteries
by Juliet Blackwell Writing as Hailey Lind**

Brush with Death

"Lind deftly combines a smart and witty sleuth with entertaining characters who are all engaged in a fascinating new adventure." —*Romantic Times*

continued ...

Shooting Gallery

"If you enjoy Janet Evanovich's Stephanie Plum books, Jonathan Gash's Lovejoy series, or Ian Pears's art history mysteries . . . then you will enjoy *Shooting Gallery*." —*Gumshoe*

"An artfully crafted new mystery series!"
—Tim Myers, Agatha Award–nominated author
of *A Mold for Murder*

"The art world is murder in this witty and entertaining mystery!"
—Cleo Coyle, national bestselling author
of *Holiday Grind*

Feint of Art

"Annie Kincaid is a wonderful cozy heroine. . . . It's a rollicking good read." —*Mystery News*

A CAST-OFF COVEN

A Witchcraft Mystery

Juliet Blackwell

AN OBSIDIAN MYSTERY

OBSIDIAN

Published by New American Library, a division of
Penguin Group (USA) Inc., 375 Hudson Street,
New York, New York 10014, USA
Penguin Group (Canada), 90 Eglinton Avenue East, Suite 700, Toronto,
Ontario M4P 2Y3, Canada (a division of Pearson Penguin Canada Inc.)
Penguin Books Ltd., 80 Strand, London WC2R 0RL, England
Penguin Ireland, 25 St. Stephen's Green, Dublin 2,
Ireland (a division of Penguin Books Ltd.)
Penguin Group (Australia), 250 Camberwell Road, Camberwell, Victoria 3124,
Australia (a division of Pearson Australia Group Pty. Ltd.)
Penguin Books India Pvt. Ltd., 11 Community Centre, Panchsheel Park,
New Delhi - 110 017, India
Penguin Group (NZ), 67 Apollo Drive, Rosedale, Auckland 0632,
New Zealand (a division of Pearson New Zealand Ltd.)
Penguin Books (South Africa) (Pty.) Ltd., 24 Sturdee Avenue,
Rosebank, Johannesburg 2196, South Africa

Penguin Books Ltd., Registered Offices:
80 Strand, London WC2R 0RL, England

First published by Obsidian, an imprint of New American Library,
a division of Penguin Group (USA) Inc.

First Printing, June 2010
10 9 8 7 6 5 4

Copyright © Julie Goodson-Lawes, 2010
All rights reserved

OBSIDIAN and logo are trademarks of Penguin Group (USA) Inc.

Printed in the United States of America

Without limiting the rights under copyright reserved above, no part of this pub-
lication may be reproduced, stored in or introduced into a retrieval system, or
transmitted, in any form, or by any means (electronic, mechanical, photocopying,
recording, or otherwise), without the prior written permission of both the copyright owner and the above publisher of this book.

PUBLISHER'S NOTE
This is a work of fiction. Names, characters, places, and incidents either are the
product of the author's imagination or are used fictitiously, and any resemblance
to actual persons, living or dead, business establishments, events, or locales is
entirely coincidental.
    The publisher does not have any control over and does not assume any re-
sponsibility for author or third-party Web sites or their content.

If you purchased this book without a cover you should be aware that this book is
stolen property. It was reported as "unsold and destroyed" to the publisher and
neither the author nor the publisher has received any payment for this "stripped
book."

The scanning, uploading, and distribution of this book via the Internet or via any
other means without the permission of the publisher is illegal and punishable by
law. Please purchase only authorized electronic editions, and do not participate
in or encourage electronic piracy of copyrighted materials. Your support of the
author's rights is appreciated.

To Robert B. Lawes,
just about the best dad a daughter ever had

Acknowledgments

Thanks as always to my wonderful agent, Kristin Lindstrom, and my great editor, Kerry Donovan. It is a privilege to work with you both.

To Sophie Littlefield, Steve Hockensmith, James Calder, Cornelia Read, and Tim Maleeny for all the writer talk. It sure is nice to know I'm not the only crazy one. And to Mario Acevedo for encouraging my witchy ways. To the Pensfatales for all the support and inspiration. Who knew a grog could be such fun?

To all the witches and wiccans who welcomed me and shared their beliefs and knowledge with pride and humor. Thanks to Karen Thompson and Peter Simoni for keeping my mind on art in addition to writing. And to my family—Jane, Bob, Susan, and Carolyn; to the whole Mira Vista Social Club; and to Oscar—who won't leave me alone.

We writers ask a lot of the people around us—friends and family alike. So special thanks to everyone for putting up with me, and to Jace and Sergio, especially. You two make this home a place of magic.

My mother says I must not pass
Too near that glass;
She is afraid that I will see
A little witch that looks like me,
With a red, red mouth to whisper low
The very thing I should not know!

—SARAH MORGAN BRYANT PIATT

Chapter 1

"I need something to guard against ghosts . . ." whispered the young woman slouching at the counter. She cast a nervous glance around my shop floor, empty but for racks upon racks of vintage clothes, cases of costume jewelry, and shelves lined with hats. "A protective . . . thingamajig."

"A talisman?" I asked.

"That's it."

"Talismans don't really guard against ghosts, per se—"

"Whatever." She shrugged. "It's better than nothing."

Her feathery bright pink hair put me in mind of a silly children's toy, the kind one might win after stuffing ten dollars' worth of quarters into the mechanical contraption at the Escape from New York Pizza parlor a few blocks down Haight Street from the store. But from the jaded look in her heavy-lidded amber eyes and the multiple piercings that marched along her left eyebrow, I suspected the overall effect she was after was "aggressively alienated youth" rather than "cuddly stuffed animal."

"You're a student at the San Francisco School of Fine

Arts?" I guessed as I opened the back of the glass display case and pulled out the black velvet–covered tray that held my rapidly diminishing collection of hand-carved wooden medallions. There had been a run on them lately.

"How did you know that?" Her eyes flew up to meet mine. *"Can you read minds?"*

"No." I shook my head and stifled a smile. "My assistant, Maya, goes to the School of Fine Arts. We've had a lot of students stop by in the past week or so asking for protection."

"Did I hear my name?" Maya emerged through the classic brocade curtains that separated the back room from the shop floor. Petite with delicate, unadorned features, she wore her hair twisted into thick locks, ending in a series of beads that clacked pleasantly against the silver rings and cuffs embellishing each ear. "Oh, hey, Andromeda."

"Um, hey," the customer said to Maya with a nearly imperceptible lift of her chin. Pink feathers swayed as she tilted her head in question. "Where do I know you from again?"

"Sculpture class," Maya answered. "We've met a few times."

"Oh, right—my bad. So, you've told her about the ghosts at the school?" Andromeda asked Maya. "The footsteps out in the hallways, the heavy breathing, doors opening and closing . . . ?"

"As a matter of fact, I have."

"It turns out that the main building"—Andromeda leaned across the counter toward Maya and me, her voice dropping to a fierce whisper—"*was built on top of an old cemetery.*"

"That's mostly a movie device," I pointed out. "It doesn't actually mean there are ghosts lingering."

"I've heard something, too, though, Lily, along with half the school," Maya put in.

The trepidation in my assistant's serious dark eyes gave me pause. Maya rarely asked for—or needed—anyone's help, and she retained a healthy dose of cynicism about the world of the paranormal. So I had been more than a little surprised a few days before when she asked me for a protective talisman, and even more so when she brokered an unusual deal with the school's provost, Dr. Marlene Mueller: If I could calm the students' fears of ghosts running amok in the campus hallways, I could help myself to the contents of a recently discovered storage room chock-full of Victorian-era gowns and frilly unmentionables.

As a purveyor of vintage clothing, I leapt at the chance.

There was only one fly in this supernatural ointment: I didn't know much about ghosts.

I'm a witch, not a necromancer. Few outside the world of magick appreciate the difference, but trust me: The two vocations don't necessarily involve the same skill set. My energy attracts spirits like flies to honey, but I can't understand a cotton-pickin' word they say. Interdimensional frustration is what I call it.

One thing I *do* know is that all of us walk over interred corpses all the time. People are born; they live; they die. It's been the same story throughout the millennia, and the physical remnants of our earthly sojourns— our bodies—have to go somewhere. If simply walking across a grave incurred a curse from beyond, none of us would live long enough to graduate from kindergarten, much less college.

"We're supposed to meet Dr. Mueller's daughter, Ginny, at the school tonight to take a look around," Maya told Andromeda.

"You're trying to see ghosts *on purpose*?" Andromeda gaped at both of us for a moment, then shivered as though a goose had just walked over her grave. "With Ginny Mueller. Huh. It figures. I hate that bi—" She stopped herself and looked up at me. "Never mind."

Looking down at the selection of talismans on the counter, she picked up a medallion, weighing the cool wooden disk in her hand. Each full moon, I make the talismans from the branch of a fruit tree, carving ancient symbols of protection and consecrating them in a ceremony of rebirth. However, just as in the natural world, there are few absolutes in the realm of the supernatural. The medallions are powerful sources of spiritual support, but they can't stop a determined force of evil on their own. I liken it to having a big dog at home: It might not chase off *every* ne'er-do-well, but your average mischief-makers go elsewhere.

"Does it matter which one I get?" Andromeda asked. "Or are they all the same, protection-wise?"

"They're—" I began.

Andromeda dropped the medallion and screamed, flattening herself against a stand of frothy wedding gowns. The rack teetered under the pressure.

"*What* the *eff* is *that*?"

Oscar, my miniature potbellied pig—and wannabe witch's familiar—snorted at her feet.

"That's Oscar, the store mascot." Maya smiled. "He sort of grows on you."

"He won't hurt you, Andromeda," I said to the pink-haired young woman still cowering against the pure white wall of silks and satins. Clearly she wasn't a pet person, or maybe she just wasn't a pet pig person. "Oscar, go on back to your bed."

Oscar snorted again, looked up at me, rolled his pink piggy eyes, and finally trotted back to his purple silk pillow.

Andromeda wiped a thin hand across her brow. "I'm a nervous wreck. Ghosts, now pigs . . . I just wish everything would get back to normal."

"This should help," I said, holding up a pendant carved with the ancient symbol of a deer—a powerful sign of support and protection—and an inscription in Aramaic. It hung on a cord made of braided and knotted silk threads in the powerful colors of red, orange, turquoise, magenta, and black. It suited her.

When Andromeda bowed her head to allow me to slip the talisman on, my gaze landed on the vulnerable curve of her pale, slender neck. Her vibrations were as clear as a bell: bright and frightened, almost tangible, and though I was only ten years her senior, I felt a surge of maternal protectiveness. Like her mythical namesake, who had been offered—bound and naked—as a sacrifice to the sea monster, this young Andromeda had a whole lot on her mind.

As we used to say back in Texas, she was scareder than a sinner in a cyclone.

But not only of a ghost, or even a pig.

Andromeda was scared of something altogether human.

"Don't you need any, ya know, ghost-hunting stuff?" Maya asked later that night after I managed to squeeze my vintage Mustang convertible into an impossibly small spot in front of Bimbo's on Columbus Avenue. Proud of my parking prowess, I led the way up Chestnut toward the San Francisco School of Fine Arts. The cool night air was fragrant with a whiff of salt off the bay, the aroma of garlic from nearby North Beach restaurants, and a heady floral perfume—early flowering brugmansia and jasmine were my guess. San Franciscans did like their flowers.

Slung over the shoulder of my vintage dress was my

trusty Filipino woven backpack, filled with a few talismans and charms; on the knotted cord at my waist was
my powerful medicine bag; and on my feet were easy-
to-flee-in Keds.

But no legitimate ghost-hunting stuff.

"Oops," I said. "Guess I left my catch-a-spirit kit in
Hong Kong."

"Very funny. Seriously . . . you don't have any special
equipment or anything?"

"Like what? Stakes and crosses?"

"Those are for vampires," Maya pointed out.

"Right. I get that mixed up. Stakes would be immaterial. Get it? Immaterial? Like ghosts?"

Maya gave me a pity smile. "The guys on that TV
show haul a lot of equipment around with them. Mostly
electronic stuff."

"No doubt they bought most of it at RadioShack's
annual clearance sale. Just how do they expect to cap-
ture energy on videotape?"

"I'm just saying"—Maya shrugged—"you should get
cable. It's very educational."

"But if I watched TV," I said with a smile, "when
would I find time to traipse around town looking for
phantoms?"

Besides, I thought to myself, *I don't need to watch a
videotape to know that ghosts are real.*

We arrived at the campus. Our footsteps echoed off
the ochre stucco walls of the covered walkway as we trod
upon earth red Saltillo tiles worn down by the feet of
scores of nuns, and now art students, for more than a century. The San Francisco School of Fine Arts was housed in
a gorgeous example of Spanish-revival architecture, complete with red-tiled roofs, intricate plasterwork, graceful arches, and a bell tower. So far the vibrations of this
convent-turned–art school felt largely positive . . . with
just enough negative thrown in to prove its claim of be-

ing a historic building. After all, bad stuff happens. Shadows are necessary in human life, if only to emphasize the light.

"Didja see anything yet?" asked an eager young woman leaning against the wall outside the heavy carved wood door of the school café.

"We just got here," said Maya. "Ginny, this is my new boss, Lily Ivory. Lily, meet Virginia Mueller."

"Hey. Call me Ginny," she said, thrusting out a hand to shake. She wore a once-white work apron over faded Levi's that clung to slender, boyish hips; her honey brown hair was cropped as short and shaggy as her paint-stained T-shirt. With her big eyes and piquant expression, Ginny had a sexy, pixyish style often found among free-spirited young artists; such were the kind of looks I had aspired to—but failed to achieve—when I was seventeen. Now, at the ripe old age of thirtysomething, I doubted the wood-sprite appearance would have aged well. Maybe that was why real elves are immortal.

Ginny's blue eyes swept over my vintage outfit, focusing on my empty hands. "Didn't you bring any, like, ghost-hunting stuff?"

"She left it in Honolulu," Maya said.

"Huh?"

"She doesn't use anything like that."

"Oh." Ginny looked disappointed. I couldn't help but notice more excitement than fear shining in her big eyes.

"I'm happy to take a look around, see what I can see," I said. "But if there *are* ghosts in the building, and you really want to communicate with them, you should probably bring in a skilled psychic."

"I thought *you* were a psychic."

"I'm no psychic; I'm . . . sensitive to things sometimes; that's all." I'm careful not to bandy about the title "witch." A lot of people were open to the idea of empaths, or people sensitive to the otherworldly. However, mucking around with special powers in order to alter reality on purpose—as in witchcraft—was another thing entirely.

"You don't have to be sensitive to hear this ghost," Maya commented.

"Most spirits aren't malevolent," I pointed out. "Has anyone been hurt?"

Ginny shook her head.

"Any property damage?"

"Only if you count when Sean Hitchins fell back on his butt into the vat of leftover clay."

"I missed that one," said Maya.

"It was classic." Ginny grinned. "We still have the imprint of his backside in the sculpture studio. You should totally check it out."

"You know," I interrupted, "my mama always used to say, *Don't trouble trouble till trouble troubles you.* All old buildings harbor a ghost or two. Couldn't y'all just ignore the noises?"

Maya and Ginny both gawked at me as if I had suggested they vote a straight Republican ticket. In San Francisco, Maya had informed me last week in no uncertain terms, artists did *not* vote for the conservative party.

"Have *you* ever tried finding the essence trapped in a hunk of stone with a *ghost* breathing down your neck at three in the morning?" Ginny demanded.

"Can't say that I have," I conceded.

"Anyway, I think I know who the ghost is . . . or was," Ginny said, pulling a tiny sketchbook from her back pocket. She handed me the pad, opened to a bold pencil sketch of a handsome young man with a heavy brow and dark, searching eyes. His hair was cut short, and he wore an honest-to-goddess high school letterman's jacket circa 1959—I had just acquired one very similar to it for the store.

A chill ran over me. If Ginny was seeing actual full-body apparitions, there could be more to this haunting than I thought.

"You've *seen* him?"

"What? Oh, nah, I was just looking into the history of the place. You know, like what tragedies occurred that might explain the noises. And I read about this guy's suicide in the old school newspaper—they had his photo and everything, and it seemed to fall into place."

Maya took the sketchbook from me and studied the picture. "What was his name?"

"John Daniels," Ginny said. "Supposedly he was, like, totally in love with this student painter. They were gonna get married and everything. But it was the early sixties, bohemia and all that. She walked away, or fell in love with someone else, or something, and he wound up throwing himself down the steps of the bell tower."

Maya and I glanced at each other before turning back to the sketch. His eyes seemed mournful.

"Can you imagine loving that strongly?" Ginny sighed. "It's *so* romantic."

"It's so melodramatic, you mean," muttered Maya. At my amused look she added, "What? He couldn't just find another girlfriend? Committing suicide is more stupid than romantic, if you ask me."

Ginny's gaze shifted to look over my shoulder.

"Uh-oh."

I swung around, half expecting to see John Daniels's lovelorn ghost.

Ginny snorted. "Here comes the Big Cheese."

Two men were walking down the hallway in our direction, heads bent as they talked in hushed tones. One wore a plush leather jacket and had a full head of snow-white hair. He looked to be in his early sixties, tanned and good-looking in a tennis-playing, gold-chain-wearing, no-comb-over-for-me kind of way. The other man was tall, lanky, and as pale as a proverbial ghost. He wore an ill-fitting brown corduroy sports jacket over outdated jeans and a baggy T-shirt.

They strode by our trio without a sideways glance and entered the café.

"Let me just take his order before we go. Be right back." Ginny slipped through the café doors after the men.

Maya and I followed, taking seats at an empty table near the entrance. It was almost midnight, but the cavernous café was abuzz with black-clad, body-pierced, and paint-spattered students. Some hunched over slim laptops and thick sketchbooks, while others downed yet one more caffeine boost before closing time while arguing over relevance and technique. A thin young man with a sparse goatee strummed on a guitar in the corner, crooning a vaguely Dylanesque tune. Plates and silverware clanged and clattered as the café staff finished washing up and putting away the last of the night's dishes.

I was happy to wait, savoring the collegiate ambience. I hadn't had the chance to go to college; in fact, I never officially graduated from high school. While other kids were memorizing French vocabulary and sweating over trigonometry, I'd been training to brew love potions and cast binding spells and interpret auras. I learned the uses and abuses of mugwort and wolfsbane and dragon's blood resin. I discovered that all sorts of "mythical" creatures were, in fact, as real as we humans. Most important, I came to understand how to call upon my spirit helper and my ancestors to focus my intentions in order to alter reality. My powers of concentration were great indeed.

I had learned all of this at the feet of a master: my adoptive grandmother, Graciela. I was lucky to have her. The small west Texas town I grew up in didn't much cotton to witches. Like many "gifted" people, I found my talents were more a burden than a boon. They had gotten me tossed out of my home, my high school, and then my hometown . . . all before I was old enough to vote.

What would it be like to hang out at midnight with like-minded folk who wanted to argue over the classics—or, in the case of the admittedly scruffy group of three at the next table, the relative merits of painters Jasper Johns and Gustav Klimt? I wondered if these kids had any inkling how fortunate they were.

I roused myself from my thoughts and followed Maya's gaze to the men standing at the counter, ordering lattes from Ginny.

"So, who's the Big Cheese?" I queried.

"Jerry Becker, one of the school's major benefactors. He's donating a cool million or so to help renovate the studio building. As daughter of the provost, Ginny's under strict instructions to be nice to him, which also means fending him off. Becker fancies himself a real ladies' man. He's been hitting on anyone and everyone even remotely young and female."

"I can't imagine he gets far with this crowd."

"You'd be surprised—he's very charming when he wants to be." Maya would have made a first-rate gossip in a small town, or a top-notch spy during the war. She had a knack for information gathering and on-the-spot, spot-on character assessments. "He arrived last week on his own private jet, flown by his own private pilot. But don't take my word for it. He'll work it into any conversation sooner or later. That and the fact that he's on a first-name basis with the staff at the Fairmont."

The Fairmont was a gorgeous, historic hotel perched atop fancy Nob Hill. It offered the kind of luxury accommodations that might cost upward of a thousand dollars a night, and it did so with a straight face.

"Must be nice," I said. "Where'd the money come from?"

"He founded a string of beauty schools throughout the South."

"Wait—this wouldn't be Jerry Becker as in Jerry's College de Beauté?" I pronounced it as I had heard it growing up in Texas: *Collage duh Bootay*.

"That would be he."

"Wow. We had one of those in my hometown. A lot of the girls in my high school went there. We ended up having more hairdressers than heads of hair to dress. How's he connected to the School of Fine Arts, of all places?"

"He's from San Francisco originally, I believe. Plus, his daughter's a student here. You met her this afternoon. Andromeda."

"With the pink hair?"

"The very one."

"Who's the other guy?" I asked, indicating the tall, gaunt fellow with him.

"That's Walker Landau. He's on the painting faculty."

"Any good?"

"Talented, but . . ." Maya trailed off with a shrug.

"Let me guess: an underappreciated genius who thinks a lot more of himself and his art than the rest of the world does?"

"Bingo. I'm surprised to see him with Jerry Becker. Landau's moody, to be kind. Probably manic-depressive, like a lot of artists. The Beckers move in high circles, with the beautiful people. Lots of parties, plenty of wardrobe changes. Seems an odd pairing."

As the men took their coffee drinks to a table by the window, another fellow strode into the café. A slight hush seemed to fall over the crowd.

Tall, dark, and handsome, he had a dashing air that made me think of an old-fashioned movie star. He reminded me of someone, but I couldn't put my finger on who. Probably Errol Flynn.

"Hey, Prof!" Ginny beamed from behind the sales counter. She glanced up at the clock hanging over the tea caddy. It was shaped like an artist's palette, with splotches of color in lieu of numbers, and paintbrushes in place of hands. "You made it right under the wire. We close at midnight. The usual?"

The man nodded, leaned one elbow on the brushed-zinc counter, and watched while Ginny busted some smooth barista moves. She preened, arched her back, played with her hair, and chatted—flirting big-time. The man smiled, and I heard his deep voice murmuring something; I couldn't make out the words, but the tone was alluring.

"And *that* is the newest sensation on campus," Maya said.

"He's very attractive."

"Smokin' hot," Maya agreed. There was a dreamy note in her voice, which was unusual for a woman who insisted romance was nothing more than a late-night fabrication of lonely women and hormonal men. "He joined the faculty this fall. In contrast to our friend Walker, this guy has done very well, represented by prestigious galleries in New York and L.A., as well as here in Union Square. Name's Luc, with a 'c.'"

"L-u-c? Is he French?"

"I don't think so. No accent, and according to rumor, he's got family around here. But he has an undeniable Continental flair; used to live in Europe."

Jerry Becker noticed the new arrival as well, and stood. Luc brought his espresso over to the table, one hand up in supplication. Luc's tone was the same as it had been with Ginny—deep, resonant, seductive.

Becker's was not. His voice grew louder and shriller until the words were bouncing off the café walls.

"And if you do, I'll kill you—do you understand me?"

The buzzing of the students, the strumming of the guitar, even the clatter of the dishes came to a sudden halt. We all held our collective breath.

Luc chuckled. I strained to hear him.

"I admire your passion, Jerry. But there's no need to go to the mats over this thing. Why don't we meet tomorrow and talk—in private?"

"This can't wait till tomorrow." Becker glanced down at a gaudy, expensive-looking gold watch that shackled his tanned wrist. "I'll meet you in your office in fifteen minutes."

Luc inclined his head, still smiling. "If you insist. See you then."

He nodded good-bye to Walker Landau before turning away.

As Luc passed my table, his dark eyes met mine, and our gazes locked. His vibrations were vivid, almost dazzling, but ultimately guarded. After a brief moment his lips formed a crooked, subtle smile, and he nodded his head, just barely.

"Evening," he said quietly.

"Hi," I said, cringing at the breathless tone of my voice.

He walked by, leaving a subtle, sweet citrus scent in his wake. I turned to watch him go.

"Nice view, huh?" Maya asked.

"What? Oh, yeah." I felt myself blush. As soon as the door closed behind him, the buzzing of the crowd came back twice as loud as before. "What do you suppose all that was about?"

Maya shrugged. "I don't know what's going on around here lately—everybody's at each other's throats. But this thing with Becker and Luc . . . ?" She shook her head. "All I know is that Becker wanted Luc to set

Andromeda up with a show at Luc's gallery off Union Square—a prestigious place—but Luc told him in no uncertain terms that he wouldn't do it."

"That hardly seems reason to issue a death threat."

"Becker's used to getting what he wants," Maya said, and stood so quickly her chair almost toppled over. "Let's go. I want to get this ghost thing over with. Kevin's waiting upstairs."

Maya caught Ginny's eye and gestured toward the door with her head. Ginny tossed her apron in a laundry basket and punched out, leaving the dishwashers to close up.

"Shall we?" Ginny said, and led the way into the main building.

There wasn't a soul in sight.

"Where is everybody?" I asked. "I know it's late, but the café was jammed."

"The former nuns' cells here on the first floor were converted into offices for administrators," Maya explained. "They're strictly nine-to-fivers. Most of the students are night owls, as you noticed, and will be working in their studios most of the night. But only the sculpture studios are in the main building. The rest of the student ateliers are housed in the new wing."

My ears were alert for untoward sounds, but the place was as quiet as the proverbial tomb. We reached the broad, tiled staircase that swept up to the second floor. On the landing waited a tall, open-faced young man wearing a security guard's uniform and a badge that read KEVIN MARINO.

He stood ramrod straight, shoulders back and chin lifted; the rough, tough security guard prepared to protect the womenfolk. I wasn't sure how he intended to do this, since as far as I could tell, the only threatening item in his possession was his rusty tin badge. I supposed tetanus could be a concern . . . eventually . . . if he stuck a miscreant with the badge's pin, but that wouldn't get him very far with a noncorporeal ghostly apparition.

"Hey," Kevin greeted us with a lift of his chin. He focused on me. "You the ghostbuster?"

"I'm Lily Ivory. Nice to meet you." We shook hands.

"Kevin." He paused. "Where's your, uh, ghost-huntin' stuff?"

"She left it in Honduras," Ginny said.

"Oh. Too bad. Well, all's quiet so far. There was a heckuva lot goin' on last night, though. Think it might be one o' them poultry heists."

"Poultry heist? Someone's stealing chickens?" I asked.

Maya nudged me. "He means *poltergeists*."

"Aah." No wonder I couldn't talk to the dead, I reflected. At times I could scarcely understand the living. "My mistake."

We started meandering down the second-floor hallway, which was laid out in a way similar to the first— a series of wooden doors leading off a broad, straight hallway—except that these roomier spaces were used as classrooms. I was enjoying the midnight outing— although I'm no artist, I am something of a night owl— but I had to admit that our foursome was one sorry excuse for a ghost-hunting team. Two anxious students; one security guard whose chief virtue, in my mind, was that he was not carrying a loaded weapon; and one bona fide witch who could not communicate with the dead, much less with the undead, if her life depended on it.

"Where'd you want to start?" asked Kevin.

"Why don't we start with the noisiest area," I suggested.

"Hmm. Lots o' those. Lots o' those indeed."

"Which one's the worst?"

"Well, now, that's hard to say. Darned hard to say."

Why would he drag this out? Was he lonely, or afraid? I forced myself to smile. "Pick one."

"The bell tower?"

"You tell me."

"Do you think . . ." Maya interrupted. "Do you think maybe we could start with the studios?"

I reminded myself that most humans—*normal* humans—aren't as sanguine as I about the supernatural. All structures have some ghosts, the whispery remnants of the souls who have passed through. Most consist of little more than residual feelings and fleeting emotions, not the apparitions of lore. And most aren't a problem. They tend to keep a low profile, noticed only by those who, like me, are . . . different. A ghost's main impact on the human world is to lend its vibrations to a place, which might make that place warm and welcoming, or cold and off-putting.

As someone who has lived a mostly solitary life, I revel in these vibrations, which make me feel connected to the past, to those who have gone before. The same feeling drew me to old clothes, which also carry a fragment of the energy of those who have worn them, but most people go through life unaware of the overlay of the past, which is just as well. On the rare occasions when they make the connection, it can be profoundly disturbing.

"Has there been activity in the studios?" I asked.

"Not really."

"Then let's not waste our time. Straight to the bell tower, I say. Let's get to the bottom of this. But listen, you really don't have to come along if you don't want to." I looked in turn at three apprehensive faces. "Any of you. I can do my best to slay the critter, then meet you all back in the café."

"I'm coming with you." Maya wasn't the kind to back down.

"Me, too," said Ginny.

"Yeah, we got your back," said Kevin.

I nodded. "Okay, great. Just remember, ghosts aren't typically malevolent. Usually they're merely a remnant of a past life, of someone who used to be just as human as the next person. Don't be afraid. Now, let's go see if we can stir up anything in the bell tower."

I may not tote around electronic equipment, but I never leave my house unprepared. My ever-present medicine bag was tied to the braided belt at my waist, and in my backpack were newly consecrated talismans for my companions. I knelt and extracted three from my backpack.

"Just in case," I said, handing them out.

Maya and Ginny accepted them gladly, but Kevin looked doubtful until Maya took the medallion and hung it around his neck. By the way he looked at her, I suspected he was the sort of "pal" who wanted to be more. They might make a cute couple. She was serious and delicate in stature; he was tall and lanky, and easygoing. But I doubted he was smart enough for my wise-beyond-her-years assistant.

"Let's go," I said, leading the way down the corridor, which ended in a T not far ahead.

Suddenly I heard something—the muffled sound of a woman weeping.

"Ya'll hear that?" I whispered.

"Yeah," Ginny said, "but that's not what we usually—"

I gestured for them to stay where they were and peered around the corner. A young woman leaned against the wall, crying. Pink feathers swayed as her shoulders shook.

"Andromeda?" I said, approaching her. "What's wrong?"

She sniffed, wiped her arm over her wet face, threw her shoulders back, and looked up at me, as though she hadn't been sobbing a moment ago.

"Nothing. Hey," she said to the others with a slight lift of her chin.

"Hey," said Kevin, mimicking her chin-rise.

"Hey," repeated Ginny.

"Hey," echoed Maya.

I gritted my teeth. I've been in California only a couple of months, so perhaps with time I'll take to the local manner of exchanging "heys" instead of actual greetings. But really . . . would a simple "How are you?" or "Pleased to meet you" kill these people?

"Gotta bounce," said Andromeda, rushing past us. "Later."

We watched her retreat down the corridor and disappear around the corner.

"Drama queen," Ginny muttered under her breath.

At my questioning look, she shrugged and clarified. "Daddy's little girl has to get everything she wants, exactly when she wants it. I should be so lucky."

"This way to the tower?" I asked, not wanting to engage in student rivalries.

Kevin nodded. "Straight ahead and to the right."

I set off down the hall, the security guard behind me, Maya following him, and Ginny taking up the rear.

I was starting to wonder if we would find anything at all. From the students' stories, I had expected to sense something the moment I set foot on campus, but so far the only odd behavior I'd seen came from flesh-and-blood humans. Maybe it was the spooks' night off, or maybe the students had freaked themselves out with too little sleep, too much caffeine, and forlorn tales of lost loves—a potent brew, I knew from personal experience.

We turned the corner into a short hallway that ended in a small, windowless square room at the foot of a circular stone stairwell.

Ginny screamed.

Chapter 2

Jerry Becker—multimillionaire, womanizer, Big Cheese—was sprawled faceup on the hard stone tile. His eyes were open, unblinking, staring into nothingness. Blood seeped from his thick white hair and pooled under his head, looking black in the dim light from the hallway. I felt a shimmering energy emanating from the blood. Essence of life.

"Eeuuuwww! Ew, ew, *ew*!" Ginny started dancing around like someone who'd gotten caught up in a huge spiderweb, flailing her arms and shuddering in an attempt to shake off the sight of the dead man. "Yuck, yuck, *yuck*!"

"*Ginny*," I said through clenched teeth, "you need to calm down."

"Ew! Gross! Yuck!"

I looked at Maya imploringly. Her trusty cell phone in one hand, already ringing 911, she wrapped the other arm around Ginny's slender shoulders and started murmuring to her, leading her over to a bench by the wall.

Kevin was silent, but his ashen face spoke volumes. He stood as if rooted in place, swaying slightly in his size-twelve work boots.

"Why don't you sit down, too, Kevin," I said, worried that at any moment he would topple over in a dead faint. "I'll handle this."

Despite my brave words, inside I felt like screaming or fainting right alongside them. I stroked my leather medicine bag for strength and concentrated on steady breathing. It might seem strange that finding a dead body could throw me so off balance, but dealing with creatures from other dimensions is not *at all* the same as dealing with sudden death. The former is a state of being, whereas the latter is a process—in this case, a violent one. I didn't have much experience with it, and I didn't want any. But I had to be sure Becker wasn't still alive. He looked dead as a doornail, but if finding a dead body was bad, mistaking a live person for a dead one was much worse. Talk about your self-fulfilling prophecies.

I studied Becker for a moment, trying to work up my nerve. I noticed a red mark around his neck, as though the chain of his heavy gold medallion had been pulled tight. One leg was twisted at an abnormal angle, obviously broken. On top of his chest was an open briefcase, and papers were scattered around the body like supersized confetti.

I took a deep breath, reached out, and touched his cheek.

Cold. The chill beyond life.

I closed my eyes and willed myself to focus on his vibrations. I sensed anger, but no fear. My gaze shifted to the steep stone staircase. Had Becker simply tripped going up them, struck his head as he tumbled, and lost consciousness before he knew what was happening? Or had he been pushed, and his last emotion was the simmering anger I sensed? And what was he doing in the bell tower in the first place?

The sound of far-off sirens approaching wrenched me from my thoughts.

Turning to look behind me, I glanced at Maya, Ginny,

and Kevin. They sat huddled together on a wooden bench against the wall, eyes wide and faces green.

"Was it the ghost?" Maya whispered.

"*You* said they weren't malevolent," accused Ginny, flinging her arm and pointing at the corpse in high dudgeon. "That—ew! *That* looks like malevolence to me!"

"There are exceptions to every rule," I mumbled. "Still, we don't know that a ghost did this."

Somewhere up the stairs, a door creaked open and slammed shut. My eyes flew toward the sound, but the stairs were empty and I couldn't see around the curve.

Loud steps echoed in the tower, descending toward us.

"You guys hear that, right?" Kevin said, looking about. "It's not just me?"

"It's not just you," Maya whispered.

"It's coming back!" Ginny yelled.

"Hush, all of you!" I said sternly, trying to get a bead on what might or might not be there. I heard loud, harsh breathing, some of it my own. But not all.

I moved to the center of the hallway and stood still, arms outstretched, trying to discern what in the world—or beyond this world—we were dealing with.

The breath became a low moan, bouncing off the corridor walls, growing in intensity, surging and swirling until it felt as though it were inside my head. The walls began to seethe with the sound, swelling and waning as though they were made of a pliable membrane rather than stucco and stone. Everything vibrated with sensations of anger, despair, and fierce jealousy.

"This is crazy!" Kevin sprang to his feet. "Let's *go*!"

He grabbed Maya's hand and yanked her down the hall, Ginny close on their heels.

"Run, Lily!" Ginny yelled. "Come *on*!"

The moaning became a roar, filling the hallway until

it screamed like a runaway freight train. And just as suddenly it stopped.

I turned tail and ran.

I may be a witch, but I'm no fool.

Within half an hour the first black and white police units to respond to Maya's 911 call were joined by the medical examiner, the coroner, the photographers, and the fingerprinters. Now I knew where all those taxes went: There must have been two dozen official personnel responding to this call in the middle of the night. Was this routine, or did it have to do with the identity of the victim, the Big Cheese?

To make the evening complete, I spied a familiar face. As always, he wore his version of a uniform: a thigh-length black leather jacket over khaki chinos, a black T-shirt, and black running shoes.

"Well, well," said Carlos Romero, SFPD homicide inspector. "If it isn't Lily Ivory."

"Inspector Romero," I said with a nod.

"You wanna tell me what you're doin' here in the middle of the night? Or wait—is this the witching hour?"

Romero and I met not long ago when he thought I might be involved in a suspicious death. One thing had led to another, and I wound up spilling the beans about being a witch. I've regretted it ever since.

"Witching hours vary. They're culturally defined," I said primly, as if lecturing an Anthropology 101 class. Carlos had that effect on me.

"That a fact? You know, that's what I like most about this job," Carlos mused. "I learn something new every damned day."

"My friend Maya goes here." I ignored his sarcasm. "The students have been hearing strange noises and footsteps, that sort of thing. I said I'd try to see if it was a ghost."

"Okay...." Skepticism shone in his dark eyes. Romero was not much taller than I—short for a man—but he carried himself as if he were six foot four. Homicide was a tough beat, and even as beautiful a city as San Francisco suffered the modern plagues of drugs, crime, and random violence. "Did you find said ghost?"

I shook my head. "Just the ... body."

"And now you're going to tell me the victim was killed by a ghost?"

"Of course not."

But I wondered. Might a ghost have pushed Becker down the stairs? We did hear a door slam, followed by footsteps, the breathing, and the moaning ... but ghosts were spirits, and spirits had no mass. As far as I knew, spectral hands would have passed right through Becker. He might not even have noticed. But then again, if a powerful spirit could open doors and windows, what would keep them from going after a human?

I was out of my league. I really didn't know that much about ghosts.

Still, even assuming a ghost *could* kill someone, why would it? Ghosts might frighten folks, of course; mess with their minds, sure thing; damage property—especially when remodeling projects disturbed their surroundings—why not? But they rarely had anything to gain by murder. And why target Jerry Becker, who had only recently flown into town?

No, I doubted it was a ghost. If only it were that simple. Truth was, I sensed something else within these walls; something beyond a ghost. A presence any sane person would fear. Something I didn't want to admit to myself, much less to homicide inspector Carlos Romero.

An evil energy, perhaps even ... a demon.

"Was Becker killed in the fall?" I asked. "Or could it have been a heart attack, something like that?"

"Why don't you just tell me everything you saw and

did here tonight, from the start?" Romero liked to ask the questions, not answer them.

I gave him the rundown: seeing Becker in the café with Walker Landau, the argument with Professor Luc-with-a-"c," and our brief ghost-hunting tour, including running into Andromeda near the bell tower stairs. He jotted notes on a thick pad of paper that had molded to the contours of his hip pocket.

"Hi there, Lily," boomed a deep voice behind me. I looked around to see Romero's partner, Inspector Neil Nordstrom, approaching us with a huge smile on his face. "How you doin'?"

"Hi, Neil," I said. "Nice to see you. Did your sister decide on that French maid's outfit?"

"She's still wavering."

"It looked great on her. Thanks for bringing her by the shop."

"Sure thing. She was happy to find it. Hey, I was thinking, do you have any outfits from the twenties? There's this big event coming up right—"

"If old home week's over," Romero interrupted, glaring at his partner, "we've got a death to investigate."

"Right you are, big guy," Nordstrom said with a wink and a jaunty salute. After I'd been cleared in the last murder, Neil had brought his sister by my shop, and we wound up chatting. He was a good guy who had a habit of bursting into song when the mood came over him, which struck me as hilarious, given that he was built like a Norwegian linebacker. Now that he wasn't threatening to haul me off to jail, I quite liked him.

I liked Romero, too, for that matter. He was smart, and no doubt a top-notch cop. I felt about police officers a lot like I did about the folks who worked urban sanitation systems: Their jobs needed to get done, but *I* sure as heck didn't want to deal with sewage of either the raw or the human variety. I was grateful they had my back.

"What did you do when you found the body?" Romero continued.

"I felt his neck, looking for a pulse."

"Find one?"

I shook my head. "He was cold to the touch."

"Cold? But you said you saw him fifteen minutes earlier, at the café."

"Not cold as in rigor mortis. Cold as in he had kicked his last bucket."

He lifted an eyebrow.

"He felt dead, Inspector. I don't know how else to describe it. He felt cold and dead."

"Did you see or hear anything else? Anything at all?"

"I didn't see a thing." I stopped there, not sure whether I wanted to admit to what I'd heard. Romero picked up on my hesitation.

"You didn't see anything. Did you *hear* anything?"

"Noises."

"Could you be more specific?"

"A door opening and closing, footsteps on the stairs, heavy breathing."

"Heavy breathing?"

I nodded. "Abnormally heavy. Moaning. And then the sound of something falling down the stairs."

"Something fell? What was it?"

"I don't know. I turned tail and ran, scareder than a cat in the dog pound."

A slight smiled hovered on Carlos's face. "A what, now?"

"Cat. In a dog pound. You know, scared witless."

"Was someone after you?"

"I didn't see a soul. If something was there, it wasn't a who. It was a what."

"A ghost?"

"Ghost, spirit, some sort of entity." I shrugged, not wanting to invoke the name of demon. "Or maybe it was all some kind of practical joke. I really don't know what caused the sounds; I just heard them. I was here to investigate some noises. We heard some noises, we found a body, and then we heard some more noises. You wanted to know everything; that's everything."

Romero nodded and blew out a breath. "Okay, thanks. I take it you're still at the same place in case I need to ask more questions?"

I nodded. "Aunt Cora's Closet, on Haight near Ashbury."

"Sounds like Neil, here, remembers the way," Romero said with a sarcastic twist of his lips.

"She has an iron maiden outfit that would suit you, Carlos," Neil suggested.

Romero had the grace to smile.

"Is that all you need from me tonight?" I asked. "I don't mean to rush you, but I've got a miniature potbellied pig waiting for me at home."

Oscar wasn't always a potbellied pig. In his natural state he resembled a cross between a goblin and a gargoyle, or maybe a gnome, but he appeared that way only to witches, and select witches at that. He was not, at any rate, conventionally handsome. His tough hide was greenish gray; he had a short snout, big batlike ears, and scaly claws on his hind legs. His hands, though, were outsized and humanlike. He was not big, at full height barely reaching my belly button.

He had barged into my life not long ago, thanks to a powerful witch named Aidan Rhodes. I wasn't sure what to make of either of them, but somehow the dynamic duo had managed to assign Oscar as my witch's familiar before I knew what hit me.

Before arriving in San Francisco a scant three months ago, I had traveled the world for years, always solo, and I'd fought against the enforced companionship of a familiar. But now . . . I still didn't trust Aidan as far as I could throw him, but I had to hand it to the little porker; Oscar had worked his way into my heart.

At the moment, the little fella was crouched on top of my old Wedgewood stove, where he was frying a grilled cheese sandwich, my old red-checked apron tied around his neck like a bib and a big spatula in hand. Melted cheese seeped out from between the slices of bread and sizzled on the hot cast-iron pan.

"Mistress!" he greeted me in his gravelly voice. "I made my own dinner!"

"I fed you hours ago, Oscar. It's nearly two in the morning." I spied the crusts of another sandwich on a plate, evidence that this wasn't his first go-round with the skillet.

"I woke up and you weren't here."

Oscar gets hungry when he's nervous. Or scared. Or happy. Or unhappy. He was pretty much a hungry guy all the way around.

"Cheese is good." He snorted happily. "Not stinky cheese. American cheese and Wonder Bread. Builds strong *bodies*. And butter! Heh, butter. I said 'butt.' "

He also wasn't the most mature familiar in the world.

I smiled and tried to ignore the mess he'd made. It was my own fault for teaching him to cook before training him to clean up.

"Oh, that *man* called earlier. It's on the machine."

My heart sped up, just a tad. "What man?"

"That man. The one who thinks I'm a dog."

"Max doesn't think you're a dog, Oscar. He just thinks you're cute. To be more precise, he thinks your piggy form is cute. I'm sure if he saw you in your natural state he would think you were very frightening indeed."

Oscar shrugged and refused to meet my eyes. Apparently familiars don't like to share.

I crossed over to the counter and hit the Message button on the sleek black machine I had installed just last week.

"It's Max. Just wanted to say hi ... let you know I was thinking about you. Are we still on for brunch tomorrow? Bring your appetite; leave the pig."

Max Carmichael was a journalist and a self-proclaimed "mythbuster" who didn't hold much with magick, much less witchcraft. Typical of me to develop a crush on a man who doubted everything I held near and dear.

But that voice ... Max's voice was deep and sexy, with a hint of weariness that made me want to tuck him into bed ... and curl up right next to him. Some people had bedroom eyes; Max had a bedroom voice.

Like the man in the café tonight—Luc something or other. What was his story? Had he met Jerry Becker as planned? Had they struggled, and Becker fell—or was pushed—down the stairs? Could it be just that simple?

Or maybe the tightly wound Andromeda, impatient for her inheritance, did her father in. If the daily stories in the newspaper were any indication, people who had everything—looks, intelligence, talent—succumbed to greed and threw their lives away like that all the time.

True, there was at least one supernatural entity lurking somewhere at the School of Fine Arts. But the mere presence of spirits didn't mean they were guilty of anything. From what I knew of humans, they were much more likely than a ghost to exact that kind of revenge.

Fortunately, none of this was my problem. Inspectors Romero and Nordstrom were on the case, and they were welcome to it.

I sat at my small bistro table and chatted with Oscar while he ate his sandwich. For reasons known only to my familiar, he was determined to teach me the ins and outs of the rules of baseball, and though I'm a reasonably intelligent person, I was having trouble following. Afterward, I insisted he help clean up the kitchen, tucked him into his sleeping cubby above the refrigerator, took a long shower with handmade rosewater soap I bought at my favorite botanicals stand at last Thursday's Civic Center farmers' market, and climbed into my old brass bed.

Unbidden, my thoughts turned to the empty, open eyes of the recently deceased Jerry Becker . . . so I tried to distract myself by visualizing Max's light gray gaze and the adorable, quizzical way he looked at me as though trying to see beyond the surface.

Just as I was dozing off, the mattress dipped as if someone had sat down on the other side of my double bed. I opened my eyes and slowly looked over my shoulder. There was nothing visible except a slight indentation on the otherwise-smooth comforter.

Great.

Uninvited spirits in my home. And in my bed.

I wasn't afraid, exactly, but I sure wasn't in the mood for this kind of harassment. I rose, grabbed a powerful amulet off my mirror, held it in my right hand, and walked the perimeter of the room in a clockwise direction, chanting:

> *I have done my day's work,*
> *I am entitled to sweet sleep.*
> *I am drawing a line on this carpet*
> *Over which you cannot pass.*
> *Powers of protection, spirits who clear,*
> *Remove all those who don't belong here.*

Demons may spook me, but your standard nighttime mares I could handle.

Still, I lay awake for a long time, wondering who had sent them.

And why.

Chapter 3

The next morning, I wrapped myself in the purple silk kimono I use as a robe and snuck down the back stairs from my second-floor apartment to Aunt Cora's Closet to go "shopping" in my own store.

Oscar trotted along at my heels, his snout studded with crumbs from the fresh blueberry muffins we had made for breakfast. Oscar's baking was as enthusiastic as his sandwich grilling, and the wonder was that after he finished "mixing" the ingredients, there was enough batter still in the bowl to make a dozen muffins.

I ate one and a half; Oscar polished off the rest.

Halfway down the stairs, as was his custom, my familiar assumed his disguise as a potbellied pig. Like most of his kind, he was adept at keeping his true identity a secret. I was grateful for this small favor: I had enough trouble explaining *myself* to my new friends, much less a shape-shifting critter like Oscar.

One of the best parts about being in the vintage clothing business was that each day began with a game of dress up. Surveying the many and varied outfits at my disposal, I felt like a kid raiding her mother's closet—not that I had ever actually done such a thing. If memory served, my mother's wardrobe held little more than cheap cotton housedresses, stained and shapeless, while there was nothing more exotic in my grandmother's closet than the black lace mantilla she wore on special occasions and a half-dozen pairs of sensible lace-up shoes, size five narrow.

Happily, my fictional aunt Cora had a kick-ass wardrobe.

Housed in the first floor of an 1890 Victorian typical in this part of San Francisco, my store was jammed with vintage clothing I had procured from every source imaginable. A few gowns dated back as far as the end of the nineteenth century; these were kept in a special display behind the counter, their aged silk too delicate for repeated try-ons. A handful of frilly, fragile specimens adorned the walls in lieu of art, their gossamer skirts and hand-embroidered bodices lending the space an authentic closetlike feel.

Crowding the main floor were racks of everything from 1930s cotton slips to 1950s prom dresses to 1980s polyester jumpsuits. Due to space limitations, I carried only women's clothes, but I interpreted this loosely. One whole alcove was dedicated to items that could be used for fantasy costumes: old uniforms, tuxedos, and cowgirl accoutrements. In the display cabinets at the register was enough glittery costume jewelry to please a magpie, along with my carved talismans. Next to the communal dressing room, stands teemed with hats of all sorts, from French berets to veiled church crowns; and plentiful shelves displayed white cotton gloves, alligator purses, a small collection of classic shoes, and even more hats.

In one rear corner of the shop floor was a little herbal stand belonging to my colleague, and new friend, Bronwyn Parrish. Bronwyn calls herself a witch and belongs to a friendly local coven, but as far as I can tell, her magic lies primarily in her open heart and loyal temperament. Bronwyn arrived in the Haight as a flower child—come-lately in 1972. She missed the neighborhood's hippie heyday by a couple of years, but she made up for lost time. By her second glass of wine, she'd start telling entertaining stories of interludes with famous rock musicians, social activists, and poets. Bronwyn was the first person I met when I arrived in San Francisco, and she had welcomed me with open arms—literally. She was a hugger.

I cherished my new friendships with her and with Maya, but I was still trying to get used to it all. . . . I had spent my life holding myself apart from people, and now for the first time I was establishing a home and becoming part of a community.

But now, also for the first time, I had something to lose.

My mind cast back to the events of last night. A chill ran through me at the visual I couldn't shake: a dead man, his life's blood seeping onto the hard stone. My uncomfortable fascination with the shimmering blood worried me—it was another sign of something amiss, an evil spirit at play within the walls of the school.

A suspicious death and supernatural entities. Never a good combo.

I tried to shake it off as I flipped through gauzy patterned summer dresses from the mid-fifties. Thinking of the changeable spring weather and my brunch date with Max, I decided upon one of my favorite styles: an early 1960s sleeveless dress with a pinch waist and wide skirt. The turquoise chintz was detailed with tiny white Xs in a wide embroidered band along the neckline, sleeves, and hem. A thin cloth-covered matching belt sat at the waist. I paired it with a cream-colored three-quarter sleeve cashmere cardigan, only one size too small.

For my feet, however, I chose sensible lavender Keds from my own closet. I adore vintage clothing but insist on shoes I can move in. As last night had demonstrated, you just never knew when you might have to outrun an out-of-control spirit or two.

I pulled my long, straight dark hair back into its customary ponytail, swiped a coat of mascara on my lashes, and applied a dab of lip gloss. Then I prepared to open Aunt Cora's Closet the way I did every morning—by making sure the crowded racks were neat, putting cash in the register, and giving the display windows and the glass cabinet a quick swab with vinegar and newspaper.

But because I was a witch, my morning ritual included a little something extra. Chanting a simple cleansing spell, I sprinkled salt water around the edges of the shop, working in a widdershins, or counterclockwise, direction; then I used a sage bundle to purify, working clockwise. Finally, I lit a white hand-dipped beeswax candle and recited a quick incantation for protection. I flipped the door sign to OPEN just a few minutes before ten.

A thin young man sat on the curb outside the store, his pale face turned into the sunshine of the chilly, late-winter day.

"Good morning, Conrad," I said as I picked up the local newspaper from the doorway.

"Duuuuuude," Conrad said as he craned his neck backward to meet my eyes. His own were red and heavy lidded from what I could only suppose were illegal substances. "What up?"

"Not much," I said, deciding against launching into tales of last night's events. It was awfully early. "You?"

"Dude, same old same old."

"The Con," as he called himself, was one of hundreds—or was it thousands?—of young people who flocked to San Francisco in search of open-mindedness and a bohemian lifestyle, only to wind up on the streets begging for food and money. The Haight-Ashbury neighborhood abounded with them; they tended to refer to themselves as gutter punks, but I just thought of them as lost souls. In the immortal words of Janis Joplin, who once lived just a few blocks from here, *Freedom's just another word for nothing left to lose.*

I knew that truth only too well.

Conrad slept in nearby Golden Gate Park and was accustomed to sitting outside my store a sizable portion of every day. Most mornings he performed a small task for me, such as sweeping the sidewalk or helping to carry in new merchandise, and I made sure he had some breakfast. I had repeatedly offered to help get him off whatever he was on, but he wasn't ready yet. My magick was powerful, but so was the human spirit. External powers could only take a person so far without a genuine desire for lasting change.

I went back into the store, spread the *San Francisco Chronicle* on the display counter before me, and hitched one hip onto a tall stool behind the counter. Jerry Becker's death had made the front page; apparently the Big Cheese rated the kind of press coverage rarely granted to more banal victims of gang violence and drug deals gone sour. The article gave more information on Becker's financial clout, but otherwise repeated most of what I already knew. What caught my eye was the byline of a related article, an in-depth analysis of Becker's business dealings, by Max Carmichael.

The Max who had called last night. The Max who was taking me out to brunch today. True, San Francisco was a small city, but what were the chances he would be investigating the man I happened to find dead last night?

The bell over the front door tinkled as it opened, and I jumped about two feet off my stool.

"Guilty much?" asked Maya with a smile.

"Sorry," I said, gathering my wits. "Deep in thought."

Maya came to stash her bag under the counter and

took a gander at what I was reading. "Aah, no wonder. Wait—this article is by Max Carmichael—is that *your* Max?"

"He's not *my* Max." I blushed.

Some folklore contends that witches can't blush, but I put a lie to that assertion. I had plenty of classic witch traits: I couldn't cry, I floated on water, and I knew who was on the phone before I answered it. But I certainly could blush.

"Uh-huh," Maya said, not believing me for a second.

We both looked up as the bell sounded again.

Andromeda.

I almost didn't recognize her. Last night's pink feathers had been replaced by jet-black hair gelled into a spiky do.

"Hey," she said, lifting her chin in greeting.

Andromeda had learned her father had died just a few short hours ago and then . . . what? Went home to dye her hair? The last time *I* made a significant change to my hairstyle I was still in high school. On the other hand, everyone mourned in their own particular way. If personal grooming made Andromeda feel better about a loved one's violent death, who was I to second-guess her?

"So you heard what happened last night?" Andromeda demanded.

Maya nodded. "We—we were the ones who found him."

Maya cast a quick glance over at me. What had been a momentary trauma for us—seeing a body at the bottom of the stairs—was a family tragedy for Andromeda. Her father had been killed.

"I'm so sorry, Andromeda," I said. "Is there anything we can do?"

Andromeda shook her head. "I just can't believe it. The police asked me what I was doing there. They didn't believe me about the ghost. Dad and I . . . We had a fight, just a few minutes before. Otherwise I would have been with him . . . and it would have gotten me, too." She looked at me, big amber eyes confused, questioning, demanding. "I thought you said ghosts don't hurt people."

"They don't, usually. We still don't know—"

"I wanna kill it. Can you kill a ghost? Is there a version of that? Can you help me?"

"Help you?"

"Kill it."

"Um . . ."

"Hurt it, then. I wanna hurt it, at least." Tears came to her eyes; her voice fell, hushed. "He was my father. I gotta do *something*, for real; I'm so whack right now."

Oscar trotted over at that moment, distracting her. Andromeda startled, but this time Oscar kept his distance, staying on the far end of the counter. He lay down and then rolled over onto his back, displaying his pale piggy belly in a newly perfected, adorable move.

"I guess the pig really is pretty cute," she conceded. When Andromeda smiled, she was transformed into the young woman she was, complete with a charming dimple in one cheek.

I had to hand it to Oscar. He might be a clueless familiar when it came to things such as cooking, but like most pets, he was good at knowing who needed solace.

"Anyway, I figured if you could make magic necklaces, you'd know how to get at a ghost."

"This really isn't my specialty," I said. "Besides, we certainly don't know that any supernatural entity was responsible for your dad's . . . for what happened last night. I hate to say it, but it's much more likely to be a person than a spirit."

"What, you're saying *I* had something to do with it?"

"No, of course not. I . . ."

"I was like, practically the only person who cared

about him," she said, tears gathering in her big eyes. "A whole lotta people wanted him dead, ya know. But I . . . He was still my dad. And I want that ghost, or whoever did this, to suffer. If you won't do it, I'll find someone who will."

She whirled around and stalked toward the door, just as Aidan Rhodes, male witch, walked in.

Andromeda stopped short and stared at him.

Women—and not a few men—react this way to Aidan. It was only in part because he was gorgeous, with periwinkle blue eyes and perfectly golden hair that curled ever so slightly at the nape of his strong, muscled neck. He also just happened to be a powerful sorcerer. His aura glittered so brightly that even people who never sensed auras were able to sense his.

"Hello," Aidan finally said, returning her gaze and holding it for a long moment, a slight, crooked smile on his beautiful mouth.

Andromeda mumbled something I didn't catch and hurried out of the store.

Aidan's eyes tracked the young woman for a moment before turning back to me.

"*Good* morning, Lily."

"A little early to be scaring customers away, isn't it?" I said as I folded the newspaper.

He chuckled and patted Oscar, who was running in manic circles around his legs, begging for attention.

"Morning, Maya."

She smiled. "Hi, Aidan. I was about to run for coffee. Could I get you anything?"

"Thank you; I'd love a cappuccino." He reached into his pocket.

"My treat," I said, handing Maya a bill from the Cuban cigar box that doubled as a petty cash till. "A mocha for me, thanks, Maya. And would you get Conrad what-

ever he wants? Food, preferably. Something with a lot
of calories."

"Will do. Be back in a few," she said as she headed
out to our favorite local throwback to San Francisco's
Summer of Love, a funky café down the block named,
appropriately enough, Coffee to the People.

Aidan waited until Maya left to turn back to me, his
bright blue gaze running down my body, then back to
meet my eyes.

"You look lovely this morning, Lily. That dress is perfect on you."

"Thank you. What do you want?"

I had no desire to make idle chitchat with this particular male witch. Aidan Rhodes made me nervous. I
had been run out of my hometown at a tender age, never
joined a coven, didn't know many witches, and no matter
where I wandered on the globe, I pretty much avoided
getting involved in any kind of local witchy politics.

But not long ago, Aidan had done me a favor, and
now I owed him—big-time. Still, I sure as shootin' didn't
trust him. So far he hadn't asked me for much in return
other than a few love potions and prosperity brews, but I
was waiting with bated breath for him to demand much
more.

Across the room, I heard the bolt on the front door
click into the locked position, and the Closed sign in the
window flipped over. Aidan hadn't touched a thing. He
didn't need to.

"Jerry Becker was a client of mine," Aidan said.

"Jerry Becker?" I repeated, as though he wasn't already on my mind. My distrust of Aidan led me to give
up as little information as possible. Normally it wouldn't
be easy to veil one's feelings around such a powerful
witch, but Aidan and I were both skilled at hiding. "As
in the man who was killed . . . ?"

He nodded.

"Did you know the gal who was here when you arrived?"

He shook his head. "Why?"

"No reason. Who killed Becker?" I asked.

"That's what I'd like you to find out."

"Me? Why me?"

"I can't be seen to be directly involved."

"What kind of client was he?"

"The paying kind."

"No, I mean, what kind of help was he asking for?"

"Frankly, Lily, that's none of your business. You know that."

I'd never been a witch-for-hire, so I was fuzzy on the ethical details of selling one's paranormal services. Apparently we were like magical versions of lawyers or doctors: We couldn't be compelled to spill confidential details.

"Isn't it enough that I'm asking for your help?" Aidan continued.

He was being polite. As we both knew, he held my marker. I was bound.

"Of course," I conceded. "Do you have any information at all on what went on last night?"

"No idea."

"There are rumors of a ghost in the building."

He nodded. "Supposedly the bell tower's inhabited. But you know as well as I do that it would be unusual for a resident ghost to suddenly take someone out. They rarely manifest in order to murder, especially years after death."

Our eyes held for a long moment.

"So you think it was the act of a human?" I asked. "Or some other entity?"

"That's what I'd like you to find out. What did you feel at the school last night?"

"How do you know I was there?"

He gave me a pained look. Aidan knew things.

"I felt . . . something," I said. "But I don't know what it was, much less what it wanted. You know how I am with spirits."

"I've got someone who can help you with that. Goes by the name of Sailor." Aidan reached into his breast pocket and took out a sleek silver case from which he extracted one of his fine ivory business cards. He turned it over and wrote on the back with a bold, black stroke.

"Sailor, as in 'Ahoy there, matie'?" I asked.

"Maybe it's a last name." He handed me the card. The word "Cerulean" and an address on Romolo Place were below the name "Sailor."

"Could you be a little more cryptic?" I asked.

"Cerulean's a club on Romolo, right off Broadway near Columbus. Sailor's a psychic. Very talented. You can find him there."

"He owns this club?"

"Not exactly. He just hangs out there."

"Uh-huh. I couldn't just call him up and ask for an appointment rather than tracking him down in a bar?"

"He's not in the business. Likes to keep a low profile, powers-wise, not unlike you."

"But he'll help me?"

"Oh, he'll help you."

"Why do I get the feeling that it will be against his will?"

Aidan just smiled and changed the subject. "How's my mandragora coming along?"

"Fine. He'll be ready in another twenty days."

Not long ago Aidan asked me to make him a mandragora, a kind of household elf made from the root of a mandrake plant. I was surprised he didn't just make it himself, but witchcraft is an enormous field of knowledge, and just as in any other profession, different witches excel in distinct areas. I'm a whiz at all things botanical, but a complete bust in the "foreseeing the future" or "talking to the dead" departments; my ornate crystal ball sat, generally unused and virtually useless, on a shelf in my bedroom.

It struck me as odd that Aidan wanted a mandragora. He claimed to be lonely. I knew there was more to it than that—probably something as simple as his selling off the imp to the highest bidder—but I still owed him.

"Wonderful." He checked his watch. The Open sign flipped back over, and the lock clicked open. "Well, I'd best be going. Lovely to see you, Lily, as always."

"Aidan," I said to his back as he moved toward the door, "would you happen to know anything about mares visiting me?"

He looked back at me, eyebrows raised in surprise. He smiled and fixed me with a quizzical look. "Nocturnal mares?"

"You know the kind I mean."

Night mares, or more specifically, incubi, are night spirits thought to sit on the chests of sleeping victims, causing fear, shortness of breath, and paralysis. Incubi have a decidedly lascivious nature, whereas mares might be underlings sent by more powerful spirits, although they, too, tend toward the bawdy and libidinous.

"Mares usually come to women sleeping alone," Aidan said.

I wasn't going to dignify that with an answer.

"Perhaps you should take a lover," he continued.

"Perhaps you should mind your own danged business."

"You asked my opinion. You and I both know the night spirits often appear in a lonely woman's bed, when her thoughts turn to . . . love." His eyes ran over the length of me. He chuckled and stroked a nearby satin and lace nightgown the color of new violets. "There's something unnatural about a witch without a lover."

I rolled my eyes.

Aidan cocked his head as though trying to understand me. "You could mesmerize any man you want, have him at your beck and call. Don't tell me you need my help."

"For cryin' out loud, I don't want to *enchant* someone to make them like me, thank you very much." I could hear that I protesteth too much. The hard truth was that I had been fighting the urge to cast a love spell over Max Carmichael since the day I met him.

"You want natural love, then?" Aidan considered me. "Hmm. A tall order for someone like you."

"Gee, thanks so much."

"You're . . . different, Lily, as you well know. You should stick with your own kind. Come out on the town with me tonight. We'll see about those pesky mares."

Unbidden, my mind flashed on what it would be like to share a bed with someone like Aidan Rhodes. Probably pretty incredible. I bit my lower lip, then looked up to see Aidan's sparkling blue eyes looking at me as though he were reading my thoughts. His warm hand closed over mine on the counter. The chemistry was undeniable, almost like an electric charge. It was enticing. But as sexy as he was, I wasn't looking for a quick fling. And at a deep, undeniable level Aidan scared me.

He had told me himself that he used to work with my father. The little I knew about my father was all bad.

Besides that, I had a date with Max. I slid my hand out from under Aidan's and started folding a bunch of silk scarves I had scored at an auction in Alameda last week. Yesterday I had hand-laundered the delicate material in a mixture of mild low-alkaline soap flakes and rosewater, then dried them overnight in the moonlight on my second-floor terrace, where I grow my herbs. Now they carried the faint scents of rosemary and lavender, and hummed with the comforting energy of the moon and their former owners.

After a long moment of silence I peeked back up at Aidan, who hadn't budged.

He smiled. I amused him—on a number of levels.

"It just so happens," I said, seemingly unable to stop myself from talking, "that I have a date for brunch today. And I didn't have to compel the man to ask me, either."

A pained expression passed over Aidan's face. He crossed his arms over his broad chest and leaned back against the counter. When he spoke, his voice dripped with disdain. "Don't tell me. It's that guy from the other night. The human."

"You say that as if it were an insult. In case you've forgotten, you're human, too, Aidan. As am I."

"Not in the same way. So, about this Mark character . . ."

"Max," I corrected him.

"Right. Max. This whole situation doesn't seem just a little *Bewitched* for you?"

"*No.*" My voice sounded defensive, even to my own ears. Old *Bewitched* reruns, highlighting the antics of Samantha, the natural witch, and Darrin, her nonmagical husband, had been a favorite staple of my youth. Certain similarities had, in fact, occurred to me. But I wasn't about to admit that to this particular male witch.

My scarf folding took on a certain frenetic quality.

Aidan continued. "Let's see. Talented witch gets together with ludicrous human who insists she deny her powers. . . ."

"Don't be ridiculous."

"I'll just start calling him Darrin."

Oscar snorted and hopped around happily at Aidan's feet, pink piggy eyes bright and interested.

"Stop it now, both of you," I snapped.

The cheery little bell on my shop door chimed. All three of us swung around to look at the door, almost guiltily.

"Speak of the devil, and the devil appears," Aidan murmured.

Oscar ran to his pillow and feigned sleep.

"Good morning, Max," I said.

Max was a handsome man in the classical sense: Tall and broad-shouldered, he had a rugged, masculine face; light gray, sad eyes; shaggy, finger-combed dark hair; and a perpetual five o'clock shadow. He was not model gorgeous, but there was something about him . . . especially that voice.

"Hello, Lily." His eyes shifted to Aidan.

The two men sized up each other. Aidan wore a mien of amused boredom; Max a quizzical, assessing look.

"Max, this is Aidan. Aidan, Max," I introduced them. They shook hands, their eyes locked.

"Nice to meet you," said Max.

"Mack," Aidan said with a nod.

"It's Max," Max responded, correcting him.

"Right. That's what I said."

The ensuing silence was broken by the bell on the front door as Maya entered with our coffees.

"Ah, look, here's your cappuccino, Aidan," I said. "Just in time. Since you were just leaving. As are Max and I."

A couple of young women, Maya's age, came in and started to poke through my small collection of vintage-band T-shirts. I left the store in Maya's capable hands; Bronwyn would be in soon after eleven to keep her company.

Aidan, Max, and I walked out onto the sidewalk, an awkward trio.

"Good-*bye*, Aidan," I said when he began walking in the same direction as Max and I.

"You'll let me know what you find out?"

"Of course."

He turned to Max, who inclined his head.

"Good to meet you, Mike."

"Max."

"Right. That's what I said."

With one more wink at me, Aidan strode off down the street.

If only he'd been wearing a cape, it would have been a picture-perfect ending.

Chapter 4

"So, you want to tell me about this guy?" Max queried after the waiter poured us each a flute of sparkling champagne.

I had been expecting a simple croissant and a coffee, so imagine my surprise when Max insisted on taking me to champagne brunch at the Cliff House, a restaurant overlooking Seal Rock, the Pacific Ocean, and the ruins of the old Sutro Baths. When I asked where we were headed as we drove across town, Max responded, "I told you I'd take you somewhere with tablecloths." Our first impromptu "date" had been at a taqueria in the Mission District, which was great by me. But there was no denying that white tablecloths, flutes of champagne, and a view of the ocean were slightly more romantic than orange vinyl booths and beer from the bottle.

"What guy?" I asked. "You mean Aidan?"

He nodded. "Is this what was so complicated in your life?"

"How do you mean?"

"Not so long ago you told me you couldn't see me because it was complicated. I thought he might be the complication."

I shook my head and tasted my champagne; it was dry and crisp, bubbly, delicious.

"I get the sense he's more than a friend," Max continued.

"He's not my lover, if that's what you're asking."

He chuckled, his gray eyes almost exactly the same color as the overcast sky on the other side of the windowpane. "You don't beat around the bush, do you?"

"Not as a general rule, no."

"So, does this Aidan person have a last name?"

"Yes. Are you planning on looking him up?"

"Just wondered what his story was."

"Tell me, Max, is this you being a journalist, or jealous, or both?"

In lieu of an answer, Max took a long pull on his champagne and stared at me, as though assessing my response. Finally he cracked a smile and shrugged one shoulder.

"Just curious."

"The truth is you and I don't know each other well enough for me to tell you all my deepest secrets."

"So he's a deep secret?"

I sat back in exasperation, folding my arms over my chest.

"Oops. Body language alert." Max held up one hand in surrender. "I'm sorry, Lily, you're right. My journalistic instincts—some would say terminal nosiness—can get out of hand. Let's make a toast to taking it slow."

He raised his champagne flute, and after a brief moment of consideration I lifted my own. We clinked glasses and drank.

Once we got over that, brunch was lovely. We visited the abundant buffet tables where Max kept putting fattening items such as éclairs and sausages on my plate, telling me I could use a little more flesh on my bones.

I'm a healthy, average-sized woman, nowhere near skinny. But I liked Max's attitude.

By the time we returned to our table by the window, our plates piled high, the waiter had refilled our flutes with champagne, and we toasted the sea lions who were trying to shove one another off Seal Rock, a fierce, angry crag that stuck up from the ocean floor.

"We used to come here when I was a kid," Max told me. "There was an old Playland on the beach with the creepiest fun house, and right here in the Cliff House was a mechanical arcade museum. I used to tell everyone I wanted to grow up to design pinball machines."

"What happened to that plan?"

He shrugged. "Pinball machines went the way of the dodo bird. Everything's electronic now. Doesn't have the same romance, somehow."

"And you're a big one for romance?"

"Mmm." He gazed at me for a moment across the table.

"Who's we?" I asked. At Max's bemused expression I clarified. "You said 'we' used to come here?"

"My brother and I. Occasionally my sister would join us, but she was a few years older and usually went off with her friends. But my brother and I would spend whole days."

"Your sister's a doctor, right?"

He nodded. "An internist over at SF General."

"And your brother? Are you two still close?"

A shadow passed over his light eyes. Max turned his attention back to his plate of food. "Not really."

I sensed he didn't want to follow that particular line of questioning.

"What happened to the arcade museum?"

"It moved over to Fisherman's Wharf. Probably a lot more foot traffic, but I liked it better before. It used to be wonderfully eerie, like a secret only you knew about, crowded and dusty. Haunted."

"I thought you didn't believe in ghosts."

"That doesn't mean I don't believe in being haunted."

True enough: Max was a haunted man. By what? I knew he was a widower, but little else about him. But that was the point of dating, right, to get to know someone? To come to trust them? I was a grown woman, but given my unconventional past, I still felt like a novice at this whole romance thing.

Distracted by the sparkle in Max's light eyes as he spoke, by the time dessert rolled around I forgot all about the plate of sugar-dusted Belgian waffles and chocolate-dipped strawberries in front of me. Max regaled me with stories of his time working as a reporter for Reuters in Europe and Africa, making me laugh until I snorted with a description of getting lost in Tangiers with an empty gas tank, a vociferous Italian photographer, and one very annoyed goat. When Max asked me about my own globe-trotting past, I found myself opening up, just the tiniest bit, about never quite fitting in ... and my protracted search for a sense of home.

Handsome, smart, funny, and heterosexual, he even had a job. Max was the elusive Holy Grail of San Francisco's single straight women. What more could any woman want?

Still, Aidan's barbs had stung. Max was ill at ease with my being a witch. But my magick was a huge part of who I was, and it had taken me a long time to accept myself. Did I want to get involved with a man who would prefer that I deny my powers? Would Max be willing to change for me instead of asking me to change for him? I reminded myself that I was in no hurry to plan a wedding, caressed my medicine bag, and willed myself to relax.

After brunch, we explored the decks around the Cliff House and looked out over the ocean. But what really fascinated me was a series of low, crumbling concrete walls, rusty pipes, and low pools that marched up the terraced hill.

"What's all that?" I asked.

"The old Sutro Baths. It was built in the late 1800s and housed a huge swimming pool complex, with separate pools of fresh water and salt water. But the place fell into disrepair and burned down in the sixties. Now it's San Francisco's version of Roman ruins. Want to climb around?"

"Could we?"

"Sure."

We descended a set of steep concrete stairs to the ruins. I was relieved I'd worn my Keds. The ground beneath our feet was wet and slippery from fog and the last high tide; had I worn a froufrou pair of sandals, I would have tumbled over the edge into the abyss. A sign warned us to climb with care, or better yet, not to climb at all, but it did not tell us to keep out. I was surprised to find the ruins open to passersby in such a litigious society: It reminded me of hiking in Europe, where the prevailing sentiment seemed to be that if you were stupid enough to fall and hurt yourself, you shouldn't expect any sympathy from the villagers.

A salt-tinged wind whipped off the ocean, making me glad I was wearing my 1940s cocoa brown wool coat, vintage Hermès scarf, and butter-soft leather gloves. Max took my gloved hand in his to help me from one wall to the next, and then didn't let go as we scampered up and down short flights of stairs, peeked into small rooms, and made our way through shadowy, briny tunnels. Wisps of fog made it easy to believe this place was haunted.

"I'd like to take you to another place I love, out near Muir Woods," Max said as we emerged from a tunnel and climbed atop a broad abutment.

"The giant redwoods? I've been dying to see them!"

He smiled and pushed strands of wind-whipped hair away from my face. His eyes were a brilliant gray, like today's sky, but his smile couldn't hide a tinge of sadness. I tried to read him, but, as usual, his guard was up.

"Then see them you shall."

He leaned in to kiss me. I felt tingly even before his lips touched mine.

His cell phone rang out. Max took a step back, reached into his jacket pocket, glanced at the display, then looked at me with regret. "I have to take this."

"Of course," I said, and walked a little farther out on the abutment to give him some privacy. Still, his voice drifted easily over to me.

"What?" His eyes flickered over to me. "Are you sure? Yeah. Twenty minutes."

When he joined me a moment later, his expression was troubled.

"Why didn't you tell me you saw Carlos Romero last night?"

"It didn't occur to me. Why would it?"

A muscle worked in his jaw. "Tell me now. Please."

I shrugged and remained mute, annoyed at this turn of events.

"Were you planning to mention anything about knowing Jerry Becker?" Max shook his head in exasperation. "It's been what, a whole *week* since you were involved in a homicide?"

"I should get back to the store." I turned and started up the damp concrete steps toward the street.

"The store can wait," he said. "I want some answers."

I paused. I felt my blood rise.

There haven't been a lot of men in my life. My father had walked out on my mother and me when I was a toddler, leaving no forwarding address. My second grade teacher, Mr. Sweeney, made me sit in the corner every recess for a week after I corrected his many spelling and grammar errors. My high school principal kicked me out of school when the star quarterback, who had been harassing me, developed a mysterious ailment that caused him to fumble the football whenever the team was first and goal.

And those were some of my better experiences with men.

So I wasn't good at deferring to male authority, especially when—as was so often the case—it arose from a sense of entitlement, rather than from earned respect.

A gust of wind snarled my tresses until they snaked around my head like Medusa's locks. I felt the cold prickle of angry power gathering along my spine and coursing down to my extremities. I closed my eyes and concentrated on reining in my anger before I hurt someone. Finally, more in control, I turned to face Max.

"I don't guess you're the one to make that decision, Max."

Our eyes held, and his expression softened. "I'm sorry. You're right. I was out of line. That phone call caught me off guard. May I ask you a question?"

"Yes. But I may not answer it."

"Fair enough. What were you doing at the School of Fine Arts in the middle of the night?"

I was torn. Should I tell him I was there looking for ghosts? Not half an hour ago I had resolved that Max would have to accept this part of me. But now I hesitated.

I liked Max—a lot. I wanted him to return the sentiment. And I didn't want to feel like a freak.

"I was having coffee with Maya and a friend of hers." I wimped out with a half-truth. "And we took a little tour of the school."

"And did you find the ghost?"

"Excuse me?"

"You heard me."

"What makes you think—"

"Give me a little credit, Lily. With your talents, it's easy to guess that your friends wanted you to look around for the things that go bump in the night."

"Hey, *I* know what we should talk about: Why doesn't Inspector Romero like you?"

"It's a long story."

"I've got time."

"I thought you had to get back to the store."

"I can be flexible. Depending on the conversation."

Max looked out over the ocean. The greenish gray of the water segued seamlessly into the ashen gray of the sky. The air was filled with the staccato caws of the gulls, the hoarse barks of the sea lions, and the rhythmic pounding of the surf. Finally, Max took a deep breath.

"My wife—my *late* wife, Deborah—was Carlos Romero's cousin." He spoke with difficulty, as though the words came at a huge cost. "Law enforcement is a tradition in Deborah's family. When I did a piece on corruption in the police department, it put us at odds. Carlos thought I was using the family's connections to investigate the story."

"Were you?"

"Maybe. I don't know, Lily. I'm an investigative journalist. It's not something I can switch on and off like a lamp."

"You said something about your wife's death. . . ."

He started up the steps. "Let's get going."

Max was usually a hard read, but as he passed by me on the steps, I felt sadness and rage emanating from him in waves.

And something nastier: guilt.

Chapter 5

All the way home Max and I ignored important subjects.
We made plans to visit the redwoods, but there was a
perceptible distance between us wrought of so much
that was not said. I reminded myself that I hardly knew
him, after all. Maybe "we" were not meant to be.

I was happy to return to Aunt Cora's Closet and all
the warm and welcoming elements of my new home:
the scent of fresh laundry and herbal sachets, the comforting hum from my inventory, the damp snout of my
miniature potbellied pig, and a plump, fiftysomething
Wiccan wearing kohl eyeliner and a garland of fresh
flowers twining through her fuzzy brown hair.

"Lily! Blessed be!" Bronwyn came out from behind
the herbal counter to envelop me in swaths of incense-
scented gauzy purple material. I let myself sink into
her embrace, savoring Bronwyn's ability to love those
around her with neither condition nor restraint.

"Maya was just telling me what happened at the
school last night." Bronwyn pulled away, concern on her
face. "Oh my *Goddess*! What a terrible thing!"

"Yes. It was . . ." I trailed off, searching for how to
describe finding someone moments after his life has

slipped away. I could feel the frigid stillness of the body. I was only human, after all. ". . . Intense."

Maya snorted at my understatement. She was sitting cross-legged on the floor near the dressing room alcove, sorting through a black plastic Hefty bag full of big band–era clothes.

"Oh, by the way, Lily," Maya said, "Ginny Mueller called earlier to see if you still wanted to pick up those clothes from the school."

I had been wondering how to snoop around the school on Aidan's behalf without seeming ghoulish. Picking up those clothes was the perfect solution. I glanced at my watch.

"Actually, if one or both of you are willing to mind the store till closing, maybe I could go get them this afternoon."

"I'll stay," Maya volunteered, then added with a shiver, "Just don't ask me to go back to school yet. I'm still dealing with last night."

"How is Ginny holding up?"

"Actually, she's over the moon. She was offered representation by a Union Square gallery."

"Wow. That's a real honor."

"You're telling me. She—"

The bell on the front door rang as Susan Rogers, fashion editor for the *San Francisco Chronicle*, swept into the shop. Susan wrote a glowing article about Aunt Cora's Closet for the newspaper's Style section after I outfitted her niece's entire wedding party with vintage gowns. Since then she had become a semiregular client, stopping in whenever she happened to be in the neighborhood. An über-stylish trendsetter in her fifties, Susan leaned toward sleek, all-black ensembles, had a propensity for swooning over fashionable but virtually unwearable shoes, and was capable of waxing philosophical about "the ever-changing hemline."

I, in contrast, knew a fair amount about the fashions of yore but next to nothing about current trends. Nonetheless, I couldn't help but respond to her ready smile and vivacious energy.

"Lily, thank goodness you're here. I'm a wreck!" said Susan. "I'm in *desperate* need of your help to find a dress to wear to my niece's wedding. I woke up at three this morning just thinking about it. I can't believe I've let it go this long!"

I smiled. The wedding wasn't for another six weeks. I was lucky if I knew what I was going to wear ten minutes before I left the house . . . but I do have an advantage, owning my own clothing store and all. Besides, until recently I had never been invited to any event for which clothes were something to fret about. Most supernatural affairs are "come as you are," while some are even "clothing optional." So when Susan invited me to her niece's wedding—the first such invite I'd ever received—I was excited beyond all measure.

Susan started flicking through a rack of 1950s formal gowns, immediately exhibiting her fashionista training by studying the inside of the collar first. For the professional in the know, labels are more important than the cut or the fabric of a garment.

"So, what are we talking about?" Susan asked no one in particular.

Before I could stop her, Bronwyn dropped her voice to a loud whisper and said with great drama, "*A man was killed last night at the San Francisco School of Fine Arts!*"

"No!" Susan whipped around to face her.

"Yes! Maya and Lily were *there*!"

"Get *out*!"

A chorus of gasps filled the room. Although there was nothing funny about a man's death, Maya met my eyes, and we shared a smile at the women's over-the-top sense of drama.

"*Do* tell," Susan said, turning to me.

"Unfortunately, it's true," I said. "Maya and I took a tour of the school last night and came across the body."

Another gasp. "Who was he? How was he killed? Who did it?"

"Probably someone after an inheritance," Maya mused.

"We don't know. . . . His body was at the bottom of the staircase leading up to the bell tower. He must have fallen."

"Who was it?" Susan repeated.

"A benefactor to the school, a man named Jerry Becker."

"*The* Jerry Becker?"

"You know him?"

"I met him once, when he was in town for a symphony fund-raiser. He was going on and on about his daughter's talent as an artist—*please*, like I haven't heard that before—and, if I recall, made several *deliciously* inappropriate remarks to me. I was with my second husband, Bradley, at the time, so I merely enjoyed the flirtation. Anyway, anyone who's anyone knows of Jerry Becker. He's got scads of money."

"*Had* scads of money," Bronwyn noted. "Can't take it with you."

"He was found in the bell tower?" Susan repeated. She looked around at Maya, Bronwyn, then back at me. "I take it you've heard the ghost stories about that place?"

"Ghosts?" said Bronwyn. "My friend Charles is a ghost hunter! Would you like me to call him? Maybe he could help."

"That's okay," I said. Charles Gosnold was precisely the kind of ludicrous, untalented ghost hunter I was making fun of just last night. "I think I can take care of it."

"There are stories about a haunting . . ." Susan went

on. "There was something else, too. . . . I can't quite remember. It just so happens I've done some research on
the school—for a while it was one of the most prestigious institutes for clothing and textile design on the
West Coast."

"I didn't know that," Maya said.

"Oh yes, ask me anything," Susan said. "I literally
wrote the book on the local fashion history a few years
ago, did you know? I'm sure Booksmith has a copy; I'll
sign one for you. Of course, the 'real' fashion design in-
dustry is in New York City, but San Francisco did its part.
Then someone at the school decided that fashion design
wasn't 'fine' enough for the School of Fine Arts, and they
phased it out in favor of painting and sculpture."

"Maybe that's why the provost is giving me some vintage clothing from the school's collection," I said. "I'm
picking it up this afternoon."

Susan's gaze, eager and just this side of greedy, fixed
on me. "What kind of items?"

"I'm not sure yet, but the provost said she thought
they were from the late Victorian era."

"Hmm . . . Too early for the school's textile program,"
Susan commented. "They must date back to the convent
days. When are you getting them?"

"Later this afternoon."

"Ooooh, could I come by tomorrow and check them
out? I would *love* to wear the perfect Victorian gown to
the wedding—can you imagine? My sister would simply
die of envy."

"Sure. We're closed on Mondays, but I'm usually here
washing and prepping inventory, anyway. Why don't you
come by around noon and I'll show you what I have?"

"Don't forget, I'll be here, too," Bronwyn put in. "I
want to learn your trade secrets."

I laughed. "As if I would turn down anyone who *wants*
to help with the wash."

Susan's brow furrowed as she began to rifle through a stand of 1940s-style dress suits. "It really is interesting, your finding a body—of Jerry Becker, no less—at the bottom of the bell tower stairs. You know, a professor from the school came to see me about a month ago, asking questions. He had seen my book."

"What professor?" Maya asked.

"A rather diffident, odd fellow ... Walter, maybe?"

"Could it have been Walker? Walker Landau?" I asked.

"That sounds right."

"What was he asking about?"

"If I knew about a death that occurred on the bell tower stairs, way back when."

"Awesome! Students!" said Oscar as I stood in my kitchen an hour later, preparing to go to the School of Fine Arts. "I *love* students. I'll come with you."

"You most certainly will not."

"I thought you said there was something fishy going on?"

"There is."

"How ya gonna know what spirits are in the building without a familiar?"

I paused from packing an assortment of charms and talismans into my satchel. It was still light out, but given what had happened yesterday, I wanted to be prepared. I had another charm bag, more talismans, a jar of special salts, and even a small bag of dust swept from the threshold of a New Orleans prison that a recent acquaintance, Hervé LaMansec, a vodou priest, had given me.

"You can detect spirits?" I asked.

Oscar crossed his arms over his scrawny chest and rolled his eyes.

A goblin just rolled his eyes at me.

"Why do you think people bring a cat to check out a house before they buy it?" Oscar asked.

"A cat?"

"Cats and guys like me, we're sensitive to such things."

"Who brings a cat to a house before they buy it?"

"Everyone."

"I know of no one who does that."

"You don't?"

I shook my head.

"Well, I'll be doggoned." His little brow wrinkled; he looked truly bemused. "I always wondered how people wound up living in haunted houses. Like that *Amityville Horror*—you ever see that movie? I guess those poor folks didn't know enough to bring a cat. Huh. Ya live, ya learn, eh?"

"You sense spirits? Can you communicate with them?"

"Nah, I can't talk to 'em, exactly."

"Then you won't be much good to me, will you?"

"But mistress! I can sense enough about them to tell what you're up against."

I hesitated. Having Oscar along might take some of the guesswork out of what I had planned. Still . . .

"Please?"

"And you'll stay in pig form?"

"Yes, mistress," he said with a sigh.

I picked up the protective amulet I had made for him two weeks before and draped it around his neck.

Oscar and I arrived at the school just after five. Oscar was in his porcine guise, whereas I was in an old pair of jeans and an even older sweater—not vintage, mind you, just old. I'd spent enough time in long-sealed, mildewy closets to know not to wear anything I cared to keep when rummaging through piles of old textiles.

I parked my purple van alongside the school's back loading dock. The graphics on the side of the van read:

AUNT CORA'S CLOSET
VINTAGE CLOTHING AND QUALITY ACCESSORIES
CORNER OF HAIGHT & ASHBURY
BUY — SELL — TRADE
IT'S NOT OLD; IT'S VINTAGE!

It was Sunday evening, and though there were students milling about, the school was quiet. Belatedly it dawned on me that I should have called ahead to see if Provost Marlene Mueller would be here. But I'm not at my best on the telephone. I don't yet trust my ability to judge people, so I still rely on sensing auras and vibrations, which don't convey through electronics and telephone wires. I was probably the last person in America under the age of eighty who didn't have a cell phone.

Besides, Ginny had invited me. Oscar and I set out to find her. We first peeked into the café, where a group of young men were shouting at one another about the birth of modernism, and then stuck our heads into a few of the artists' studios, where we interrupted a couple in the middle of a loud breakup—but no one had seen Ginny. Walking down the hall, we passed a cluster of young women bickering over the relative merits of oil sticks versus traditional chalk pastels.

Artists made for a volatile student body.

Wherever we went, Oscar caused a sensation. He preened and snorted, lapping up the attention. Not for the first time I wondered, given that Oscar could choose to transform into anything he wanted, why he had chosen to be a pig. I'm allergic to cats, but I quite like dogs. Having a dog as a familiar would have made my life a lot simpler. Then again, I reminded myself, Oscar's duty was to make my spell casting, not my life, easier.

As we passed the administration offices, I noticed a light was on. A large oak door sported a sign, MARLENE MUELLER, PROVOST.

"Wait here. Do not move," I told Oscar, and knocked.

There was a long pause and then scuffling sounds before a woman's voice beckoned me to enter. When I did, I felt as though I had interrupted something. Marlene Mueller sat behind her desk, her face flushed, and a young man stood near her chair.

"Lily, what are you doing here?" Marlene asked.

"I hope it's all right," I said. "I never got a chance to look at the clothes last night."

"Oh ... I see." She glanced up at the young man standing beside her. He was lanky and blond, good-looking in a sort of surfer-dude-meets-boy band way. He appeared to be in his early twenties, around Ginny's age. Did Marlene have a son?

"Well, since the incident ... That is, I don't think ..." Marlene trailed off.

"I won't disturb the crime scene," I said.

"Still ..." She trailed off once more, her light eyes again searching out the young man. Marlene was not nearly the lithe pixie her daughter, Ginny, was, but she had a delicate manner that suggested she might faint at the sight of blood. She wore her golden brown hair in a romantic upsweep, with artful curls framing her fine-boned face. An asymmetrical, rainbow-patchwork jacket and lots of chunky handmade jewelry made her look artistic and businesslike at the same time, but tonight she seemed pale and pinched.

Having one's school associated with the suspicious death of its most generous benefactor must be a potent double whammy for someone in her position.

"It can't hurt if she gathers the clothes, Marley," the young man told her, his voice soft but sure.

"We haven't met," I said, and held out my hand. "I'm Lily Ivory."

"Todd Jacobs. Nice to meet you." He shook my hand. His blue-eyed gaze met mine, and I could see he had a certain charm about him, to be sure, but his vibrations were careful, standoffish, as though he were assessing me just as I was him. I also detected a surprising sense of control, rare for one so young.

"Oh, I'm sorry, where is my head?" Still seated, Marlene reached up and took Todd's hand, leaned in to him, and beamed. "This is my husband, Todd."

Husband?

"I can't tell you how wonderful it is, to have someone by your side when going through an ordeal like this," Marlene said. "Do you know, one of our very own faculty members has been accused of this hideous crime."

"That Luc fellow?" I asked.

"No, of course not. Why would Luc be involved? I was thinking of poor Walker—Walker Landau. Do you happen to know him?"

"I don't really know anybody . . ." I began.

"Poor Walker—"

"Walker wouldn't hurt a fly," Todd interrupted. "This whole thing is ridiculous. Fact is, everyone wanted that man dead."

"Wanted Walker dead?"

"No, Jerry Becker," Todd said.

Marlene's face had gone pale and drawn, and she averted her eyes. She looked suddenly older. I felt waves of sadness and . . . was it embarrassment? I caught the scent of something akin to must, dank and closed off: shame.

"Well," she said with a nervous laugh, fluttering her hands over her chest, "be that as it may, it's in the hands of the police now."

"Walker's in police custody?" I asked.

"No, they haven't arrested anyone as far as I know. Anyway, perhaps it *is* a good thing you're back. After all, the police aren't going to help us with the school's being ... haunted," Marlene said, her gaze holding mine. "I hadn't wanted to say before, but it's getting worse. And now everyone's so ratcheted up, their nerves are shot, it's as if there's something in the air. There have been skirmishes amongst the students, and even the faculty. Professional jealousies are running amok. And now, well, this ... tragedy ... certainly hasn't helped things. I even had someone in here messing with my ephemera!"

"Breathe, Marley," Todd said in a quiet voice.

Marlene smiled up at him and took a deep breath, letting it out slowly.

"Messing with your ephemera?" I asked. Was that a euphemism?

"Marley's a collage artist," Todd explained, yanking his chin toward a drafting table set up in the corner. Every surface was covered with tiny bits of clipped magazine pages, letters, advertisements, and patterned papers. "She seems to think someone was going through her things yesterday."

"No one thinks I could possibly notice, but I know these things," said Marlene. "It may look like a mess, but it's *my* mess."

"Why would anyone want your ephemera, Marlene?" Todd asked.

"Some student with an overdue project, no doubt." She turned back to me. "Anyway, if you can figure out what's going on with the noises, without getting involved in the police investigation, I suppose that would be all right."

"I'll do my best. So, it's all right to collect the clothing?"

Marlene glanced up again at Todd, who nodded. She flashed me a brilliant smile. "Of course."

"The closet's on the third floor, on your right at the end of the hall," said Todd. "Marlene and Ginny had to break the handle to get it open. There's a hole in the door, so you can't miss it. Want me to go with you?"

"No, thanks, I'm good," I said. "But I do appreciate the offer."

The stairs leading from the main building's first floor to the second were broad and formal, but the steps to the third story were steep and encased in a narrow, enclosed stairwell. Oscar and I climbed slowly. I hadn't taken the students' concerns seriously enough the last time I was here at the school, assuming they were overreacting. I had been almost flippant about it, and I should have known better. Jerry Becker's death, not to mention the sounds I had heard on the bell tower stairs, had sobered me.

As had the sense that there was an evil spirit involved. I hadn't said as much to Oscar because I wanted his untainted version of what might be present. Plus, I was hoping maybe I'd gotten it wrong. But unaccustomed fighting, jealousy, and petty theft were potential signs of demonic activity. The wretched creatures really did love to stir things up.

We took our time mounting the stairs, searching for the sensations encased within the rough stucco walls, the smooth stone steps, the slick wooden banister. Thousands of souls had passed through these hallways for more than a century, leaving faint traces of themselves each time. I felt hints of misery amongst the whispers of everyday human experience, but nothing out of the ordinary.

Oscar and I paused at the top of the stairs, which opened onto the third-floor hallway. The long corridor, flanked by a series of simple wooden doors and a few small windows, was much narrower than the floor below.

I wondered which unlucky nuns had been banished up here under the eaves.

The empty hallway stretched out before us. Strong shafts of afternoon light slanted in through the window-panes, dust motes floating lazily in the brilliant orange beams. Evening would soon be upon us. I crouched and, concentrating, put my hands, palms down, on the floor. I listened and looked, but I also smelled.

Mildew and the sickeningly sweet aroma of death. Unhappy death.

"Whose offices are these?"

I jumped at the sound of Oscar's loud whisper.

"I think they're just storage closets, by the looks of it," I said in a low voice.

"Nuns used to live up here?"

"A long time ago."

"Guess you gotta be dedicated if yer gonna give up everything and live in a dreary place like this, huh?"

I didn't answer, as I was straining to hear, to feel.

"Mistress?"

"Hush, Oscar. I'm trying to feel for something."

"Sorry."

He was silent for maybe ten seconds.

"I knew a nun once, in Heidelberg. She was a hoot and a half when she started drinking that sacramental wine. She told me a great joke: 'This nun walks into a ratskeller—'"

"Sssh."

I began moving gingerly down the hall, senses alert. The last door on the right had a hole where the handle used to be, big enough for a hand to pass through. To one side was a heavy mahogany bureau that appeared to have been moved from its place in front of the door, judging by a dark rectangle on the wooden floor where it had stood, and by scrapes along the floorboards.

What drew my attention, though, was the door at the very end of the hall. It was slightly larger than the others, and there was something about it. . . . As I stared, the door started to shimmer, fading in and out, as if beckoning. I wondered where it led—to the bell tower stairwell?

Halfway down the hall, Oscar suddenly grabbed the back of my sweater and pulled.

"Don't go farther, mistress!"

"You feel something? What is it?"

"Dunno exactly. . . . It's not safe."

Oscar is something of a drama queen, and despite his fearsome looks, he's a big chicken. I pried his fingers off my sweater, made sure my amulet was attached, and cradled my medicine bag in my hand.

"It's okay, Oscar. I've got this under control."

"What's the plan, mistress?"

"You stay here while I check it out."

"That's the plan?"

"I didn't say it was complicated. Now hush."

I took a step down the hall but stopped dead in my tracks at the unmistakable sound of footsteps on the stairs behind us. Oscar and I turned toward the noise, goggle-eyed and speechless as in a cartoon.

Something was approaching.

Oscar leapt into my arms, transformed into his pig guise, and squealed. I stumbled back against the wall and tried to ready myself for a repeat of last night's haunting.

I began to murmur a protective chant.

It was upon us.

Chapter 6

"Is someone there?"

I stopped chanting.

It was the handsome professor from the café last night—Luc something or other. Wearing worn jeans and a dusty black T-shirt, he had a sheaf of papers in his hands. He seemed a little surprised to see me, and a lot surprised to see Oscar.

"Hello again," he said with that amazing voice. As he neared us in the hall, a slow smile spread across his sensuous mouth.

"Hi. Again." I breathed, trying to still my heart. Oscar kicked his cloven feet, and I set him down.

"Great pig," Luc said, and crouched down. Oscar snuffled his open hand and wagged his curly tail. "What's his name?"

"He's, um . . . Oscar."

"Hey there, Oscar." Luc stood and smiled at me. "I saw you recently—where was it?"

"In the café."

"Ah, yes, that was it. I'm Luc, by the way."

"Lily. Lily Ivory. Pleased to meet you."

He held out his hand, then realized it was wet from

Oscar's greeting. With a rueful smile Luc wiped his palm on the thigh of his worn jeans.

"The pleasure's all mine."

"What brings you up here?" I asked.

"My office." He gestured to one of the doors.

"They exiled the new kid on the block all the way up here?"

Luc smiled. "Probably would have, but I asked for it. If it's easy for folks to drop by, then they will, and I never get any work done."

I returned his smile, and our eyes lingered for a moment until it occurred to me that I was on the deserted third floor, alone—except for a pig—with a possible murder suspect. I had mentioned Luc's name when I told the police about the argument he had with Jerry Becker in the café. Surely if the authorities had anything on him, he wouldn't be walking around free—would he?

Oscar was winding around our legs, eager for attention. What would he do if I were in real danger? Was he doglike in that way, willing to throw himself into the fray to save his mistress?

More likely he would hightail it to the nearest exit.

I didn't pick up any threatening vibrations from being near Luc, though; that much was certain. Just sumptuous, sensuous ones; they felt round and voluptuous, almost tactile, wrapping around my arms and legs. I breathed in his pleasant, fresh citrus scent. Still, I wished I had been able to touch him, to shake his hand. Nothing takes the place of skin-to-skin contact when it comes to reading someone's vibrations, especially when they're guarded.

"What are *you* doing up here?" Luc leaned down to pet Oscar again, almost absentmindedly. "Most of the other spaces are used for storage."

"I was promised the contents of the closet at the end of the hall."

"Ah." He nodded. "There must be something good in there. I hear people going in and out all the time."

"That must be a different room. This one's been locked up until recently."

"I don't think so. The one at the end, on the right? I hear it creaking open and slamming shut all hours of the day and night. I've been wondering what was in there, but when I tried it, the door didn't open. Served me right; I have no business in there."

"Supposedly there's a bunch of old clothes."

His eyes swept over me. "And you need old clothes because . . . ? Maybe a smock so you don't get dirty?"

"No, nothing like that." I smiled, absurdly pleased that he thought I might be making art. It made me feel as though I fit in, just your average everyday art student . . . who just happened to be a witch. "I sell vintage attire, and I'm hoping there's some great stuff here."

"Why would vintage clothes be kept in the closet of an art school?"

"Good question."

In the short time I've been in this business, I've happened upon fabulous finds in attics, basements, closets, storage units, trunks of cars, moldy cardboard boxes, office storerooms, and on one memorable occasion from an abandoned yacht. So I hadn't given much thought as to why there might be clothes in a cubby tucked under the eaves in an art school, no matter that it was from an era when the building served as a convent. Now that Luc had mentioned it, it did seem odd. Why would nuns have beautiful gowns? Had the women brought the clothes with them when they came to the convent but given them to the church when they took their vows and donned the order's habit? If so, why were the clothes still here? I knew nothing about this sort of thing, much less the building's history. For all I knew, the nuns had supported the convent by putting on theater productions of bawdy French farces. It would behoove me to spend some time in the massive San Francisco Public Library.

Oscar nudged my hand, bringing me back to the present. What to do, what to do. . . . I could play it safe and leave, do my research, and come back knowing more about what I was dealing with. Or I could give in to my curiosity, assume I was a strong-enough witch to deal with whatever I might find, and look in the closet.

I wasn't one to play it safe. And after all, as they say back in Texas, this weren't my first rodeo.

"Wait here a minute," I told Luc and Oscar. I caressed my medicine bundle, took a deep breath, and proceeded down the hall. The door at the very end still shimmered, but I ignored it. One investigation at a time.

Gingerly, I pushed on the door with the broken handle. It gave a creaky protest as it swung open. The room was under the eaves, more a cubby than a closet, and though I'm only of average height, I had to duck to avoid knocking my head on the ceiling's steep angles.

The good news was that the space was warm, dry, and dark, the only source of light a small screen vent to the outside.

The bad news was it reeked of age and dust, the musty smell of a room long closed off, a stench the clothes would absorb.

The really bad news was that it also reeked of something acrid, malevolent; something profoundly wrong.

There was an evil here, that much was clear, and not only by the conspicuous absence of my piggy familiar, whose clicking hooves could be heard retreating down to the far end of the hallway. Very old scrapes in the wooden floor showed symbols and a triangle within a pentagram within a circle, along with scattered powder and stems that might once have been herbs. Five little piles of what looked like ashes sat at regular intervals on the dusty floor. Several candle stubs littered the floor as well. Someone had been working the craft here, long ago. It looked like a binding spell.

I stood still and concentrated, but it was very hard to read, hovering as it did just out of mental reach.... It was like trying to remember the details of a vivid dream the morning after. I steeled myself against a strong yearning, a seductive need. The sensations were unfocused and vague, but undeniably present.

The room was dim, illuminated only by the lamps in the hall and the scant late-afternoon light that managed to work its way through the vent. I looked around for a light switch before noticing there was no overhead lamp. Two candelabra, their misshapen stearin candles half burned, rested on a bureau near the door. Had this room been shut off before the building was wired for electricity?

The small space was packed with remnants of a long-ago era: a huge black steamer trunk; old leather-bound books written in French; wooden boxes of all shapes; a massive chest of drawers against one wall; an ornate, almost thronelike wooden chair; a freestanding full-length mirror, its silver backing flaking and corroded in spots.

And in that mirror . . . a face?

The ghostly visage was gone so fast that one might convince one's rational mind that it was a trick of the light. But this wisp of a spirit was accompanied by an undeniable tingle of energy and a blast of icy air. It was trying to make contact. Whether that was helpful or threatening, I had no way of knowing.

Right about now I was wishing I had some of that RadioShack equipment, not to mention a psychic ghostbuster at my side—a burly, muscle-bound psychic ghostbuster. I'm not frightened of spirits per se, but there was something wrong in this room.

Crouching down, I kept my eyes on the mirror while

reaching into my satchel and extracting a megawatt flashlight.

"Were you a Girl Scout, by any chance?"

Luc's voice startled me. I had forgotten about him. My witchcraft training had taught me first and foremost to focus my intent to the exclusion of all else, a skill I had mastered early on. This otherwise admirable power of concentration got me into trouble at times like these.

"Not hardly," I said as I stood and gently shoved him out of the room. "Stay in the hall, please."

Luc smiled but looked curious. "Want to keep the treasure to yourself? I won't steal it."

"Just stay outside until I say so."

Turning back to the room, I knelt before a large black trunk covered in tooled leather, bearing still-colorful stamps from France and Hungary. I slowly undid the brass latches that held it closed, took a deep breath, and inched it open, praying it didn't contain a skeleton or something equally macabre.

It stuck at first, then opened with a poof of dust. I peeked inside.

Ruffles, lace, Victorian-era underthings. Frilly cotton petticoats and silk camisoles. I breathed a sigh of relief.

Clothes were my strong suit. Finally, something I could read.

The clothes smelled of aromatic cedar. A cursory inspection revealed some light stains, but nothing I couldn't handle, and the fabric was in great shape. One by one I picked the pieces up and held them to my chest, feeling for their vibrations. There was some darkness, yes, but an overarching feeling of excitement and purpose. The particulars weren't easy to understand—the sensations were frustrating and elusive; very old and vague.

I held a corset up to myself. It was made of delicate ivory silk and ice blue satin ribbons. Looking in the full-length mirror, I felt a strong, outlandish impulse to strip, right then and there, and don the garment.

"I'm trying not to get hot here."

I whirled around.

Luc was right behind me. *Why does no one do what I ask?*

"I *told* you to stay outside."

Luc gestured to the corset I was clutching to my chest. "Now *that's* fodder for any number of adolescent fantasies. Fortunately, I am urbane and sophisticated."

I tossed the undergarment into the chest. Grabbing my satchel, I rooted around for one of the extra protective amulets I always carry with me.

"At least wear this," I said as I stood and hung the pendant around his neck. I laid my hands flat on his chest and murmured a brief protective incantation. "Don't touch anything. And don't look in the mirror."

"Oookaaaay." He picked the carved medallion up off his chest to study it, then cast an interested look back at me, raising one eyebrow. "What's this?"

"It's a . . . um . . . good luck charm."

Luc gave me a slow, curious smile. "Kind of creepy in here, isn't it?"

I nodded, looking up at him. Our gaze held a beat too long. I was finding it a little hard to breathe.

"And what's in the mirror?" he asked, looking over at it.

I grabbed one of the petticoats from the trunk and used it to cover the looking glass. It was one thing for a powerful witch to shrug off visions in a haunted mirror; quite another for a normal human to do so.

Suddenly, the closet door slammed shut. There were heavy footsteps out in the hallway and loud, unnatural breathing, growing in intensity.

And the loud squeal of a pig, with the clatter of small hooves rushing toward us down the hallway.

"Oscar!" I yelled, flinging the door open, but it slammed shut before I could take a step. I opened it again, and it banged closed. I tried it once more.

"I think it wants to stay shut," said Luc, his voice loud enough to be heard over the moaning that began to swirl around us.

Luc pushed me aside and opened the door easily enough, then threw a chair into the opening before it slammed shut once again. With remarkable athletic prowess, Oscar sailed over the chair into the room, accidentally kicking the chair into the hallway, and the door slammed shut again.

"What the—"

Luc bent over to peer through the hole in the door. I grabbed him by the shoulders and yanked him back just as a burst of light and burning hot air blew through the open keyhole.

The breathy moaning swirled about us, echoing off the angled walls, so intense it was painful. I clutched my medicine bag and wrapped Luc's hand around it as well, my other hand caressing the top of Oscar's head. Luc twined his arm around me and held me tight, whether to protect me or to comfort himself, I wasn't sure. Either way I was grateful: In the supernatural pandemonium, the vibrations and breath of another human being were a lifeline, tethering us to this plane of existence. Oscar, Luc, and I backed away from the door to the far corner of the room behind the steamer trunk, where we sank to the floor. Oscar jumped into my lap, shaking. We covered our ears and huddled together against the wall as the ashes on the floor swirled up in the whirlwind, careening through the small space.

The chaos showed no signs of abating. This was ridiculous.

I lifted Oscar into Luc's lap, grabbed my backpack,

and extracted a jar of salts. Casting a circle around us, I drew symbols of protection with the salts and chanted.

> *Spirits of protection, spirits who*
> *clear, remove all those who don't*
> *belong here. Wrap us, protect us,*
> *keep us from harm.*

At first I had to shout to be heard. I closed my eyes and called on my guiding spirit as I cast. I repeated the chant over and over, working myself into a near trance as the sounds subsided, becoming fainter until things fell silent.

Just as suddenly as it had arrived, it was gone.

"You okay?" Luc asked.

I nodded. "You?"

"I'm fine. That . . ." He trailed off and shook his head. "That was the damnedest thing. Are you a priestess of some sort?"

"Not exactly," I said. I noticed that Luc seemed more intrigued than frightened. I didn't know whether to be relieved by his relatively calm reaction . . . or suspicious.

Oscar started running around the room in circles like a mad pig.

Luc chuckled. "He needs a piggy sedative."

"Don't we all."

I tried the door, which swung open easily—and stayed open. Luc and I peered up and down the hallway. Nothing. Within our cramped closet, all was back to normal, including the neat little piles of ashes.

The immediate danger having passed, I wanted to look around the closet some more. Luc seemed to be on the same wavelength. Evening had fallen. There was no more sun through the grate, and the light cast from the hallway was dim. My flashlight had given up the ghost when I dropped it.

A Bic lighter sat on the bureau next to the candelabra, left over, I imagined, from when Marlene and
Ginny opened the closet; no doubt they had no light,
either.

As I was looking down the hall, Luc lit the candles.

"Wait!"

"What?"

Too late. He had already lit them. I held my breath
and listened. Candles set out in a certain configuration
could be a sign of a spell, and if they were lit in a particular way, the spell could be activated.

Or they could simply be used for light in a room without a lamp.

"Nothing," I said when all seemed normal. "Never
mind."

"Take a look at this," said Luc. He held some papers
near the candle. "A letter. Do you read French?"

I shook my head. "Just Spanish."

"*We don't know how long you can expect to stay, but
our lord will be with you for eternity,*" he translated
out loud. He looked at the envelope, then rummaged
through the box some more. "From France. Looks like
the only one. What do you suppose all this is? Why would
they have kept it all in here for all these years?"

"I have no idea." Was it deliberately hidden in here, or
had it simply been forgotten? I started looking through
the clothes hanging in the armoire—a few simple skirts
and blouses, more underthings.

I noted a floral scent, like perfume.

And music.

Annoyed, I said to Luc, "I told you not to touch
anything."

"I didn't." Luc gestured toward a music box sitting
atop the bureau. "It started on its own."

It was a simple wooden box; when it was opened,
a glass plate allowed you to see the movement of the

metal drum and comb. It was twirling around slowly, playing a ditty at once familiar yet foreign sounding.

Luc started singing, " 'There's a place in France where the naked ladies dance . . .' "

"That's how the song goes?"

"You don't know that one? It was all the rage in the third grade."

"I must have been out that week."

"It's also the snake charmer song, 'Dee dee *dee* dee dee . . .' "

"Oh. Is the song significant in some way?"

Luc laughed. "I have no idea."

"Do you know if it's old? Would this be original to this room?"

"I wouldn't be surprised. You know how kids' culture keeps old things alive, like that 'Ring Around the Rosy' song."

"Which song?"

"Were you homeschooled, by any chance?"

"Kind of."

" 'Ring around the rosy, pocket full of posy'—it's a holdover from the plague days. Ring around the rosy is the pox; a posy was to stave off the disease, something like that. Ashes actually referred to cremation of the bodies."

"And little *children* repeat this?"

Luc took my hands and guided me in a circle, as he chanted:

> *Ring around the rosy,*
> *Pocket full of posy,*
> *Ashes, Ashes, we all fall . . . down.*

I wrenched my hands away. There was an odd look on Luc's face, and something off about his vibrations.

The gleam in his eyes was too beautiful, strange, seductive.

Chapter 7

As I watched, wary, Luc seemed to shake it off.

"This place really is . . . odd. Do you think the noises were related to our being in here?"

Another strong floral scent, a sensation that we were not alone, and more cold air.

I nodded.

"Where did all this stuff come from again? And why do you suppose the door was blocked by a bureau?"

"Marlene Mueller told me they couldn't find the key, so it was closed up and no one came in, probably for decades."

"That doesn't explain why it was all put in here in the first place."

"Aren't you supposed to give up all your worldly possessions when you join a convent? Perhaps the girls arrived from France as novices, and their things were stored here, then forgotten."

"I went to Catholic school. You're telling me those sour-faced nuns wore this sort of thing under their habits?"

Luc held a petticoat up to himself. The odd juxtaposition of such a manly man in the lacey white ruffles made me smile.

"I don't think it was considered sexy lingerie back then," I pointed out. "Just plain underwear that no respectable woman would go without."

"Uh huh," he grunted, unconvinced.

"Could I ask you . . . what were you and Jerry Becker arguing about last night in the café?"

He shrugged. "The usual. Jerry was under the impression he could control everyone he met. He was wrong."

"How did you know him?"

"His daughter's in a couple of my classes."

"I heard he wanted you to help her get a show at a gallery?"

He nodded. "You heard right. But my refusal didn't bother him nearly as much as Andromeda's posing for one of my sculptures."

"Why would he object to that?"

"He didn't. He wanted a cut of the money I got for the sculpture."

"And you refused?"

"Absolutely. It doesn't work that way. I paid Andromeda for her time, and when it sold, I offered her a portion of the profits toward her tuition. She declined; said she didn't need the money."

"Oh."

"Mostly I think Becker thought Andromeda and I were having an affair. And that's what bothered him—I didn't fit into his game plan for her."

"But you weren't seeing her?"

He gave a bark of laughter. "No. She's not my type."

"What *was* Becker's game plan?"

"Walker Landau."

I was still sorting through the items in the trunk, but that brought me up short.

"Walker Landau? The . . . um . . . thin fellow?"

"The very one."

"Becker wanted Andromeda to be with Walker?"

He nodded.

"Why on earth . . . ?"

"I have no idea. I barely knew him, but it seems to me Jerry was a goal-oriented kind of guy. He had his reasons for manipulating his friends and family."

"How odd."

"Listen, do you still want these clothes? I'll help you take them downstairs, if you like."

"Actually, I'd like to speak to Walker Landau before I go. Do you happen to know if he's around this late, and on a Sunday?"

"Probably. He's like the rest of us, here all the time. When you're an artist, your work is also your fun, so there's not much point in going elsewhere. Why are you investigating Becker's death, exactly?"

"I'm not, really. Marlene asked me to look into . . . whatever's going on here."

"Going on?"

"Weird noise-wise."

"Ah. You're a ghost hunter?" he asked, a gleam entering his eyes. "Do you use any of that high-tech equipment?"

"Not exactly. I'm just sensitive to such things, though to paraphrase a friend, you don't have to be sensitive to hear what you and I experienced today." I looked him up and down. "I have to say, Luc, you're pretty nonchalant for someone who was just assailed by the unexplainable."

"I lived in Europe for some time. In an old castle. You want to talk about spirits . . . Let's just say I've seen enough to try to keep an open mind."

That was refreshing.

"Just be more careful, okay?" I said. "If I hadn't pulled you away earlier, you might have lost your eyesight. No joke."

"I'll be careful. Come to my office, and I'll call down

and see if Walker's around. He set up shop in my studio. A pipe burst in his ground-floor space not long ago."

Luc led me down the now-quiet hall to his small office. A number of scale models and small sculptures adorned simple wood shelves, and there were papers everywhere, not stacked but seemingly tossed willy-nilly. Lots of fine-point Sharpie pens and sketches in black ink on thick white paper, mostly nudes and details of the human body.

"I do my actual sculpting work in my studio. This space is just for the paperwork, and the thought. Two different processes. Thinking through one's work, then bringing it to fruition."

"I always thought artists came up with their ideas on the spot. You know, moved by the muse, that sort of thing."

He shook his head. "If only. Sculpting stone involves taking away rather than building up, so a mistake can't be undone. If you rush in and start carving, you'll end up with nothing. A lot of consideration goes into it. It's as though you're freeing the very essence of the stone."

"I think I heard someone quote you on that just last night. Is Ginny Mueller one of your students?

"She is."

"I hear she was just offered gallery representation."

"Ginny?"

"That's what I hear. You're surprised?"

"Frankly, yes. Her work shows a lot of promise, but her technique's immature. Nothing time won't solve, but she's not there yet. Not by a long shot."

"Maybe you're a better teacher than you think."

He smiled. "Well, like I always say, it's better than working for a living."

Luc reached over to the beige institutional phone and dialed Walker Landau. They had a brief exchange, and

Luc told him I was on my way down. He drew a little map on a pad of scratch paper.

"He's just one floor down," Luc said. "Feel free to leave your pig here with me if you'd like."

"You wouldn't mind?"

"After our little incident, I could use the company. It does get creepy up here occasionally." He took a Pay-Day candy bar out of his desk drawer and gestured to Oscar. "Does he like peanuts?"

"As far as I can tell, he likes everything, with the possible exception of ham." I watched as Oscar proved my point by sitting prettily for a portion of the candy bar. "Thank you so much."

I patted Oscar and headed down the hall to the narrow stairs.

As I rounded the landing, I realized there was a subtle hint of scent on me—Luc's scent. It was a heady aroma. He was charming. I didn't trust him, but was that because of him or me? Partly he was too good-looking, *too* charming—I had the sense that he got whatever he wanted, not through magic as did Aidan, but as a favored heir to the throne. He had probably been voted Most Popular in high school.

I had not been exactly popular in high school, and had an innate distrust of those who were.

Down on the second floor, I found Walker Landau easily enough. The door was open and the light on, and he waved me in eagerly.

"Hello, hello, come on in," he said. My second impression was the same as the first: He was almost cadaverlike in appearance; not ugly, just . . . odd. Still, he looked better in his paint-splattered smock than he had in last night's ill-fitting jacket; more at home.

The studio was large and airy, with white dust covering much of the floor. There were sculptures in varying states, male and female nudes, some nearly finished, others barely more than blocks of marble with a few gouges in them. A few were covered with drop cloths, giving them humanoid, vaguely threatening shapes.

In the center of the room was a circle of easels ringed around a raised platform, ready for a painting seminar. Along one side of the room sat canvases of varying sizes featuring somber compositions of black and gray streaks on a white background, or white and black streaks on a gray background, or gray and white streaks on a black background. I was sensing a theme.

In another corner of the room were canvases of a completely different style. These were figurative, full of rich oil colors that reminded me of the Pre-Raphaelites. These paintings were in varying states of completion with a single unifying theme: A spiral staircase of stone steps led into a tormented sea, and a naked young woman who looked a lot like Andromeda stood bound on the bottom stair, menaced at the water's edge.

I stopped and studied one particularly large canvas on the wall. It was Andromeda, all right, right down to the hint of a dimple on one cheek. Her face showed the anxiety of the waiting, the horror of knowing that your father has willingly sacrificed you to the monster.

"Do you like it?" asked Walker from right behind me.

"I . . . um . . ." I'm not great at lying, even little white social lies. "It's well done, but it's a bit . . ."

"Disturbing? It's supposed to be."

"Oh. Why?"

"Art isn't only about beauty, you know. It's about making people see what they can't necessarily see with their own eyes."

He was right about one thing: The painting made me feel something more than just a simple response to a fabricated scene.

"Is that your work as well?" I asked, pointing toward the black, gray, and white canvases.

"My old stuff. But it seems so tedious now. I've been working like crazy lately, going in a whole new direction," Walker said, a feverish look in his eye. "It's so exciting; it feels like a blur when I paint it. I'm so absorbed in the work, I hardly notice the time going by."

"What does Andromeda think of it?"

"Andi? She poses for me when she can. Her story—actually the story of her name—inspires me. Do you know the myth?"

"I do, yes." I nodded, turning away from the disturbing paintings. I wasn't sure I was up for a long monologue about Walker Landau's artistic process. "Andromeda seems to be a popular model. Luc mentioned using her for a sculpture, as well."

"Who are you, again?" Walker asked.

"I'm Lily Ivory," I said, realizing I hadn't introduced myself. I held out my hand to shake, but he held up his paint-spattered one and declined. "I was hoping I could ask you a few questions about Jerry Becker. Did you know him well?"

"As well as anyone, I guess," Landau said as he began cleaning his brushes in mineral spirits, then wiping them with a rag that used to be a white T-shirt. "He wasn't the kind to let people get close. But when his daughter enrolled here, he started coming around more often. He was very supportive of my painting."

As Landau spoke, I concentrated, not so much on his words as on his aura. His vibrations were sincere, but confused. My mind flashed on those sociopaths who can fool lie detectors because they genuinely don't feel guilt, or shame, or other emotions that make us healthy human beings. But Landau was no sociopath; just a nerdy artist wrapped up in himself and his art.

"Yes, I was with Jerry right before . . . before he was

killed, but so were a lot of other people." A petulant note
crept into Landau's voice. "And there must have been
two dozen people who heard that fight between Jerry
and Luc last night. Why aren't they going after *him*?"

"I think the police are talking to a lot of people," I
said. "It's standard to speak to anyone who might have
been with the victim in the time before death."

"They've got it in for me."

"Have they said anything to make you think you're a
person of interest?"

"Not in so many words. But I can tell by the way
they look at me. You know, I've always been socially
awkward, an outcast. Sometimes my reactions . . . well,
they're misunderstood."

My heart went out to him. True, there was something
off-putting about Walker Landau, but I of all people understood what it meant to be an outsider. It became a
Catch-22: The more you tried to fit in, the more awkward everything became. Social misfits were doomed
before the first school bell rang in the morning.

"Walker, why were you asking Susan Rogers about
the bell tower?"

"I found her book, and I thought she might be able
to cast some light on the history of the building. This is
going to sound crazy, but there's something inspirational
about the bell tower. Whenever I get stuck, I go climb
those stairs—it's also part of the new get-fit program
Todd's been helping me with."

It was beyond me why anyone would climb indoors
when San Francisco's famous hills—not to mention the
steep, scenic stairs to Coit Tower—beckoned right outside the school's doors.

"That explains the pull-up bar," I said, gesturing to
the chrome bar suspended in an archway.

Walker curled one arm as though to show me his biceps, an amusing but unfortunate gesture that reminded

me of the old cartoon about a ninety-eight-pound weakling . . . in this case writ very tall.

"Anyway, the kids say the bell tower's haunted," Walker said. "That's crazy, isn't it? But I started hearing things myself, and wondered. Besides, I wanted to know the story; thought it might inspire my work even more. So I looked into it."

"And do you think the stairs are haunted?"

He shrugged. "They've brought me nothing but luck, personally."

"Luck with your painting?"

"That and . . . other things as well."

"Walker, is it true that Jerry Becker wanted you and Andromeda to get together?"

He blushed. "Yes, you see, that's another point in my favor. Unlike a lot of people, I *wanted* him to live—he was in favor of my marrying Andromeda."

"Please don't take this the wrong way, but . . . why would he want you to marry his daughter, in particular?"

"Why not?" he asked, sounding defensive.

"I don't mean to suggest she shouldn't. But were you two . . . involved?"

He blushed again. "Not really."

"This is the modern world, Walker. Fathers don't arrange their daughters' marriages anymore."

"Jerry wasn't your average father. He knew what was best for him, and for his daughter. And if you don't believe me, talk to Andromeda yourself."

He ripped a corner off a sketch and wrote down a number and address. "She lives on Russian Hill, not far away. Ask her. She'll back me up on this."

By the time I left Landau's studio, I was feeling a lot like Alice down the rabbit hole. What did a group of turn-of-the-last-century nuns—and the supernatural assault on the closet upstairs—have to do with a suicidal ghost on the bell tower stairs? And should I presume said ghost killed Jerry Becker, who was trying to force his talented and pretty young daughter to marry a not particularly successful artist fifteen years her senior?

Maybe Andromeda was right—a situation this convoluted sounded as if it grew out of some kind of ancient-cemetery curse. It was enough to make a witch consider recommending razing this historic building and starting from scratch.

Snap out of it, I scolded myself. If *I* was ready to run away, imagine how everyone else must feel.

After all, there was a death to consider. If an evil spirit had pushed Becker to his death, and the students were bickering and hearing noises . . . could things be ratcheting up to an all-out slaughter of innocents?

One thing was sure: However talented and wise SFPD Inspectors Romero and Nordstrom might be, they weren't half ready for something like that.

Despite my pledge to steer clear of the murder scene, I wanted to take another look at the bell tower stairs. I descended to the main floor and made my way down the corridor, turning right at the T where our ghost-hunting quartet had encountered Andromeda last night. I felt mounting trepidation as I approached, but that was normal. Scenes of trauma are difficult for anyone, normal or witchy.

Another right turn, then straight ahead.

A line of A-frame signs, meant to signal the presence of a wet floor, formed a symbolic barrier, their black silhouettes of a person falling making subtle parody of last night's tragedy. Bright yellow crime scene tape also cordoned off the scene. I ducked under the police tape, crouched, and laid my hand on the stone within the chalk outline, trying to feel something more than I had last night.

I heard a noise and swung around.

Todd Jacobs was leaning up against the stone wall,

hands deep in his pockets, looking at the same time younger than, yet older than his twentysomething years. In the dim amber light, framed by the medieval-inspired architecture, he looked like a tortured, romantic version of a surfer-dude boy toy.

"Needed another look?" Todd asked.

I nodded.

"Even though I didn't like the guy, it's still a tragedy," Todd continued. "It's been pretty traumatic for everyone, Marlene especially. And Ginny."

"Ginny?" I hadn't seen her since she was taken aside for an interview by the police last night. She had been pretty upset at the sight of the body, but I didn't have the impression she would care much about Becker.

"She's been beside herself."

"I thought she had some good news about her art."

"Yes, she called earlier. It's a great opportunity. But last night her mother had to put her to bed with chamomile tea and a sleeping pill, she was so upset. She was still asleep when we left about noon."

"She lives with you?"

He nodded. "I know what you're thinking."

I doubted that.

"How does Ginny deal with living with a stepfather only two years older than she is?"

Okay, he *did* know what I was thinking.

"Rent around here is killer, and when Marlene and I got together . . . well, the last thing I wanted to do was displace Ginny. The relationship between Marley and me is unusual, I know." He pushed away from the wall and walked slowly toward me. "We're both artistic, so maybe it's easier for us to think outside the box. All I know is that when true love comes along, it's awfully hard to say no, no matter what package it comes in."

"I suppose that's true." I had spent much of my life being unfairly judged by others, and now I found it a struggle not to judge others with the same vehemence. It was a lesson I needed to learn over and over, it seemed. "But why would Ginny be so upset about Jerry Becker? I didn't get the sense she was fond of him."

"I would imagine it was the drama of the scene, more than the identity of the victim himself."

We both fell silent for a moment, eyes on the chalk outline.

"Did you hear about the suicide here back in the early sixties?" Todd asked. "Some poor schmuck was so in love that he threw himself down these same stairs."

"I've heard the tale."

"Sad what love will make people do."

"You're not suggesting Becker threw *himself* down the stairs, are you?" I asked. That Becker's death might be a suicide had never occurred to me.

Apparently Todd shared my opinion. He shook his head. "I can't imagine someone like Jerry Becker feeling *any* emotion that strongly, least of all love. He struck me as more *destructive* than self-destructive."

We fell silent again, looking at the bleak scene.

"Hey, did you find the clothes upstairs?" Todd asked.

"I did, thanks."

"Need help carrying them out to your car?"

I had considered not taking the clothes at all, given what-all had gone on tonight in that closet. But my curiosity was almost as strong as my magical abilities; I wanted to take the garments into a more controlled situation and see whether they could tell me anything further. Besides, I had the perfect cleansing spell to cast out whatever evil might lurk within.

"If you don't mind, that would be great," I answered. "Luc offered as well, but with all three of us, we could make short work of it. Thank you."

"The closet's directly up the tower stairs here," Todd said, gazing up toward the curve in the steps . . . beyond which lay a mystery. "But to tell the truth, I usually take the stairs on the other end of the building. Call me superstitious."

"I'm right there with you," I said.

I needed some face-time with the supernatural entity, but not with a civilian at my side. I would come back and explore the bell tower stairwell armed with more knowledge about what I was dealing with, some spells at the ready, and maybe even some ghost-busting equipment.

Todd and I walked the maze to the other side of the building and climbed the more utilitarian, less-haunted stairs.

"About Marley's reaction earlier . . . She's not trying to be obstructionist," Todd said as we started climbing. "It's just that she's so wrapped up in this school, it's as if something happened to one of her children. First the talk of ghosts, and now Becker's death . . . It's been a really tough week."

"I can imagine," I said. "Todd, do you know anything about Walker Landau and Andromeda Becker?"

"Anything . . . like what?"

"I don't know. Did she take a lot of classes with him, anything like that?"

Todd hesitated so long, I thought he wasn't going to answer. Finally, as we mounted the last flight of stairs, he spoke.

"He's a little—what's the word? 'Obsessed' is a little strong. It's not like he's a stalker or anything, but his studio is full of paintings of her. She poses for him, but my overall impression is that she doesn't return his interest."

"Any idea what Jerry Becker thought of it?"

"Yeah, that part was weird. He actually seemed in favor of the two of them getting together, was even sort of pressuring Andromeda to spend time with Walker. Or at least it seemed like it, but to tell you the truth, I didn't like to spend much time around Becker."

"I hear he was a bit overbearing."

"That, and I didn't like the way he treated his daughter."

"Andromeda? How did he treat her?"

We walked down the hallway toward Luc's open office door.

"Same way he treated everyone, but . . . she was his daughter, after all. Shouldn't you treat your own daughter like a princess?"

We reached Luc's office. He and Todd shook hands.

"Looks like you and I are on moving duty tonight," Todd said.

"We live to serve," Luc said solemnly.

Together the two men wrestled the big black trunk down two flights of stairs and out to my van at the loading dock, while I followed with Hefty bags I'd filled with clothes from the chest of drawers. Oscar stuck close to me on the stairs, nearly treading on my heels, his snout banging into the backs of my calves every time I slowed down. After one more trip up and back down the stairs with wooden boxes full of miscellaneous frilly underthings, we were good to go.

I gave each of the men one of the new business cards I had made up for Aunt Cora's Closet, thanked them, and invited them to come by the store anytime. Oscar jumped into the cab, eager to leave this haunted academy. I joined him with a similar sense of relief.

Todd banged the side of the van and gave us a little wave as we drove off.

Chapter 8

As soon as we rounded the corner, Oscar reverted to his natural form—a goblin with an overactive voice box. He started jumping back and forth over the seats, recounting our adventure in the closet.

"What in the *heck* happened back there? I totally thought we were goners when the light flashed and the noise and the cold . . ."

"Could you tell what it was?"

"Scary as *heck* is what it was."

"But was it a ghost, or a demon, or some sort of angry spirit?"

Big, glass green eyes stared at me. "Yup."

"Which one?"

"All of 'em."

"*All* of them?"

He nodded vigorously, his talisman thudding against the tough scales on his chest.

"Any specifics—male, female, anything?"

"Most demons do both, mistress. They're andro-whatchamacallit."

"Androgynous?"

"*Red—light—means—stop!*"

I braked for the light on Columbus Avenue and let Oscar's words sink in. I had been hoping I was wrong.

"So you're sure there was a demon," I said.

He looked over at me with an incredulous look on his face. "D—"

"*Stop* right there." I held out a finger to him. "Do *not* say, 'Duh' and roll your eyes at me, young man. I am *not* in the mood."

"Yes, mistress."

"And don't sigh and be petulant, either."

"Yes, mistress," he said with a petulant sigh. Oscar turned to look out the window, then breathed heavily on the glass, idly drawing a pentagram on the fogged surface.

"So tell me again, just to be sure: demon?"

"Demon."

"Do you know who? Do you know its name?"

"No, mistress."

"Any distinguishing characteristics?"

"No, mistress."

I signaled to make a U-turn toward Fisherman's Wharf. "I need to talk to Aidan."

"Can't. Out of town."

"And you know this how?" If Aidan had a phone number, I was not privy to it, but somehow Oscar always knew about Aidan's comings and goings. A suspicious witch might think a certain gnomish critter wasn't being entirely forthcoming.

"Um . . ." Oscar continued. "That Sailor guy ought to be able to help."

"Sailor guy?"

"Didn't Aidan give you Sailor's name and tell you to speak to him about the school?"

"Oh. Right. Some faceless guy in a bar is my best hope. Great."

"The bar's right around the corner," Oscar pointed out.

We pulled up to another stoplight and I studied my wide-eyed familiar. I felt a lot of unexpected—for me—affection for the porcine guy, but we had only been to-gether a short time, and I was still figuring out how much to trust him and his take on the supernatural. Besides, though he called me "mistress," he had a connection to Aidan Rhodes, powerful male witch. I just had no idea why Aidan would want Oscar to spy on me, much less whether Aidan was working for good or for evil . . . or simply for the highest bidder.

Oscar shivered. I could feel his vibrations: excited but fearful. I pulled him over to my side and gave him a quick squeeze. The little goblin was undeniably helpful to have nearby when I was brewing potions—he seemed to facilitate my powers sliding through the otherworldly portals, helping me to focus my intentions—but I made a mental note to leave him at home, where he would be safe and safely out of my way, whenever I might be go-ing toe to toe with anything frightening in the future.

That included anything scary of the human variety.

And that reminded me: The first time I met Androm-eda in the shop, I sensed she was frightened of some-one—a human someone. Could it have been her father? Or Walker? I found Walker Landau's paintings of her disturbing at best, but then again he himself suggested I speak to Andromeda to support his claims about Jerry Becker. Would he have done that if he were menacing her?

None of this changed the salient point, however: If there was a demon at the San Francisco School of Fine Arts, it had to be bound and expelled before all hell broke loose, whether or not it was directly involved in Becker's death. And I was guessing I was the best woman—the *only* woman—for the job.

I had felt the spirits myself; I didn't need Oscar to tell me that something was there, though he did confirm what I already knew. What I really needed, though, was someone who could *communicate* with spirits. Oscar was right.

Time to go talk to a Sailor in a bar.

The corner of Broadway and Columbus is a vibrant, somewhat sleazy area featuring a spicy variety of sex shops and girlie shows. In between are plenty of restaurants and cafés, mostly Italian, as well as a few intriguing features such as the Beat Museum, highlighting the neighborhood's role in the beatnik movement of the 1950s and 1960s. The Hustler Club and the Lusty Lady were doing a brisk business, even on a Sunday. I found a parking space a couple of blocks from my destination, and after a cursory complaint about being left alone in the van with eerie dresses, Oscar curled up to take a nap.

Romolo Place is a quiet side street off busy Broadway. The grade of this mostly residential street is so steep that there are shallow steps carved into the sidewalk. In the way of neighborhood clubs trying to maintain their insider chic, there was no actual sign for the bar. I followed a deep blue light outside the door and the sound of a pulsing bass.

I paused in the doorway to get my bearings—bright blue vinyl couches, sleek chrome, neon. The music was thump-thump-thumping some monotonous tune I didn't recognize. The crowd was not the typical North Beach mélange of tourists, aging hippies, and beatnik wannabes; this group was young and artsy, and chicly dressed. At the moment I felt like a construction worker in my dusty jeans-and-sweater ensemble, but I would have felt like a 1950s hausfrau wearing one of my typical old-fashioned, wide-skirted dresses amongst all these toned, tanned young bodies clad only in skimpy handkerchief halters and brief polyester shifts—scraps of cloth that wouldn't have qualified even as proper petticoats in days of yore. I fit in okay in scruffier bars and Moose Lodges, but at Cerulean I stood out like a sore thumb.

Just an ordinary day in my less-than-ordinary life.

I stood on tiptoe to see over and around the packed crowd, searching for Sailor. The only thing I knew about him was that he was a man, which ruled out less than half the people in the place. I elbowed my way across the room and slid into an open spot at the bar.

"Help ya?" the bartender asked with a lift of his chin. His spiky brown hair was frosted white at the tips, and blue eyeliner complemented his eyes.

"I'm looking for Sailor," I said, leaning across the bar and yelling to be heard over the throbbing alternative rock music from the jukebox.

The bartender's pale eyes swept over me, lingering on the cleavage I had unintentionally displayed as I leaned toward him.

"Broadway."

"Excuse me?" Was Sailor living the dream in the Big Apple?

"The sailors hang out at the girlie shows on Broadway. But if you're looking for a quickie, I'll give you a go."

It took a moment for his words to sink in. "Um, thanks. I mean, *no*. Thank you. I guess."

The bartender shrugged, and the tall, thin woman standing next to me with a Celtic cross tattooed on her exposed shoulder offered to assist me if I was *looking to play for the other team*.

Flustered, I shook my head and stepped away from the bar, my cheeks burning.

As I surveyed the room, my eyes met the dark gaze of a man sitting at a booth on the other side of the room. He was slouched low, his back up against the wall, one arm resting along the top of the booth and one long black-jeans-clad leg stretched out on the seat. He wore big black leather motorcycle boots and an uninviting scowl.

After a brief moment, he averted his eyes and shook his head in a gesture of exasperation. You didn't have to be supernaturally sensitive to pick up on the fact that the man was *not* looking for company. Aidan had told me I would be looking for a psychic reluctant to use his rare talents. . . . Had I found my guy?

I made my way over to him and stood beside the table.

"Excuse me . . . Mr. Sailor?"

He ran his eyes over the length of my body, tossed back the remains of the amber liquid in his shot glass, and then looked around at the other bar patrons. When he spoke, he did not meet my eyes. World-weariness dripped from every word.

"Let me guess. Rhodes sent you."

I nodded.

He blew out an exasperated breath.

"Just Sailor," he said.

"I'm sorry?"

"It's not 'Mister' anything. Just Sailor."

"Oh. Hello, Sailor." I smiled. "Sounds like a pickup line: Hello there, Sailor. Lookin' for a date?"

"Gee, never heard that one before."

"Sorry. I'm Lily, by the way. Lily Ivory."

"Nothing personal, but I really don't care."

"Mind if I join you?" I persisted. "Buy you a drink?"

Sailor's eyes were dark, heavy lidded, and brooding— nothing at all like any of the psychics I'd ever known. I wondered if Aidan was playing a practical joke on me. Could this guy be for real? What was his story?

Sailor picked up his empty glass and shook it. "Scotch. Neat. The good stuff, none of that blended crap."

I made my way back to the bar and flagged down the bartender.

"Found your man?" he asked.

"Two scotches, neat. The good stuff." I tossed a twenty on the bar, but the bartender demanded another five. That had better be darned good stuff, I thought. On the way back to Sailor's booth I spilled about six dollars' worth when I tripped over a man in a zippered pantsuit lying on the floor. It seemed best not to ask why he was there.

I placed Sailor's drink in front of him and slid into the booth across from him.

"To your health. And it had better be good; it cost a fortune."

"Only the best." He ignored my raised glass and took a deep drink.

I took a sip. And coughed. Tears filled my eyes. Wow. Single malt.

Sailor's gloomy gaze strafed the room, as if he was searching for a more-interesting companion—or an escape route. Apparently finding none, he glowered at me.

"Well? What do you want?" he demanded.

"An entity of some sort has taken up residence at the San Francisco School of Fine Arts. I was hoping you could help me figure out what I'm dealing with."

He gave a mirthless chuckle. "Why should I?"

"Aidan said you could help. He gave me your name."

"I'll just bet he did." He threw back his head and tossed down the rest of his scotch. My glass was still nearly full.

He slid out of the booth and nodded toward the exit. I left my expensive drink on the table and hustled after him, following in his wake as he stormed through the crowd. After an awkward dance with a man built like a rugby player, I stumbled out to the street.

The night was cool; the air damp and foggy. Down

at the end of Romolo Place shone the garish lights of Broadway. For a moment, I thought my quarry had vamoosed, but then I spotted him leaning against the building a few yards uphill.

Sailor removed a small pouch and a packet of rolling papers from his jacket pocket, placed tobacco into a paper square without dropping a single shred, and deftly rolled a cigarette with his long, graceful fingers. He neatly licked the edge of the rolling paper, sealed it, pulled a box of wooden matches from his front pants pocket, lit the cigarette, sucked tobacco smoke deep into his lungs, and blew out curlicues of smoke from his nostrils.

Performance over, Sailor looked at me and shrugged.

"I know, I know. No one smokes tobacco in California." He looked down at the cigarette in his hand. "Lucky for me I'm psychic, so I know for a fact I'm not going to die from lung cancer."

"Really?"

He gave me a cutting look. "*Please*. I'm just a stubborn ass with a nicotine addiction and a death wish, like everybody else. Listen . . . *Lily*, was it? . . . That drink only bought you ten minutes of my time, so if I were you, I'd start talking."

"I thought you'd have guessed already. You know, since you're a psychic and what-all. I thought you might read my mind."

"Couldn't even if I wanted to, which I don't." He blew out a smoke ring. "Do you have *any* idea how tedious most people's thoughts are? It's enough to make a man lose faith in humankind."

I was willing to bet that Sailor's faith had been challenged by something other than mere tedium. What had happened to him to cause such darkness to hover around him like this? And why would such a misanthrope hang out in a crowded bar?

Sailor smoked and watched the passersby while I gave him a brief rundown of the spooky events at the School of Fine Arts and Jerry Becker's death. For the first time, a glimmer of interest sparked in his eyes.

"Doesn't sound like you're dealing with your average everyday ghost," he said. "Ghosts are human dead who haven't crossed over for some reason. They might make noises or slam the occasional door, but they're unlikely to manifest with overt physical pranks or violence. Not unless they were practicing magicks before they died. You'll be a loud one, I'll bet."

"Excuse me?"

"When you pass on. You're the kind who'll stick around and will have plenty to say to those left behind, as well as the power to say it."

"That's a disturbing thought."

"Living takes courage. So does dying."

"Anyway, I thought you said you couldn't read my mind."

"That's how I know what you are." He took a drag on his cigarette and shrugged. "Your thoughts are blocked, and power's radiating off you like waves of cheap perfume. I could sense it before you even stepped foot in the bar tonight."

I lowered my head and surreptitiously sniffed my shoulder.

Sailor snorted. "It's a metaphor, peaches. I don't mean real perfume. Your essence. Take my word for it—you can't wash it off."

A pair of good-looking young women dressed in skimpy negligee-like dresses brushed past us on the way into the bar.

"Heya, Sailor," cooed one, her lip gloss shining in the lamplight.

"Angelina, Britney." Sailor nodded. "Lookin' good tonight."

Lookin' cold *tonight*, I thought.

They giggled and jiggled.

"Aren't you coming in?" Angelina or maybe Britney asked.

"Only if you promise to buy me a drink."

"It's a deal," she said with a look that promised much more than alcohol.

Sailor and I watched as the two bounced into the bar. He met my eyes, lifted his eyebrows, and one corner of his mouth kicked up in a semblance of a smile.

"What can I say? It's the boots."

"I think it's that sardonic your-mama's-gonna-hate-me aura you wear like a crown."

He flashed a genuine smile. "Makes me irresistible to women."

"To *some* women, maybe."

"Not to you, I take it?"

"My mother never cared who I was with. Besides, she had terrible taste in men herself. I'm not drawn to the dark side. I get plenty of darkness all on my own, thanks very much. Getting back to ghosts . . ."

He shrugged. "Hauntings can also be the result of energy imprinting on the physical surroundings, like a movie or a record playing over and over on a constant loop, with no awareness of what's going on around it. Highly charged situations—your violent murders, your mutilations, that sort of thing—leave an energy trace. Do you know the history of the building?"

"A little. Not enough."

"Bump that up to the top of your agenda. Find out if there was a murder, act of violence, or some extreme human emotion."

"Supposedly there was a suicide."

"That might do it, though suicides can go either way. If the suicide comes at the end of an otherwise well-adjusted life, probably not. If it was a way to strike out at the world or someone in particular, then it might very well be a good basis for a haunting in which the scene plays itself out over and over again for an eternity. Sort of like giving the cosmos the finger."

"Sounds dreary."

"Hey, ghosts are just dead people, and people aren't always famous for their maturity or smarts."

"Could a ghostly loop like what you're describing interact with the living? Use them as stand-ins to replay the scene of death, something like that?"

Sailor shook his head and exhaled cigarette smoke. It wrapped around him in a swirl, lifting up toward the yellow glow of the streetlamp.

"Nah. They don't even know you're there."

"Could it be a poltergeist?"

"Poltergeists are obnoxious and noisy and partial to breaking things—sort of like a bratty child. But like a child, their powers are limited, and because they're bratty, as opposed to malevolent, it's exceedingly rare for a poltergeist to harm someone. The worst that usually happens is people get so scared, they end up hurting themselves. Besides, a lot of so-called poltergeist activity is actually out-of-control PK."

"PK?"

"Psychokinetic energy. A result of unsettled human minds, not something supernatural."

"You're saying that if the art students got themselves all worked up about what was going on in the school, then . . ."

"Their belief alone could be sufficient to create the manifestation. Sort of like a form of mass hysteria brought to life. If they truly believe they will hear noises, they start to manifest those noises."

"But that still wouldn't explain Becker's death."

"No, it wouldn't."

"What about an evil spirit?"

"Possible. A spirit is a human who died and crossed over but retains the ability to move between the planes of existence, from this plane to the next and back again. A spirit can be vengeful or helpful, like a guardian angel. Unlike ghosts, spirits can touch us. Sometimes they're harmful, but sometimes they're downright friendly."

"Friendly?"

"Sure. What? You've never felt you were being hugged or comforted by something from the Great Beyond?"

I shook my head. Our eyes held for a moment, and I felt an unexpected shock of kindred understanding. That surprised me. I wasn't kidding when I told Sailor I had more than enough darkness on my own. But looking at him now, I wondered: Do I walk around with a black cloud over me, too?

"You said spirits were of human origin," I clarified. "What about nonhuman types?"

"Demons can take corporeal form and are more than capable of reaching out to humans with the intent to harm." He gazed at me steadily, his eyes black in the dim light. "But I don't need to tell you this, do I?"

Before I could answer, two young men stumbled out of the bar and swayed down the street. Sailor and I watched until they were out of earshot.

"So you think there's a demon at the school?" I asked.

"No, I think there are a bunch of kids with overactive imaginations. A demon can't just show up, you know. It has to be summoned to this world. It's not that hard to do, and it occasionally happens by accident, but it's a pretty big deal. Did you feel a sense of yearning, desire?"

I nodded.

"Not a good sign. Anyway, if you've got a homicidal demon on your hands, you'll know for sure soon enough. He wouldn't stop at one death." He puffed on his cigarette and shook his head. "But you know that old medical school saying about diagnosing illness—'If you hear hooves, think horses, not zebras'? Same thing here. If a man is murdered, think human perpetrator, not demon."

"I've been snooping a bit, but the demon is sending out a lot more signals that any human suspect."

"Ha. They usually do. A murder in the building would stir up the demon, that much is true. Or the demon itself might have helped to inspire jealousy or passion amongst the students; it might have spurred on the murder. What's it to you, anyway?"

"Aidan asked me to look into it."

"What're you into him for?"

"What do you mean?"

"What do you owe him?"

"A lot. My life, maybe."

He let out a loud bark of mirthless laughter. "Well, best of luck to you in that case."

"I take it you don't trust him."

"Aidan Rhodes, godfather of the West Coast spooks? Not exactly, no. And if you're smart, you'll keep away from him as well."

"I'm afraid it's a little late for that. So will you come with me to the school?"

"Nope."

"But Aidan—"

"If Aidan Rhodes wants something from me, he can put on his big-boy pants and come talk to me, man to man. Sending a little witch like yourself won't cut it."

"I'm not here for him, Sailor. I need your help to communicate with whatever's at the school."

"You'll have to find help elsewhere, then. I'm not in the charity business."

"I'm not asking you to work for free. How much do you want?"

"I'm not in *business* business, either. Not anymore."

"But why?"

He pushed himself away from the wall, agitated.

"Because I don't goddamned well feel like it—that's why. Do you have *any* idea what it's like to open yourself up to that sort of thing? The agony of souls in torment, unable to move on? The horror of demons, all the way down in your marrow?" Sailor threw his stub to the pavement and squashed it with one heavy boot. He seemed abashed at his outburst and spoke in a quieter voice. "I can do without it, thank you very much."

He headed toward the bar entrance.

"Sailor—" I called out to him.

He halted with one hand on the door. "Yeah?"

"It was . . . nice to meet you."

He laughed bitterly. "Yeah. Right."

And he disappeared inside the bar.

Chapter 9

"What was Sailor like?" Oscar asked excitedly when I returned to the van.

"Sullen. Dressed in black to match his mood. Why?"

He shrugged. "He's like a legend in this town."

"Really?" I asked as I pulled away from the curb and fought heavy North Beach traffic for a block or two until it thinned out in the financial district, mellow on this Sunday evening. "That guy's a legend? What's he done?"

"He *knows* things."

"He doesn't know much about civility."

"*Big* things."

"He's no fan of Aidan's—I tell you that."

"It's complicated."

"It always is."

I'm the first to admit I'm not what you'd call a good judge of character. Not surprising, since I hadn't had much practice interacting with humans. Growing up as a (super) natural witch in a small Texas town, I learned early to stay out of people's way. The other children, the teachers, even my own *mother*, were afraid of me. If it hadn't been for Graciela, my grandmother, herself a talented midwife and *curandera* who taught me how to harness my considerable powers, I wouldn't have known a moment of tenderness. One of the many curses my powers bestowed was a near-perfect memory, which meant I recalled every alienating episode, every isolating incident, every personal and social humiliation visited upon me in my thirty-one years.

In brief, I had a few "trust issues," as they say here in California.

Still, this Sailor character was off the charts on the peculiarity scale. Undeniably good-looking in a bad-boy way, he oozed a kind of overt, primal sensuality. But the man had a chip on his shoulder the size of Lake Tahoe. What was up with that? And why would Aidan send me to see him?

On the other hand, Sailor did know a great deal about spirits. And he had confirmed a few things for me; chief among them was that whatever was going on at the San Francisco School of Fine Arts spelled trouble with a capital T.

Ghosts were one thing; demons quite another. Who was it? What did it want? How had it come to be at the school? As Sailor had pointed out, demons didn't just show up; they were summoned. Who could have summoned it, and why? And what, if anything, did it have to do with Becker's death?

Sailor was probably right about that, as well: Jerry Becker had most likely been killed by a human. He had money—was it as simple as that? They always say "follow the money" . . . but who *was* Jerry Becker? Why were people so intrigued with him? I should read Max's article about him, and soon.

The streets of San Francisco were quiet as I steered the van home to Haight Street, near the corner of Ashbury. This hippie-turned-hipster enclave was now a bustling neighborhood full of stylish restaurants, chic artists, and trendsetting young celebrities, but like the rest of

San Francisco, it closed up early. My stomach growled, and Oscar's belly answered with a growl of its own. After years spent in Europe, I found it shocking that it was so hard to find a meal past nine thirty in this otherwise urbane city. It was tough on night stalkers like me. Good thing I liked to cook.

But none of that now. I was tooling around in a van full of possibly haunted Victorian garments. Given where these clothes had come from, I wanted to drive out any lingering traces of evil posthaste. What I needed now was a potent cleansing spell. And for that, I needed the tools of my witchy trade.

Oscar and I entered the front door of Aunt Cora's Closet, made our way across the main floor, and passed through the rear storage room that housed the industrial front-loading washer and dryer, a jade green linoleum kitchen table and chairs circa 1962, a hot pot, a microwave, and a roomy storage closet. We climbed the narrow staircase that led from the rear storage room to the cozy one-bedroom apartment on the second floor.

I showered, then dressed in a freshly laundered white skirt and plain white T-shirt. Many witches wear special spell-casting garments, but I've never bothered with those sorts of details. For me, being clean and dressed in black or white was sufficient, but even that wasn't really necessary. Most ritual preparation was about helping the practitioner to focus her intent, and since I already had more power than I knew what to do with, I didn't need to harness still more.

In the kitchen, I filled my iron cauldron with fresh springwater and set it to boil on the old Wedgewood stove, then went up on tiptoe to retrieve a massive red leather tome from a high shelf—my bible, my Book of Shadows. Graciela had given it to me when I was eight years old. Already fat with spells, chants, and blessings that she had written down over the years, the book was one I had been adding to ever since, jotting down notes on what worked and what didn't, inserting new spells and lists of potent ingredients, as well as inspirational quotes and newspaper clippings—some positive, and some regarding things I must remember whether I wanted to or not.

I laid the massive Book of Shadows on the counter and started flipping through it in search of the appropriate cleansing spell. I knew virtually all my spells by heart, but looking them up like this was how I began my casting ritual and got myself focused and in the right frame of mind.

Besides, every once in a while my Book of Shadows had something to tell me. It might change the order of a familiar spell, add or subtract a page or a few lines of writing. This used to bother me—where did this information come from?—but I could only surmise that the book, like my power itself, had a life force of its own. It literally hummed with memories and rare knowledge.

I checked the lunar calendar that hung over a collection of jars of special salts: It was a waning moon, late in the month . . . perfect for the potent cleansing spell I wanted to use.

Oscar munched on Goldfish crackers and followed on my heels as I carried my basket and white-handled *boline*, a sickle-shaped knife used to cut magical herbs, out onto my lush terrace garden. I gathered sprigs of lavender and Syrian rue, bits of blackthorn and devil's pod, eupatorium and galangal. I brought the fragrant botanicals into the kitchen and chanted while crushing them with the ancient mortar and pestle I had taken with me when I left home.

Graciela swore the stone set had been handed down to her from an Aztec *curandero* who worked his magic long before Cortez had arrived on the scene and mucked things up ... but she tended to exaggerate. Either way, the mortar and pestle always reminded me of home and history.

I continued to chant while I dropped the herbs, one by one, into the boiling cauldron, then added a thin slice of unleavened bread, a tiny crumb at a time. I stirred the concoction deosil, or clockwise, until it began to swirl on its own. The brew continued to boil after I removed it from the fire, a sign of a proper brewing. Thirteen drops of raw goat's milk, two pine needles, and three threads of a spiderweb.

And finally, I cut a small X in my palm, adding two drops of my own blood.

A great burst of vapor rose from the brew, and an amorphous, barely there face emerged above me. Vaguely, I heard Oscar squeal and run away. I couldn't blame him. My helping spirit was awe inspiring, an indication of my power.

While the cauldron bubbled, I gathered the remainder of my materials. In my pantry-cum–supplies closet I found a rusty square-headed nail I had picked up from a New Mexico ghost town, the site of a major silver-mining accident that killed twenty-two men; a small spherical stone smoothed by the rushing waters of a sacred river in Nepal; and a length of red silk twine, which I knotted as I intoned my spell, one rhyme for each knot.

Finally, I brought my supplies down to the van. Oscar and I climbed in and I closed the doors behind us, then set out candles and lit them. Opening the black tooled-leather trunk and the boxes, I spread the clothes about, sprinkling them with my brew.

I set the small flat stone atop a strong wooden box and cast a circle, then set the nail upon the stone.

Striking the nail thrice with an iron hammer, I intoned:

Clavus Ferreus Malleus ...
Ferreus Ferrum Refilum ...
Ferrum Nobilis.

I scored the stone three times with the nail's point, then added the nail to the charm bag securely tied around my waist.

Next I wrapped the stone with the knotted silk twine, saying, "*I ward thee to keep harm at bay. As I will it, so mote it be.*" I repeated the lines in Spanish, then in broken Nahautl, the language of the Aztecs and Graciela's native tongue, as I had been taught. What mattered were not the exact words, but the focus of my intentions. And my powers were focused.

The air hummed with energy as I slipped into a semitrance. Scraps of paper and bits of material floated through the air on the vibrations, and the metal of the van reverberated. I subsumed myself, becoming a conduit of mystical powers, a vessel of the craft. I felt the touch of my helping spirit and my ancestors reaching through me.

Casting a spell, especially a potent one, always reminded me that what I was doing wasn't about little old me, or Jerry Becker, or the students at the School of Fine Arts. We were all interconnected.

Afterward, Oscar curled up asleep in the passenger's seat while I drove across town. Parking in the official View Area on the San Francisco side of the Golden Gate Bridge, I walked halfway across the span with my tied, treasured stone in hand.

I turned up the collar of my wool coat against the cutting, damp wind blowing across the mouth of the bay. The beguiling beauty of the Golden Gate Bridge, the way it drew tourists and locals alike, might be explained as aesthetics, a marvelous feat of engineering. But I knew it was more than that. The Golden Gate was a magical point, uniting two important bodies of water: the wind-tossed, powerful Pacific Ocean and the sheltering refuge of the San Francisco Bay. At this point, far below me, wildness joined with serenity, ceaseless motion with calm tranquility.

Not long ago I had been dragged down into those icy bay waters to face a malevolent spirit called *La Llorona*. I survived through the help and intervention of my new friends, including Maya, as well as Bronwyn and her coven . . . and lest I forget, the invaluable assistance of Aidan Rhodes, the witch Sailor had warned me against so vehemently.

I took a deep breath and steeled myself against a profound sense of isolation. I stood alone at the center of a massive bridge painted not gold, as its name implied, but the warm red of the earth. It reminded me of the precariousness of my new life. All those years wandering the globe, I tried to put the loneliness out of my mind, seeking only safety and security. But now I wanted more. A community of friends. And . . . to be brave enough to call Max and ask him over so I could jump his bones. But we had toasted to taking it slow, and that made sense—for lots of reasons, not the least of which were that he was a journalist who had just written a story on the same man I found dead, and all I knew about his wife's death was that he felt a sense of guilt far beyond the norm.

I forced my thoughts back to the task at hand. This was, arguably, the most important step of the spell: casting the danger where it would no longer be a problem.

I kissed the stone, thanking it for helping me by binding the evil within its flinty core. Like most witches, I felt a fierce affection toward what most of the world sees as inanimate objects; an innate, profound sense of kinship with the natural world, which offers solace and cloaks us with protection and fortitude . . . whether we humans recognized it or not.

Bringing my arm back, I hurled the stone as far as I could over the railing, out to the mouth of the ocean. Forever to rest in the deep, brackish realms of the sea spirits.

The next morning I had to deal with a cleansing of an entirely different and much more prosaic kind. Monday is Wash Day at Aunt Cora's Closet, the most important day in a vintage clothes dealer's week. Fans of vintage clothes take nips and tucks and mends in stride, but they have zero tolerance for dirt. Wash Day was labor-intensive, and though it tired me out, I was usually excited to spend the day just handling the clothes, and reveling in the sense of accomplishment.

But not this Wash Day. I hadn't slept well. The mares were back, despite last night's incantation. I walked my bedroom again last night, casting them out temporarily, but I could sense they were not cowed.

Clearly, I needed to stop thinking about my love life late at night.

The main challenge with vintage clothes is that almost by definition, they've been worn before—repeatedly. The only exception is "dead stock," stashes of unopened, never-before-used items long locked away in warehouses or store basements or factory sheds and forgotten. In my experience, dead stock usually consisted of items such as stockings, lingerie, and accessories, and occasionally shoes.

But most of my acquisitions had to be thoroughly cleaned before I could put them up for sale. Unfortunately, few vintage garments could be popped into my jumbo washer and dryer like modern clothing.

I glanced up at my antique mantelpiece clock. Bronwyn would arrive at nine, so I took some time to complete a little commerce-related paperwork—sales tax reports, quarterly estimates—and write checks to my

mother and Graciela. I hung my Brazilian market-
ing basket on my arm, said good morning to Conrad,
and then slipped down the street to the Coffee to the
People café. This bastion of 1960s style, decorated with
political slogans and the portraits of Che Guevara and
Harriet Tubman, remained much as it must have been
during San Francisco's famed Summer of Love, except
that these days most of the patrons were grooving to
iPods and computers rather than to transistor radios
and newspapers.

"Good morning, Xander, Wendy," I said to the baristas behind the counter.

"Hey, Lily," said Xander with a thrust of his chin. Silver glinted with each move of his head. He was a tall,
lanky young man with a sweet expression, if you could
see past his numerous, painful-looking piercings.

"Hey, Lily," Wendy echoed. "What's up?"

Today Wendy was wearing a cotton-candy pink slip
I had sold her last week, but rather than using it as intended, she was wearing it as a dress. She had paired it
with heavy black boots, fishnet stockings, and studded
black leather wristbands. Wendy was an ample young
woman, far plumper than current fashion dictated, but
she didn't let that hold her back. On the contrary, she
wore her black bob in dramatic bangs across her forehead, favored heavy eye makeup, and never went without bright red lipstick. In spite of the black leather, she
looked like a voluptuous pinup girl from the 1950s. . . .
the kind of girl mamas in my hometown would have
warned their sons about.

Wendy also happened to be a high priestess in Bronwyn's friendly Wicca coven.

Not long ago the sometimes surly baristas had decided that I was cool enough to acknowledge. I felt a
little thrill, as though I had been invited to sit at the popular kids' table during lunch.

"Lily, you've got art deco stuff at the shop, don't you?" asked Wendy as she prepared my drinks. I had ordered a cayenne mocha for myself, a blend of espresso, chai, and soy milk called Flower Power for Conrad, and three bagels with avocado and jalapeño peppers.

"Some, yes," I said. "I've got several flapper costumes and a couple of 1930s-style evening gowns."

"Perfect."

"What's up?"

"There's this dance called the Preservation Ball. It's put on every year at the Paramount Theater in Oakland, sponsored by the Art Deco Society."

"There's a society for art deco?"

"Cool, huh? Anyway, I put Aunt Cora's Closet in the newsletter."

"There's an art deco newsletter?"

"You bet." Wendy placed my drinks on the counter and started to prep the bagels, fresh from the toaster. "These folks are organized."

"What do they do?"

"Throw parties, mostly. Everybody dresses up in period costume and there's music from the era, lots of big band stuff. The Preservation Ball raises money to save old art deco buildings."

"So it's just a group of people who like the style?"

"Pretty much. I mean, I don't think they have a social agenda or anything like that. But it makes for some kick-ass parties."

"I can imagine." I pondered the idea of a social club that existed simply to enjoy a particular historical and stylistic era. Sounded like fun. Maybe Max and I—maybe we could go sometime? Did he even still like me, or had he decided he'd had enough of spooks? I shook my head and brought my thoughts back to the current conversation. "So what does it mean that we're in the newsletter?"

"It means you're sure to have your deco wardrobe scouted, and soon. Competition for really great costumes is fierce. I'll make it over in the next day or two myself."

"You go?"

"Sure. You should join us."

"Really? Would I need . . . a date?"

Wendy laughed. "It's San Francisco in the twenty-first century, sweetheart. Going stag is considered cool, not lame."

"Good to know. I'll think about it. And thanks for putting our name in the newsletter. That was thoughtful."

"Any time."

I loaded the food and drink into my basket and returned to Aunt Cora's Closet, offering Conrad his breakfast and scootching down to sit with him on the curb. Oscar joined us; I had brought him a bagel, too, even though he'd already eaten a peanut butter sandwich up in the apartment. The morning was surprisingly sunny—uncommon in coastal San Francisco, where most mornings come in gray and overcast, with the sun making a leisurely appearance after noon. The changeable weather made dressing for a day out a constant challenge and was famous for driving unsuspecting tourists into the welcoming arms of the sidewalk sweatshirt vendors.

We ate in companionable silence. Afterward, Conrad helped me unload the newly cleansed clothes from the van—we carried in the black trunk, the bags and boxes of clothes, and the music box. I looked around for the letter from France that Luc had been looking at. I checked the back of the van and amongst the clothing. No sign of it. I must have left it in the closet.

Rats. I didn't relish the thought of going back into that chamber of horrors without having a better handle on what was going on.

The bell tinkled as Bronwyn walked into the shop, coffee in hand.

"Good morning, Lily, and blessed be," she said.

"Morning, Bronwyn," I said, slipping a Pink Martini album onto the little CD player behind the counter. "There's still time to escape. Are you sure you want to spend your day off up to your elbows in sudsy water?"

She gave me a huge, generous smile. "But I'm spending my time with one of my favorite people. What could be better? And you know me; I love to learn something new every day."

I returned her smile as I started sorting through the new Victorian-era acquisitions. Bronwyn truly was one of a kind, and I wasn't sure what I'd ever done in my life to deserve her steadfast friendship.

"Those look like bloodstains." Bronwyn frowned, pointing to the brownish streaks on the ruffled ivory petticoat I was holding. "Is that normal or creepy?"

"Both," I answered. It wasn't all that unusual to find all kinds of stains, including bloodstains, on old fabric. And whatever had happened, it took place long ago. I had faith in the power of the spell I cast last night—no one would be hurt by anything here. Still, it gave a person pause.

"My mother always got bloodstains out with a little peroxide on a cloth, wiping it out," Bronwyn said. "But I don't know if it would work on such old stains. You can also leave salt on top to draw the blood out."

"We could try that. Sometimes I use lemon juice or a little white vinegar."

"Oh hey, Max stopped by yesterday afternoon," Bronwyn said.

"Oh?" My head whipped around at the mention of his name. Very cool witch. I caught myself and tried to make my voice sound nonchalant. "What did he have to say?"

"He said he was in the neighborhood and wanted to apologize to you for acting like an ass."

"Really? He said that?"

Bronwyn nodded. "Eventually. We chatted for a while, and he confessed he hasn't been sleeping well. I told him he might have been visited by mares, and that you could probably help with a spell, but he insisted there was a logical explanation and that he'd find out what it was. I told him to come by this morning."

I felt that now-familiar fluttering in my belly, and momentarily considered changing into something more flattering than the stained T-shirt and simple patterned cotton skirt I was wearing. But it was Wash Day, and somehow I thought Max was a strong enough man not to be put off by a sloppy T-shirt or two.

Bronwyn and I had our work cut out for us. Waiting to be laundered were not only all the Victorian items from the school, but everything else I had acquired over the past week. Maya gathered old clothes from the elders she met through her oral history project, and I usually hit at least two or three garage sales or estate auctions each weekend. And by now Aunt Cora's Closet was developing a reputation; I paid well for good items, and news traveled fast.

We started by separating the clothing into four piles: dry-clean only, machine wash, hand wash, and hard cases. As usual, the machine-washables pile was the smallest. Into this pile we tossed only the most recently manufactured items: vintage T-shirts, classic jeans, and cotton-blend shirts made later than the sixties. Because Bronwyn had come here to learn, I explained the process as we went along.

"As a rule of thumb," I told Bronwyn, "nylon goods or mixtures were introduced after 1940, acrylics after 1950, and labels marked polyester after 1960. Some fabrics from the sixties have specific registered trademark names such as Crimplene. They're usually clearly marked on the tag."

"What is Crimplene?"

"It's a kind of high-bulk polyester. With lukewarm water and a cold rinse, it washes and drip-dries beautifully."

"Is lukewarm a specific temperature?"

"Blood temperature."

"Again with the blood," Bronwyn said with a smile. The CD had finished, and Bronwyn started humming the song from last night. "Dee dee dum dum dum . . ." I glanced at the music box I'd found in the closet. It sat upon the sales counter, but it was not playing.

"Where did you hear that tune?" I asked.

"What?" Bronwyn threw a voluminous plaid skirt into the hard-case pile.

"That song."

"What song?"

"The one you're humming. The French naked lady song."

Bronwyn's expression suggested I was nuts. Was it possible that I was thinking about the tune and projecting it? I looked over at Oscar. Could he be doing so?

Any danger locked within the clothes had been bound and cleansed, I felt sure. Still, there was a powerful force at work if any of those vibrations came through.

I scooped up several of the Victorian dresses and petticoats and concentrated on their vibrations. They were calm, serene. Foreign, but that was normal.

"Lily, is everything all right?" Bronwyn laid a hand on my shoulder, startling me.

"Yes, just fine," I said. "Would you mind putting another CD on the player?"

Bronwyn chose classic Jimmy Hendrix, and we continued sorting.

The wash-by-hand pile included cotton, linen, and

wool items, especially those mixed with nylon and acrylics.

The largest pile by far was the "hard cases." These were silks or wools likely to "shatter" with washing, quite literally falling to pieces. Any garments decorated with old lace or ribbons also needed special treatment; improperly treated lace would lose its crispness. Taffeta or other stiff material that rustled when it moved, as well as antique items with whalebone cages, celluloid inserts, or special finishes like watermark moiré, also had to be handled with particular care.

A few pieces weren't candidates for traditional washing at all. They could be "valeted" by hanging in the fresh air.

"But don't hang white or creamy wools or silks in the sun. They yellow in direct sunlight," I reminded Bronwyn.

"I thought sunlight bleached fabrics?"

"It does with cottons, but wool and silk fibers contain cystine, which is sulfur bearing and causes a discoloring reaction in direct sunlight. I hang them in a room with a bowl of white vinegar for a few days and let the vinegar absorb any smells. On a breezy day, open the window and let fresh air into the room."

"Did you get a degree in home economics?" Bronwyn asked, awed at my knowledge of fabric.

"School of Hard Knocks, I'm afraid," I said, thinking ruefully of a number of pieces I had ruined when I first began. "You should see the meticulous method I saw a clothing conservationist use once. I'll spare you the details."

Sorting finished, we started on the hand-wash pile.

After cleansing the garments with low-alkaline flake soap in a large zinc tub, I placed them, one by one, on a white towel and blotted them dry or rolled them in the towel to soak up the excess water. We let the items air dry on wooden racks, or used a blow-dryer set on cool, finger-blocking and coaxing the garments into shape. The goal was to keep the amount of ironing to a minimum.

"Okay, now I'm sorry I volunteered to help," said Bronwyn. I noted the sheen of sweat on her brow. Slogging wet clothes was great for the upper arms, but it did make one's back ache.

I laughed. "It really makes you appreciate modern fabrics, doesn't it?"

"I'll say."

I felt a tingle and glanced at the front door where the Closed sign was displayed. It was Max.

"Sorry to bother you on your day off," he said, his eyes flitting over my soaked T-shirt as I opened the door. "Catch you in the middle of something?"

"Washing clothes. The backsplash is an occupational hazard."

We exchanged smiles. He looked tired, with dark rings under his eyes, but he was still handsome. It made me wish I had called him last night after all—if we weren't going to get any sleep, we might as well have been wide-awake together. Neither of us spoke for a long moment.

I sighed inwardly—I was a goner.

"Morning, Max," Bronwyn shouted from the back room, hands up to her elbows in rinse water.

"Morning, Bronwyn. Doesn't your boss give you a single day off?"

"Not hardly," she twanged, mimicking my Texan accent. "She's a real rhymes-with-bitch."

"Very funny," I said. "Did you stop by for a reason, or just for the wet T-shirt contest?"

"I am a man of reason. In this case, several. First, I wanted to apologize for the way I acted yesterday. I was out of line."

"Apology accepted," I said. "I wasn't at my best, either."

"Second, I wanted to set Bronwyn straight on something." He turned to address her. "The sensation of being visited by entities while sleeping is a recognized physiological condition, a form of sleep paralysis called 'hag syndrome.' I looked it up. A perfectly plausible scientific explanation."

"That's correct, dear," Bronwyn said. "But did you ever wonder *why* you're experiencing sleep paralysis? What if the 'hags' for which the syndrome is named are making you enter that so-called physiological state?"

Max grinned. "Why do I bother arguing with a true believer?"

"Because you're stubborn?" I suggested.

"Must be."

"Besides," Bronwyn added, "*witches* are called hags, did you know that?"

A bang on the front door signaled someone else trying to open the locked front door. It was Luc, the sculpture professor from the School of Fine Arts, carrying two cardboard cups of coffee. He spilled some coffee on himself, jumped and swore, and shook his hand.

"Luc," I said, opening the door. "What—"

"The hell are *you* doing here?" Max interrupted.

"I was about to ask you the same thing," Luc said, eyes on Max.

"Lily's my . . ." Max paused, and I wondered how he'd complete that sentence. What were we to each other, after all? "Friend."

"I take it you two know each other?" I asked the men.

"You could say that," Luc muttered.

"Luc's my brother," Max said. "My *baby* brother."

I now realized why Luc felt familiar—the men shared

a family resemblance. Luc was the pretty one; Max the more mature, manlier one, rougher around the edges and with those heart-stopping light eyes.

"Who's no longer an infant," Luc said. "Lily and I are . . . 'friends' . . . as well. As a matter of fact, she and I were trying on corsets together, just last night."

I rolled my eyes.

"You were doing *what*?" Max demanded.

"It's an ancient bonding ritual," I said, annoyed with both men. What, were they thirteen years old? "Invoked to ward off childish displays of sibling rivalry. Obviously, it didn't work."

Bronwyn laughed, and Luc smiled a crooked, sexy smile. "I, for one, was letting my imagination run free."

"Run amok, more like," Max grumbled.

"Stop it, both of you," I said. "Luc, you're deliberately provoking your brother. And Max, it would help if you didn't rise to the bait."

Max glowered. Luc grinned.

"I brought you coffee," said Luc, handing me a paper cup.

"Thank you—how kind. What can I do for you?" I asked. Luc looked around the shop floor, but his gaze seemed to settle on Bronwyn's herbal stand and the painted sign with the amiable slogan from the Wiccan Rede: AN IT HARM NONE, DO WHAT YE WILL.

"I was hoping to talk to you about something . . . odd."

Max snorted, arms crossed over his chest.

Luc's happy-go-lucky visage hardened. "You can leave now, Max. I came to talk with Lily, not you."

"I was here first. Anything you have to say to her you can say in front of me."

I was hoping I wasn't about to be treated to a Carmichael family smack-down.

"Oooo, this is so exciting. So manly," Bronwyn sang out above her energetic rinsing of the clothes. "I can't wait to see how this turns out."

The tension in the room eased a bit.

Luc shrugged. "Here's the deal. I think I'm ... That is, I'm afraid I might be"—he took a deep breath and blew it out—"possessed."

I choked on my coffee.

"Possessed," I repeated.

"Possessed?" Bronwyn asked.

"Possessed," Luc confirmed.

"Give me a break," Max scoffed. He leaned back against a jewelry display case, the picture of world-weary cynicism.

"Max, I'd appreciate it if you'd keep an open mind," Luc said, and I noted his vibrations shimmering with anger—and fear. "Just because you had a bad experience doesn't mean everyone who believes in these things is nuts."

"Sure, little bro, whatever you say."

"Max, please," I said. "Luc, what makes you think such a thing?"

"I've been blacking out, losing time. It's happened a few times now."

"When?"

"Last night, after you left. I've got a half-finished sculpture, but the thing is ... I don't remember doing it."

"Did you ... hurt anyone?"

He shook his head.

"Tell me exactly what happened. What's your last recollection?"

"I remember I was working in my office, but I went back into the closet because that damned music box we found kept on playing."

"The music box? You're sure?"

"Positive. I saw something in the mirror, something indistinct, kind of like mist. And that's the last thing I remember." He paused. "But there's something worse."

Max sighed, and I glared at him.

"Go on," I said.

"Now I'm afraid I may have killed Jerry Becker."

Chapter 10

Max gave a loud, dismissive snort.

"Max," I said, "feel free to leave, if you'd rather."

Arms crossed over his chest, Max looked as though he was here to stay.

"What happened, Luc?"

"That night, I remember being at the café. I remember seeing Becker there, and you, and walking back up the bell tower stairs toward my office. But that's it. When I came to, I was sitting in the third-floor hallway."

"So why would you think you killed Jerry Becker?"

"It's hard to explain. It's as though I felt a sense of blind rage, like in a nightmare."

Luc might have been sensing the fury of the demon, I thought . . . but would he have acted on that rage?

"And," Luc continued, "I lied to you yesterday about what Becker and I were arguing about. He actually accused me . . . of sending him a blackmail note."

"A blackmail note? About what?"

"I don't know; we didn't get that far. That's what he was coming up to talk to me about."

"But you didn't send anything?"

"I don't think so, but like I say, I haven't exactly been in complete control of all my actions lately. I can't imagine what I would be blackmailing him over, though, since I don't know anything about him, except that he's a cold-hearted jerk, and the whole world knew that. Anyway," Luc said, downing the last of his coffee and tossing the paper cup into the trash basket by the register, "I've got to go. I'm already late for an appointment down the street. This stuff has just been preying on my mind, and after I saw you in action yesterday, then happened to pass by your store, I thought I should get your opinion."

"Here," I said, taking a small ball pendant from my display and crossing over to gather herbs from Bronwyn's stand. The filigree ball opened to form a little pocket, in which I placed some black cohosh, eupatoriam, and Devil's Pod. "Wear this. It's a little stinky, but it will help. Is there any chance you could stay away from the school for a few days?"

"We're in the middle of midterm projects. But I'll be more careful; won't hang out alone up on the third floor anymore."

"Good idea," I said.

With a pat for Oscar, a smile at me and Bronwyn, and a curt nod to his brother, Luc left the shop. The door had barely closed before Max started in.

"Don't tell me you believe that cockamamie story?" Max demanded.

"I didn't say I believed it. But I think he does."

"And he's virtually admitted killing Becker?"

"He did no such thing. He said he was *afraid* he might have but didn't remember it."

My mind was racing ahead: How in tarnation would a person explain that if Luc killed Jerry Becker, it wasn't his fault? I was no lawyer, but I was pretty sure the state of California would not recognize a plea of innocent-by-reason-of-demon-possession. Back in the burning days, a person could claim that "the devil made me do it," though all that ever accomplished was a conviction and execution for witchcraft rather than the original crime. Indeed, in past centuries, the mentally ill, or people suffering from occasional "fits" such as epileptics, were often branded as possessed by evil and subjected to torturous exorcisms. But today, the pendulum has swung the other way; those who might actually be demonized are given enough anti-psychotic medication to turn them into walking zombies.

Just as the old exorcisms failed to help those with mental illnesses, modern pharmaceuticals were of no use to the demon-possessed.

By far the easiest way to go about this, I decided, was to first see if there was another explanation for Becker's death. Still, I couldn't help but ask myself whether, if I learned that Luc had indeed pushed the Big Cheese down the stairs to his death, would I inform the police?

"But you agree he's possessed?" Max persisted.

"Not at the moment."

"Lily, please. You've *got* to be kidding me."

" 'Fraid not. What did Luc mean about your having had a bad experience with the supernatural?"

Max shrugged and pressed his lips together. His hands rested on his hips. Tension and anxiety pulsed around him. "It wasn't something supernatural, exactly."

"What was it, exactly?"

"Bad experience with a so-called psychic."

"What happened?"

"It doesn't matter. What worries me at the moment is that you believe my brother when he says he's been possessed. Call me a cynic, but I'm thinking you both need help."

"You think he's making it up? What reason would he have to do such a thing?"

"Luc's always been a drama queen. He's probably having trouble sleeping, just as I have been lately, and fell asleep at his desk. Or . . ." He trailed off.

"What?"

Max shrugged. "Luc's had a drinking problem. He's been sober for almost a year, but . . . it's possible he relapsed and just blacked out."

"Oh, I see. Still, I need to look into it, at the very least."

"Why? Why are you mucking around over at the scene of a criminal investigation in the first place? It's not your job. You're not a cop, or a private investigator. Just walk away."

"Whatever is going on at the School of Fine Arts is well outside the expertise of the SFPD."

"And this requires your intervention why, exactly?"

I took a deep breath. "This is who I am, Max. If there's some sort of spiritual entity terrorizing people, and I can help . . . well, I feel obligated to do what I can. Can you understand that?"

There was a long pause. Finally, he said, "I don't know."

That irked me. But at least it was honest. And what did I expect from a self-declared "mythbuster"? A proclamation of love and affection despite our diametrically opposed views of the natural—and supernatural—world?

"Well, then, I suggest you figure it out. Now, tell me, why were *you* looking into Jerry Becker's death?"

"Checking out his finances, mostly. I heard about Becker when Luc took the position at the school, and got curious. His was one of those meteoric rags to riches tales that folks love to read about. It's all laid out in the article. Unlike some people, I don't keep secrets."

"Really. What happened with your wife, Max?"

The muscle in his jaw clenched.

"I'm going to run upstairs, find something for Oscar to eat. Don't mind me," Bronwyn said. At the sound of her voice, Max and I both jumped. We'd forgotten she was there.

"I'd best be going, anyway," Max remarked. "Let you

two get some work done. Besides, my attempt to apologize seems to be something of a bust."

"Not entirely," I said.

"I'll call you later, if that's all right."

"Of course."

The bell jingled as he left. My eyes followed his tall, broad-shouldered form as he made his way down the street. I hated to admit it, but maybe Aidan Rhodes was right: Max was my Darrin, and I was his Samantha . . . unfortunately, this *Bewitched* redux wasn't very funny.

Bronwyn and I washed slips, bloomers, camisoles, skirts, and dresses until our shoulders ached. Two hours later, we both looked up at the door, grateful to see Susan Rogers.

"I brought you a copy of my book!"

I dried my hands and flipped through the large coffee-table book. It included fine-colored illustrations, historical photos, and pictures of the movers and shakers in Bay Area fashion design, past and present.

"I believe it sold at *least* fifty copies, probably forty-nine of those to my mother and her friends," Susan said with a rueful smile. "But Booksmith still keeps a handful of copies on the shelf, since I'm local. They're a great bookstore. Pages twenty-six and twenty-seven have the bit about the School of Fine Arts."

I turned to the pages and noted an old photograph of the school, appearing essentially the same as it did now. There was also a reprint of a brochure with a description of the school from back in its designer days. And finally, there was an even earlier, sepia-toned image that chilled me: It showed a group of five young nuns.

The caption read, *Novices newly arrived in America from France, mere weeks before the 1906 earthquake.*

"Do you know anything more about this group of novices from France?" I asked.

Susan shook her head and looked over my shoulder at the photo. "I got that from the California Historical Society, down on Mission. It was the only photo I could find from the days when the school building was a nunnery. There's very little information about what convent they came from in France. No one knew them, and they spoke no English when they arrived. The only interesting thing I remember reading about was that not long after they moved in to the convent, they were disciplined for 'immodest behavior.'"

"What would qualify as immodest behavior for a nun back then?" Maybe they really *had* been performing in bawdy plays?

"I don't know," Susan said. "I suppose drinking, dancing, fraternizing with men . . . maybe worse. Those were quite the wild days in San Francisco history, you know. It was called the Barbary Coast for a reason: Barbarous amounts of drinking, gambling, and whoring went on."

"You're not suggesting the nuns ran a brothel out of the convent, are you?" Bronwyn asked.

"Of course not . . . All we know is that there were some scandals of untoward behavior. Then the whole group of them disappeared during the 1906 earthquake."

"Disappeared?" I said.

"Like poof? Up in a cloud of smoke?" Bronwyn asked.

"Oh, they probably just left, moved someplace safer," said Susan. "A lot of displaced San Franciscans made their way across the bay to Oakland. Nobody saw the nuns go, but it was a madhouse. Certainly no one was keeping records in the chaos after the quake, and worse, the fire."

"Fire?" I asked.

Bronwyn nodded. "The earthquake was bad and destroyed a good many buildings. But the real devastation was caused by a massive fire that broke out afterward, when gas mains ruptured. The fire raged for days and wiped out huge portions of the city."

"But not the convent?"

"No, it survived, but it was shut up for more than a decade, before it was renovated and turned into the school," Susan said.

"Hmmm. Anything else odd about the building's history?"

"A few decades ago," Susan said, "a young man threw himself down the bell tower stairs. Suicide."

"So I've heard."

Susan extracted a lime green file from her satchel, from which she drew several photocopied articles. "I pulled these off the microfiche." She spread the articles out on my sales counter, and we all perused them. "Looks as though the school tried to keep it quiet, but I found a mention of the death in the *Examiner* newspaper."

"No photo of the deceased?"

She shook her head.

"This doesn't mention suicide, or even where the death occurred," I said.

"The school must have hoped the death notice would fly under the radar. A suicide would be dramatic, bring unwanted attention to the school."

Something bothered me: Ginny claimed to have read about the suicide and made her sketch from a photo of John Daniels. Where did she get the photo?

"But what does this have to do with the clothes in the closet?" I wondered aloud.

"I don't know—maybe nothing," Susan said. "But want to hear the kicker?"

"There's a kicker?"

"The woman in question in that little romantic tragedy still lives nearby—right across the bay in Sausalito."

"How in the world did you find her?" Bronwyn asked.

Susan smiled. "I have my sources . . . and then I just

looked her up in the phone book. Seems she kept her name—Eugenia Morisett. I gave her a call last night; she's happy to talk to us. And here's the best part: She has some old clothing she's willing to part with." Susan favored Bronwyn and me with a cat-and-canary smile. "Anyone feel like having lunch in Sausalito?"

Bronwyn and I left several dresses to drip-dry over the big tub, a few others blocked out on mesh boards, several hanging in the fresh breeze, and one very disgruntled potbellied pig who was told he had to stay home.

As we left the store, Conrad shuffled over and said in an urgent whisper, "Dudettes, run!"

"What is it?" My question was answered a second later when I spied Inspector Carlos Romero ambling across the street toward us.

"Don't worry, Conrad," I said. "He's a . . . friend."

"He's a *cop*," Conrad mumbled as he disappeared around the corner.

Romero reached the sidewalk and nodded. "Good afternoon, ladies."

"Hello, Inspector," I replied. "I'm afraid we were just leaving."

"I have a couple of things I'd like to go over with you first."

"Susan and I'll pop into Coffee to the People for a few minutes," Bronwyn said. "Get you anything?"

Carlos and I declined, and I let him inside the quiet shop.

Oscar was beside himself with joy, convinced I had come to my senses and decided to bring him along. He ran circles around us, bringing a reluctant smile to Carlos's typically solemn face. Poor Oscar would be doubly upset to learn I was going again; I was sure my familiar would have a few choice words for me when I returned home later that day.

The inspector's dark eyes alit on the frilly garments hanging from a nearby rack. He reached out and rubbed a piece of delicate hand-tatted lace between thumb and forefinger. I watched with interest—I would have thought Romero too serious of mind to be distracted by such things as corsets and lingerie. Then again, as Luc had pointed out yesterday, adolescent fantasies ran deep.

"Inspector?" I urged at his continued silence.

He dropped the lace, almost guiltily. "I hear you were hanging around campus yesterday, asking questions."

"Not the whole day—I just passed by there in the afternoon. I wanted to retrieve the vintage clothing Marlene Mueller had promised me."

"Who did you speak to while you were there?"

"I met Luc Carmichael, whose office is near the third-floor closet where the clothes were kept, and then I stopped by to speak to Walker Landau before I left." I decided not to mention the supernatural light-and-sound show Luc and I had been treated to in the closet.

"Why did you want to talk to Landau?"

I shrugged. "He was in the café with Becker the night he died. And Marlene said he was nervous."

"Provost Mueller? You spoke to her as well?"

"Oh, yes, to confirm it was all right to pick up the clothes. And her husband, Todd."

"Anyone else?"

I thought for a moment and shook my head.

"Uh-huh." Romero's dark eyes swept around the shop. "Okay, what I'm still not getting here is why you're involved in this investigation at all."

"I wouldn't say I'm involved...."

The inspector fixed me with a cross between a stare and a glare.

"I asked a few questions yesterday when my curiosity got the better of me. I suppose I thought maybe people would open up to me more easily than to you. No offense."

His lip curled up in the barest semblance of a smile. "Did you find out anything?"

"I think Walker Landau's telling the truth, for what it's worth. Becker was useful to him alive. He stood to gain nothing by murdering him."

Romero let out an exasperated breath. "I don't know why Walker Landau's so fixated on his being the number one suspect. At this point his guilty response is the only thing making me look at him."

"He does seem a little high-strung," I said.

"That's the understatement of the year. Truth is, Landau's no more a person of interest than anyone else. Jerry Becker had more enemies than Adolf Hitler. We've got suspects coming out our ears. This was not a well-liked man."

"Well, you know what they say," I said. "Some people are all right till they get two sets of britches."

"Excuse me?"

"Wealth doesn't suit some people."

"Have I ever told you how much I appreciate your homespun wisdom?"

I laughed. "What about Luc Carmichael? Is he a suspect as well?"

"As far as I'm concerned, until this case is closed, my own mother's a suspect."

I smiled, but Romero looked serious.

"Tell me once again who was with you when you were ghost hunting?"

"The security guard, Kevin something, Ginny Mueller, and Maya Jackson."

"Ginny's an unexpected beneficiary of Becker's death—lucky for her you gave her an alibi."

"What do you mean she's a beneficiary?"

He ignored the question, but clearly had something

else to add. He cleared his throat, looked down at the medallions in my display case, over at Bronwyn's jars of herbs, then finally back at me.

"Inspector Romero?" I asked.

"I think I might have heard that bumping you were so interested in."

"Bumping?"

Romero shifted his weight uneasily. "Sounds. Strange sounds. At the school."

"I see."

"If you repeat any of this to anyone I'll arrest you and lose the paperwork."

I smiled. "It's not a crime to admit you heard strange noises."

"I'm a rational man, Lily. A police officer. An SFPD Homicide Inspector. I can't exactly go around telling people the building's haunted, much less that maybe a ghost killed Jerry Becker."

"For what it's worth, I do believe in this stuff, but I don't think a ghost was responsible, either. It's really not normal spectral behavior."

"That would reassure me, except that I find myself discussing what is and what is not 'normal' ghost behavior."

"You'll get used to it."

"No, I don't think I will."

There was something of an awkward pause.

"Oh, by the way," said Carlos, "I've been meaning to tell you that you can get your clothes back."

My mind was blank. "What clothes?"

"The ones we confiscated when you were involved in the last death."

"I wasn't *involved*."

He shrugged. "Whatever. You've been in town three months, and you've been associated with two suspicious deaths. Given what the police from your hometown tell me about your unusual ... 'upbringing'? ... and what you were accused of back in Texas, it gives me the willies."

"Is that a technical police term?"

The corner of his mouth kicked up in another slight smile. "What can I say? I listen to my intuition, for better or for worse."

I nodded. He didn't trust me. Maybe Conrad was right; we weren't friends after all. . . . Carlos Romero was first, last, and always, a cop.

"Anyway," he continued, "you can get the clothes back now that the case is closed. I'll make sure they're released."

"Thanks. So, back to the School of Fine Arts—is it all right with you if I poke around a little more? I won't interfere with your investigation. I'm just trying to figure out what we're dealing with here. Until I do, the, uh, 'bumping' will continue."

He nodded. "Tell you what: You do what you do, and I'm going to keep doing what I do, namely search for a real live person who was responsible for this. But if you run across anything, however crazy it sounds, I want to be your first call." He reached into his jacket pocket and laid a business card on the table. "Your *very* first call."

"I'm proud of you, Inspector Romero. It's not easy to admit you've experienced something unexplainable."

He snorted and turned to leave.

"Inspector, could I ask you a question about Max? Max Carmichael?"

His expression shifted, almost imperceptibly. "What about him?"

"I don't . . . I mean this is probably going to sound rather forward, but he tells me his late wife was related to you."

"My cousin," he said with a curt nod. I noticed a small tic at the corner of his eye.

"And her death . . ."

"Was his fault."

Romero's dark eyes were deep and unfathomable. I wished I could read what he was thinking.

"His fault?"

"And he's the first to admit it. Unfortunately, all the regret in the world won't bring her back." He started to turn away, but hesitated and looked back over his shoulder. "It's none of my business, but if I were you, I'd be careful around the man. He doesn't have the greatest track record with women."

"Shall we take my car?" I offered. "We can put down the top and enjoy the sunny day."

Bronwyn and Susan agreed with enthusiasm, and I breathed a sigh of relief. Last week, Bronwyn drove me across town to pick up some fresh goat's milk from a new source in the Mission, and within three few blocks I vowed never again to enter a vehicle with her at the wheel. She was full of good intentions, but drove as she did everything else—with joyful abandon and sweeping gestures, which sent us careening all over the road.

My companions directed me to head north across the majestic Golden Gate Bridge. The day was perfect: A robin's egg blue sky provided the ideal backdrop to cottony clouds that looked made to cradle angels. Hawks and seagulls swooped overhead while tourists crammed the bridge's walkways, taking souvenir photographs and relishing the famous vistas. The rugged Marin headlands, just on the other side of the span, jutted out into the Pacific Ocean.

I was so busy enjoying the view myself that I managed to miss the first Sausalito exit. Instead I took the second, which dropped us off in an unmarked residential area.

"Just keep heading downhill," said Bronwyn.

That was easier said than done.

Sausalito's narrow streets wind about the hills like a meandering river that defies gravity. The road started out downhill, then snaked back up before heading down again. I found San Francisco twisty and hilly, but compared to Sausalito, it's positively tame. The area is overgrown and wooded, with the houses built right on the streets so that meeting a car coming the other way requires one or both vehicles to pull into a nearby driveway or cling to the edge of the road. Old Victorians, simple beach bungalows, Italianate manors, and sleek modern structures pepper the hillsides in a fascinating mélange.

We looped and swooped around zigzagging hairpin turns, avoiding bicyclists, walkers, and children in strollers until we finally reached a main drag on the edge of the water, a natural inlet of the bay directly across from what locals refer to simply as "the City." Looking past the jostling crowd of tourists thronging the sidewalks, one could see the architectural remnants of Sausalito's history as a sleepy fishing village. The bay was jammed with sailboats, a passenger ferry, and two tugboat-escorted freighters lumbering past on their way to the port of Oakland.

We turned right, went straight up a hill so steep I had to shift into first, made another turn down an impossibly tight street, and finally nosed into a driveway of an older Mediterranean home with white stucco walls decorated with brightly painted tiles. The entrance was on the top floor, while the rest of the house was on descending floors following the grade of the hill.

A lovely elderly woman answered the door. Her pure white hair was thick and artfully styled in a relaxed bob; her eyes were a deep, startling sapphire blue.

"Come in, come in. Do excuse the mess, but the place is in quite the uproar," she said, gesturing to various cardboard boxes and items strewn about. "We've been working all morning."

In the entryway hung a large, riveting oil portrait, obviously Eugenia Morisett as a young woman. There was no mistaking those eyes.

"Thank you so much for meeting with us," I said as Eugenia led the way to a glass-enclosed garden room. We passed through a living room studded with original art work, sculptures, as well as paintings, both classical and modern.

Eugenia gestured for us to take seats on comfy overstuffed couches covered in floral chintz. Quaint leaded windows overlooked the town of Sausalito and out to the bay.

"Don't mention it. I'm happy to unload these items; I've spent weeks just cleaning out the closets. I'm thinking I'll probably sell the house as soon as the market improves. Now that my husband, Richard, has passed, it hardly seems worth the time and energy to keep it up. Only in the summertime when the kids come with the grandchildren—that's when I truly enjoy it. But one can't shape one's entire life around three weeks in the summer, can one? I might just move into the Nob Hill apartment full-time."

Must be nice, I thought.

"It's such a fabulous place," said Susan. "But I can see how it would be a lot of work to maintain. Still, it's the perfect place to display all your artwork."

"Isn't it just?" Eugenia said, preening. "I like to think of myself as a patroness of the arts. I'm on the board at the MOMA. I think art is essential to any civilized town, don't you?"

"Is some of it your work?" I asked. "You're an artist as well, aren't you?"

"Oh, good gracious, that was a long time ago."

"When you were at the School of Fine Arts?" I asked.

"Yes. Such a long time ago,"

Susan leaned forward, a delighted look in her eye. "Oh, do tell! What was it like, back in the day?"

I watched with interest as Susan coaxed Eugenia into talking about her days at the school, and I realized for the first time why Susan was such a successful journalist. She had a way of simultaneously flattering and acting so interested that a person wanted to tell her everything— even I, who never confided in anyone, felt like spilling my secrets when she gave me her undivided attention and probed.

Perhaps Eugenia really *had* been a talented artist, I thought after she had gone on for some time about how gifted she had been, and how popular. She certainly had a way of painting herself in a good light.

"I hear there was a sad incident, regarding a young man?" I asked when she started to wind down.

"Dear, sweet John," Eugenia said with a dramatic sigh, looking out over the ocean. "He painted that portrait of me that hangs in the entry."

"It's lovely."

"He adored me."

"I heard you two were engaged?"

"He gave me a ring, but it was a tiny thing," she said with a laugh. "He hardly had enough money to support himself, much less a wife. We talked about getting married, but it was mostly idle daydreaming. Among other things, at the time I thought it might be too bourgeois. The bohemian ideology was strong back then. Ah, we had such fun right there in North Beach. I really enjoyed that area, but now it's so dirty, overrun with tourists, such a pity. Oh, and the homeless . . ." She gave a delicate shiver of her slender shoulders.

"I like North Beach," said Bronwyn.

"Me, too," I said.

"Ah," Eugenia said, sitting up. "Here's Amanda now."

A tall woman entered the room, lugging two bulging

plastic garbage bags. My own arms ached in sympathy—it never ceased to amaze me how heavy clothing was in bulk.

"I can't tell you how much work there is to be done," Eugenia exclaimed. "Amanda, bring us some iced tea, will you? Please, don't stand on ceremony; look through the clothing."

I started rummaging through the big bags. It didn't take much investigation to determine that Eugenia's clothing was quality stuff.

"It looks wonderful," I said. "We don't have to unpack the bags, I'm happy to take it all. Even if I can't sell it, I'm sure we can find needy folk who would appreciate it."

Amanda came back in the room, carrying a tray of four glasses of iced tea garnished with thin slices of lemon.

"It is *so* exhausting taking care of this place," Eugenia repeated with a grand sigh as she helped herself to tea. "And now we're cleaning out the closets. There's just *so* much to do."

I met Amanda's eyes. We shared a smile. I was willing to bet that the lion's share of the work around here was done by Amanda and her colleagues. But perhaps issuing orders was exhausting as well. I wouldn't know.

"Those were magical times, though, back at the school," Eugenia continued. "We traipsed around North Beach, listened to the Beat poets. . . ."

"What happened with John?" I asked.

She gestured with her hand, as though waving away emotions. "He was desperately in love with me, but I wasn't really ready to settle down. And I was distracted by another man."

"This was Richard, your late husband?"

"Good heavens no."

"You fell in love with another man?" Bronwyn asked.

"Love had very little to do with it," Eugenia said with a laugh. "I was attracted to him. Incredible body, very manly. Very aggressive. John, on the other hand, was a dreamer, an artist."

"Did this other man go to the school also?"

"Not exactly. Believe it or not, it was the delivery boy. I know, I know, it sounds like a cliché. But he used to bring rolls of canvas, other supplies to the school. Drove the truck, hoisted the goods. I can still recall how I used to love watching those biceps gleam in the sunshine."

Bronwyn, Susan, and I exchanged glances.

"I was the belle of the ball in those days, I can tell you that. I was beautiful, and they were all in love with me." She sighed. "John, Jerry, Richard ..."

"Jerry?"

"Jerry Becker. The delivery boy."

"Whatever happened to him?"

"He ran off shortly after John killed himself. I guess it was all too much, and he realized he didn't really have a chance with me. I enjoyed our time together, but what was I going to do—live like a bohemian my whole life? If I wanted that, I could have married John, after all."

She took a drink of her tea, shrugged a delicate shoulder, and continued. "I was raised in privilege. I know people don't like to say it, but I wasn't used to anything else. This is the lifestyle I was accustomed to. I couldn't stay a student forever. Oh, look!" She reached over to a nearby bookcase. "I unearthed an old album from my student days."

She flipped through large pages of aging snapshots, showing us numerous pictures of herself with a few other students, including a very young, long-haired, beatnik-looking Jerry Becker. He had been handsome and buff back in the day, she was right about that.

"Do you have any pictures of John Daniels?" I asked.

"No. He never let anyone take his picture. He had a superstition about it; said it would steal his soul." She laughed again. The high-pitched sound was beginning to annoy me. "Silly boy."

"Then what happened to Jerry?" Susan asked.

"He went off and made a fortune—he established a line of hairdressing schools, if you can believe it. He came back at one point and declared his love for me, but it was too late. I'd already set my cap for my Richard. Richard's father was a U.S. senator, you know."

"This is going to sound odd," I said, "but did you ever have a sense that the bell tower at the School of Fine Arts was haunted?"

"Ghosts? Pfff." She gave a dismissive breath and waved her hand. "I've heard that. After the . . . incident, people said it was John's ghost. As though he would be the type. The only ghost stories *I* knew came from the sealed closet they opened up under the eaves."

I choked on a big swallow of iced tea. "The what?"

She seemed amused by my reaction.

"It was just a tale we students used to tell to scare one another, though I do believe that Jerry believed it—I remember once finding him poking around in that dusty old closet, looking through the old corsets, of all things. He even wanted me to try one on and admire myself in the mirror." She let loose yet another peal of laughter. "I refused, of course. Then there was some tale about a nun fighting off a demon. . . . Supposedly there was a group of novices that came from France and brought something spooky with them when they arrived. I guess, strictly speaking, they were more a coven than a group of nuns, but in any case, you were never supposed to go in because the demon was somehow trapped in there. And then something happened. I remember the school was closed for a few days after John's sad death, and when we came back, the closet was all sealed up."

Chapter 11

My mind raced. A coven of nuns? Did she mean that literally, as in a group of witches, or was she using the term as a derogatory reference to a group of women bent on evil? What was the "spooky" thing they brought with them?

The women's conversation had moved on while I was lost in thought. Eugenia started regaling Susan and Bronwyn with tales of student hijinks back in the day, including a fad for panty raids in the residence halls.

"I'm sorry," I interrupted, "if we could go back to the story about the nuns just for a second—do you know anything about what kind of demon it was supposed to be? Anything at all?"

"Just your everyday closet demon, so far as I know." Eugenia smiled and shrugged. "You don't actually believe in this stuff, do you?"

I ignored that question. "What happened to the French nuns?"

"I have no idea. This was all before the 1906 earthquake, you know, a very long time ago. The building was damaged in the quake, and closed for a time. When it reopened, it became the art school. I imagine the nuns went wherever it is they go . . . to a nunnery somewhere else."

"San Francisco's not a very Catholic city," Susan mentioned. "Perhaps they found an area more accommodating."

"You know, it's so odd . . ." Eugenia said with a faraway look in her eye. "I talked about this not long ago, for the first time in years. Some fellow who teaches there now—Landau is it? He called to ask about it. Isn't it funny how you can go ages without thinking of something, and then it's absolutely everywhere—just in the air, I guess."

In the air and on Walker Landau's mind. That was the second instance of his setting out to interview folks about the odd goings-on at the school. Had I missed something when I talked to him? Why was I so convinced he was innocent? Could he be cloaking his intentions somehow? I was usually quite confident in my assessments of such things, but not so long ago I had been led astray, so I knew I was fallible. I needed to speak with Landau further.

Susan, Bronwyn, and I gathered up the bags of clothes, and I wrote Eugenia my standard check in return. It seemed strange—usually I was paying elders and humble folk who really needed the cash. I had half expected Eugenia to suggest I give the money to charity in her name, but she seemed more than happy to accept the check. I suppose that's how rich people stay wealthy.

"Wait," Eugenia said. She left the room and returned a moment later with a leather and cloth letterman's jacket.

"Here. This was John Daniels's jacket. I don't know why I've kept it all these years. Why don't you go ahead and take it."

"Are you sure?" I asked. "I wouldn't want you to regret losing it."

There was a flicker of doubt in her deep blue eyes, but it passed quickly.

"No, no. You take it. It was a reminder of those care-free days of youth, but now it's just one more thing cluttering up the closets. I'm having a closet designer in next week; I've always admired how organized they manage to make things. We don't have room for silly memories."

Eugenia stood at the door and waved good-bye to us as we pulled away. Our trio was silent for a good stretch, the mood almost somber.

"What a vain, pathetic excuse for a woman," Susan finally said as we turned onto Sausalito's charming Main Street, dodging tourists on bright red rented bicycles, some built for two.

"Maybe she was trying to cover up her feelings," suggested kindhearted Bronwyn.

I knew from her vibrations that it wasn't so. There was no underlying sadness there, no genuine grief. Eugenia was self-involved to the point of being self-obsessed, and probably always had been. Still, like the rest of us, she was also plagued by moments of self-doubt. None of us escaped the human condition.

"I'm starving," I said as to avoid more dismal themes.

"Well, it seems I lured you two out here with the promise of lunch, didn't I?" Susan said brightly, good humor restored. "I know the perfect place on such a pretty day. Let's go to Le Garage and sit outside."

On the way to the restaurant, Susan regaled us with stories about Sausalito, which, like much of the Bay Area—and in particular the Barbary Coast—laid claim to a rather picaresque past. Besides fishing, the town was known for harboring rumrunners during Prohibition. And Sally Stanford, the famous madam of a popular San Francisco bordello nestled on the south slope of Nob Hill, established the Valhalla restaurant in Sausalito in 1950. Some years later she won election as town mayor.

We found a parking space in a lot behind the main square and walked to Le Garage bistro, an open-air café that reminded me of the charming sidewalk cafés of Florence. Shooing away curious seagulls looking for scraps, we took our seats at a wire mesh café table.

"I'll have a Co'cola," I said to the waiter who asked for our drink orders.

"I love how she says that," teased Bronwyn. *"I'll have a Co'cola."*

"Nonsense. Bring us a wine list. This is our day off," Susan declared with a flourish. "Today we are the proverbial ladies-who-lunch."

I had a million things to do, including getting back to my clothes washing and tracking down a demon. But the temptations were too strong to deny—the warm sun, the cool ocean breeze, the lure of new friendship. I relaxed and accepted a glass of refreshing, buttery-smooth Chardonnay.

"I tell you what, that Jerry Becker always was quite the ladies' man," said Susan. "He cut a swath in his day. He was a charmer, no denying that."

"I'm still amazed that the mighty Jerry Becker started out as a delivery boy," I said.

"Do you suppose he was so ambitious because he was trying to get Eugenia back?" Bronwyn asked.

"It sounds like *The Great Gatsby*, doesn't it?" remarked Susan. "The green light at the end of the pier and all that."

"The green light? What does that refer to?" I asked.

"You know, the light was a symbol of Gatsby's dreams of winning Daisy over. . . ."

"Oh, I never read the book," I said.

"How'd you get out of high school without reading *The Great Gatsby*?" Bronwyn asked.

"I uh . . . didn't exactly make it through high school."

Both of my companions gaped at me across the table.

"I mean, I studied, just not traditionally," I hedged. "I don't have an official diploma or anything."

"You were homeschooled?"

"Sort of. I read a lot, but somehow I missed F. Scott Fitzgerald. But I'm planning on going to the library soon, anyway, so I'll check it out and read it this week, I promise. Mmm, these breadsticks sure look good," I said in a blatant attempt to change the subject. "I bet I could eat a boot if you boiled it long enough."

I took a big gulp of wine. Me and my big mouth. I've never had friends before, so I wasn't used to having to mind what I said. Rats. This sort of thing never came up when social interaction was limited to exchanging basic pleasantries.

"What about your GED?" Bronwyn asked. "Did you get that?"

"What's a GED?"

Again with the gaping.

"It's the high school equivalency exam."

"I left the country when I was seventeen." I shrugged. "I guess I missed out on a few things."

"I should say," said Susan.

"Oh, honey, we really should get you a GED," said Bronwyn.

"How do you get it?" I asked.

"Just pass a basic exam. You're smart; you could do it."

"I don't know. . . . Me and tests don't really mix. Me and math, especially."

"I'll help you prep for it," said Bronwyn. "I'm good at math."

"Me, too!" said Susan. "Ooh, a project. I love projects."

The waiter returned. We each ordered a *salade niçoise*,

and shared ample plates of glistening mussels and crispy *pommes frites*. Bronwyn began recounting some of her flower-child stories, and Susan reminisced about her own experiences during the sixties, when she was a student at Bryn Mawr, the all-girls college. After the second glass of wine I relaxed enough to forget about demons for a while, and just basked in the unfamiliar, gorgeous setting and the company of my new friends.

Eventually I reverted to Co'cola so I could drive us home. On the way, I veered off the road at a handwritten sign for a garage sale. This was an occupational hazard: I careen as recklessly as Bronwyn when I see a sign for a sale. And the handwritten ones are, by far, the best.

Half a dozen people meandered about a scraggly lawn, poking at the myriad bits and pieces laid out on card tables, holding up the occasional item to the sun for inspection. A sixtyish woman sat in a folding beach chair; her floppy sun hat and glasses made her look as if she were sitting on a tropical beach. She smiled a welcome at us newcomers, then turned her attention back to her thick historical novel.

Garage sales are a uniquely North American institution. Sure, there are flea markets all over the world where people sell secondhand goods, but the garage sale is a different animal entirely. You have a bunch of stuff you don't want anymore, but rather than toss it or give it away, you spend an entire weekend just sitting out with your goods, making money a dollar at a time. A pewter tankard for a quarter; a hand-knitted scarf for a dollar, or seventy-five cents if you haggle; old 45s; a slightly used tricycle—the offerings are always different and almost always interesting.

Home-based sales are especially attractive to me because the goods are attached to their place of origin, so I can get a sense of locale, as well as just the vibrations from the items. This sale had no great vintage clothing, but I ferreted out a Public Enemy T-shirt and three pairs of faded classic Levi's, perfect for my Haight-Ashbury clientele.

I picked up a Scrabble board marked for sale at fifty cents, but almost put it back when I realized it was missing most of its little wooden letters. Then I thought of Marlene's love of ephemera, and wondered whether she could use the remaining dozen or so letters in one of her collages. I decided to invest two quarters, just in case, and moved on to a small collection of shoes, where I found a pair of tooled and stitched cowboy boots in metallic copper leather, and the pièce de résistance, a pair of platform gladiator sandals. That made the trip worthwhile right there.

Finally I turned my attention to the kitchenware.

Unlike a lot of collectors, I was not drawn to typical antiques such as fine furniture or porcelain figurines. Instead, I adored kitchen items. They were used day in and day out, and they carried the precious vibrations of steady, tranquil, quotidian human interactions. I found several items made of milky jade green and rosy pink depression-era glass, which reminded me of the hodgepodge in my mother's kitchen cabinets when I was growing up. Mama was always embarrassed that we couldn't afford a matching set of modern dinnerware, but I loved the different colors and patterns. It made the table seem bright and festive—one of the few such examples in our lives at the time.

As I added a vintage grater, egg beater, and iron corn bread mold to my collection of garage sale loot, I thought I might have to create a separate section for vintage kitchenwares in Aunt Cora's Closet. Maybe I could rename it Aunt Cora's Closet and Pantry? Though as Maya had pointed out to me last time I brought home a bright yellow vintage Sunbeam mixer, I was going to have to annex the neighbor's shop space soon if I kept acquiring goods.

"What's that?" Susan asked of the iron pan.

"You use it for corn bread. My mama had one. I think I was a teenager before I saw corn bread that wasn't shaped like little cobs of corn."

"That's adorable! I love good corn bread."

"I'll have you over," I said impulsively. Though I liked to cook, in my life I had never had people over for a dinner I had prepared. Not long ago, Bronwyn and Maya had joined me in my apartment and we ordered Chinese food, and already that was a first. But this friendship thing was seductive. "Do you like gumbo? My mama's people were from Louisiana, so she cooked Cajun."

"I *adore* Cajun!" gushed Susan, making me smile. I imagined that Susan would adore anything I had suggested; snake stew, even. Her enthusiasm was delightful.

Susan found a charming watercolor of Stinson Beach, the carved frame for which was probably worth more than the painting, and Bronwyn bought a few old paperback romance novels for herself and a Madame Alexander doll for her granddaughter. I wound up buying much more than I needed, but especially given the mystery that was unwinding before me, I felt drawn to the normalness of these items. They pulsated with wholesome, straightforward vibrations.

It was nearly five o'clock by the time we climbed back into the Mustang, crossed the Golden Gate, and paused to pay our six dollars at the toll booth. Luckily we were traveling in the noncommute direction; rush hour traffic was bumper-to-bumper coming out of the city.

While Susan and Bronwyn chatted about their favorite spots in Marin County, I pondered what Eugenia had told us about Jerry Becker, John Daniels, and a group of mysterious nuns.

I knew I was probably jumping to conclusions, but I couldn't seem to help myself. Could a young, jealous

Jerry have pushed his rival, John Daniels, down the stairs those many years ago? And then would Daniels's ghost have waited all this time to exact his revenge? But even if so, how did any of that relate to the demon in the nuns' closet, or were they related at all? If there were multiple spirits inhabiting the building, it was hard to believe they wouldn't interact at some point. Could Jerry Becker really have discovered something untoward in that closet? Something like a demon? Could it have helped him with his ambitious ways? One thing was clear: I needed to know much more than I did about Becker's past, and the undead.

Chapter 12

"Back to our washing?" Bronwyn asked after we lugged the Hefty bags from Eugenia's house into Aunt Cora's Closet. She acted as game as ever, but I didn't have to read her vibrations to know she was not looking forward to more backbreaking work.

"Why don't you go on home and relax? I'm actually fixin' to meet with a friend this evening."

That was a stretch. It was more that I wanted to have a little chat with someone who had known Jerry Becker well, or at least the paternal aspect of the man.

"If you're sure . . . but I don't want to leave you with all this."

"Go on—I'm sure your granddaughter will be excited to get her present. Really, I'm not going to do any more washing today."

I dug the scrap of paper Walker had given me out of my backpack and dialed Andromeda Becker, woman of the pink feathers and black spikes.

"What do you want to talk about?" Andromeda asked over the phone.

"About your dad. But I do better in person—would it be all right if I dropped by?" I asked.

It sounded as though she put her hand over the speaker; I heard muffled voices.

"Okay," she said when she came back. "Wanna come over now?"

"Perfect," I said, hung up, and looked down at my grumpy, neglected familiar. "Want to come for a ride? You'll have to stay in the car, but you're welcome to join me."

Oscar seemed torn between sullenness and eagerness. Given his visage, it was hard to tell. Finally he decided to come along, sailing into the front passenger seat.

I checked the map before making my way to the address on Russian Hill, not far from the school. The neighborhood was tidy and obviously well-to-do, though cramped. Narrow streets were laid out in a stubborn grid on the steep hills, resulting in some of the most precipitous grades in the city—the kind where the nose of your car goes over the ledge and you just have to have faith there's a road under you somewhere. Some stretches did away with auto-accessible roadways altogether, replacing them with staircases. A few tourist-laden cars were backed up at the top of Lombard Street, a brick stretch of road characterized by sharp switchbacks and featured in any number of movies and TV shows.

I squeezed my car into a narrow space between a late-model Jaguar and a shiny Lexus. On the other side of a four-foot wall along the dead end of the street was a sheer two-hundred-foot cliff of rock all the way to Chestnut Street below, interrupted only by a few tenacious scrub bushes.

The address Andromeda gave me was spelled out in brass numbers on a plain wooden door. It was a modern structure, with lots of wood and glass, taking advantage of the incredible view—not exactly the cold-water walk-up of your average starving artist.

While waiting for someone to answer the bell, I tried to quell my nervousness. After a childhood spent being turned away from doors in my hometown, I still felt out of place when asking permission to enter a house.

Andromeda Becker opened the door. Now her hair was purple, but she'd gone back to soft feathers rather than gelled spikes.

"Hey," she said.

"Hi," I said. "Thanks for seeing me."

"Sure." She turned and led the way into the apartment. I trailed her in, closing the door behind me. A great bank of sliding glass doors stood open to reveal a man sitting at a table out on the deck.

He stood and came toward us.

"Dave Kessler," he said in that hale and hearty way common to athletic men of a certain age. He was in his mid- to late forties, average looking, probably bald on top, and wearing a faded black and orange Giants baseball cap to hide it.

He held out his hand and we shook.

"Lily Ivory," I said, sorry Andromeda and I weren't alone. Dave's vibrations were confident and cautious. Self-protective, self-satisfied . . . self-interested.

"I didn't mean to interrupt your meal," I said.

"Don't be silly," said Dave, gesturing to a chair at the table on the deck. "Have a seat and join us. It's just some wine and cheese, a nice vintage I picked up last week in Sonoma, a Seghesio Rockpile Zinfandel. Do you know it?"

"I'm just beginning to learn about wine," I said, slipping into a wrought-iron chair. "I don't know much."

"Where are you from?" he asked.

"West Texas, originally."

"Not many vineyards there."

"Not hardly. Moonshine's more likely."

He chuckled and poured me a glass of the deep red wine. I took a sip; it was rich and full-bodied.

"Andi and I were just going over recent events," Dave said.

"The cops keep talking to me. I don't get why this is such a deal," Andromeda said as she sank into a chair, putting one foot up on the seat like a child. "About Dad . . . being killed. That ghost did it—we've all heard it. Anyway, he'll get his."

Dave rolled his eyes and raised his eyebrows, looking over at me as if to say, *Can you believe this?*

I smiled, but my thoughts were on Andromeda's posture on the chair. Graciela, my grandmother, would have given me a withering look at best—a smart rap on the head was more likely—for sitting like that. She had drummed it into me: A lady sits with her feet flat on the floor and her legs together. Not that I worried much about being considered ladylike these days, but youthful training ran deep.

"Andromeda, babe," Dave said with a pained look on his face, "we all know you were raised in a somewhat unconventional manner in Berkeley, but please, you're a grown woman. There's no such thing as ghosts, for Pete's sake."

His condescending tone put me on edge like fingernails on a chalkboard. At his words, or perhaps just his tone, the brash Andromeda seemed to fold in on herself.

"How would *you* explain the noises?" I asked Dave.

"The sounds?" He shrugged. "Old pipes, wind knocking at the windows. Imagination run amok, most likely."

"I take it you haven't spent the night on the grounds?"

"You're telling me you believe this stuff?"

"I'm saying I don't dismiss things out of hand without checking them out."

He sat back, let out a mirthless chuckle, and fixed Andromeda and me, one after the other, with a look.

"So you think a ghost killed Jerry," he said in a patronizing tone. He shook his head, then peered through the wine in his glass, as though concentrating on the way the light streamed through it.

"No," I conceded. "But I think something very odd is going on at that school."

"Well, tell you what," Dave chuckled again, "if anyone could get a ghost mad enough to kill him, that'd be our Jerry. He was like a walking motive to murder."

"How so?"

"A couple of ex-wives, just to start. His kids hated him. Business associates who've been burned. And you wanna get started on the lovers?"

"Maybe later."

"On top of everything else, he was a real bastard, through and through."

"What's your association with him?"

"I'm a friend of the family."

Could've fooled me.

"Or I was," Dave clarified. "Jerry and I had a bit of a falling-out ourselves."

"What kind of falling-out?"

"A business deal gone awry, what else? I set up a big deal, and he swooped in at the last moment to steal it out from under me. Classic Jerry. Don't worry, I told all this to the police."

"So who do you think killed Becker?" I asked.

"Well, it certainly wasn't Andi, here, and I told the police they should leave her alone already. Either charge her with something, or let it drop. She didn't have any motive, anyway—his money's slated to go to the school, not to his kids."

"He wrote you out of the will?" I asked Andromeda. She opened her mouth to speak, but Kessler beat her to it. "Not entirely. She'll still be comfortable; I'm just saying that the bulk of his wealth is going elsewhere."

"So are you thinking someone connected to the school killed Becker?"

"Personally, I'd check out sweet little Ginny Mueller."

"*Ginny?* What's she got to do with it?"

"She was jealous of Andi here. Crazy jealous. Plus, Jerry was . . . well, let's just say that Ginny had reason to be jealous on a number of fronts."

"Aside from the fact that there's a big leap from being angry at someone to actually killing them," I said, "Ginny couldn't have done it. She was with me at the time of Jerry's death. Andromeda saw us."

"Then there's that whack-job, Walker—" Dave began.

"Could you give me a ride to school?" Andromeda asked, jumping up and knocking over her chair in her haste.

"Oh, um, sure." The cheese plate remained untouched. "Nice to meet you, Dave."

He nodded but did not get up. Andromeda grabbed her purple backpack and left the house without saying good-bye.

"Are you . . . Do you not want to talk about Walker?" I asked as we closed the door behind us.

"I'm just tired of all these guys talking about each other, running each other down. And I am *so* sick of people telling me what to do."

We walked the rest of the way to the car in silence. Andromeda went to the curbside to climb in the passenger's seat, but she lingered for a moment, looking down over the cliff.

"A few months ago some poor guy was breaking into cars right here on this street," Andromeda said. "And when some cop chased him, he jumped over this wall and fell to his death. He didn't mean to—he thought it was just a low wall."

She stood looking down over the cliff for so long that I started to get worried. I went to stand beside her.

"But sometimes when you jump," she continued, "you don't know how far down the other side is."

"Andromeda, are you okay?"

"Sure. How do you mean?" She strode past me and climbed into the car. "Hi, pig," she said to Oscar, who was snorting in the backseat.

I pulled out of the parking space and started making my way down the hill.

"Is there anything more you could tell me about your father's death, about what happened?" I asked. "When I saw you that night, you were crying. You said you two had an argument?"

"We did, but that wasn't what I was crying about."

"What *were* you crying about?"

"I saw Todd. You know him? Marlene's boy toy? He tried to talk to me about the whole Walker thing." She shrugged. "Dave's right, you know. My dad really was a head case, or at least made everyone around him a head case."

"But Dave still counts himself a friend of the family?"

"Yeah, well, he's still friends with the rest of us."

"What was Todd going to tell you about Walker?"

"He thought Walker had some hold over Dad."

"What kind of hold? About what?"

Andromeda shrugged and looked out the window. Several minutes of silence ensued.

"And your mother was which wife?" I changed the subject.

"Number two. Dad had two kids with his first, then me with my mom, Connie. The police have been talking to all of us, asking a lot of questions. I guess when people get murdered they look to the family, right?"

"That's what I hear. Do *you* think any of the family was involved?"

"One of my half brothers lives in London, the other in Bangkok, trying to get as far away from Dad as possible, I think. So I guess they're off the hook."

"But you think one of them might have done this, if they were given the chance?"

She shrugged but started tearing up. Suddenly the mask of haughty artist and self-obsessed youth fell away, and she just looked like a child. My heart went out to her.

"Dad used to call us worthless, that sort of thing. He just wasn't very nice. I mean, even my name. Walker told me about the myth I was named after—there was this father who gave his daughter as a sacrifice to the sea monster; had her tied up naked at the water's edge. What kind of backstory is that to give a kid?"

Good question. Luckily, Andromeda was looking out her side window, so I didn't have to come up with a response. We drove past one neat flowering garden after another, full of early-spring color.

"I heard something about your dad wanting you and Walker Landau to get together?"

"Yeah, that was weird. Like all of a sudden, he decided I should settle down already, and he sure didn't mean with Dave. Dad said I had to go out with Walker some, at least give him a try."

"Do you like Walker?"

"He's okay. But he's like the last guy I'd think of ... that way. I mean, I guess I shouldn't talk. I've got bad taste in men, like my dad always told me." Andromeda ran chipped black-painted fingernails through her short purple hair. "But the weird thing is, Dad could be really . . . I don't know, easy to talk to about things like my love life. It was strange, as if I knew he would tell me the absolute truth. There aren't a lot of people who will do that, right?"

"True."

"He was kind of hard to pin down. He kept reinventing himself: son of a poor immigrant, high school drop-out, then hippie guy, then hardheaded businessman. I guess my dad had to be pretty tough, to get where he did, given his background. Here's something I bet you didn't know: He actually funded a scholarship for kids of immigrants. Sent a whole bunch of kids to school. But he kept it a secret."

I *was* surprised. That was the thing about people. They're multifaceted. Maybe Andromeda was right; Jerry Becker had to be tough to achieve what he had. Either that, or he'd had help.

"And your mom?" I asked. "Did the police talk to her as well?"

"Dunno. She's been up a tree the last two months, so I doubt they can even talk to her. But then at least that gives her an alibi, right?"

"Up a tree?" I asked. Was that slang for something?

"You know, at Berkeley."

I must have looked blank.

"You really aren't from around here, are you?" Andromeda asked. "I noticed the accent."

"People say I twang."

"It's cute. You make one-syllable words sound like two." She studied my profile for a moment. "And you've got great skin tone, pale but really olive. Hey! Would you model for me sometime?"

I could feel myself blush. "I really don't think . . ."

"Don't be embarrassed. You'd be great. You don't have to go all naked or anything, though that's a plus. Luc Carmichael says we should all think about modeling naked at some point in our lives. It frees us."

"Really. Luc said that?"

"I pose naked for him sometimes, along with half the student body. Ha! Sounds like a pun. Naked student body . . ."

Interesting, Luc had left out that little tidbit about the source of a father's anger.

I could hear Oscar snorting loudly in the backseat.

"So your mom is where . . . ?

"She's one of the tree-sitters in Berkeley."

"A tree-sitter?" An image flashed in my brain of a woman holding a sapling in her lap, watering it with a baby's bottle.

"The university fascists want to cut down some old redwoods, so a bunch of people are living up there. You never heard of Julia Butterfly Hill?"

I shook my head.

"Where are you from, Mars?" She started riffling through her backpack.

"I've been traveling."

"Must have been gone for a while."

"A good while."

"Anyway, these folks live in the trees so no one can cut them down. Aha!" Triumphant, she held up a crumpled pack of strawberry-flavored sugarless bubble gum. "Piece of gum?"

"No, thank you. So you mean they live in the trees full-time?"

"Duh," she said, shoving two pieces into her mouth. The car soon took on the sweet, distinctive aroma of artificial strawberry.

Though I was raised in a small town, I had traveled the world and rarely felt provincial. Still, the Bay Area denizens had a way of throwing me for a loop. Try as I might, I just couldn't envision living in a tree.

"How do they sleep? How do they . . . you know . . . go to the bathroom?"

Andromeda looked over at me with the first real glint of humor to enter her eyes since I had met her. "First off, there is no bathroom to go to. They pee and poo in a pot they lower to the ground."

"Are you serious?"

"It's worth it to save the life of a redwood."

I was appalled. Before I perched on a branch trying to do my business in a pot that I lowered to my earth-dwelling associates, I think I'd volunteer to cut down the danged tree myself. On the other hand, this was one of the things that had drawn me to the San Francisco Bay Area: People were crazy in really interesting, socially conscious ways.

Clearing my throat, I got back to the subject at hand.

"Did you ever see your dad with anything strange, sort of occult-seeming?"

"Like the talisman you sold me?"

I inclined my head, hating to hear my own items referred to as occult. "Any medallions, jars of powders, old books of symbols . . . ?"

"He always wore a medallion. But that's about it."

"Was there a symbol on it?"

"Yeah, but nothing I recognized. Kind of like a horoscope sign or something like that."

"Would you be able to draw a picture of it?"

"Nah. All I remember was it was kind of spiky, like a fork sort of, with four crosses at the tips. Something like that."

"Why were you the one child still hanging around your dad?"

"He paid my way."

"It's that simple?"

She shrugged.

It seemed odd to me, but then I wasn't sure what normal family dynamics looked like. My father had walked out before my first birthday, and my mother, overwhelmed, essentially gave me over to Graciela—the woman I called Grandmother—at the age of eight, when she figured out I wasn't merely a strange misfit, but an out-of-control force of nature.

"My therapist says it's more than that," Andromeda said. "She says I'm trying to work things out. She says that that's why I sleep with Dave, 'cause he's older and kinda Dad-like and used to work with my dad, so there's a parallel there, and transference stuff."

Sleeping with Dave? As Ginny would say, eee-uuuwww.

"Do you think your therapist is right?" I managed.

Andromeda shrugged. "Maybe. I never slept with my dad, though," she clarified with a quick, sidelong glance.

Thank goodness for small favors.

Andromeda thanked me for the ride and climbed out when we arrived at the school. I idled in the car for a moment, pondering what my next move should be. If only Sailor had agreed to come to the school and help to communicate with the restless spirits, I might know what the heck was going on. Then again, I might not be able to understand what they were trying to say, but at least after Sunday's supersized dose of supernatural sensations, I was starting to tease out some distinct vibrations.

As I sat at the green curb in front of the school building, a student streaked by—quite literally. The young man continued running down the street, buck naked.

Oscar gaped at the boy's pale posterior.

"Didja see *that*?"

Another nude student ran past. I tried not to look.

"This is one *nutty* school," said Oscar, shaking his head and cackling.

"You can say that again," I muttered, noting a small cluster of students in the covered hallway, arguing. Meanwhile, two couples embraced passionately under a bank of brilliant fuchsia bougainvillea.

"Wait here," I told Oscar.

"Yes, mistress." For once he didn't argue; he must have had enough the last time he'd volunteered to accompany me.

I entered the doors to the main hall. There were a

few papers strewn about the floor, and a smear of chalk dust and colored pigments near the entry looked like a modern expressionist painting. A dozen or so students lingered in the hallway or headed from one class to another; a few small groups argued about painting methods and materials.

"Kevin," I called out as I spied the tall security guard breaking up a fight between two young women.

"Oh, hey," he said. "I don't know what's going on with these kids lately."

I smiled. Kevin wasn't any older that the "kids" he was referring to, but in my experience, full-time employment tended to mature a person quickly.

"Do you happen to know Walker Landau?" I asked him.

"Sure. Why?"

"Have you heard anything . . . odd . . . about his relationship to Jerry Becker, or Andromeda Becker?"

"Not really. But I'm not really part of the gossip mill here. I work for a living."

I nodded.

"Only weird thing I noticed was Landau changed his whole style of painting lately. Then last week I saw him working on a collage, of all things."

"A collage?"

He nodded. "I always thought that was like, for kids? But a lot of folks here do it as legitimate art. Guess it takes all kinds."

"I guess so."

"He did have the grace to seem kinda embarrassed about it, though, when I walked in. I was just closing up; didn't know he was there. He doesn't usually work past midnight."

"Was he alone? Was anyone posing for him or anything?"

"No one posing, but yeah, now that you mention it, there was somebody else in the studio."

"Who?"

He shrugged. "Dunno. The whole back of the studio was pretty dark; I could tell someone sort of slipped behind the partition when I walked in, but I didn't see enough to even tell you whether it was a man or a woman. Wasn't really my business, though, right? I felt kinda bad. I try not to interrupt artists at work. They're doing some important stuff here. Look, I'd better get back to work."

"Of course. Thanks for talking to me."

"See you around," he said as he loped off down the hallway.

I headed in the opposite direction, toward the bell tower stairwell. This time the ghost—was it John Daniels?—wasn't wasting any time. As soon as I arrived, the breathing and footsteps began to sound.

Scattered herbs, a pentagram drawn in chalk, and the stubs of three candles had been set up on the second stone step. Was someone casting spells? I held the sage bundle to my nose and inhaled. Stale. No witch worth her salt would use less than potent herbs, especially when going up against an entity from beyond. And there were no strong vibrations here, no remnants of power. Strictly amateur hour.

That was good. Unless, of course, whoever was fooling around had managed to rouse a spirit anyway, without any idea what to do with it. People didn't realize what they were fooling around with when they failed to take such things seriously. I was a powerful witch, but things like Ouija boards scared the heck out of me. And they were sold to little children, in the *toy* section.

The ghostly sounds grew louder in intensity, making the stucco walls vibrate.

"I can't understand you," I said to the empty stairs.

The moaning intensified.

"For cryin' out loud, I hear you already. Hearing is not understanding, you get me?" This ghost was treading on my last nerve. I had no idea if he could understand me, but it was worth a shot. "Either *do* something, or figure out a way to communicate, or shut the heck up."

The noises subsided.

"I'm sorry," I said in the general direction of the stairwell. "I didn't mean to yell."

"Who are you talking to?"

I whirled around to see Ginny standing behind me.

"Ginny! Good to see you," I said.

She looked around, a question in her eyes. "Who were you talking to?"

"The, um. . . . the ghost."

"You're apologizing to a ghost?"

"Sort of."

Now her eyes looked wary. "Isn't this the ghost that, like, pushed the Big Cheese down the stairs?"

I shook my head. "I don't think it was responsible."

"Then who was?"

"I have no idea."

"Oh." Her vibrations were frightened, and angry. Very angry. A bitter smell of chicory floated over to me.

"Hey, I hear you're to be congratulated on your deal with the gallery," I said, moving aside as a trio of squabbling students jostled by us. "That's great news."

"Yeah, thanks," Ginny said, decidedly lacking in enthusiasm. "I've got a show coming up. Will you come?"

"I'd love to. Are you working at the café today?" I asked, noting the coffee-stained apron she was wearing.

"I was, but . . . everybody's sniping at each other. I bounced."

"I don't think anyone's intending to do it," I said. "There's something going on. . . ."

"Something to do with the ghost?"

"Sort of, yes. Ginny, could you tell me, when you were with Jerry Becker, did he ever have anything strange with him?"

"Strange?"

"Odd symbols, or jars of salts or powders . . ." As I said the words I realized how peculiar they sounded. "Just anything out of the ordinary?"

She shook her head. "But we weren't exactly best buddies or anything. Except for the fact that he was . . . 'close' . . . to my mom, we didn't have a lot of connection."

Again, the wafting scent of bitter chicory. It reminded me of the cheap, weak coffee we drank in my hometown.

"How about when you and your mom opened the closet upstairs? Did you notice anything unusual?"

"Unusual how?"

"I don't know . . . just anything out of the ordinary?"

She shook her head. "It smelled kind of funky. But there wasn't anything cool in there—no offense, but I couldn't care less about old clothes, if you get my drift. That's my mom's deal. She was Miss Fashion back when this place was a fashion institute. But I'm all about real art."

"Your mom was a student here?"

"Yeah. Didn't you know? Anyway, I gotta go. Maya's picking me up, and we're gonna take some of my paintings to get gallery framed for the show, and start packing some of the sculptures. She said you probably wouldn't mind if we borrowed the van."

"She knows she's welcome to borrow it anytime." For a young artist with a major gallery show coming up, Ginny didn't seem very happy. On the other hand, she had just walked away from her job, and her home life seemed to leave a bit to be desired. Maybe those things were weighing on her mind.

I made a note to talk to her mother about the good old student days. Marlene wasn't old enough to have gone to school with Eugenia and John Daniels, but it was an interesting tidbit nonetheless.

"Ginny, one more thing before you go: How did you know what John Daniels looked like?"

"What?"

"John Daniels. You showed me a sketch of him, but I can't find any photos of the man."

Ginny's big eyes looked anywhere but at me.

"Ginny?" I persisted.

After a long moment of silence, she mumbled, "I saw him."

"Saw him where? How?"

"In the mirror. Up in that creepy closet."

A chill came over me. "How did you know it was him?"

She shrugged.

"This is very important, Ginny. What did you do after you saw him in the mirror?"

"I got scared, so I just left. That was why Maya thought you might be able to help."

Just then a fire alarm sounded. Everyone evacuated the building.

It turned out to be a false alarm, but Ginny disappeared into the crowd before I could ask her any more questions.

Chapter 13

"You're prob'ly pretty hungry after your day running around, huh?" Oscar said as soon as I let us in to Aunt Cora's Closet.

My familiar was many things; subtle was not one of them.

"Prob'ly you're feeling just a might peckish?"

"Give me just a minute, Oscar," I said.

My familiar harrumphed and curled up, pouting, on his silk pillow.

I took a moment to hold Eugenia's designer clothing in my arms, feeling the sensations. There were mostly light wool skirt suits and Jackie O–type sheaths. They gave off a confident, arrogant, self-satisfied hum, much like the woman herself. They wouldn't be right for everyone, but perfect for some, such as the customer who needed a brash, self-assured outfit to take on a corporate board, or to face a soon-to-be-ex-husband during divorce proceedings.

A few of the outfits went beyond arrogant. I didn't sell items that seemed to contain overwhelming amounts of negativity, anguish, or evil, certainly, but many darker items had their matches. A lot of people in the world were drawn to the dark side, in need of gravity, even solemnity, in their surroundings. For them, shadows were necessary to underscore the lightness.

Lastly, I drew John Daniels's coat into my arms. The letterman's jacket smelled of leather and old fabric, and creaked slightly as I hugged it. The vibrations were subtle, aged. I felt profound melancholy, betrayal, grief—all emotions in keeping with a suicidal personality, to be sure. But the sentiments could also apply to a man who had just discovered that the sapphire-eyed love of his life was boffing the art supplies delivery boy. Maybe—

"I'm sooooo hungry," Oscar said, interrupting my thoughts. His little belly growled loudly enough for me to hear it across the room.

"I know, Oscar, I'm sorry," I said, laying down the jacket. Enough of death; it was time to focus on the living for a while. "Let's go upstairs and start dinner. You can make the salad dressing, just like I taught you. And afterward we'll practice cleaning the kitchen."

He made a face, I think. Given Oscar's gruesome, gray-skinned countenance, it was sort of hard to tell.

"So you said Aidan was out of town?" I asked Oscar a couple of hours later, as we were finishing up washing the dishes after a meal of jambalaya and red beans and rice. Discussing Cajun food with Susan earlier had put me in a nostalgic mood; the mere aroma of sassafras filet gumbo was enough to bring me back to humid, lazy evenings at home in Texas. Though my mother and I weren't what you might call "close," there were times I missed her with a visceral yearning. And don't even get me started on my grandmother.

"Where did he go?" I continued.

In nonanswer to my question, Oscar shrugged a scaly shoulder.

"When will he be back?" I persisted.

He gave me a wide-eyed look and shook his head.

"Oscar, how are you connected to Aidan? How do you know so much about his comings and goings?"

"Could we make cookies?"

I wasn't sure how far to push my familiar. I knew Aidan well enough to know he wouldn't like being crossed, and if he had sworn Oscar to secrecy, the little guy might be vulnerable to some sort of punishment if he told me the truth. Knowing Oscar, he wouldn't be able to keep the guilt off his gnarled face.

Besides, did it matter? If Oscar was spying on me, could he be telling Aidan anything I wouldn't be willing to tell him myself? *Only the details of my love life*, I thought to myself. Or more to the point, my current lack of a love life. I had checked the message machine first thing upon walking into my apartment. Max hadn't called.

After whipping up a batch of Toll House cookies using local Ghirardelli chocolate chunks, Oscar and I both overindulged while discussing the further details of the shortstop position and the San Francisco Giants' current pitching lineup, and then he curled up in his cubby atop the refrigerator to sleep.

I brought out yesterday's paper and read Max's article on Jerry Becker's meteoric rise. Interestingly, it was entitled *The Devil's Own Luck*. The son of a poor immigrant, Jerry grew up in a poverty-stricken neighborhood in the city of Richmond, across the bay. He dropped out of high school by his sophomore year and got a job driving a delivery truck. Finally, he went back to school at night, managed to secure a small loan to develop a hair-curling device, and then attracted one investor after another as he founded one of the nation's most successful chains of hairdressing schools. He then diversified into auto mechanic training and business schools, and had fingers in real estate and several pharmaceutical companies.

Indeed, despite his humble beginnings Becker seemed to have had the devil's own luck: He won a scholarship to go back to school when the first-place winner was killed in an auto accident; he sold off his first business mere days before the stock plummeted upon announcement of a new invention that would make his obsolete; his business partner went blind from a rare condition and eventually killed himself, leaving his half of the business to Becker.

I sat back and pondered for a moment. The article had only whetted my appetite. Clearly, I needed to do some further research on the Internet. But technology makes me nervous. Since my senses are so primal, I feel put off by cyberspace and all those bits of code jumping around, uncontrolled. Theoretically the computer programs had all been developed and engineered by humans, so they had no inherent spirit of their own, but I had seen energy attracted to too many odd places not to believe that some opportunistic entity might jump right into the high-tech world. And then where would we all be?

Still and all, search engines were useful research tools.

Feeling rather silly, I laid out stones of hematite, malachite, and amethyst on the kitchen table, then lit a white anointed candle for protection before starting up my notebook computer and logging on to the Internet.

I searched for "nuns in San Francisco." Up came a site for an "order" of gay male nuns called the Sisters of Perpetual Indulgence, established by a Sister Hysterectoria. Apparently they were huge in the Castro. Next I found a used clothing store in the Richmond district called Get Thee to a Nunnery. I made a note of the address, figuring I should check out the competition the next time I was in that part of town. Finally, there was a punk rock group called the Nuns who once opened for the Sex Pistols.

These were not exactly the nuns I was looking for.

Neither could I find anything significant with regard to the building that housed the San Francisco School of Fine Arts. I did find that Andromeda was right; there had been a cemetery on the site a long time hence. But it turned out that there were small graveyards all over San Francisco at one time; most of the bodies had been exhumed and moved to Colma and Oakland a century ago.

As usual, there was an overwhelming amount of information on the Internet but nothing pertinent to my particular questions, odd as they were. Tomorrow I would go to the California Historical Society, where Susan had found the photo of the French novices, and talk to a human. I liked my chances there better.

"Funny that the nuns left right after the earthquake." Oscar's voice startled me.

"What are you doing up?"

He shrugged and shoved one of the few remaining cookies into his mouth. "Couldn't sleep. Hungry."

"Why do you think it's strange the nuns left after the quake? Everyone left the building; it needed to be repaired."

He nodded. "It's just that . . . sometimes when you summon a demon, all hell breaks loose."

"Are you saying these nuns caused the earthquake by calling the demon?"

"It's possible."

"Can demons even cause an earthquake? If they were that powerful, wouldn't they be wreaking major havoc every day?"

Oscar shook his big head. "They like to play too much.

If they'd wanted to wipe out humanity, they woulda done it back during the Holy Roman Empire, I reckon."

I had to smile at Oscar's unconscious parroting of my Texan phrases. But then I considered what he was saying. It made a certain amount of sense.

Speaking of nuns . . . I had intended to check in the closet for the missing letter while I was at the school earlier, but after my meeting with Ginny, and the fire alarm, I forgot all about it. Rats. I would love to get that missive fully translated, just in case it could shed some light on this whole affair.

"Oscar, you didn't happen to notice an old letter with all the clothes we took from the closet at the School of Fine Arts, did you?"

He shook his big head.

"Durn it," I sighed under my breath. "How much do you know about demons, Oscar? Is there any way to tell who we're dealing with exactly? The entity in the closet?"

Oscar's bottle green eyes widened. "I don't know nothin'," he said breathlessly. "They scare me. Can't say their names."

I nodded. Those of us with powers and connections to the other realms had to be careful about these sorts of things. Regular humans might be able to talk about things like demons and elves and brownies without fear, but as for the rest of us, we adhered to the old saw, "Speak of the devil and the devil appears."

"You know who you should talk to, the one who knows everything. . . ."

"Aidan? I thought you said he was out of town."

"Nah, not Aidan on this sort of thing. Sailor. He's your man."

I sighed and rubbed my eyes. The last thing I wanted to think about was dealing, yet again, with the recalcitrant man in the bar. Not only was his negative attitude frustrating, but Sailor made me feel ... strangely vulnerable. He said he couldn't read my mind, but it seemed almost as though there was an elevated level of understanding between us—something beyond the norm. Given his apparent character—or lack thereof—this was not a comforting feeling.

"Let's get some sleep," I said, switching off the computer.

I tucked Oscar in his nest, showered, and crawled into bed.

Night mares circled the room again, but I think I was on sensory overload. When I was riled, my powers were focused just fine. I merely shouted at the mares to go away, and they did.

I spent the next morning finishing up laundry left over from the previous day's washing marathon and opened the store on time at ten. Foot traffic was slow, as usual for a Tuesday morning. I enjoyed the quiet and used it to rearrange the shelves of gloves, folded scarves, and miscellanea, and to lay out some new talismans I had charged over the weekend.

When Maya arrived to start her shift at noon, the store was empty of customers.

"Maya, could I ask you a couple questions?"

"Sure," she said, stowing her shoulder bag under the counter and popping the lid on a travel mug of what smelled like chai tea. "What's up?"

"I ran into Ginny yesterday. She said she's been hearing and seeing things at school."

Maya nodded, uncharacteristically quiet. Maya was no chatterbox under the best of circumstances, but neither was she as solemn as she had been lately.

"You didn't tell me that," I said.

"We've all been hearing things. You know that."

"Hearing things, yes. But she's *seeing* things, too."

Maya nodded.

"Seeing things," I explained gently, "is a whole different matter, supernaturally speaking."

"Huh. Guess I never thought of it that way."

"Are you okay, Maya? Is something bothering you?"

Maya shrugged. "Nothing special."

"Maya?" I pressed. "What is it?"

"It's just that . . . this whole situation is making me . . . I don't know . . . really . . ."

"Uncomfortable?" I guessed. Maya was supportive of me as my friend, but she wasn't intrigued by my abilities the way Bronwyn was. When it came to magic and mayhem, she was nearly as skeptical as Max.

"Yes! I mean, I'm trying to be cool and all, and you know I really respect you and everything you've been through, but it's not easy accepting what it all means."

"That there are other dimensions out there, and that our worlds sometimes overlap?"

Maya looked sheepish. "Exactly. It's all very hard to reconcile with the way I was raised. There aren't a lot of ghosts and spirits in the Baptist church. Other than the Holy Ghost, of course."

"Of course."

"Of course," Maya said, returning my smile.

"I know it's hard," I said, "and I don't want you too close to any of it, really, especially if it makes you uncomfortable."

"I'm all right. Maybe just a little at a time, okay?"

"It's a deal. Did Ginny say anything to you about the closet where we found the clothes we got from the school?"

"Nothing much. She was a little odd, I remember, when she mentioned it. I think she was just scared, but you know the sounds have been getting worse. Besides, she's been pretty upset about Andromeda's doing so well, while she wasn't."

"Those two don't like each other much, do they?"

"In your immortal words, boss, 'not hardly.' "

"Why is that? Just a student rivalry, or something more?"

"I think it's mostly just a personality clash. But on top of that . . . Ginny thinks Andromeda's dad was fooling around with her mom."

"Marlene Mueller and Jerry Becker?"

Maya shrugged and straightened a stack of promotional store postcards. "I imagine Ginny'll calm down now that she has a show coming up. Did she mention it?"

"She did."

"The reception is tonight. Want to go together?"

"So soon? I thought she just signed with them."

"It's fast; I know. But another exhibit that was supposed to be coming from Europe fell through. A ship holding the artwork sank, or something," Maya said. "But Ginny's been pretty optimistic about all of this; had her work prepped for the show already. I guess she's not wanting to waste any time."

I left Maya in charge of the store while I ran to the North Baker Library at the California Historical Society on Mission Street. To my surprise I found Marlene Mueller working at a computer.

"Marlene, how nice to see you here. This is a pleasant surprise."

"Lily," Marlene said, looking shocked, and decidedly *not* pleased to see me. "What are you doing here?"

"I wanted to look into the school building's history. And you?"

She shrugged. "The same. Trying to figure out what's going on. Do you—how can I phrase this?—Lily, Ginny thinks Jerry Becker was murdered by a ghost." She paused. Her delicate hands fluttered, and her voice dropped. "I can't believe I actually just said that. Do you think such a thing is possible?"

"No, I don't," I said, deciding it was best not to explain why.

She looked relieved. "Me neither."

"Marlene, you were a student at the school, weren't you?"

"Yes, back in the early eighties. God, that seems so long ago, doesn't it? I studied collage, paper arts in general." She gave a little laugh. "Looking at all this stuff in here makes me want to go make art. I feel the urge to cut it up—if it weren't historical, of course."

"Oh, that reminds me. I was at a garage sale, and I bought an old Scrabble game. It only has some of its letter tiles, but I thought you might be able to use them in your art."

"You bought it for me?"

"It cost all of fifty cents. Don't you love garage sales?"

Marlene smiled and seemed to relax a little.

"Was there anything unusual going on at the school when you were a student there?" I asked.

"I don't think so. I mean, people talked about the bell tower's being haunted just as they do now, and there were occasional rumors of something up under the eaves, but nothing more specific. Mostly the kind of stories young people like to tell one another about things that go bump in the night."

"But you never heard or saw anything yourself?"

She shook her head.

"Never knew anyone who claimed to have experienced something?"

"No."

"How about recently? Did you see or hear anything the night Jerry Becker was killed?"

"I wasn't on campus when that happened. Todd had

a 'boys' night out' at a concert that evening, so I got together with a girlfriend."

"How about earlier in the day? Anything strange happen?"

"No." She shook her head again. "It was just another day. Meetings, phone calls with parents, e-mailing faculty. The usual. Well, except . . ."

"Yes?"

"Just what I mentioned before. That someone took some things from my collage table. It happened a couple of weeks ago, as well. It just bothers me that anyone would have come into my office unannounced."

"No idea who?"

"No. Why would anyone want to? Couldn't they tear up their own magazines? It seems strange, doesn't it?"

"When did you notice this?"

"Right after lunch. I ran into Jerry . . . I mean, Mr. Becker. He seemed preoccupied, hardly even said hello to me. As if he were looking right through me, and after . . ." She trailed off. Again I detected the smell of shame. Her pretty eyes looked hurt and confused. "How can men be so cold?"

"That's a hard one. I think sometimes—"

"We . . . he and I . . ." Her vibrations zigzagged from shame to grief to red-hot anger. "He even made a pass at Ginny. Bastard."

So says the woman apparently cheating on her much-younger husband with a wealthy man. Being nonjudgmental was a tough gig at times. *Those who cast spells do not have the luxury of casting judgments, Lily,* I remembered Graciela lecturing.

"When you and Ginny first opened the closet on the third floor, did you notice anything unusual?"

"Like what?"

"Oh, anything at all . . . strange noises . . . ?"

"Like the ghost?"

"Sure. Or did you hear music playing, maybe? See anything in the mirror?"

She frowned and shook her head. Her vibrations were tense, closed off. She was guarded around me.

"Did you do anything unusual while you were there?"

"Like what?"

"Sing a song? Hum a chant? Accidentally set fire to a bundle of sage?" I was trying to determine if Marlene or Ginny had inadvertently conjured a demon. But it couldn't be that easy, could it? If demons were that easy to summon, this world would have been overrun by their kind millennia ago.

"Accidentally. . . . what?" Marlene's expression suggested that I had gone completely insane, but then she didn't know the full truth about me, and I wasn't about to enlighten her. Admitting that you might have a resident ghost and bringing in a "psychic" investigator is one thing; casting witches' spells quite another. Most people fear witches. The people around me in the Haight had been so open and accepting that I was starting to forget how unusual that was.

"Are you saying there's something strange in that closet? I thought it was just the stairwell."

"Never mind," I said. "It's probably nothing."

"You might ask Ginny. She's the one who discovered it in the first place." Marlene stood and hoisted her huge designer purse onto her shoulder. "Anyway, I have to dash. How do I close this computer search?"

"Click the x in the top right-hand corner," I said.

And with the click of a mouse Marlene was gone. I watched her go, then glanced down at the computer screen. She hadn't closed the program as she had thought, and a search engine showed results for "demon possession."

I wish people would stop lying to me, I thought

grumpily. How am I supposed to rid their schools of evil spirits when they keep lying to me?

"I'm Dean. What can I do you for?"

The unfamiliar voice belonged to a young man with thick black glasses and a fifties do, short on the sides, puffed up in the front, and slick in the back, à la Buddy Holly. He wore narrow black jeans and a crisp white T-shirt, and both actually fit him, unusual in the land of low-slung jeans and extra-extra-large T-shirts. It both amused and annoyed me that the local street toughs chose to dress like droopy-drawered babies in ill-fitting hand-me-downs.

Not Dean. Dean was someone a girl would be proud to bring home to meet Ward and June Cleaver, back in the day.

"I'm looking for information on a group of French nuns who arrived in San Francisco at the turn of the last century. They joined a convent here in the city, but disappeared sometime after the 1906 earthquake."

Dean looked thoughtful. "That's a familiar story. A lot of people disappear from the public records after the quake. No surprise there, since only a small percentage of the refugees were ever officially processed. Besides, the fire destroyed all kinds of records; it took years to get the bureaucracy back on track. We might find some evidence of their being at the convent, but I doubt there will be any way to trace their steps afterward. Let's look at the Ephemera Project."

For a second I thought he was referring to Marlene's collage table.

"What's the Ephemera Project?" I followed Dean to another bank of computers at a table in the center of the room.

"It's a searchable, online database linking the collections of several history groups and archives: The California Historical Society, the Gay, Lesbian, Bisexual,

Transgender Historical Society, the San Francisco Public Library, and the Society of California Pioneers," he said. "It's what we in the history business call 'nifty.'"

He took a seat at one of the computers and started typing. I pulled up a chair and looked over his shoulder, in the process noticing an intricate, tribal-inspired tattoo that peeked out from beneath his sleeve when he moved the mouse around. I wasn't sure what Ward and June would make of that.

"What is ephemera, exactly?" I asked.

"Ephemera refers to the kind of materials intended to be short-lived or discarded, such as brochures, catalogs, menus, billheads, mining certificates, theater programs, bylaws, political flyers, travel guides, wine labels . . . and sometimes letters. Precisely because they weren't created to last, they sometimes contain information that is not otherwise documented. Let's just see. . . ." He squinted at the screen. "Bingo. Here's one cross-referenced as *Five young nuns from France disappear during earthquake.*"

Looking over his shoulder, I read the facsimile copy on the computer screen. The writing was spidery and unfamiliar, with the swoops and flourishes of another era. But as my eyes grew accustomed to the style, I read more quickly.

On Saturday morning, the Sisters, who had arisen at five o'clock, were dressing when the first shock occurred. The dear old tumbledown rookery withstood the tremor. Of course, plaster and articles fell, but our old Convent remained firm. There followed the usual excitement, and they camped out in the garden that night watching the progress of the flames and snatching winks of sleep. . . . Five French Sisters had swelled our party at St. Peter's. Poor little frightened, foreign birds. They must think San Francisco a very shaky place. The procession, headed and guarded by the Brothers and some Priests, started walking all the way out to St. Mary's College. The foreign birds were agitated, carrying with them a number of items they would not let loose.

Of course, hunger and thirst assailed them. Then one of the Priests and a Sister of Mercy escorted the French Sisters by a most circuitous route, taking the entire day, returning to our old tumbledown Convent rather than reaching the ferry and, in the end, Oakland. Only the Priest escaped, having left the women behind. They are there now, all enveloped in silence, if not in smoke. We have not heard from them. However, we possess our souls in patience and pray they are not lost to us.

"Fascinating," Dean murmured. "Why would they have gone back to the convent, rather than going to Oakland?"

"Good question."

"Hey, here's something else—there's an official note here, disciplining one sister from this convent for 'un-Christianlike' acts of pagan religion, just a day before the earthquake."

I looked over his shoulder at the facsimile of a church document, complete with the stamp of the archdiocese. The handwritten scrawl was faded and hard to read, and there were no details, but Dean was right: A nun had been practicing some sort of ritual unapproved of by the official church.

"Do you know what happened to that part of town in the aftermath of the quake?" I asked. "The old building didn't burn; it's now the School of Fine Arts."

Dean's expression took on a wary edge. "You're looking into *that* building?"

"Yes. Why?"

"That's a whole other ball game." His chair squeaked as he leaned back and looked around at his colleagues, as though checking to see if anyone was overhearing our conversation. His voice dropped. "I'm not sure how to say this, so I'm just going to ask outright: Do you, uh, have an open mind about . . . certain things?"

"Certain things?"

"There's a lot of speculation about that building." His serious, horn-rimmed visage studied me. "Remains were found in the attic. They say it's haunted."

"Human remains?"

"Really old remains," he said, fingers flying over the keyboard once again. "It was like, they did this whole remodel to turn it into the School of Fine Arts, after it had been closed for a number of years after the earthquake. They say some people had died in there, got trapped in an attic room."

"But there is no attic. Could it be one of the top-floor rooms?"

"Let's take a look. Here it is: a newspaper reference." He pointed to the computer monitor. "Hmm, doesn't say much. Remains were found, but rather than remove them, the building's owners decided to seal up the room. If that's not grounds for a haunting, I'd like to know what is."

No, you wouldn't, I thought.

"But why seal in the remains?" And if they were left in the closet, why hadn't I found bones or mummified bodies?

He shrugged. "Got me," he said. "Maybe they were scared? There wasn't time? The cemetery was full? In any event, that seems to be when the rumors of hauntings started."

"So you're thinking maybe they died there? The French nuns?"

"Maybe. Oh, look: there's a photo." He clicked on the photo file, and it filled the screen.

I leaned forward to see it while Dean dropped back in his chair, as if shoved by an unseen hand. The grainy photo was of the small room where I had been just two days ago. Everything looked exactly the same. And if you looked closely, you could make out a vague image of a woman's face reflected in the mirror, as well as round balls or streaks of light: orbs.

"Is that—?" Dean asked.

"I think so," I confirmed.

He looked at me, wide-eyed. "There's an ancient belief that after someone has died in a house, the mirrors must be covered or else the soul will be trapped in the mirror. Which is bad enough, if you think about it. But it gets worse: The ghost will steal the soul of anyone who admires his or her reflection in the mirror."

"I've heard that, too," I said. But I had never known whether to believe it. I should spend more time in libraries. Clearly, one can learn a lot.

"Maybe the women went back to the convent," Dean breathed, "and *died* up there in this room, and their souls are now trapped in the looking glass."

"We might be getting a little ahead of ourselves," I said, though I feared maybe old Dean was on to something. That mirror shimmered too brightly, and I had seen something in it myself—as had Luc, and Ginny . . . "The face in the mirror could be a trick of the light, or a flaw in the developing process. Photography was still pretty primitive back then."

"Maybe," he said, clearly unconvinced. "Hey, did you know that vampires and witches have no reflections in mirrors because they have no souls?"

I looked into his innocent, young eyes. Why did it still hurt so much when people said things like that?

"Everyone has a soul, Dean," I said, my voice sounding hollow to my ears.

"Not necess—oh." Realization dawned in his eyes. "My bad. No offense. Some of my, um, best friends are witches."

"Personally, I don't hold with that sort of nonsense," I joked, hoping to put Dean at ease. Judging by his rapid retreat behind a door marked STAFF ONLY, it's safe to say I failed.

Chapter 14

Having a world of information at my fingertips should have felt exhilarating. Instead, I felt like scum.

This was because I had moved on to the public library, and opened the *San Francisco Chronicle*'s online database to look up Max Carmichael.

Not that I doubted Max's intentions, and I certainly didn't *really* think he had anything to hide. But I felt compelled to check just in case he was a wanted serial killer whose psycho vibrations I had somehow failed to pick up. Or, say, because Deborah was his fifth wife to die under mysterious circumstances. I felt disloyal, but when I was a child, *Blackbeard* had been a favorite, albeit macabre, bedtime story. No wonder I grew up to be so different. The scene of the curious new woman finding the heads of Blackbeard's previous wives . . . Well, let's just say I've always been too curious for my own good.

I read that Max had been married for six years to Deborah Morales, during which time they lived downtown, near the Ferry Building. Her obituary did not mention a cause of death, but she had been only thirty-two years old. In lieu of flowers, donations had been directed toward Children's Hospital Oakland. She was survived by her husband, Max, and a truly impressive list of relatives.

Other than the obituary, I found nothing naming Max except a long list of professional accomplishments, and references to his byline on what seemed to be thousands of newspaper and magazine articles. The man was a successful journalist, after all.

Next I turned to the library's holdings on demonology, which proved to be limited mostly to "New Age" materials. This sort of thing frustrated me. Demonology was a deadly serious subject, not to be treated lightly.

Just before leaving, I remembered to check out a copy of *The Great Gatsby*, as I had promised Susan and Bronwyn. Maybe it would shed some light on Jerry Becker's character, or, at least, distract me from thoughts of love late at night. And even if not, it would fill a gap in my literary education. An encyclopedic knowledge of fairy tales—most of which were true even though normal humans thought of them as harmless legends—could only take a witch so far.

I parked in the driveway I rented several doors down from my store—parking was impossible in Haight-Ashbury, even for me—and walked back to Aunt Cora's Closet. As I passed by my neighbor's shop, Peaceful Things, I remembered the owner's showing me her copy of the *Malleus Mallificarum*, the witch hunters' bible. The *Malleus* dealt with witches, not demons, but it reminded me of something: In past centuries, folks knew better how to deal with demons. Medieval monks, unburdened by the distractions or cynicism of the modern world, spent their lives detailing the names, characteristics, and behaviors of demons; most important, they noted methods of exorcising a demon.

That's what I needed, I realized. An old-fashioned

demonology would help me figure out what I was dealing with, and how to get rid of it.

And if that failed, I would have to find a way to force Aidan to tell me what the heck was going on.

Peaceful Things also had an unusual mirror in the front display window: It was framed on only three sides. Such mirrors were used by witches for scrying, or "seeing" as one would in a crystal ball, presuming one had more talent for such visions than I.

I thought about the mirror in the closet at the School of Fine Arts. I knew I couldn't avoid it any longer; the mirror needed to be destroyed before more innocent folks looked into it.

My mind was burdened by the time I walked into Aunt Cora's Closet, but as usual I was heartened simply by walking through my front door. I had made new moth-chasing sachets last week, and the whole store was scented with the essence of rosemary and mint. Eight or nine customers wandered the aisles, smiling and talking as they held up outfits to themselves. Bronwyn was chatting with a friend while she packed herbs in a small burlap sack, and Maya was exchanging pleasantries with a customer while she rang up her purchases on my antique register.

I *love* my job.

"Lily, thank goodness you're here," Maya said as her customer gathered her bags and left. "A customer is looking for a special dress for the upcoming Art Deco Society ball."

"Hi, I'm Claudia," said a woman about thirty years old, with mocha-colored skin, long straight hair, and exotic features. She held out a hand to shake, and a mischievous grin lit up her face. I liked her immediately. "I write the newsletter for the Art Deco Society, so I've got a jump on the competition. I need a fabulous dress for the dance at Oakland's Paramount Theater. Another thing . . . I don't suppose you or your friend there"— she motioned to Bronwyn—"know anything about love potions?"

"As it just so happens, I do," I said, a bit breathless. Until a few days ago, I would have denied knowing anything about any kind of spell or charm. I was becoming braver around these Bay Area people.

"The important thing to remember about love spells is that the object of your affection needs to be inclined that way, anyway," I explained. "A charm can help overcome a hurdle, but it can't force someone to feel something they otherwise wouldn't."

I was not entirely forthcoming. There were stronger "love" spells, more than capable of compelling a person to exhibit a certain kind of behavior . . . but I gave them a wide berth. Such spells crossed the sometimes-too-thin line between heartfelt love and mindless obsession. Witchcraft could be scary.

"I understand," Claudia said. "I just want him to realize I'm alive and possibly perfect for him, know what I mean?"

"I'll mix something up. But first things first: I have a couple of dresses in the back that I think would be perfect for you."

I brought out a few treasures. First was a 1920s gold lamé flapper gown I bought from an estate sale at a Pacific Heights mansion; it was in almost-mint condition, having been worn only once or twice. The gorgeous chemise-style gown was made with an under bodice that snapped closed in front, as well as at the front-left waist. The drape was gathered up into a large bow over the hip and secured with a rhinestone-embellished metal ornament. The dress featured a woven pattern of lotus blossoms, a symbol of the sun and rebirth.

"Cool Egyptian motif," Maya commented.

"The discovery of King Tut's tomb in the early 1920s sparked a craze for all things Egyptian," I explained. "It also influenced interior design and fashion."

"It's very nice," Claudia said, but her voice betrayed her doubt. The twenties style, cut large and meant to drape on the body, tended to look droopy on the hanger. Claudia was more drawn to a full-length bias-cut floral dinner dress in purple and gold, with a surplice-style wrapped bodice, an attached belt with a jeweled buckle, and a plunging back. I could tell it wouldn't suit her as well, and not for the first time I wondered why we humans were so often drawn to things not right for us.

Recently I had attained a smidgen of local fame for finding suitable items for my patrons by matching the vibrations of clothing to customers' auras. Most of them just felt better about themselves in the clothes; they didn't attribute this to anything magical, but to the little lift we all feel when wearing something flattering.

I brought both dresses into the large communal dressing room and helped Claudia put them on. Dressy clothes from earlier than the forties were famously difficult to adjust properly by oneself; the nice stuff, especially, was made with the assumption that the woman wearing the clothes had a maid to help.

Claudia tried the floor-length gown first. It was a lovely piece, but didn't do much for her. Next I helped her put on the flapper dress.

"Like a lot of flapper dresses, it's easier to leave all the snaps and hooks closed and simply slip the dress over your head," I said, carefully bunching the lamé in my hands to make it easier. The ample fabric slunk down the length of her body, over her hips and chest.

We both stood back and looked at her reflection in the mirror.

"You look just lovely," I said. Though the dress was a

tad large for her petite frame, its looseness fit the style. "A few nips and tucks and it'll be perfect."

Claudia looked delighted. "Is that really me?"

"Wow, that dress looks *perfect* on you!" exclaimed Maya. I smiled at her wide-eyed expression. Maya wasn't usually much for gushing. She glanced at me and smiled, a little sheepish. "It didn't look like much on the hanger."

"They never do."

"It's really perfect," said Claudia, smiling and twisting around to see herself at various angles in the full-length mirrors.

"Would this go with it?" Maya asked, holding up a posh embroidered raw silk duster. Simply tailored, the coat was quintessential art deco, wrapping asymmetrically with a large button and loop closure and single interior snap. The collar, cuffs, patch pockets, and wide band around the hemline were all heavily embroidered by hand in silk floss. The only flaw was a very slight bleeding of the silk floss onto the raw silk, but this was faint and hardly noticeable.

Claudia pulled it on over the gold lamé dress. It was as though they were made for each other.

"Good call, Maya," I said.

I made note of a few simple alterations, promising to have it ready for her in two weeks.

While Claudia poked around the shop, Bronwyn and I mixed some herbs for a simple love charm. I had to run upstairs to my garden to supplement Bronwyn's stash with a few items.

The recipe for the love spell read a little bit like a recipe for muffins, if you ignored the rocks and tree bark. I gathered together an orange slice, two sticks of cinnamon, a handful of cloves, two teaspoons of garlic, a tiger lily petal, a dash of muddy water, chips of tiger's eye and rose quartz, and a tablespoon of olive oil. I folded these ingredients together and added a handful of dark chocolate chips, one pinch each of sugar, sage, and ginger, a drop of amber oil and one of vanilla, a piece of bark from a witch hazel tree. Finally I added one smooth rock from a riverbed and a chip of real gold.

After mixing all of this together, I placed the ingredients into a black silk bag.

"Keep this with you at all times," I told Claudia. "Stroke it, hold it, and think about the object of your desire. Concentrate on that person, but think only about positive things. And here's the weird part: Bodily fluids enhance the power of the potion, so if you want, you can add a drop of your saliva or even blood."

"Ew," she said.

I laughed. "I told you it was the weird part. It's not necessary to the charm, but it does intensify the effects. Just FYI."

"Aren't you supposed to ..." She looked embarrassed. "You know, say something?"

"You mean like 'abracadabra'?" I held out my hand and said the word. "Just kidding. It's more a token than a spoken charm."

Claudia laughed, eyes shining. "I'm so excited! Hey, you should come to the dance, Lily. You'd love it. We have a great time."

"I think I might, thanks," I said, exhilarated at being invited not once, but twice, to the ball, just like a witchy Cinderella.

"So, Lily," Bronwyn said, turning to me after we watched our excited customer leave, "I got you a present."

"A present?"

She handed me a heavy rectangle wrapped in birthday paper. I ripped it open to find a used copy of *Introduction to Algebra* and a slick new math workbook. My heart sank.

"Oh," I said. "Thank you, Bronwyn," I managed, trying to keep the loathing from my voice, but failing. I wasn't that good a witch.

"Don't think of it as algebra," she said. "Think of it as the route to a high school diploma. It's pretty exciting when you think about it that way."

"Where did you find the book?"

"Believe it or not, I still had the textbook in my daughter's old room. It's a little outdated, but the great thing about math is that the answers are always the same. The methods of teaching it might change, but the results never do."

That was precisely what I *didn't* like about math, I thought. Nothing in life should be that predictable.

"Shall we get started?" Bronwyn asked.

"Now?"

"No time like the present, I always say."

I looked around the shop, hoping for a reprieve. But the half-dozen customers on the floor were absorbed in their private searches, the clothes racks were neat, and Maya was staffing the register. I was trapped.

We started my first algebra tutorial. Bronwyn was gifted at math and was a patient teacher, guiding but not doing the work for me. I could feel my brain getting smarter as it tried to wrap itself around the unfamiliar material. But after about forty minutes, my eyes were bleary and my mind felt like mush. Give me a musty tome of ancient spells over a slick algebra workbook any day. Recipes that called for blood and claws and teeth, no problem. But solving for the mysterious "x"? Torture.

Just as it had during math class as a child, my mind wandered.

I was willing to bet Jerry Becker had made some sort of deal with a demon, given his meteoric rise from obscure delivery boy to billionaire entrepreneur, his "dev-

il's own luck," his consistent success with women. Was
Aidan helping him? I had known Aidan only a short
time, and my first instinct had been not to trust him. Still,
after he stood by me the last time I faced down a phantom, I thought perhaps I had misjudged him. But if he
was assisting humans to make deals with demons ...

I took a couple of deep breaths to calm myself. It was
a big deal to accuse someone of making a deal with a
demon. I may not have read *The Great Gatsby*, but I was
pretty familiar with Goethe's *Faust*. Faust's deal with the
devil has been an enduring theme in movies and literature, and it was even sometimes played for comedy. But
actually calling up a demon to achieve a goal required a
level of audacity bordering on the psychotic. It was kind
of like conjuring a tsunami to put out a campfire; effective to be sure, but you'd have to be crazy to try it. And
there was always a whole lot of collateral damage.

What really bothered me was Aidan's inconvenient
disappearance. Had he been part of the earlier antics at
the school? But how? I didn't know his exact age, but he
couldn't be more than forty. He wasn't even born when
Jerry was romancing Eugenia, was he?

"Lily?" Bronwyn interrupted my thoughts.

"Hmm?"

"I don't think you're concentrating. You've been staring at that same problem for ten minutes now."

"I ... oh look, here's Susan!"

Susan Rogers swept into the shop with a flourish. She
had a woman of similar age and coloring at her side.

"I decided it was simply too evil of me to outshine my
sister on her baby's wedding day," Susan said. "So here
we are! Lily, this is my sister, Joanne. Make of us what
you will. I've been simply *dying* to try on some of those
old dresses you dug up at the art school."

Susan donned a few of the Victorian-era garments
and fell in love with an exquisite jet-beaded Victorian

cape, but in general the style didn't suit her. Besides, all the dresses from the closet were sized too small; no way around that one. Instead, I pulled out a 1960s Pat Sandler floral gold and copper brocade. Both sisters loved it.

"It's a size fourteen," Susan said. "I'm a twelve at most."

"There's no way you're a twelve if I'm a fourteen," said Joanne. "Have you looked in a full-length mirror lately? You might want to check out the rear view, is all I'm saying."

"You're just jealous. You've had three children, Joanne. It's only natural that I would have kept my figure."

"I'm not saying you didn't keep your figure—you've always been at least a fourteen."

"Says *you*," Susan said with a gasp.

Their sniping made me nervous until I noticed that Bronwyn was chuckling at their quips. Then I leaned back against the sales counter, observing their obvious closeness. I envied them the ease of their teasing sibling relationship.

"Sizing has changed over time," I pointed out. "I always advise people to ignore labels, rather to look at the fit. Besides that, if it's slightly too big, we can take it in. That's an easy fix. The other way around is a lot tougher."

People used to be smaller than they are now; not just skinnier, but more petite all the way around. Daily vitamins and improved year-round nutrition had grown a healthier populace, in general, than our forebears. But this made it tough for today's average adult to find vintage clothes that actually fit.

Maya's mother, Lucille, was an excellent seamstress, and she had come up with many clever ways to modify old clothes for twenty-first-century dimensions: Inserting extra panels when we replaced old zippers in the back, for instance, to broaden the waist; or releasing darts for more ample busts and wider shoulders. Lately Lucille and I had been planning a new venture: making patterns from old styles and cuts to be manufactured in any size. But that plan was still on the cutting board, so to speak.

"Would it be too over-the-top if I wore the dress with these great cowboy boots?" Susan asked. She was standing in front of the three-panel mirror, trying to see herself from the back. The "mod" Pat Sandler style suited her perfectly, and the fit was just right.

Joanne just chuckled and rolled her eyes.

"If the *Chronicle* fashion editor can't get away with it, I don't know who can," I said with a smile.

"I like your attitude, Lily," Susan said, giving her sister a significant look. "*Some* people know original style when they see it."

"Uh-huh. Whatever floats your boat, there, my dear sister."

Joanne tried on the same dinner dress that Claudia had just an hour ago, but on her it looked perfect. Twenty minutes later Maya rang up the satisfied customers, wrapping the dresses carefully. They didn't even need to be altered.

"Lily, what time do you want to leave for Ginny's opening?" Maya asked.

"Is this Ginny Mueller's art show? I'm going to that," mentioned Susan. "I just got the assignment to cover the opening. There's buzz about it already."

"I thought you were the fashion editor," I said.

"I am, but they've laid off half of us at the paper. Now I'm Arts and Entertainment as well, as though I know anything about the subject."

"Don't be so modest," said Bronwyn. "I'll bet you have a great eye for art. And entertainment, for that matter."

"I don't know about that, but what little I've seen so far of Ginny's work, I do think it's just stellar."

"Who knew, right?" said Maya. "I mean, she's my friend and all, but I couldn't believe how she pulled it all together. Everyone's really excited about the show."

Chapter 15

The gallery was right downtown, on Geary not far from Union Square. It was a lovely, airy space with brick walls, arched windows, and soaring white walls. Ginny's works, both paintings and sculptures, were mounted and hung very professionally; unfortunately, all the lovely curating in the world couldn't make up for the fact that the art wasn't very good.

Or at least, it didn't seem very good to me. Apparently, I was the only one in the room who remained underwhelmed . . . but what did I know about modern art? I found it hard to enjoy pictures and shapes I couldn't decipher. I had enough hard-to-understand murk in my life as it was.

The gallery was jammed with people, some of whom I recognized: Marlene and Todd, of course; Kevin Marino, the security guard; and even Wendy and Xander from the café.

And one man who looked vaguely familiar: handsome, rather corporate looking, with slick, styled hair and blue eyes. He stood next to a pretty, noticeably pregnant woman. I couldn't quite place him but felt as if I had seen him before.

"Would ya look at that," Wendy said, solving the mystery for me. "The freaking *mayor* is here with his wife. Ginny must be pretty connected."

"Maybe they come to everyone's opening," suggested Maya, sipping the bright glass of Chardonnay Kevin had brought to her. "Support the arts and all that."

"Ginny *is* the provost's daughter," I said. "And the school's important to the city, I would imagine."

As if on cue, Marlene Mueller ambled by, holding tight to Todd's arm. He looked especially handsome in a nice gray suit, and she was chic as always in an artsy, hand-crocheted coat worn over a plain black shift. The couple seemed relaxed and happy; Todd was leaning down to hear what Marlene was saying, and they smiled into each other's eyes.

"What do you make of the whole cougar thing?" Kevin asked us after the pair passed by.

Wendy and Maya shrugged.

"I like all the big cats," I said.

Maya laughed. "Not that kind of cougar. He means the older woman–younger man thing."

"What does that have to do with mountain lions?"

"The older woman in that kind of relationship is called a cougar," Kevin explained.

"Really? Why?" I asked.

"I have no idea, now that you ask," he said with a laugh. "All's I know is that when you get a woman in her forties with a man in his twenties, they call the woman a cougar."

"Interesting."

"I hear Todd lost his mom early—she walked out on him and his dad. Maybe he's looking for a substitute," Kevin suggested, not unkindly.

"Could be, though I'm not sure a big difference in age is necessarily a result of trauma," I said. "Maybe it's just one of those strange quirks, where they fell in love with each other despite the obvious differences."

"You're a romantic at heart, Lily," teased Maya.

"I just think people can fall in love, even if they come from really different backgrounds," I said. Or at least I hoped they could.

Just then I noticed Dave Kessler walk into the gallery with Andromeda Becker. I was surprised to see them; from our talk the other day, I had gathered that neither of them was a big Ginny Mueller fan.

"So what do you call that guy, then?" They all turned to look. "Dave Kessler, the man with Andromeda? There's at least as much of an age difference between them as with Todd and Marlene."

"That guy's dating Andromeda Becker?" Kevin asked, surprise in his voice.

I nodded. "So what would you call him? A tiger?"

"More like a dirty old man," Kevin said.

"That sounds about right," Wendy agreed with a smile.

The crowd sipped wine and oohed and aahed over Ginny's bright, abstract canvases and even more difficult-to-decipher sculptures. Fellow students and outsiders alike seemed to be bowled over by the work. I even saw Dave Kessler put a red dot sticker, signaling a sale, on the frame of one expansive, colorful oil painting.

I noticed Todd standing off to the side while Marlene chatted with a group of what looked to be potentially wealthy donors. I took the opportunity to talk with him alone.

"Hi, Todd. How's it going?"

"Well, thanks. Great turnout, isn't it?"

"I'm so glad for Ginny. Todd, I know this is awkward timing, but I wanted to ask you: Andromeda mentioned you two talked the night Becker was killed. She was upset."

Todd's eyes looked wary. His nostrils flared slightly.

"Becker was trying to talk Andromeda into pursuing a relationship with Walker Landau. I thought it was just plain creepy."

"Isn't Andromeda old enough to make her own decisions?"

"I guess ... but Becker was a hard one to go up against. So I thought I could talk to Walker, get him to lay off."

Speaking of Walker Landau, it dawned on me that he was rather conspicuous by his absence tonight.

"Did Walker have some sort of pull over Becker?"

I could feel Todd's aura shift. He looked over at me, startled. Then he relaxed and shrugged.

"I guess now that Becker's dead, it doesn't really matter. You know the suicide that supposedly took place on the bell tower stairs? Walker thought Jerry Becker actually pushed the guy down the stairs all those years ago."

"Did he say what made him think that?"

He shook his head. "Personally, I hated the idea. I was always rather taken by the romance of the suicide, loving someone that much. It sort of ruins it to think it was actually murder."

"Murder? What was murder?" asked Marlene as she came up to us.

"These art openings are murder," Todd responded smoothly. "How long do we have to stay?"

"Oh, you naughty boy." Marlene poked him in the side and favored him with a coy smile. All I could think of was wildcats. "You know perfectly well we have to act as host and hostess tonight. Poor Ginny is overwhelmed."

I followed Marlene's gaze to her daughter, who lurked in the corner, looking glum. She was wearing her usual ripped jeans, but she had dressed them up with a black top slit asymmetrically on one shoulder, her short hair artistically tousled; lots of eye makeup; heavy lip gloss; huge chandelier earrings of worked silver that caught the light whenever she turned her head. She looked good as always, piquant and big eyed . . . but lost. One thing was certain: She did not have the mien of an artist whose dream had come true.

"Is she okay?" I asked.

"It's all a bit much," Marlene said. "With art openings, you work your fingers to the bone up until the last second, and it can be hard to be scintillating after that."

"Marlene, I know this isn't the best time to talk about this, but I think you should consider closing the school. Just for a few days."

Her sherry-colored eyes fixed on me. "What are you talking about?"

"You know yourself that things are getting out of hand there. The students are bickering; they can't be getting much done."

"I just don't know. . . . I'll think about it," she said, sounding distracted and looking over my shoulder.

"If you could close for a few days, I could . . ."

My attention was caught by something stuck to Marlene's intricately crocheted coat—a small piece of paper. I picked it off.

"Oh, that's nothing," Marlene said. "I was working on a collage piece earlier."

I studied it. Faded ink on yellowed parchment paper. I could make out part of a word; it looked French.

"Where did you get this?" I asked her, but Marlene had already moved on, fulfilling her hostess duties, chatting now with the mayor and his wife.

Todd began to follow in her wake, but I grasped his arm.

"Todd, you didn't happen to take a letter from the third-floor closet, did you?"

"What?"

"There was a letter, written in French. It was with the

stuff in the closet; it must have been written to one of the nuns."

"I don't remember seeing anything like that. Sorry. I'd better get back to Marlene," he said, and headed after her.

I stood staring down at the little scrap of paper, trying to glean something from it.

"Did you buy the smallest painting Ginny had for sale?"

I looked up and smiled at Luc.

"Not exactly. Luc, do you know what happened to the French letter you started reading in the closet the other night?"

"I put it back in the box where I found it."

"And I have the box at my store, but not the letter. Strange."

"Maybe it's still in the closet?"

"Maybe. Anyway, how are you?"

"Do you mean in the sense of making polite party chitchat, or in the larger sense?"

"The larger, I guess. How is . . . what we talked about yesterday?"

"Nothing new to report. Some weirdness to be sure, but I'm getting a lot of work done. I just don't always remember doing it."

"Luc, I told you yesterday: You should stay away from the school. It could be dangerous."

"It's not that easy. I work there."

"Couldn't you go stay with Max, or your father? Doesn't he live around here? I think you should be around people you can trust. Just for a few days. I'm hoping to figure out what's going on."

"I have to hand it to Ginny," Luc said, looking around the room and nodding absentmindedly. "This is some amazing artwork."

"You like it?"

He nodded. "Very much."

"Oh, me, too," said Bronwyn as she joined us.

"Isn't it something?" Susan said breathlessly as she whirled by, gushing about the newest young artistic talent, snapping pictures with a tiny digital camera, and jotting down notes in a leather-bound book.

Not for the first time, I was the pariah in the room.

Okay, so I wasn't a modern-art lover. I really never even understood Pablo Picasso's appeal; I could see that the cubist revolution was important to the art world, but I didn't particularly care. Anything later than his blue period failed to evoke any emotional response from me. And don't even get me started on Jasper Johns, or Jackson Pollock, or Rothko.

I tried to keep an open mind, but all I could think about was yet another story I knew from childhood: *The Emperor's New Clothes*.

I ducked out of the reception early, not wanting to come up with one more polite way of not answering when people asked me what I thought of Ginny's style.

Besides, something else had occurred to me. Maya mentioned that Jerry Becker had been staying at the Fairmont Hotel, on Nob Hill. Since the murder investigation was still open, surely the room would still be intact?

It was a long shot at best. If Inspectors Romero and Nordstrom had found something amongst Becker's possessions that looked to be occult in any way, they would have asked me about it already, wouldn't they? But that was presuming they would recognize it. Even I didn't know what I was looking for. What might Becker have used to conjure a fiend?

I drove to the top of Nob Hill and used my parking charm—one of the best things about being an urban witch—to secure a good spot right in front of the revered Fairmont Hotel. I took my athletic bag from the trunk of the car and then climbed into the backseat, going through what magical tools I had on hand. I suppose some nonwitchy women could talk their way into a sealed hotel room without using witchcraft, but I fell back on old reliable methods. I mixed a few ingredients together, said a quick chant, and completed a spell of truth telling and persuasion on a stitched *paket kongo*.

I walked into the lobby and paused to take it all in. The interior of the historic Fairmont building, completed right after the great quake of 1906, was decorated in sumptuous shades of cream and gold. A white marble floor and massive gold-veined ionic columns set the tone. Soaring potted palms reached toward the ornate ceilings. A venerable building. I supposed that if people had to have obscene amounts of money, at least a place like this let them spend it in good taste.

At the reception desk I asked to see the manager. He bustled out a moment later from a back office, a paunchy little fellow in his fifties, with male-patterned baldness, a round face, and an eager expression. His discreet gold name tag read LOU GARNER.

"Call me Lou," he said as he held out his hand to shake. I held it in mine and cupped it with my other hand. I fixed my eyes on his, focusing my intention. I could feel the *paket* hum in my pocket, echoing my purpose. I couldn't sway folks just willy-nilly, but luckily Lou was already inclined to be helpful.

"I need to see the room Jerry Becker was staying in," I said.

"Well now," Lou said with a toothy smile, "normally that would have been the Penthouse Suite, of course, since that's the best, but Mr. Becker had no need of three bedrooms, four baths, so he took the Tower Suite instead."

"Has it been closed off since the death?"

"Oh, yes. The police asked us to keep everyone out.

All we've done is change the sheets. But we even had to cancel a reservation for the room—moved them to a Deluxe King Tower Suite—so, as you can imagine—"

"You'll take me there now, won't you?" I interrupted.

"Of course."

Garner got a key card from behind the reception desk and met me back at the elevator, where I now suffered under the one unfortunate result of this spell that I never managed to eliminate: Once the target was doing what you asked of him, he felt compelled to tell you all his secrets. I really did not want to know that good old Lou had a mad crush on his wife's sister, Patsy, or that there had been a skirmish amongst the personnel because someone had been stealing Veronica's special yogurt from the communal refrigerator in the break room.

I nodded, watching the lobby, only half listening while we waited for the elevator and Lou droned on.

A tall man in motorcycle boots, a dark gray trench coat, and a generally bad attitude stormed through the main doors, paused, and looked straight at me. He then turned and scurried down the side hallway.

Chapter 16

What was *Sailor* doing at the Fairmont?

"Wait for me here," I told the manager.

"Yes, ma'am. Happy to do it. Wait for you here." Lou was a people pleaser.

I hurried down the hallway after Sailor. Where had he gone? Out a side exit? Into the gift shop?

There was one other alternative—the men's room.

I hesitated for a fraction of second before pushing open the heavy cherry door and stepping in.

A large redheaded man standing at a urinal quickly covered up and fled, blatantly ignoring signs exhorting all to wash their hands for the sake of public decency.

"You can't just waltz in here," Sailor said, indignant, as he stood over the sink, splashing water on his face.

"I most certainly can. I just did."

"Is nothing sacred anymore? The last place on earth a man could escape for a little peace, and now you just make yourself at home." He reached for one of the linen towels in a neat stack on the marble counter. "You women want it all, is that it? Even urinals?"

I ignored his bluster, intent on taking in the rare scene before me. The only other time I'd been in a men's bathroom was an emergency situation at a gas station in

Arkansas, and in that case I was pretty sure those women's and men's rooms were just about the same level of disgusting. The Fairmont men's room, in contrast, was as refined and dazzling as the lobby; it looked pretty much as I imagined the women's room did, but for a line of urinals rather than a fainting couch or makeup mirrors.

My attention shifted back to Sailor, and I realized he looked haggard under the restroom's fluorescent lights. I hadn't noticed it in the dimness of the bar the other night.

"What are you doing here?" I asked.

"Washing my face."

"I mean at the Fairmont."

"Booking a room for my honeymoon."

"Really?"

He gave me a disgusted look.

"I do beg your pardon," I said. "I'll try harder to keep up with your sarcastic wit."

He gave a humorless bark of laughter, leaned back against the sink, and crossed his arms over his chest. He looked up at the bathroom door a moment before it opened and a gray-haired suit-clad businessman type entered.

"*Out*," Sailor commanded. The man stopped in his tracks, looked at me, then up at the sign on the men's room door, and then ducked back out.

"What do you know about possession?"

"Excuse me?"

"Demon possession."

"Happens a lot when demons are a bit weaker; easier than manifesting whole. When coming out of conjuring, for example. On the other hand, some of them just enjoy it, since it freaks people out. They usually go after weaker personality types, folks with temptations and flaws."

"That sounds like all of us."

"Some are easier to convince than others."

I pondered that for a moment. "I reckon you're here to look through Jerry Becker's room?"

He just looked at me, not answering.

"Shall we go?" I asked.

Sailor let out another exasperated breath, but he followed me out of the restroom. The businessman he had ordered out was standing to the side of the door, waiting.

"It's all yours," Sailor said to him. "Enjoy."

I led the way back to Lou, who was bouncing up and down on his tiptoes at the elevator, apparently agitated.

"Oh, thank goodness you're back. There's a problem with a reservation, and I need to get back to the main desk. Have you heard of Akon? He's a well-known rap star, and apparently there's a mix-up. . . ."

He trailed off as his watery blue gaze fell on Sailor. "And who's this strapping fellow?"

"My . . . fiancé." I put my arm through Sailor's. He looked down at me, aghast at the suggestion of intimacy.

"Well, that's some woman you've got there, young man," Lou said with an ingratiating smile.

"Oh, yeah," Sailor said, yanking me closer to him, his hand digging into my side. "She's a pistol."

"We just need to check through poor uncle Jerry's things," I said, tugging away from Sailor's too-tight grip. "We won't be long."

"If you don't mind, I won't escort you up," Lou said. "Here's the key card, and you can let yourselves in. Just give me a buzz if there's anything more I can do."

"That's perfect," I said, staring into his eyes. "We won't be long. And we won't be disturbed."

"You won't be long," Lou repeated with an energetic nod. "And you won't be disturbed."

Lou reached into the elevator, hit the appropriate

button, and stood back, holding up his hand in a wave. The elevator doors slid closed between us.

"That's a neat trick," Sailor said, giving me a heavy-lidded once-over. "That some sort of Jedi mind control?"

"Excuse me?"

"Like in *Star Wars. These aren't the droids you're looking for.*"

"I never saw that movie."

"You never saw *Star Wars*?"

I shook my head, watching the old-fashioned elevator dial tick off the floors.

"What are you, some kind of an alien? How could any red-blooded American not see that movie?"

I sighed. I was feeling a mite sensitive—this sort of thing was coming up a lot lately. "I think we have more important things to think about right at the moment, not the least of which is what in the sam hill you're doing here at the Fairmont."

"I could ask you the very same thing."

"*I'm* investigating Jerry Becker's death, whereas you claimed you wanted nothing to do with it."

"Yeah, well, we can't always get what we want."

The elevator doors slid open with a muted ding and a refined swoosh. We walked down the hill to the room marked with an elegant brass plate: THE TOWER SUITE.

I used the key card and swung the door open. Sailor and I hesitated in the threshold, taking a moment to feel for sensations before proceeding.

The suite was made up of a parlor with a bedroom and bath. It was decorated in standard, ho-hum hotel chic—still in shades of cream and gold, but lacking either the charm or the grandeur of the lobby and main historic hotel. The only thing out of the ordinary was a telescope set up on a tripod in the main window, which opened onto an amazing view of Coit Tower and the bay.

Sailor started right in tossing pillows, opening bureau drawers, and looking under the furniture in the sitting room.

I headed for the bedroom and felt the sheets—you could usually pick up a lot from the sleeping area—but they had been changed since Jerry Becker slept here. His clothes still hung in the closet—a single suit, two shirts, one pair of shiny black dress shoes, one pair of athletic trainers. I tried holding each piece, but still picked up nothing distinct. Next, I tried the bathroom, riffling through Becker's personal toiletries, sniffing at his shaving gel, poking through his bag, which contained a toothbrush, toothpaste, a small bottle of cologne, blood pressure pills, and a vial of Viagra.

Housekeeping hadn't been here—there was a dirty towel on the floor, his things scattered about. Still, I couldn't get much of a read from his personal effects.

Defeated, I sat on the bed. There were signs the police had been here; perhaps they had already confiscated anything of interest.

"Anything?" Sailor asked from the doorway.

I shook my head. My eyes alighted on a framed photo of a smiling Jerry Becker, surrounded by two young men—his sons, I assumed—and Andromeda. I felt a surge of grief for Becker, the father. He had traveled with this photograph, set beside his bed so it was the last thing he would see at night. I held it to my chest. Yes, it had been cherished.

There was something else: a small collage on thick, hand-pressed paper. It was very well done, and featured hearts and roses. *With love, from M.* Marlene, I presumed. I was finding it hard to reconcile the beaming, seemingly content Marlene I had seen with Todd with the unfolding story: a woman in love with Jerry Becker. What could she have seen in him? Unless, of course, he was playing with a deck supernaturally stacked in his favor.

Sailor slumped onto the bed beside me, leaning forward, elbows perched on thighs. With his coat and boots he reminded me of some European rock star, or a futuristic road warrior. This close, I could feel his exhaustion; could smell his subtle aroma of spice and perfume.

"Sailor?"

"Yup."

"What are you looking for in Jerry Becker's hotel room? For real."

"Probably the same thing you are. I wanted to take a look at where Becker was staying while he was here. Looking for clues."

"Last time we talked, I had the distinct impression you weren't going to pursue this."

"I don't have much choice. Aidan contacted me."

"I heard he was out of town."

"You heard wrong."

"I don't get it," I said. "What kind of control does Aidan have over you? Why don't you just move away?"

Sailor's dark eyes rested back on me.

"What kind of control does he have over *you*?"

"I told you—he helped me out once. I owe him. And besides, this isn't about Aidan anymore. I have to find out what's going on at that school before things get any worse. First a murder, and now . . ."

"What?"

I shook my head.

"I told you I can't read your mind. Tell me what happened."

"Possible case of possession. Things are ratcheting up. I can feel it."

Sailor swore under his breath, blew out a breath, and fell backward onto the bed. He pressed the palms of his hands into his eyes. "I was trying to avoid going to the school. Thought I could figure it out from here. But nothing has any of his vibrations."

"I was thinking the same thing. Cloaking of some sort?"

"I'd say more serious than that. It's as though the guy wasn't even human."

"He was human enough to die when pushed down the stairs."

"You've got me there."

We sat together in surprisingly companionable silence. For some reason my thoughts turned to my familiar. I felt a bit betrayed by the little porker, even though I had known he was working with Aidan. Still, I couldn't believe he lied to me about Aidan's being out of town. I thought about Oscar blowing on the van window and drawing a pentagram on the fogged glass. . . .

Something occurred to me.

I went into the bathroom and breathed on the mirror.

A drawing appeared. Almost crownlike, it was a big U topped with a straight line, then three crosses at the top, four small circles below the line, and one at the bottom of the U.

"A sigil," Sailor said from right behind me. "God *damn* it."

A sigil is a demon's seal. Demons might have several names, varying appearances, or pronunciations that shift across geography, history, and cultures. But the sigil stays constant.

"Do you know whose?"

He shook his head. "But that doesn't mean much. I only know a few of the most obvious. As I'm sure you know, there are thousands."

"Tens of thousands," I muttered.

"*Shit*," Sailor swore again, and banged the door frame. He had a decidedly green-around-the-gills look on his face.

"Why are you so surprised? I told you I suspected demonic activity."

"I assumed you were being histrionic."

"You *hoped* I was being histrionic."

He shrugged one big shoulder.

"So how do we find out whom we're dealing with?" I asked as I tried to commit the drawing to memory. I feared sketching it, as with my powers I could inadvertently call something up before I was ready to deal with it. That would be bad—really bad.

Sailor shook his head. "Look up the sigil, I guess."

Even reading about demons made me nervous. They were so serious and so numerous. It was overwhelming—and frightening. I closed my eyes, took a deep breath, and released it very slowly.

Then I felt the large, comforting pressure of a hand on my head. I opened my eyes and saw Sailor in front of me. His dark eyes looked worried, and there was a surprisingly open, vulnerable look on his face. After the briefest of moments, the sardonic, cynical mien returned. He dropped his hand and turned away.

"I thought you couldn't read my mind," I said to his back as he retreated out of the bedroom.

"No need. Your face is like an open book."

I trailed him into the main room, unsure what to do now. I studied Sailor's profile for a moment as he bent over to look through the telescope at the view. He had an elegant nose, pouty lips, long eyelashes, a distinctive chin. He was rugged, strong—and yet so unhappy.

"Sailor, do you think Aidan is capable . . . Would he have helped Becker to conjure the demon?"

Sailor turned to me and put a finger to his lips, gesturing for me to hush. He assumed a fighter's stance, arms at his side with his fingers twitching ever so slightly. It was an unconsciously masculine pose that I had seen men all over the globe strike when under threat; it must have something to do with testosterone.

He took me by the upper arm and urged me toward the door.

"Let's get out of here. We can talk elsewhere."

Out in the hall, two housekeepers were pushing a cart of clean towels and supplies past the door. The elevator was open and waiting.

As we descended, I heard Sailor's voice, low and grumbling.

"Just my luck to get mixed up with a bunch of crazy witches."

"Be that as it may, you apparently owe Aidan. You need to help me figure this thing out."

He blew out an exasperated breath as the elevator doors opened onto the lobby.

"Come on, Sailor, he's obviously got you on a leash somehow. If you help me find out who—or what—I'm dealing with at the school, you're off the hook."

"For the moment."

We proceeded out the front glass doors. Outside, the night was chilly; the damp air carried the scent of fog and the sea. I breathed deeply, relishing the freshness of the evening after the oppressive feeling in Becker's room.

"I need to get a few things from home before I can do a proper reading," Sailor said as we paused in front of the building.

"You mean you'll come to the school?"

"I don't appear to have much choice in the matter."

"Great. Thank you."

"Anyway, I have to stop by my place."

"I'll go with you."

Sailor pressed his lips together. His hands rested lightly on his hips, and he looked around as though searching for escape.

"Whatever," he finally said under his breath.

"Do you have a car here?" I asked.

"Motorcycle."

I laughed.

"What's funny about that?"

"I was just wondering if you could hit any more clichés. The attitude, the boots, the bike . . ."

He looked at me, frowning in perplexity. "If I didn't have the bike, why would I need the boots?"

Now I laughed at the sincere bewilderment on his somber face. I was still chuckling when I turned to see Max Carmichael, of all people, striding toward the front doors of the Fairmont. He stopped in his tracks when he saw me.

"Max," I said.

"Lily," he replied, surprised.

Sailor swore under his breath. Max's gaze shifted to him. A black cloud passed over his face, and he strode toward Sailor.

"It wasn't *me*," Sailor said, putting his hands up in supplication and backing away.

Without pausing, Max stormed over and punched him, clipping his jaw with a wicked left hook.

Chapter 17

"Max!" I said, grabbing his arm. Sailor staggered into the wall of the hotel, then steadied himself. "What's gotten into you?"

The doorman whistled loudly and jogged up to us.

"Hey, what's going on here? Take this somewheres else—hear me?"

"What are you doing with this guy?" Max demanded of me as he pulled his arm away from my grip. His voice was harsh.

"He's helping me with something," I said.

He glared at Sailor, who leaned back against the wall, his hand rubbing his jaw and his tongue feeling around on the inside. Then Max stalked off.

"It's okay," I told the hovering doorman. "We're leaving."

Grumbling loudly about Certain Kinds of People, the uniformed man went back to assume his position at the main entrance.

"Wait, Max!" I called out.

He didn't slow his pace, so I ran to catch up with him.

"Max, what in the world was all that about?"

Max looked down at me, his eyes full of torment and sorrow. "Don't trust that guy, Lily. Take my word for it."

"He's just doing me a favor," I said. "It's nothing—"

"I'll talk to you about this later. I—I can't talk about it right now."

"All right."

He briefly cupped my face in his hand, gave me a sad little smile, and walked away.

I returned to Sailor, who was still leaning back against the building. I held a hand up to touch his face. "Are you all right?"

"Fine," he muttered, pushing my hand away. "He didn't give it his all."

"You didn't punch back. I'm impressed."

"Yeah, well, if it had been *my* wife, I would've taken his head off. He had cause."

We started walking toward my car.

"What about Max's wife?"

"I thought you knew him."

"I do."

"But you don't know about his wife?"

I shook my head.

He shrugged. "You should probably let him tell it."

"You slept with his wife?"

Sailor stopped in his tracks and gaped at me, appalled.

"Now how is it that you go right to the down and dirty, not stopping to think that I might have a few scruples? Good Lord, woman."

I tried not to smile at his outraged sense of morality. "Sorry. My bad."

"You'd better believe it is," he grumbled. "Fact is, I used to be in the business. Used my so-called abilities to make money. I had a business partner. Max's wife came to us, looking for help."

"What kind of help?"

"She couldn't get pregnant."

"Why would she go to psychics?"

"She'd tried every legitimate route, I guess. She was in pretty bad shape, to tell you the truth—seeing a shrink, on meds. I guess she was stable enough but really desperate for a kid. I counseled her to adopt. Unfortunately, my partner took her on as a client, saw her for quite a while, and eventually told her she should go off her meds."

I let out a little sigh of distress. "Oh, no."

"You can say that again. She was clinically depressed, you know, not just fooling around. Like I said, this psychic bullshit is dangerous."

"I can't believe this."

"Believe it."

"Poor Max."

We reached my car.

"There's my bike," he said as he gestured toward a Kawasaki 750 just down the block. "Follow me."

I pulled up my Mustang behind Sailor's motorcycle, thinking about Max's poor wife—and about poor Max. No wonder he was so tormented.

Sailor led the way across Nob Hill to Clay Street, then straight down the hill to nearby Chinatown. We crossed Stockton, where even at this hour folks flocked across the street, delaying traffic. We drove down Waverly Place, and took another right onto Sacramento. Sailor parked his bike and gestured to a spot for me on the crowded street.

"The alley's pedestrian-only," Sailor explained as we walked down the alley, past a dim sum parlor called Hang Ah Teahouse on the left, and a children's playground surrounded by a chain-link fence on the right. There were lots of vibrations here; big, boisterous families, plenty of history.

"If you enter from the Clay Street side, the street's called Hang Ah Alley. Enter from Sacramento Street and it's Pagoda Alley, which is the Western name for it. Hang Ah means 'fragrant' in Chinese."

I noticed a strong aroma of perfume; this was the scent I had noticed on Sailor earlier this evening. I met Sailor's gaze.

"Yeah, I know," he said. "There used to be a German perfume maker down here, back in the day. A few of us can still smell it."

I noticed alternating English and Chinese text on the ground, telling about the history of the alley.

"What a great place!" I exclaimed.

Sailor seemed amused at my reaction. "I like it here. People mind their own business," he said pointedly.

Right past an informal mah-jongg parlor, we entered a nondescript door and started up a dim stairwell. Coming down the stairs was a short Chinese man. He started yelling at Sailor as he passed.

"Yeah, yeah, tomorrow," Sailor said.

The man continued down past us, shaking his head.

"Rent's due," Sailor explained. "Maybe a little past due."

"You understand Mandarin?"

"It's Cantonese. And I understand thoughts, remember? The language is just the verbal expression. I can pretty much understand all languages, but I can't speak them."

"So you understand but remain misunderstood?"

"Something like that."

"That seems like a metaphor for something," I said as I trailed him up the stairs. "Your life, maybe?"

"You know your problem?"

"I have an idea you're going to tell me."

"You think too damned much."

At the second landing, Sailor pulled out his key and started to open the door. I stopped short. Something chilled me to the core.

Our eyes met.

"A homicide over a bad gambling debt, sometime

in the 1920s," said Sailor with a shrug. "Mah-jongg. It's harmless, just repeating itself."

"And you live with it?"

"I'm not afraid. I know what it is."

"Yes, but . . ." I trailed off. No wonder he was in such a bad mood all the time. That sort of despair would have to seep into you eventually, wouldn't it? Unless, of course, it reflected emotions he already had and gave him a strange kind of comfort, a feeling of kinship.

"Besides, the rent's cheap. And it encourages people to keep their distance," Sailor explained. "They all know what happened here, so they think I'm nuts."

"Not that I'm telling you what to do, but did you ever think maybe you *are* nuts?"

"Only every damned day."

The studio apartment featured a sad-looking couch covered with a bedspread, a neatly made bed—the only tidy thing in the place—and stacks of cardboard boxes full of files and papers. Tall stacks of books had dirty coffee cups atop them. An iMac computer sat on a scarred wooden coffee table. The apartment looked ugly, but it smelled surprisingly good, like spices and jasmine tea, with whiffs of ghostly perfume emanating from the alley.

As Sailor packed a few items into a leather knapsack, I decided to indulge my curiosity.

"Sailor, were you born with your psychic abilities?"

He snorted. "Nope."

"Then how did you become psychic?"

"Ask your BFF Aidan."

"BFF?"

"'Best friend forever.' You don't know basic texting?"

"I don't even know basic algebra," I grumbled.

"Algebra's tough. I was better at geometry."

"I suck at that, too. So how does your psychic ability work, exactly?" I asked. "I mean, if you can't read minds . . ."

"I can read plenty of minds. I choose not to."

"But not mine."

"Not yours. What, you think you're a regular person?"

"Can you pick the winning lotto numbers?"

He gave me a pained look. "I can't predict the future—I might have a premonition from time to time, but I'll bet you have that as well. I'm more a medium—souls that have passed on seem to be able to communicate with me, or more precisely, *through* me."

"And you with them."

"Yeah, no. It's more like they talk to me than the other way around. They seek me out. It's not what you'd call my idea of fun."

I picked up a few nearby books, looked at their spines, and read the titles. "*The Afterlife and Other Questions, The Enigma of the Psyche, Psychics: Charlatans or Seers?*"

Sailor watched me looking through his things, extracted a bottle of tequila from a crowded cupboard, and took a swig. He gestured with the bottle toward me.

I shook my head. "No, thanks. Does that help with your psychic reading?"

"It helps get me through the day. Not to mention the night."

Our eyes met. A long moment passed.

"What happened to you, Sailor?"

He paused, continuing to look at me so long, I thought he might actually be about to confide in me. But then that sardonic look came over his features, once again.

"Anyone ever tell you that you ask way too many personal questions?"

"Not really. I don't usually ask personal questions at all."

"But I inspire nosiness?"

"A bit, yes. You're something of a puzzle, as if you didn't know."

"And you're not?"

"I guess we're a matched set, then."

He walked slowly toward me, his eyes never dropping from mine. I felt my heart speed up, my mouth open to speak, but no words came out. Sailor didn't stop until he stood right in front of me; too close. He reached out and placed his hand around my neck, as though throttling me, but he held me very gently.

"You and I are not a matched *anything*. Get that straight."

He let go, reached around me, and grabbed another small duffel bag off a nail in the wall. "Come on. Let's get this over with."

Obviously, Marlene had not implemented my suggestion. The school had not been closed. As we walked along the hallways, dozens of students lingered between classes, and several small groups bickered. I noticed blue paint had been smeared upon several of the old stucco walls.

Sailor and I had maintained a mutual silence since we left his apartment. But as we walked down the main hallway, he stopped in his tracks.

"Wait," he said, eyes wide, "No, is it . . . It couldn't be! It's—it's . . ."

"Sailor? What is it?" I asked, my heart pounding.

"It's a *Snapple machine*."

I hit him in the arm. "That's *not* funny."

He laughed and rubbed his bicep, feigning hurt from my punch.

"I shouldn't have to remind you that this is serious business," I said, sounding prim to my own ears.

"Why haven't you shut the school down if it's so serious?"

"I'm working on it."

We arrived at the bottom of the bell tower stairs. The minute we entered the antechamber, footsteps rang out on the stairs and the moaning began.

"Holy hell," Sailor muttered. "You sure you want to stir things up here?"

"They're already stirred up," I said grimly. "I have to do something to regain control."

We started climbing the bell tower stairs, me leading the way. I peeked back at Sailor, but he was concentrating, his attention fixed on the walls and the ground. The noises swirled around us, building to a crescendo when we reached the top and opened the door to the third floor. The closet was directly to our left.

I swung the door open. Sailor paused a long time on the threshold.

"You removed something from here?"

"Clothes," I said, "and a few other items. A music box."

"I trust you did a cleansing? Beyond your average wash cycle, I mean."

I nodded.

He took a deep breath and walked in.

Sailor set up an incense censer and candles, then asked me to draw a circle of protection for us. We both sat cross-legged on the floor within the circle, facing each other. He held out his hands, palms up.

"Lay your hands on mine."

He blew out a deep breath and shook out his shoulders, as though shaking off a chill.

"I hate this stuff," he grumbled. "It feels so cheesy."

"There's nothing cheesy about a genuine séance."

He grunted and closed his eyes. He took a series of deep breaths. I could see his lips moving slightly as though he were chanting to himself. After a few minutes his head fell back so his face was toward the ceiling.

The closet was so small that the incense soon filled

the air with a haze that reeked of a moldy bonfire. This was no pleasant, patchouli-oil incense. It was stinky, almost noxious.

I heard Sailor breathing harshly, murmuring something unintelligible but urgent, in different-sounding voices, as though several people were having a low, mumbled conversation. He remained seated, his hands touching mine, but his head whipped back and forth, and I could see his eyes rolling under his eyelids.

I felt him using me as a power source. The energy coursed through my palms into his, making my hands burn and itch. As I watched, the quality of the haze changed. At first almost imperceptible, the smoke began to morph into faces. Horrible faces. They cried and moaned and whimpered, fading in and out. I smelled a strong floral perfume, then heard giggling, sobbing, humming all around us.

The piles of ashes started to fly, swooping around the room, joining with the smoke and mist.

Suddenly the tinny notes of the music box rang out, playing "There's a place in France . . ." but the music box was still at my shop.

And then a voice sounded. It was coming from Sailor but was not his.

"I am John Daniels. Why haven't you heard me? You must help me. There is an evil one. There is . . ."

The voice trailed off. Sailor's head dropped down again.

The next voice was effeminate, giggling. "Our lord, our master." Then came another giggle, another distinct voice, also high-pitched. *"Notre Père, nous aimons . . ."*

And then everything stopped; all sound came to an end.

Sailor's head hung limply on his chest, his eyes closed.

Power marched up and down my spine. Evil. *Wrong.*

A ghastly sound assailed my ears, at first like the rushing of wind through reeds . . . but then it sounded as though thousands were wailing, crying out in agony and despair. It was the beating of wings, horrible wings.

I looked up to see a winged big cat—a jaguar, or maybe a leopard. Each beat of its wings cast that horrific, screaming noise through the room.

The demon. *No.* I wasn't ready for him. We weren't ready; we hadn't contained him.

But he quickly dissolved in the ether, just like the other images. I sagged with relief. He wasn't manifesting; it was just an image of him—a potent image. But when a powerful witch thought about a demon, it could be almost as effective as summoning him on purpose. . . .

I let out a great burst of energy to break our connection. Sailor and I repelled from one another. Sailor flew back and landed prone; I was thrown up against the chest of drawers, banging my head.

All sound ceased.

I jumped up to check on Sailor, but he was already sitting up and dusting off his jacket.

"I *hate* this crap. Look at this mess."

"I . . . are you all right?"

"Sure. Why?"

"I . . ." I looked around the room, still full of incense smoke, but not images. The ashes were back in their five neat piles.

"What did you see?" Sailor asked.

"Too much."

"Let's get the hell out of here."

We took the other, safer set of stairs down to the first floor and hurried out the front doors. Only when we were safely outside the building did Sailor talk to me.

"The ghost from the bell tower isn't your problem.

He's just a lovelorn schmuck. Actually, though, he was murdered—he didn't kill himself."

"Did he say by whom?"

"Couldn't say. Quite literally couldn't. We were interrupted. But he's harmless, scared to death as a matter of fact."

"A scared ghost?"

"A lot of them are terrified. It's very confusing to be caught in between. But this one was happy enough here at the school until a new guy came on the scene."

"New guy?"

"What did you see, Lily?"

I swallowed hard. "An image of the demon."

He nodded. "Uh-huh. The poor ghost—John something—has been trying to warn you. God *damn* it. Why couldn't you just stay out of it?"

"Did the demon kill Becker?"

"No. It's hard to explain how I know . . . but I didn't smell death on him. Not yet. I think he's looking for a host."

"A host?"

"He's looking to possess someone. Permanently. Didn't you tell me that was a concern already?"

"Unfortunately, yes. So what do we do about it?"

"*We* aren't doing anything about it. I sure as hell can't bind a demon. I don't want any part of this."

"I need help, Sailor."

"*You're* the damned witch. Act like it and bind that thing. I did my part and have to live with those images for the rest of my life, thank you so much."

I hurried after him as he hustled down the sidewalk, headed toward his motorcycle.

"Damned witchy freaks," he muttered under his breath.

"*Excuse* me?" I hated that word, and I was itching for a fight myself. "You're calling *me* names?"

"Why shouldn't I? You're a freak."

"It takes one to know one."

"Absolutely. I'm a freak show myself."

As much as I wanted to argue with the man, that just struck me as sad.

"No, you're not, and neither am I," I said.

"Look at yourself. You sound like a parody of *The Wizard of Oz. I'm a good witch*," he mocked in a falsetto, singsong voice, then snorted. "Good or bad, it's the same power source. Just embrace what you are, I say."

"You're saying I'm evil?"

"I'm saying there's no such thing as an evil witch or a good witch. You're just a plain old witch. Haven't you ever heard that old saw, 'With great power comes great responsibility'? What you choose to do with those powers, in the moment, may be good or bad, but you're still a freak of nature."

We reached his bike. He swung one long leg over the seat and pulled on his helmet.

"You sure as hell had better find a way to bind that thing before he finds a permanent host. Given his growing strength, I'd say you have a couple of days, tops. A moonless night's coming up, isn't it? That'd be good timing."

I nodded. "What are *you* going to do?"

"Me? I'm gonna go drink. Someplace where nobody asks questions."

I lingered in the doorway, watching while he roared off on his motorcycle. He was scared, and how could I blame him? Sailor could communicate with spirits, but he didn't have any powers to protect himself from them.

Vaguely, I noted the echoes of students arguing behind me. I had to get someone to close the school, or at the very least to board up the bell tower stairs for a while—and maybe the third-floor hallway. And I had to go up against a demon. And I *still* didn't know who had killed Jerry Becker.

Next on my agenda were talking with Walker Landau and seeing why he had been asking so many pointed questions. Walker hadn't come to Ginny's event tonight; could he still be working at this hour? It was worth a try to find out. I made my way back into the school and up to the dusty second-floor studio he was sharing with Luc.

The door was ajar. Walker stood before a large canvas propped on an easel, painting frenetically. As I came closer, I could see the theme of his composition. A chill ran over me.

It was a self-portrait. Walker sat in a thronelike chair, the one I had seen in the third-story closet, surrounded by a bevy of dark-haired young women dressed in frothy Victorian garb. The painting was nearly complete, but as I watched, Walker began jabbing at his own likeness on the canvas, his paintbrush dipped in a brutal red pigment. He seemed to stab at the painting, gouging, while the paint ran down the canvas in bizarre crimson streams.

"Walker, what are you doing?" I asked quietly.

He whirled around to face me. His face looked exactly like the face on the canvas, grotesque and melted, bloodied.

Chapter 18

As I watched, it worsened.

I retched. Forcing myself to overcome my shock and revulsion, I began chanting, holding my medicine bundle in one hand, wishing I had my ceremonial knife with me. I needed my salts. I needed Bronwyn's coven at my back, or Aidan's power, or some idea of what in the world to do. I didn't have any of them. My witchcraft is more the brew-in-the-peace-and-quiet-of-my-home kind of talent than the middle-of-the-action, throw-down-situation kind.

I took a deep breath and calmed my lurching stomach.

The biggest advantage I had at my disposal was less fear of the supernatural than your average person.

I am powerful, I reminded myself. If Sailor was right, supernatural entities should be able to smell me like so much cheap perfume.

Besides, I reminded myself, *what I am seeing is not real*.

I hoped.

"Who are you?" I demanded, surprised at the steadiness of my voice.

Walker—or whatever Walker had become—threw back his head and laughed, his jaw flapping strangely as though about to disconnect from his skull. He seemed to be trying to talk but was making a strange grunting noise instead.

With my left hand holding tight to my medicine bundle, I held my right hand, palm-out toward him, focusing my intent on visualizing a line of light from the palm of my hand to Walker Landau.

"Demon be gone!" I yelled. "Leave this man, I compel you!"

There was a rasping, terrible sound. Walker's neck distended, as though something were inside, fighting to get out. Finally he stopped and smiled a grotesque, deformed smile, his face twisting further in front of me.

Dropping his paint-covered hands to his sides, he started backing away from me and stepping straight toward the open window.

"No! Walker, don't!"

"*Demon. Be. Gone*," he rasped, still smiling, and flipped backward out the window.

Stunned, I stood unmoving for a second, the harsh rasping of my own breath the only sound in the void.

I heard a lone scream, then far-off shouts, then more screaming.

I ran to the window and stuck my head out. Walker Landau had landed faceup on top of a thick evergreen hedge. To my great relief, that face no longer looked melted, but back to normal. His eyes were closed, but he was moving. He was alive. I sagged in relief against the window frame. A splinter of wood cut into the palm of my hand, but I welcomed the pain, appreciating the normalcy of it.

I fell to my knees, focusing on breathing.

In front of me were footprints in the dust: one a normal man's shoe print; the other a paw, like that of a big cat. And under a small painting cabinet, I noticed three small cut-out letters, as from a collage.

Something moved behind me.

I jumped and whirled around, landing on my butt on the floor.

Luc stood in the doorway, his features sketched with concern.

"Lily? Are you all right? What happened?"

I struggled to my feet and ran across the room, throwing myself at him. Stone dust poofed up from his white T-shirt, but I didn't care. I grabbed on to him as to a lifeline. Strong arms wrapped around me as I laid my head on his warm, broad chest.

"*Luc*. It's Walker. . . . He threw himself out the window."

Luc's large hand caressed the back of my head, smoothing my hair.

"Poor thing, you're shivering," he said. "It's okay. . . . You're okay."

"I should never have confronted him, I—"

"It's true. You shouldn't have."

He started humming. It was the music box tune, "There's a place in France . . ." Luc was still petting my head, but his other hand started to caress me just a little too intimately, dropping from my waist to my hip. I tried to pull away, but the hand on my head grabbed my ponytail, holding me to him, not letting me go.

"Luc, what—"

"Just calm down now, Miss Fancy Pants." His voice was off-kilter, whispery, so it was hard to tell whether he was actually speaking or whether it was someone— something—else. "Big bad witch gonna take on the demon?"

I pushed against his chest with all my strength. Luc wasn't budging. He laughed; I heard the rumble in his chest under my ear.

"Where do you think you're going, spitfire?"

"Luc, listen to me. This isn't you. Fight it."

"Why would anyone want to fight this?" He pulled my head back, and his mouth came down on mine. But it wasn't Luc who was kissing me; I was very sure of that.

I centered myself and began kissing him back. When he was off guard, I yanked my knee up, as hard as I could, into his groin. I jumped back as he doubled over, then grabbed his head and brought my knee up into his nose. I let out a blast of energy from the palm of my hand. He tumbled to the ground and rolled.

Invoking the power of my spirit guardian to help me, I held up my medicine bundle and began chanting a protective spell.

Luc rolled in the dust on the floor, eyes tearing, in the fetal position. He changed as I watched him, his eyes glassy, almost glowing, his neck extending oddly as though he were fighting to swallow, or to breathe. There were choking sounds beyond anything I had caused.

I held my hand out to him to hold him at bay, the blood on my palm practically glowing.

Quickly, I drew a circle in the dust around him, and within that a pentagram, and within that, a triangle.

I compel you . . .

Luc looked up at me now, and it *was* Luc. His eyes were confused; he was looking around, still blinking back his tears, and bringing a hand up to touch his nose.

"Are you all right?" I asked.

"What happened?"

I leaned in to help him up.

He sat up and smiled at me. A smile of evil intent.

I ran.

Sirens were approaching the school by the time I reached my vehicle. My heart was pounding; my stomach was taught with tension and fear. I couldn't block out the sight of the hapless Walker Landau flipping backward out that window . . . or the memory of my powerlessness to do anything about it.

I shouldn't have come on so strong or been so scared. I should have tried to communicate with the creature rather than immediately trying to cast it out. Maybe it was trying to tell me something.

Stupid. This is what came of not having the proper preparation and training.

Poor Walker. Even if he wasn't physically damaged, I could only imagine what his memory of tonight would be like. He didn't possess much strength of personality in the first place.

And what about Luc? Given how easily he had returned when I trapped him within the triangle, I judged he was already back to himself, confused but free of the demon. On the other hand, when I leaned in at the last moment, the evil creature had smiled at me . . . but that was my fault. I reached out too soon, breaking the circle myself. The demon must have been still hovering nearby, ready and able to come back to inhabit Luc's corporeal form. By now it would have fled; Luc wouldn't be able to cross the circle until the demon had left him, and the evil spirit would slip through the portal formed by the triangle rather than remain trapped.

All of this boiled down to one thing: Sailor was right. I needed to figure out how to exorcise the creature before it gained sufficient strength to take over whomever it wanted, whenever it wanted. At least the demon was still contained within the school.

Somehow it had been awakened, and I imagined Jerry Becker's murder further spurred him on. That kind of strife and rancor was like Miracle-Gro to those of evil intent. I had seen a set of footprints in the dust, one human, one animal. That was the classic sign of an incubus, but it might also belong to a higher demon.

Demons adhered to a clear hierarchy, and some commanded legions. Could I have stirred something up on my first visit with Maya, when we found Becker, and the demon sent the lesser spirits to harass me and Max and others at night?

Several students stood by the front entrance, avidly taking in the scene of firefighters plucking Walker from atop the high hedge. The flashing lights of a multitude of emergency vehicles gave the night a strange blue-white-red strobe-light effect.

"Could I borrow your phone?" I asked a young man with a backpack. He jumped at the sound of my voice behind him.

"Oh, uh, sure," he said.

"Sorry, I didn't mean to scare you."

"S'okay," he said as he handed me a sleek, lime green phone. "Did you see what happened? Some guy jumped. A real genius, he fell into the bushes."

I just nodded but didn't respond. I didn't feel up to making small talk, to pretending things were anything close to normal.

I called Carlos Romero.

"It's Lily Ivory. I don't know how to tell you this, but I'm at the School of Fine Arts—"

"I already got the call. I'm on my way to the scene. Wait for me there," Romero answered in a clipped tone.

"I—I can't," I said. "I have to check something out first."

I was spooked. I felt out of my league. I needed more information before I had an in-depth discussion with police officials.

"Lily—" Romero began, and then stopped, as though intending to try talking me out of it but then reconsidering. "All right. Call me back in an hour. I want to talk to you about this, in person."

I agreed. Before giving back the phone, I made one more phone call, to Max, asking him to get his brother from the school and take him home. I told him I couldn't give him an explanation but asked him to trust me. He agreed with obvious reluctance.

Then I headed to the San Francisco Wax Museum, located at Fisherman's Wharf.

Aidan Rhodes had gotten me into this mess; he was refusing to help me, and I wanted to know why. Even if he really was out of town, maybe I could snoop around his office, see if I turned up anything telling.

In the ticket kiosk of the Wax Museum sat a bored young woman, very Queen of the Dead in her Goth outfit of dyed black hair, heavy kohl eyeliner, and multiple piercings. She grudgingly put down the worn paperback romance novel she was reading when I approached.

"One adult?" she asked with a sigh, leaning her head in her hand as though she could barely stay awake.

"Not for the museum, but is Aidan Rhodes here?"

"Nuh-uh."

"Do you know when he'll be back?"

"Nuh-uh."

Did I really want to risk going through Aidan's office without his permission? I had a moment of self-doubt. What did I think I was, a one-woman crusade able to hold off powerful witches? But as I was thinking, it dawned on me that I couldn't tell whether the young woman in the ticket booth was lying or not; I couldn't get a read on her aura at all. That was odd. I assessed her. She didn't have powers . . . unless the booth was enchanted. I placed my hand on the metal railing and perceived a faint hum. Clever; Aidan didn't want her giving anything away.

"I don't suppose you'll come out here and talk to me?" I said.

She screwed up her forehead as if I had suggested she eat nails. "Say what? Could you step aside? There's other customers."

I waited while she served a large multigenerational family speaking some sort of eastern European language. The children were teasing one another, ratcheting up their titillation about visiting the Chamber of Horrors. I was right there with them. The whole Wax Museum put me on edge. There were too many possibilities for transfiguration. Wax figures in the form of humans, otherwise known as poppets, are used too often for destruction, in my experience.

As the family hustled up the main stairwell, I followed them.

"Hey!" I heard the booth attendant yell at me.

I figured given her level of investment in this job and her probable minimum wage paycheck, she wouldn't care enough to make it out of the booth. She didn't.

I moved quickly past the entrance to the Chamber of Horrors, and slipped behind a small display of European explorers next to a heavy walnut door.

I banged on it. No answer.

"Aidan?" I called.

Nothing.

I banged some more. Then I spotted Aidan's familiar: The elegant, white long-haired cat sat on a small ledge near the corner, absolutely still, as though made of wax itself. I looked into its intelligent eyes. It was acting as guardian. If I tried anything, I reckoned I'd be dealing with cat scratch fever.

But it also meant that Aidan was *not* out of town.

Graciela had always told me I had more power than I knew. It was time to stop screwing around.

I focused my rage—and I had plenty—on the door, and flung it open with my mind.

Aidan Rhodes, male witch, sat behind his large walnut desk.

"What in tarnation's going on?" I demanded as I stormed in.

Aidan's eyes shifted to the chair in front of his desk.

"I apologize for my friend's intrusion, Garrett," Aidan said. "We'll finish this up later."

Only then did I realize Aidan was not alone. I turned to see a man in a well-cut, expensive-looking charcoal gray suit that was now covered in a generous helping of white cat hair. With a jolt, I realized I had seen him earlier at Ginny's art opening. Garrett Jones, the mayor of San Francisco, sprang out of his seat, looking ashen.

"I'm sorry, I—" I began, but the damage was done.

The mayor scurried by me, frightened. I gave him what I hoped was a reassuring smile as he scooted out of the office. I cringed inwardly, feeling chagrined at my impulsive behavior.

"Don't stop now, Lily," Aidan said to me, looking simultaneously amused, bemused, and irritated. "Come on in, by all means. My door is, evidently, always open to you."

I shut the door behind me and took the seat the mayor had just left.

"Tell me what Jerry Becker wanted you to do for him," I demanded.

"I can't do that."

"He wanted something . . . wrong from you, didn't he? Wanted the strength of a demon at his beck and call, something like that?"

"Why don't you calm down and tell me what's happened before you start accusing the most powerful witch in California with dabbling in the dark arts."

Aidan sat back in his chair, steepling his fingers in front of him. He always acted so laid back and relaxed, the ultimate West Coast witch. But I had seen him in action and had felt the tingle of his power. He was warning me off, and with good reason. I stroked my medicine bag and got a grip on my emotions. It wasn't like me—and it was profoundly unwise around someone like Aidan Rhodes—to lose my temper.

I looked into his apparently guileless eyes for a long moment before responding.

"If it's any consolation, I would never accuse you of dabbling," I said. "I imagine that anything you do, you do expertly. Besides, I thought *I* was the most powerful witch in California."

He grinned. "Let's call it a draw. I doubt either of us would come out well should we put it to the test."

Aidan's snow-white familiar jumped into my lap, and I leaned away from her. I love the beauty and grace of cats, but I'm allergic. I imagined whatever witchy gods and goddesses there might be would enjoy the idea of making a natural witch feline-phobic.

"What's going on, Lily? Why are you so upset?"

"There's a demon at the School of Fine Arts."

"You're sure?"

"Darned sure. Someone summoned it."

"Do you have the demon's name, characteristics?"

Having failed to get the proper attention from me, the cat jumped onto the desk, sauntered across the expanse of gleaming walnut, and leapt into her master's waiting arms. Aidan stroked her long, white hair with his graceful fingers.

"Not really. But he's out of control." I described tonight's incident to him.

He nodded thoughtfully. "Jerry Becker thought it was some kind of demon. That's why he came to me."

"To try to harness the demon's power?"

"Get your mind out of the spiritual gutter, there,

missy. I won't tell you the details, but Becker came to me for help."

"Why do I find that hard to believe?"

"Because you're a cynic when it comes to men? Powerful men, in particular?"

"That's not true."

"Isn't it?"

"I . . . It doesn't sound as though Becker was a very nice man."

"No, he wasn't. But that doesn't justify a death sentence."

True. "So how can we tell how much of a danger this demon poses for the school community?"

"Most demons are more about mischief than actual violence. Unless, of course, he killed Becker. Have you ruled out the human factor?"

"Not really, but Sailor doesn't think it was the demon."

"Sailor should know."

"So you're saying Jerry Becker didn't strike some sort of deal with the demon, back in the sixties when he was hanging around the school? His success—"

Aidan laughed. "I can guarantee you that Becker's success had much more to do with the drive of a man trying to escape death, rather than embracing it."

"From what I've put together, it seems the demon's been conjured, then bound, twice: once back with the group of nuns in the closet, and then in the sixties—after John Daniels was killed. Who conjured it this time?"

"I have no idea. Does it really matter? Clearly, whoever conjured the demon did not have the skill, or the intention, to bind it. So you'll need to do the honors. And make sure it stays that way, this time. How difficult that task will be depends on who he or she is."

Aidan stood, placed the cat gently atop the desk,

and studied the books on the shelf, his brow wrinkled in concentration. I watched, wondering what to make of him. I didn't trust this male witch, but I did feel a certain kinship. As much as I loved my new friends, someone like Aidan understood me in a way that Bronwyn never could, much less Maya or Susan or any of the gang, coven members or no. He was my kind. It was as simple . . . and as complicated . . . as that.

If Aidan really was what he said he was, just a wickedly talented witch working for the side of good, then I was prejudiced unfairly against him because of his talents, which was something I had always accused the world of doing to me.

On the other hand, Aidan had told me himself that he knew my father. Even if I believed him in all the other realms, that knowledge alone was enough to put me off. Still, I went out with Max, who didn't really believe in magick despite what he had witnessed in my presence. So what did that make me? Was I a self-hating witch?

"Lily?" Aidan was asking me something.

"I'm sorry? I drifted off there for a minute."

"Are you still having trouble sleeping? Those pesky mares at it again?"

"They wouldn't have anything to do with the demon at the school, would they?"

"I'm not sure. Tell me, is Matt having troubles as well?"

"You know very well his name is Max."

"Right, Max. That's what I said."

I couldn't help but smile. "You're incorrigible."

"I'm just waiting for the right witch to come along and 'corrige' me," he said with a crooked smile.

He pulled a huge parchment-covered tome off a cherry bookcase, handing the heavy volume to me. On the front cover the title was written in a bold, Gothic script: *Pseudomonarchia daemonum*, by Johann Wier,

1583. And down came another tome, *Lemegeton Clavicula Salomonis*, or *The Lesser Key of Solomon*. Aidan tapped on the second one.

"The Lesser Key of Solomon is an anonymous seventeenth-century grimoire containing detailed descriptions of spirits, as well as the conjurations needed to invoke and oblige them to do the will of the conjurer, or exorcist. That would be you, in case you weren't clear." He smiled. "It details the protective signs and rituals to be performed, the actions necessary to prevent the spirits from gaining control, the preparations prior to the evocations, and instructions on how to make the necessary instruments for the execution of those rituals."

Aidan placed the books in my arms and gently but firmly pushed me toward the door.

"Look up your demon and figure out what you're dealing with. This is what I'm paying you for."

"You're not paying me anything."

"Okay, this is what I'm canceling your debt for."

"But—"

"A minute ago you were bragging about your powers. Now, live up to your inflated image of yourself and figure this thing out. I'm busy."

"I don't know what I'm doing, Aidan. I need help."

"You've got plenty of help. You've got Oscar, and Sailor, and a whole coven behind you, if I'm not mistaken."

"They're a peace-and-nature-loving neo-pagan Wiccan coven. They like to thank the Goddesses and eat baked goods. They don't usually deal with this kind of thing."

"Time they started."

"Aidan, I was never trained for this. I'm . . . scared."

Aidan let out an exasperated breath. "Did anything actually hurt you?"

"No, I guess not," I conceded. "It was mostly a lot of

noise and visual tricks. Disgusting visuals. It kissed me, though."

Aidan's eyebrows rose, and he gave me a crooked smile. "It *kissed* you?"

I nodded.

"What guise was it under when it kissed you?"

"Luc Carmichael, a teacher at the school."

"Cute."

"It wasn't cute. It was . . . weird. Very weird."

"Do you like this Luc fellow?"

"I do. He's Max's brother, among other things."

Aidan let out a sharp bark of laughter. "Oh, that's a good one. This demon sounds like a real character. Does Max know about you and his brother?"

"There's nothing to 'know.' And no, I don't plan on mentioning it."

Aidan was still grinning. "You see? He's playing with your mind. You know how these demons are—they're mischief-makers mostly, only ratcheting up toward violence over time. They don't normally cause so much havoc up-front that people call in experts and exorcise them, that's the last thing they want. They want to stay and play. Besides, if he was only recently conjured, he's probably not strong enough to do much real harm. Now, if you'll excuse me, I'm busy."

"Doing what?"

"In case you didn't recognize him, that was the mayor of San Francisco you just tossed out on his ear."

"What's he doing here?"

"We're coming up with an evil scheme to transform all elected officials into my puppets. Come on, Lily, what do you take me for?"

I ignored that question. "Why are you so shy about going on campus and just taking care of this yourself?"

"I have my reasons."

"Which you won't share with me, no doubt."

Aidan grinned again. "It's almost as though we have telepathy, you and I. We understand each other so well."

Before I knew it, I had been escorted out of the office and found myself on the other side of Aidan's closed, and locked, door.

Chapter 19

I lugged the big leather research books down the stairs, past the glowering young woman in the ticket booth, and out to my car. Jostled by the tourists flocking to Fisherman's Wharf, I found a rare pay phone outside a restaurant and called Carlos Romero.

"How is Walker Landau?" I asked.

"He seems okay—physically, at least. Psychologically might be another matter," Romero said. "Listen, I want to talk to you in person. Someplace we won't be overheard. Meet me at a club called El Valenciano, near Valencia and Twenty-fourth Street in the Mission."

I agreed.

It took me nearly half an hour to cross town and find parking in the bustling Mission District. Carlos Romero was waiting for me at the bar, but as soon as he saw me enter, he led the way across the dance floor, where a salsa band was playing a cumbia. The floor was jammed with couples dancing with abandon, some so young they didn't look legally eligible for drinks while others were white haired and wrinkled. A "wedding crowd" I'd heard it called.

"One thing you can say about Latinos," the inspector shouted as we made our way to a dark, slightly quieter corner on the far side. He held up four fingers to the overly made-up waitress on the other side of the strobe-lit dance floor. "We like to dance."

"Isn't that a generalization?" I asked.

"Doesn't mean it's not true. Never did understand these clubs where women are standing alone, not dancing. Come to this place or Rockapulco or El Rio, and you'll be dancing before you order your first drink."

As if on cue, a man came up to the table, met Carlos's eyes, and asked me to dance. I supposed he was asking permission for my company. Carlos sent him away with a barely noticeable shake of his head.

It was hard to hear over the live band. We leaned toward each other across the small café table, like conspiratorial smugglers.

"Landau's not seriously hurt," Romero told me. "More shook up than anything. We've got him in the psych ward at S.F. General."

"Just to clarify—this was no suicide attempt."

"Then what was it?"

"I think Landau was temporarily possessed."

The inspector sat back and gave me a skeptical look.

"I'm afraid our little haunting is getting out of hand. The students are already at one another's throats. It's only a matter of time till more serious problems develop and someone gets hurt." I took a drink of water. "You need to close the school."

"What do you think is going on?"

"There's a demon entering through a third-floor closet."

"A demon."

"Demons typically sow chaos and discontent, and it ratchets up from there."

"I would assume, based on the careful study of horror movies, that a demon would disembowel, that sort of thing."

"It might well be building up to that. He's just playing with us right now."

Carlos folded his arms over his chest and fixed me with that unconvinced mien. "I was kidding."

"This is no joke."

The band ended the cumbia and started in on a merengue. The beat was catchy, and dancers flooded the floor. I looked over the crowd, taking comfort in their high spirits. It was a welcome reminder of life, and of joy.

"Right now he's just playing around," I continued. "Trying to see how far he can push people before they crack. Demons love to see humans display their basest emotions—jealousy, greed, fear. But I don't know where it will go from here. I fear for the students' safety."

The waitress came over with four shots of tequila, cut limes, and a salt shaker. I watched as Carlos licked the back of his hand, applied salt, downed his shot, and bit into a lime wedge. I did my best to mimic him, but sipped the tequila rather than shooting the whole thing. I'm a lightweight. Besides, I needed all my wits about me.

"I feel like I'm going from zero to sixty here," Carlos said after he was fortified. "I admit to you—and to myself—that I've actually heard haunted house noises. And now we're going straight to the concept of a homicidal demon?"

"I'm sorry, Inspector, but I don't have a lot of time to sugarcoat it."

"I have the sense you're not into sugarcoating, time or no."

"I need to ask you a couple of questions about Becker's death. Would it be possible for me to see the evidence, the body?"

"I thought of that. But frankly, I don't know how I would explain you. If anyone finds out a secondhand-clothes dealer is looking at evidence, I'm a laughing-stock. But I do have this."

He extracted an iPhone from his pocket.

He pushed some buttons before handing it to me. Photos showed the body at the bottom of the stairs, and afterward, on the table at the morgue. I remembered the red marks I had noted on his neck when I first saw him. The medallion that Andromeda mentioned was still around his neck—and there were marks as though the symbol had been burned into the skin. It was hard to make out, but it looked a lot like the sigil Sailor and I had found in the hotel room.

"What were the papers scattered about the body?" I asked.

"Mostly standard business documents. The only thing notable was a blackmail note."

"A blackmail note? About what?"

He handed a copy to me, which I read aloud. *"I know about John Daniels. You know what I want in return for silence."* It was written in the classic kidnap-note way, with letters torn from a magazine.

"It was done carefully," Carlos said. "We haven't come up with any detailed forensic information on it yet. But trying to get lab work done around here takes forever— this isn't like cop shows on television, I'm afraid."

"Any ideas about who wrote it?"

"Like I said, Becker had a lot of enemies. But as you probably know, it's usually the blackmailer who is killed in these cases, not the blackmailee."

"And you understand the reference to John Daniels?"

"Supposed suicide, decades ago, when Becker was a young man—a delivery truck driver who often hung around the School of Fine Arts. So I guess we're assuming now that Becker was involved in John Daniels's early demise." Carlos paused and took another taste of tequila. "I asked you once; I'll ask again: Do you think this ghost killed Becker?"

"No. I think it was a human." The band switched to a ranchero-style ballad, and the crowd went wild. I smiled, watching a tiny old man with a pencil-thin mustache lead a woman twice his size around the dance floor. "I have an odd question for you: What would happen if a person committed such a crime while possessed by a demon?"

He gave a humorless laugh and shook his head. "I have no idea. This is all new to me." Then his dark gaze drilled into me. "Are you saying you have a suspect you think was possessed?"

"No, of course not. Just thinking about how demons act, is all." I was glad the room was dim so he wouldn't take note of my blush. I wasn't a great liar. "So, about closing the school . . ."

"I'll see what I can do," said Carlos.

"What will you tell your cop buddies?"

"I'll figure something out." Carlos rubbed his eyes. It was hard to tell in the dim light, but he struck me as pale. A fine sheen of perspiration gleamed on his forehead. "Just promise me you'll get to the bottom of this, as soon as humanly possible—or should I say 'witchly' possible?"

"Do you feel okay, Carlos?"

"I haven't been sleeping well." He shrugged.

"There's a lot of that going around." Fishing around, I found a carved talisman in the bottom of my backpack. I wrote out the words of a protective chant on a small pad of paper.

"Wear this tonight, and walk the perimeter of your room saying these words."

Carlos looked at me askance, doubt shining in his dark eyes.

"Trust me," I said. "It will help." It occurred to me that I should track down Max and do the same thing, or offer to set up a protection spell at his place. Yeah, right. That ought to go over big.

"Just figure out what's going on so we can finish it," said Carlos, "and then I'll be able to get some rest already."

I raised my shot glass of tequila to him.

"I'll drink to that."

I dragged myself back home to Aunt Cora's Closet, wondering who might have summoned the demon. I knew Aidan had said it didn't matter, but I disagreed. Knowing how the creature got here, I thought, might help me decide how to get rid of it—once I figured out who "it" was, of course.

Time to do my homework, and I didn't mean algebra. If the past few weeks were any indication, a thorough knowledge of demonology would be much more useful to me—and to the city of San Francisco—than arithmetic.

I lugged the huge tomes Aidan had lent me through the front door of the shop. Oscar ran to greet me, in his piggy guise. Shifting the books in my arms, I turned to lock up as it sank in that Oscar would be in his natural form, unless—

A man stood in the doorway.

"*Max.* Are you all right?" He didn't look all right. He looked terrible, as though he hadn't slept in days.

Max reached out to take the heavy books from my arms. "Where do you want 'em?"

"Anywhere's fine. On the counter. Come upstairs and I'll make us some tea." I noted his haggard, haunted expression. "Or better yet, a stiff drink."

He trailed me through the store and up the rear staircase to my apartment. In the tiny foyer he paused, taking in the mirror set up to repel evil spirits, the sachets tied with black ribbons, and the bundles of rosemary hanging over the door.

I poured us both a glass of wine, then set a peanut butter and jelly sandwich on the floor for Oscar.

Max remained mute. I swallowed hard, wondering whether he was trying to think of the best way to break up with me. We'd had only one real date, true, but he struck me as the kind of man who wouldn't just stop calling. He seemed like the type to let a witch know where she stood.

"How is Luc?" I asked, finally, breaking the silence.

"He seemed okay. Sort of vague. I didn't smell anything on him, but I'm really afraid he's drinking again."

"I don't think so, Max. Where is he now?"

"At our dad's house, in Mill Valley."

"You need to keep him from going back to the school. It's going to be shut down for a while, anyway."

"Why? As a crime scene?"

"As a potential crime scene. In the future."

"You're reading the future now?"

"Max, listen. Luc's fears were not unfounded. He can't be allowed to go to the school building. I'm asking you to be your brother's keeper, just for a few days."

There was a pause; then Max gave a curt nod.

"I'm sorry about what happened earlier at the hotel," Max said.

"There's no need to apologize."

"That man, that 'Sailor' person, took me by surprise. Seeing him there, with you . . ." He shook his head. "I lost it. I completely overreacted."

"I understand. He told me a little about what happened between the two of you."

Max sipped his wine and wandered through the sitting room, then out onto the terrace. I followed. It was a dark night with little moonlight, and the air was fragrant with the scents of my lush herbs and flowering bushes. He leaned back against the balustrade.

"My wife's name was Deborah."

"I know. I read about her, a little bit."

"You looked me up?" Max asked.

"Like you haven't looked *me* up."

"Actually, I haven't."

"Oh. What happened to not being able to turn off the journalist inside you?"

"I guess I was trying not to be that person with you. I was trying to trust you."

"I'm sorry." Now I *really* felt guilty. "Please, go on with what you were saying."

"Deborah wanted children—she came from a huge family—and I've always loved kids. We tried to get pregnant for a long time, then moved on to fertility treatments. After a while I wanted to stop trying, wanted to adopt a child instead. The need to become pregnant was becoming an obsession. It . . . seemed to take over our lives, somehow." He took another sip of wine and looked up at the stars.

"Deborah was very gentle. Very soft. Kind. A wonderful woman, but . . . not the strongest person in the world. I talked her into seeing a psychiatrist, a friend of my sister's. The meds helped some, but it was still tough, living with a depressed person. She was like a shadow of the woman I once knew. I was traveling a lot at that time, working freelance but scrambling to find a more permanent situation since Deborah didn't want to leave the Bay Area. She finally found her way to a so-called psychic. I didn't realize how close they had become, how this so-called *seer* had wormed his way into her confidence . . . while I had dropped out."

He cleared his throat and balanced his wineglass on the balustrade.

"Apparently, he told her to quit taking the meds. The truth is, I wasn't around enough to know. I was on assignment in Europe when it happened. I called every day, but it wasn't uncommon for Deborah to ignore the phone. By the third day of silence, I called Carlos and asked him to check on her. She had overdosed on pills. Killed herself."

"Oh, Max." I cast a comforting spell, but it repelled right off him. He couldn't receive it.

"The worst part is knowing she was there, on the floor, with no one there to comfort her." His deep voice wavered. "I might as well have killed her myself."

"No, Max. That's not true."

He turned away, hands on his hips.

"Look at me, Max. It was a tragedy, but it wasn't your fault. You're only human. You did try."

"Did I? Not enough, obviously. I failed her."

He tilted his head back, taking a deep breath in through his nose, then released it in a rush. "I walked around in a daze afterward. For years. Then, that first day I saw you at the shop . . . it was as if I were waking up from a coma." He shook his head and turned back to me. "I can't explain it. I don't know whether it's pheromones, or fate, or your damned magic, but I can't stop thinking about you."

I moved into his arms. We held each other for a long moment. Finally he drew back, studied my face, pushed the hair out of my eyes.

And then came a kiss. His lips were warm, soft but hard, seeking. The kiss deepened, becoming more demanding, almost urgent.

Without pausing to think, or to talk myself out of it, I took Max's hand and led him into the bedroom.

Where neither of us was bothered by nightmares at all.

Chapter 20

I awoke at four in the morning. It wasn't mares that disturbed my sleep, but faint music. Tinny notes from a music box, playing that now-familiar ditty. "There's a place in France . . ."

And a pig snuffling at my side of the bed.

I slipped out of bed, careful not to wake Max. He slept flat on his back, splayed, with one beefy arm crooked over his head. He looked rumpled and sexy and gorgeous . . . and the memories of the past few hours brought a blush to my cheeks. Unfamiliar muscles made themselves known as I pulled on my robe. I felt deliciously relaxed, with a deep sense of well-being despite the events of the past few days.

Oscar and I scooted out of the bedroom, and I closed the door behind me.

"What is it?" I whispered.

"You stirred something up," said Oscar, transformed back into his goblin form. He crossed his arms over his chest, tapped a toe, and gave me a schoolmarm look.

"What are you talking about?"

"A witch like you, doing you-know-what half the night? That sure as heck stirs things up." His glare made me feel like a sixteen-year-old caught sneaking in the window after curfew with straw in her hair. "It's no surprise, what with your . . . carrying on and what-all."

Sex magic. Had I really let myself go that much? Did I release something?

"It wasn't like that," I insisted.

"Then it's quite the coincidence," Oscar said, cynicism dripping from every word.

The music droned on from downstairs. "Dee dee *dee* dee dee . . ." And I thought I heard something banging around now, as well.

I grabbed my medicine bag, tied it around my waist, and hung a talisman around my neck. Chanting a protection spell under my breath, I cautiously descended the stairs.

Everything was as it should be in the back room, but through the opening in the curtains I could see movement out in the dim shop.

I approached the curtains, slowly pulling them back. Oscar stayed under the table.

Dancing. The clothes I had liberated from the closet were dancing about my store; Victorian frills swaying and swooping, keeping time to the music emanating from the old box on the counter.

"Stop!" I yelled. I repeated the command in Latin, then Spanish, and even Nahuatl.

Nothing.

I tried closing the music box, but opened or closed, it continued playing its tinny tune.

What had I been thinking about when . . . when Max and I were together under the sheets? Joy. And freedom. And connectedness.

As strange as it seemed, the clothes were happy for me.

I leaned back against the counter, let out a long sigh, and shook my head.

Oscar mimicked me, taking up a similar posture at my side, shaking his big head, and tsking.

Other people had sex and all they had to worry about were questions of morality, unintended pregnancy, and STDs. *I* had to contend with accidentally setting off supernatural forces, inspiring the equivalent of a ghostly dance hall.

Life's just not fair.

"What's this?" Bronwyn asked the next day, holding the thick demonology grimoire in her hands.

"It's a ... uh ..."

"Demonology?" Bronwyn said, reading the spine. "As in, an encyclopedia of demons?"

I nodded.

"You believe in such things?"

"You don't?"

"Our coven focuses on the holidays, the good stuff. People often make the mistake of thinking that Wiccans are about devil worship, that sort of thing, and I always correct them. We're pagans, but we're all about the good." She lifted troubled eyes to mine. "I always assumed such negative creatures as demons were just the invention of the official church hierarchy, not reality."

I didn't know what to say. Bronwyn had an inordinate faith in my abilities; a faith much stronger than mine. She also seemed to think I had some sort of handle on what such evil was all about. But truth to tell, even during my training with Graciela, I was always better with practice—spells and brews—than with theory. I had left town before we got through much of the important history of the craft, hence my formal training left something to be desired.

So I really didn't know *why* evil existed, or where it came from; I knew only that, indeed, it did exist.

"The last time we went up against something evil like this . . . it scared me, Lily. It scared all of us."

"I know that, and I don't know how to thank you. I couldn't have done it without all of you. But this isn't the same sort of situation. *La Llorona* was a malevolent spirit; this is a classic demon."

"What's the difference?"

"I'm trying to figure that out. I think it's mostly about motivation. *La Llorona* was a mother who committed a terrible crime and is condemned to feel the anguish over and over, as well as to inflict it on others. A regular demon, a real demon, is a creature as old as the earth, and I'm not sure what demons are after, beyond spreading misery and fooling around with people's minds. To tell you the truth, I don't know much about them myself. Hence the demonology."

Just then, Max came into the shop from the back. He looked sleepy, despite the strong coffee I had made for us earlier in the apartment. Still, the haggard, haunted look had lessened. Though he and I had been up a good part of the night, he had gotten some rest, sleeping in until almost ten.

"Morning, Max," Bronwyn said, cool as a cucumber. But she looked over at me, lifted her eyebrows, and winked.

"Good morning," he answered.

Oscar snorted loudly and ran to his pillow.

I blushed and closed the demonology. I didn't want to remind Max, right at this moment, that he was now officially sleeping with a demon-hunting witch.

"I'm late for work," Max said. "Are you free for lunch?"

"Actually, I have plans. With Hervé LaMansec. Remember him?"

He gave me a rueful smile. "My girlfriend is having

lunch with a vodou priest. Never thought I'd see the day. I'll call you later, then?"

"I'd like that," I replied with a smile.

He kissed me good-bye. The feel of his lips made me want more—much more. I watched him let himself out the door.

"What's the expression?" Bronwyn asked. "Hate to see you go, but love to watch you as you leave?"

"Very funny," I said. But I surely did enjoy watching that man stride down the street.

"Soooo . . . did you have a nice evening?" asked Bronwyn, Ms. Innocent.

"Very, thank you." Except for incidents of possession and what-all. But the later part of the night was just perfect.

The bell over the door tinkled as Maya walked into the shop. Bronwyn grinned at her.

"What?" Maya asked.

"Ms. Lily here got lucky."

"Bronwyn!" I gasped.

"Max or Aidan?" Maya asked with an interested smile as she hung up her jacket. "Or someone new?"

"Max," Bronwyn replied.

"Bronwyn, we don't need to hire the Goodyear blimp to announce it, do we?" I asked.

She laughed. "Get used to it, girlfriend. We're happy for you. Max is a good guy."

"Lily," Maya said, "have you heard from Ginny Mueller lately, by any chance?"

I shook my head. "No, I haven't seen her since the art opening."

"Me neither. She's not answering her phone, and she stood me up this morning. We were supposed to have coffee," Maya said. "I'll try calling Marlene, just to be sure everything's okay."

"You sound worried."

"She just seemed sort of out of it at the art show. And then she slipped out without even saying good-bye." Maya noticed the demonology books splayed on the counter. "What's all this?"

"Lily's trying to figure out what demon's been menacing the School of Fine Arts," Bronwyn replied.

"Really? It's in here?"

"Maybe," I said. "There are tens of thousands of them. I know what his sigil, or sign looks like, but I can't draw it."

"Why not?"

"It's . . . dangerous for someone like me. I could accidentally conjure it before I'm ready."

Bronwyn and Maya exchanged a look.

"I know, it sounds bad."

Bronwyn started flipping through the pages, reading various descriptions to us. The demons listed were a fascinating mélange of wickedness and surprisingly entertaining attributes. The monks had written meticulous details about their propensity for the lustier side of life, especially.

"Here's a good one: *Beleth, also spelled Bilet, Bileth, and Byleth, is a mighty and terrible king of hell, who has eighty-five legions of demons under his command. He rides a pale horse, and all kind of music is heard before him.* Didn't you mention hearing music, Lily?"

"I did, but there was no pale horse. The fellow I'm looking for looks like a Griffin, with wings of an eagle and the head of a big cat, a leopard maybe."

"This is interesting, though," Bronwyn said. "According to this, Ham, Noah's son, was the first in invoking him after the flood, and wrote a book on mathematics with his help. I thought demons were fierce, and to be feared?"

"They are—it's kind of hard to explain. Some people

feel their powers can be harnessed, and they can help you by lending you their powers," I said as I folded and rehung the dresses that had been scattered about the shop last night. I had gathered them this morning when they finally stopped their dancing with the arrival of the dawn. "I remember one fellow, for example, named Dantalion, who is supposed to be Lord of Arts and Letters, and used to be invoked by students. I guess demons can be of service, but you have to be darned sure you know how to control them before you call on them."

"I see what you mean," said Bronwyn. "It says that when Bethel appears, he tries to frighten the conjurer. The conjurer should hold a hazel wand in his hand and draw a triangle by striking toward the south, east, and upward, then commanding Beleth into it by means of special conjurations. Otherwise . . ."

"Okay, I think that's enough for now, Bronwyn," I said, noticing the uncomfortable look on Maya's face.

"Oh, just one more. This is a good one; looks like a Griffin, too. His name is Sitri, also known as Set, Bitru, or Sytry."

"What's with the aliases?" Maya asked. "It's as if they were undercover."

"They cross a lot of cultures," I said. "I guess a lot of different folks have categorized them."

Bronwyn read aloud. *"The twelfth spirit, called Sitri, alias Bitru, is a great prince, appearing at first with the face of a leopard, and having wings as a Griffin; but afterward at the command of the Exorcist, he putteth on a human shape; he is very beautiful, he inflameth a man with a woman's love, and also stirreth up women to love men. Being commanded, he willingly detaineth secrets of women, laughing at them and mocking them, and causeth them to shew themselves luxuriously naked if he be desired, etcetera. He governeth sixty legions of spirits; and his seal to be worn is this . . ."*

"He maketh women naked?" I asked as I tossed a petticoat onto the to-be-washed pile.

"That's what it says."

"Okay ... Does it say anything about faces melting? Because that was the part that really worried me. Give me naked women over melting faces any day of the danged week."

"You saw melting *what*?" Maya looked slightly gray.

"It was just an illusion," I clarified. "A disgusting illusion."

"Have you seen this anywhere?" Bronwyn asked, holding the book open for me.

I looked up to see a beautiful, hand-tipped illustration of a figure with the face of a leopard and wings of a Griffin. And below it was his sigil: a big U bisected by a line with four circles, and topped by three Gothic-looking crosses. That was the sigil Jerry Becker had drawn on the mirror in his hotel room.

"That's him," I said, not exactly comforted by the knowledge. But at least I now had an identity. I was dealing with Sitri, a great prince, who commanded sixty legions.

"He mocks women?" Maya asked.

"Mocking I can handle," I said. "I grew up being mocked. Mocking never killed anybody."

"So what does this mean, exactly, Lily?" Bronwyn asked.

I crossed over to stand beside her and read the entire entry. Besides listing his attributes, the author gave very explicit instructions for binding the demon, as well as describing possible mayhem if the demon was not exorcised properly. I felt butterflies dance in my stomach.

"It means I know whom I'm dealing with, and there are a few tricks described here to keep him in line. But it also means that unless I can figure out a way around it, I have to go up against a powerful demon, and soon. Like tonight."

"And you need help," Bronwyn said, her voice uncharacteristically subdued.

"I think I do, if it's offered. I'd limit your exposure to the actual demon, but it would be a huge help to piggyback on your coven's power. . . . I'm sorry, Bronwyn. You're probably regretting getting to know me about now."

Bronwyn smiled and came over to give me a hug. "Never, sweetie. Never. I'll talk to the coven women and let you know what they say."

"We've got your back, Lily," put in Maya. "We wouldn't let you go it alone."

Oscar trotted over to join in the love fest.

How did I ever get so lucky?

I got together with Hervé LaMansec, my new friend at the Ramp, an informal restaurant with tables outside by the water, near China Basin.

Hervé and I met not long ago when I was investigating the haunting by *La Llorona*. Though his vodou belief system, methods, and power source were completely different from mine, I felt a certain kinship with him as a fellow power-bearer, just as I did with Aidan.

I watched as he wound through the tables toward me. A man of medium height but with a thick, football player's build, his dark skin gleamed in the sun. Everything about Hervé was formidable—you could see people unconsciously making way for him, as though he were royalty. When he drew near to my table, his rather severe face split in a huge grin. I stood and we hugged.

"Lily, wonderful to see you," he said as he took a seat. "I keep hearing about your exploits in the bay. Each version more exaggerated than the last. That was one for the ages."

"Thank you, I think."

The waiter approached, and we both ordered sweet tea. I asked for clam chowder and salad, while Hervé ordered a vegetarian Gardenburger with fries. I noticed Hervé used a thick Caribbean inflection when he spoke to the waiter. With me, he switched back to his genuine L.A. accent. He told me once that the Caribbean persona was part of the package his customers paid for, and I saw his point. Most people wanted the "beyond" to be exotic; for some reason it was easier to believe in oddities from a faraway locale rather than from one's oh-so-familiar backyard. It made me wonder whether practitioners of magic in the Caribbean used an "exotic" California accent to please their customers.

I gave Hervé a quick rundown of the problems at the School of Fine Arts. He wasn't fazed by talk of ghosts, but he reared back at the mention of a demon.

"Those guys scare me," he said.

"Me, too," I replied.

"How has it been manifesting?"

"Sowing discontent amongst the students, a couple of cases of temporary possession, and someone jumped out a window...."

Hervé chuckled. "Busy little fella, huh?"

"Oh, and there was one murder that sort of kicked things off, though, that seems to have been human caused."

"The demon might have stirred someone up, inspired him or her to do something they might not have otherwise. Or it could have been the other way round—the murder could have fed the demon."

I nodded.

"Keep an eye on anyone who was possessed, temporarily or not," he said.

I nodded again, and handed him a Xeroxed copy of the page from the demonology. "This is him."

"As you know, we have a different pantheon in vodou. I did have a case once, a few years ago, where I actually worked with a Catholic priest to dispel a demonic presence."

"A priest worked with you?" I was surprised to hear that.

"A very open-minded priest. He and I had worked together to provide services for at-risk populations, homeless kids, and the like. What I do know is that a fellow like this"—he held up the piece of paper, seemingly unwilling to mention his name—"might be conjured easily, especially within a portal, or without imposed restraints. But the opposite, the binding, must have been done intentionally, and with great power. Is Aidan Rhodes involved?"

"How do you mean, involved?"

"Is he one of those who trapped the creature the last time?"

"I don't think so. It was before his time."

Hervé stared at me for a long moment.

"What?" I asked

"I wouldn't be so sure."

"Sure about . . . ?"

"Aidan looks good for his age."

The waitress came with our food. Savory aromas wafted up to us.

"By the way," Hervé said, "I've had recent visits from two young women who go to the School of Fine Arts. One was Andromeda something. She told me she knew you. She wanted something to hurt a ghost she thought had killed her father."

"You're kidding me." I put my glass of iced tea down with a clunk. "What did you tell her?"

"I tried logic first, but soon resorted to trickery." He smiled and shrugged at my surprised look, then dipped a French fry in a puddle of ketchup mixed with Tabasco sauce. "I gave her some old herbs and salts, wrote down a few meaningless words, and told her they would cause great pain and torment to the ghost's ears."

"Do ghosts even *have* ears?"

He laughed, a pleasant rumble from deep within his chest. "She was looking for guidance, feeling out of control. As you know, in such cases as these, the belief is more important than the actual result."

"True enough. You said there were a couple of girls?"

"The other came by just yesterday. Virginia something."

"Virginia? Could it have been Ginny?"

"She said Virginia. She mentioned that her mother runs the school?"

"What did *she* want?"

He had a pensive look on his face, and a slightly bemused frown. "Sulfur. And protective herbs."

"Did she say what she wanted them for?"

"Looked to me like she was looking for ways to deal with a demon. I told her to speak to you, but she said she couldn't. I didn't give her anything she could hurt herself with, but it's worth noting. In any case," Hervé continued, "if Rhodes was involved, that would explain why he's so interested in the current case, and yet why he's not becoming directly involved."

"Why would Aidan hesitate to get involved?"

He shrugged. "Once you are known to the demon, he can eat away at you. Bound or not, he's probably figured out a way through Rhodes's defenses by now. Can't go back without all hell breaking loose." He took a huge bite of his Gardenburger.

I was impressed. This wasn't Hervé's area. It wasn't even his belief system; yet he knew much more than I about how things worked. Not for the first time I regretted having left home before my training was complete. I needed to remedy that, and soon, if I was going to keep on getting enmeshed in such things. My naïve desire to keep the whole witch thing under wraps seemed less and less likely as each demonic day passed.

"I guess what I need is to develop an exorcism plan," I thought aloud.

"Consult the demonology for suggestions, but I would recommend you rely primarily upon your own power sources. Given your talents, you'll be more effective with your own approach. Brew something, chant, or whatever it is you do that focuses your power."

"So basically you're telling me I need to handle this. By myself."

Hervé grinned and winked at me. "Go get 'em, tiger. You're stronger than you know."

I wished I had his faith.

Chapter 21

After lunch I sat in my car watching the seagulls swoop and dive and dance on the breeze, and wondering what my next move should be.

The good news was I *wasn't* in this alone; I felt sure Bronwyn's coven would come through, and though they didn't have a fraction of my power, the focused and unyielding faith of a group of women was no small addition to my arsenal. I also decided to call Graciela and ask for long-distance backup for my spell. While I was at it, I would see if she had any further advice.

The bad news was that I had to deal with the demon. The worse news was there was still a murderer of the human variety on the loose.

I started up the car. There were a few more people I wanted to talk to before I could put this demon, and this case, to rest. First stop: San Francisco General's psychiatric ward.

I was pleasantly surprised that Walker Landau agreed to talk to me. He shuffled into the rec room wearing a blue bathrobe over a dingy gray T-shirt and navy blue sweatpants. Sluggish movements and speech suggested the effects of heavy medication.

We took seats at a small table with a checkerboard on top.

"Andromeda says you're decent," Walker began, staring down at the checkerboard. "She came to see me, for a quick visit. She vouched for you."

"I'm glad to hear that."

"Is Todd still angry at me?"

"Todd? Why would he be angry?"

"Because of Andromeda and me."

Why was Todd so interested in what happened to Andromeda? I wondered. He seemed so in love with Marlene. . . .

"Because of the note."

"What note?"

Walker paused, as if the mental energy required to process my question were overwhelming.

"The one he wanted me to write to Becker."

"What about?"

"Blackmail. Because I figured out Jerry killed that art student long ago. So very long ago . . ." He sighed, and seemed to rally.

"You're referring to the death of John Daniels?"

He nodded, picking at a loose string on his bathrobe.

"How did you figure that out?"

"Ginny said something once. I was already curious because I'd been looking into the so-called haunting on the staircase. I managed to track down Jerry's former girlfriend in Sausalito; she was the victim's girlfriend, too. Then I hinted around, and Jerry basically confessed."

"Becker confessed to you that he killed John Daniels?"

"It was a coupla weeks ago, after Andromeda's art show at a gallery on Chestnut Street. Jerry'd heard the noises on the stairs—you know, the ones you heard?— the previous night. He was upset, had been drinking a lot. I guess he'd been living with the guilt for a long time. That sort of thing can, you know, eat away at you over the years."

Couldn't it just?

"When I shared what I learned with Todd, he told me to demand money in exchange for my silence," Walker continued. "But I asked for Andi instead."

"What do you mean you 'asked' for Andromeda? She's a woman, not a possession." I caught myself. I needed Walker to answer my questions. "And her father agreed?"

"I told Jerry I would keep his secret if he got Andromeda to marry me."

"How was he supposed to arrange that?"

Walker shrugged.

"So you wrote the blackmail note and ... ?"

His eyes darted around the room. "I gave it to him a coupla days before he was killed. Todd helped. He brought me the cut-out letters; even told me what to write. It wasn't my fault. But then I asked for Andi instead of the money. I guess that part was sort of my fault."

Gee, you think? I wanted to ask, but controlled myself. "Let me get this straight: Todd encouraged you to blackmail Jerry Becker for money. Were you supposed to share it with him?"

"You know, that's the funny part. I don't think Todd cared about the money, not really. Mostly he hated Jerry, so he targeted what Jerry valued most."

"His money."

"That's right."

"Not his daughter?" And the Father of the Year Award lost another contender.

"He said rich people only felt pain in their pocket-books."

"Did Becker know Todd was involved?"

"No." He shook his head vigorously. "Anyway, I never told him about Todd. He seemed pretty sure I had a partner, but he thought it was Luc. That was what they were arguing about in the café the night Jerry died."

"Walker, don't you think you should tell the police what you know?"

"They wouldn't believe me. I'm in the loony bin, after all."

"Call this number." I handed him Carlos Romero's card. I had memorized the number by now, anyway. "Inspector Romero's familiar with what's been going on at the school. He'll listen to your side of things. You can trust him."

Walker stared at the business card for a moment, then nodded.

"So we still don't know who killed Becker," I pondered aloud.

"Oh, I know who killed him."

"You do?" That'll teach me not to ask the obvious questions.

A look of confusion came into his eyes. "Haven't you been listening? I thought you understood."

"What? Who?"

"Daniels."

"John Daniels?"

"Well, his ghost. To avenge his death."

I shook my head and blew out a frustrated breath. "The ghost didn't kill anyone. Becker was killed by a human, Walker."

"Really? You're sure?"

"Positive."

"Wow. Who would do such a thing? Maybe Ginny? She didn't like that Jerry was sleeping with her mom. Or that security guard—Kevin something? He's always hanging around. Or Luc. He was going to meet Jerry that night. Or—"

Time to wrap this up. "Thanks, Walker. I really appreciate your taking the time to talk to me. I'm afraid I have to run."

"Do you think Andromeda is still interested in me?"

I sighed, though he had my sympathy. Poor Walker Landau was acting like people did when under the spell of the sort of love magic I refused to perform—mindlessly devoted and smitten unto obnoxiousness.

"Why don't you focus on getting well? Make yourself strong in mind and body, take some time with your art and what-all, and when you're feeling good again, *then* go talk to Andromeda. She's pretty vulnerable herself right now. She just lost her dad. Not a time to make important life decisions."

"Of course," Walker said, though the feverish gleam of unrequited love—or obsession—shone in his eyes. "You're right."

Somehow I doubted he would take my advice.

I took a deep breath when I got outside, lifting my face to the sun, feeling its warmth and thinking about how easy it was to be a fool for love. In some ways I was just beginning to get to know Max, but already he'd made me doubt my vow to be true to myself. That was pretty profound, not to mention disturbing. And speaking of Max . . .

The demon had temporarily possessed two people, which meant he had some kind of connection to them. Walker Landau was in a locked facility, so he wouldn't be drawn to the School of Fine Arts during tonight's exorcism. He'd be safe.

But the same couldn't be said for Luc.

I hurried back into the hospital lobby, found a pay phone, and dialed Max's cell phone. He answered, sounding distracted, and in the background I heard raised voices and shouting, the sounds of a newsroom.

"Miss me already, huh?"

I smiled. "I do. Max, is Luc still staying with your dad?"

"For the moment."

"I need you to do me a favor, and I need you to do it without asking questions."

"Again?" There was a pause. "Is this one of those relationship exercises like in those women's magazines, 'Ten Ways to Know If Your Man Really Trusts You'?"

"I wish. Will you do it?"

"What do you want me to do?"

"Go over to your dad's house tonight, and make sure Luc stays there. Physically restrain him if necessary. Under no circumstances is he to go to the school tonight."

"What's going on?"

"No questions, remember? Just do this for me, please."

"All right." I could practically hear Max, proud myth-buster and self-described man of reason, grinding his teeth as he imagined the magical hijinks I would be getting up to tonight. "But we need to talk about this, and soon."

"I know. We will."

After we hung up, I felt gnarled fingers of self-doubt wrap themselves around my heart. Last night had been magical—and not only in the witchy sense—but could I ever be completely myself around Max? Would I have to deal with his doubt at every turn?

I fished in my bag for more coins and called the store to see if Maya had gotten in touch with Ginny. She hadn't, and Maya said Marlene wasn't answering the phone, either, so I asked for their home address along with directions. I would bet my familiar Ginny was somehow involved. It was past time for us to have a heart-to-heart chat.

Ginny had seen something in the mirror in the closet,

I was sure of it. She had also said something to Walker Landau about a long-ago murder. And she had experienced sudden—and improbable—career success.

Funny, elfin little Ginny, who hadn't been smiling much of late despite her artistic dreams having come true.

Thirty minutes later, I nosed the van into the driveway of a well-tended stucco row house in Glen Park. Pretty flowering plants in terra-cotta Mexican pots adorned the short flight of terrazzo stairs up to the landing. On the front door was a modern version of the traditional welcoming wreath, made of scraps of colored paper that fluttered in the afternoon breeze.

"Lily. What a surprise," Todd said as he answered my knock. His eyes flickered behind me, as if to check on whether I'd brought backup. He made no move to invite me in.

"Hi, Todd." All the way over I had debated whether to confront Todd with what Walker had told me about the blackmail note. I decided, for now at least, to keep mum. Presuming Walker talked to the police, it would be a moot point, anyway. And if Walker didn't speak with Carlos Romero soon, I would tell the inspector everything I knew. For the moment, I thought, discretion would be the better part of valor. "Is Ginny here?"

"As a matter of fact, she's not."

"How about Marlene?"

"Now's probably not the best time—"

"You told the police I had to *close* my school!" Marlene shouted as she came to the door. She was dressed in an old pair of blue jeans, her hair was loose and unkempt, and I caught a strong whiff of alcohol. "How dare you!"

"It's necessary, Marlene," I said. "Just for a few days."

"You—"

"Marley," Todd said quietly. Marlene glared at me, spun on her heel in a huff, and retreated.

"Is she okay?" I asked.

"She'll be fine. Sorry about this, but Marley's not quite herself at the moment."

"Do you know where Ginny is?"

He shook his head.

"I know this is going to sound weird, but could I take a quick look at her room?"

"Her room? I don't think—"

"Todd, this is important."

"What are you looking for?"

"I don't know. But I need to see if there's anything . . . unusual. It's related to the haunting of the school."

"You think Ginny's involved?"

"Unwittingly involved, yes."

After another brief hesitation, and a glance behind him, Todd stepped back and let me in. "This way," he said.

About halfway down a short hallway, I noticed the unmistakable aroma of rotten eggs—sulfur.

Todd opened a door and nodded. I noted a line of salt had been poured across the threshold as though to keep out evil spirits.

On Ginny's desk and tacked to the walls were dozens of pieces of paper with Sitri's sigil sketched upon them. Some of the drawings were elaborate, in full color with curlicue embellishments; others were crude and childlike, as if drawn by another hand entirely.

A black cloth was draped over what I guessed was a mirror atop a cherry dresser. Several books on witchcraft—all of which looked to be of the peace-loving Wiccan variety—were scattered near the bed. A Ouija board was set out on the floor, alongside a splayed tarot deck and a thick tome, *How to Interpret the Magical Tarot*. Protective sachets hung over the doors and

window, and the room was filled with white candles—
lots and lots of white candles.

The sensations in the room were chaotic. Portals
were half opened, spirits half formed. Someone here
had been playing with magic, and she'd had enough
power to get into trouble but nowhere near enough to
get herself out.

My concentration was broken by the sound of a tussle
in another part of the house. Female voices—Marlene's
and Ginny's—were raised in argument. The voices drew
nearer.

"Don't go in there!" Marlene said. "Don't—"

"It was an accident," Ginny cried. She was pale, with
dark circles under her eyes. "I never meant to do anything, Lily!"

Marlene started into the room, but Todd stopped her,
his voice low and reassuring. "Let them talk, Marley.
Maybe Lily can help."

"Ginny, this is important," I said. "Tell me everything
that's been going on, how it all started."

"I can't. You'll think I'm crazy." Ginny cried softly,
wiping her tears with the sleeve of her sweater.

"I really won't."

"It was the closet. On the third floor. Before we even
opened it, there was something about it—it felt like
it was calling to me. As though the door . . . as though
something wanted me to open the door. I couldn't stand
it. I had to know what was in there."

I nodded. Ginny clearly had some psychic ability,
however untrained. I wasn't surprised she would have
felt the energy emanating from such a place of bound
power.

"What happened when you opened the door?"

"Nothing, at first. Mom had to break the handle to
get it open, but then it was just a regular old closet, kind

of. It was hard to see, and there was no light switch, so I lit the candelabra sitting on the dresser."

"Do you remember the order you lit the candles in? Think carefully."

"Order?" She had pushed up one sleeve and was picking at her forearm; I noticed a series of scratches, red and angry looking.

"All in a row, one after the other, or randomly?"

"Randomly, I think." She shrugged. "I wasn't really paying attention. But after I lit them, I felt something. I've always been a little . . . you know—I could feel things, see things sometimes. And then I found this."

From under the drawings on her desk she extracted a piece of paper, crumbly and yellowed with age. On it was sketched Sitri's sigil.

"It was in the middle of the floor, with a knife stuck through it, pinned to the floorboards. Mom got weirded out and left. But I figured, if there really was some . . . *thing* in the closet, that was, like, his avatar." She twined a finger in her hair, and I noticed several strands came loose. Ginny was falling apart.

"Did you pull the knife out?"

She nodded, then opened a desk drawer and handed me a beautiful, antique *athame*, a ceremonial knife used for spells.

"And then I saw something in the mirror . . ." Ginny continued. "And I started thinking about that damned Andi, with her big art show, and I remember thinking that if I had a rich father like she did, I'd be famous, too . . . and it was almost like the face in the mirror *wanted* me to ask for help. I must have fallen asleep or something. I must have been dreaming. But I asked for help."

"You called on the demon?"

"No. No way. I wouldn't do that."

"What *did* you do?"

"This sounds crazy, I know, but it was like the voices in the mirror were telling me to ask *our lord* for help. I didn't know what they meant. It kind of scared the crap out of me, but they said it would grant my wish. Sort of like a genie."

Or a demon.

"Was this when the sounds of the bell tower started getting louder?"

"Yeah, how'd you know? I mean, a few of us had heard things for, like, years, but nothing like it's been lately. But you're right—it sorta started after we opened the closet. I tried to, like, sort of like stop it."

"Stop it, how? Did you do anything to bind him?"

"Him who?"

"The demon."

"The *what*?" Marlene hovered at the door, though Todd kept her from entering the room. I concentrated on Ginny.

"It wasn't a Genie?"

"Not by a long shot, I'm afraid. Ginny, please. This is very important. The one the voices referred to as *our lord*. Did you try to bind him?"

"What does that even mean?" Ginny coughed into her hand and squeezed her eyes shut. "I don't feel very good."

She looked awful, too, and no wonder. Ginny had compromised her soul, however unwittingly.

"Tell me what you did to try to stop it. Did you perform an exorcism, cast a spell?"

"An *exorcism*?" Ginny looked at me as if I were nuts. "Like in the movie? Are you crazy?"

I reined in my impatience and fear. "Just tell me what you did."

"I was afraid to go back to the closet, so I tried to communicate through my old Ouija board. We used to do it at slumber parties when we were kids, and even though my friends thought it was just a game, I always felt like I actually heard something. And then I tried to read the tarot, but I don't know that much about it and didn't make it through the book. There's more to that stuff than you'd think."

"Yes, there is," I said.

"Ginny had nothing to do with Jerry's death!" Marlene interrupted from the doorway.

"I know that, Marlene," I said. "She was with me when it happened."

"He left her money for a scholarship in his will." Marlene started to cry. "So the police are saying she had a motive."

"Not a very strong one," I replied, my eyes still on Ginny, who was looking more and more distressed. "And it's a moot point, anyway. Ginny didn't hurt anyone."

"It was the ghost," Ginny said with another cough and a sniff. "I don't know why nobody believes it, what with everything that's been going on. I mean, *hello*. Even Mom believes it."

I glanced at Todd, who was watching Ginny closely.

"Lily, can you help me? Make this stop?" Ginny sank onto her bed. "I don't know what's going on. . . . I'm so confused. And I feel like crap. I think I've got the flu."

"I'll help you, Ginny—of course I will. But you *have* to stay here tonight. Do *not* go near the school. Understood?" Ginny nodded, looking relieved. I turned to Todd and Marlene. "Whatever you may think of me, trust me on this: You must keep Ginny at home tonight. Tie her down and sit on her, if you have to. Under no circumstances allow her to leave the house. Clear on that?"

Todd and Marlene nodded.

"What else can we do?" Todd asked.

"Fetch me a large garbage bag. Let's get this Ouija board out of here. Grab all the sigils, too."

"The what?"

"These drawings."

Marlene started collecting the sigils as Todd returned with the trash bag.

"No! I need those for a project I'm working on!" Ginny gasped, a feverish glint in her eyes.

"Trust me," I said. "This is one project you do *not* want to finish."

Ginny was in bad shape, but modern medicine could do nothing for her, and neither could my botanicals and brews. The only thing that would help Ginny was for me to confront and disable Sitri. If only I knew exactly how.

On my way back to Aunt Cora's Closet, I decided it was worth one more stop by Aidan's place, just to clarify a few issues, and to be sure I wasn't still lacking anything obvious.

After another brief verbal skirmish with the young woman in the booth, I made my way up the stairs and through the wax figures to Aidan's office. This time, before I had even knocked, I heard a voice beckoning me to enter.

"Lily! What a lovely surprise. Stop by for tea?"

"Not exactly. I'm going up against the demon tonight, and I think I figured out why you can't help me. You know him, don't you?"

Aidan looked at me so long, I thought he wasn't going to answer.

"I do. Many years ago, Jerry Becker came to me. He told me about releasing the demon and making a deal with him. But he wanted out of their agreement. He needed my help to exorcise the demon."

"I thought it wasn't possible to renege on that kind of agreement."

"It's not easy. The cost is prohibitive for most. Becker

forfeited part of his soul. He was never a whole man afterward."

"When was this?"

"Some time ago."

"When Jerry was a young man? But you couldn't be more than, what, thirty-five or forty?" I may not know algebra, but I did know how to add and subtract.

Aidan gave me a crooked grin, his blue eyes twinkling, and then he ignored my question.

"Your father and I helped Becker come up with a plan of exorcism. Gave him the necessary tools, and the ritual. We hoped to stay out of the actual conjuration, but that connection was enough for the demon to know us."

"My father? He helped as well?"

Aidan just nodded.

"And you sent me in there alone, without my knowing?"

"I couldn't be sure what was going on. Jerry Becker came back recently, told me he thought the demon was loose again. But I didn't know whether to believe him—he did have a dramatic streak. I didn't want you to go in with ideas and accidentally conjure the nasty fellow. You know how these guys are. I can't so much as say the name without summoning him. Anyway, I knew you were strong enough to deal with whatever you encountered."

I wished people wouldn't assume I was so doggoned strong all the time.

Besides . . . something else occurred to me.

"It's not that. You weren't sure which side I'd go to," I said.

Aidan raised his eyebrows and shrugged. "What can I say? The seductiveness of the demon is strong indeed. And we both know about your father."

"Yes. We do."

"Those nuns, the ones who invoked him all those years

ago, they died in that room. They sacrificed themselves for his benefit. That's powerful stuff. Luckily, someone realized what was going on and trapped him."

"I think it was one of the other nuns, a sister one who escorted them back to the convent. She had been disciplined for 'practicing pagan something or other' at one point. But I think she was just trying to stop whatever was going on."

"Lucky for all of us."

I nodded. "So, how do I stop him this time?"

"There's no one way to do it. It's like the rest of what we do, Lily. You do whatever it takes to channel more power than he can. It's heart, not any particular dogma."

One last question occurred to me as I turned to leave.

"Aidan, how did Sailor get his psychic abilities?"

"We made a deal."

"What kind of deal?"

"I thought you understood I couldn't discuss issues about my clients."

"He was a client?"

"In a manner of speaking. Anyway, why are you so interested in Sailor?"

I shrugged. "He's . . . enigmatic."

"Aren't we all, my dear Lily? Aren't we all?"

Tonight was the dark moon, which boded well for a demonic exorcism. Ginny's deteriorating condition had given me a sense of urgency. I had taken Hervé's words to heart, and now I added Aidan's. I would memorize the recommended method for conjuring and binding the demon from the Lesser Key of Solomon, but most of all I would rely on my powers . . . bolstered by all the help I could muster.

When I got back to Aunt Cora's Closet, Bronwyn

told me she had arranged a meeting with Wendy and another priestess, Starr, at a Haight Street café named Coco Luxe. We sat and talked over creamy mochas and homemade marshmallows.

"Have a praline," said Wendy, holding out a small plate of candies.

"Mmm, thank you. But, just for the record, these aren't pralines. They're caramels with pecans," I said.

"But Coco-Luxe pralines are famous!" said Starr.

"Real pralines aren't caramels," I said. "My mama used to make them." I took another bite. "They're incredible, all right. They just aren't pralines."

"Told you," said Bronwyn with a smile. "Our Lily's a praline purist."

Starr turned to me, a serious look on her face. "Bronwyn tells us you need help with a demon. What does she mean?"

"I always thought demons were invented by the church hierarchy," said Wendy. "You know, to scare the crap out of people so they'd be good and go to church."

"That's what *I* said," said Bronwyn.

"I'm afraid not. I mean, I have no idea where they come from, whether they're connected to some entity called the devil, or any religious tradition. I just know they exist, and there were writings about them long before Christianity arose. They cross historical as well as religious traditions."

"What are the risks involved?" Wendy asked.

"There's always some risk, but in this case it should be minor. You won't even enter the building. I just need the coven's powers for the setup. I'll be doing the actual exorcism. The demon won't be able to touch you, but he might try to tempt you."

"What should we look for?" Bronwyn asked.

"Usually some offer of power or wealth, youth or beauty. But he'll probably realize that won't work with the coven, so I'm guessing he'll try something else. Beware of sensuous feelings; feelings of love, of being wanted, desired. It's like being high on booze or drugs; the feeling is real, but it's not based on anything tangible. Draw strength from one another, as you always do within the circle. I'll be there, too, to battle with him if I need to. But unless I miss my guess, he'll wait for me to come to him."

Starr looked at Wendy, and Wendy at Bronwyn. They nodded.

"Okay," declared Wendy, "but we're gonna need some more marshmallows."

These were my kind of Wiccans.

Chapter 22

"I missed out on *marshmallows*?" Oscar whined when I returned to my apartment to brew. My mind was so focused that I had forgotten to bring him a piggy bag.

"Sorry, Oscar," I said. "I'm a little under the gun at the moment, but I'll make it up to you. I promise. Just as soon as I have this demon under control."

Oscar shivered, and I did the same. Just the thought of that demon would scare any sane person or pig.

I laid a clean white cloth on the counter, placing upon it my *athame*, a few sprigs of Sorcerer's Violet, a segment of sacred rope, a selection of crystals, a handful of enchanter's nightshade, and three apples sliced horizontally to display their secret pentacles, or stars. After opening my Book of Shadows to tonight's spell, I filled my cauldron half with springwater and half with fresh goat's milk, then set it on the stove to boil.

I sliced another apple for Oscar, and while the pot came to a boil, I placed a call to my *abuela*, my adoptive grandmother, Graciela. A formidable woman of few words but great powers, she had taken me in during the dark, frightening days of my out-of-control youth, just as she had my father before me.

Years ago she had lost my father to the wrong side

of the power, and I knew she was angry with me still, as well. When circumstances conspired to make me leave my hometown of Jarod, Texas, Graciela had sent me to finish my training with a powerful friend of hers in Chiapas, but instead I had gone looking for my father. Big mistake.

Graciela and I still hadn't talked about our estrangement; in fact, I had spoken to her for the first time just a couple of weeks ago, when I needed her advice and help to go up against *La Llorona*. And here I was asking for help yet again. Graciela quickly outlined what she thought I would need to brew for optimal strength and focus during an exorcism.

She also told me, in no uncertain terms, that if San Francisco was as rife with spirits as it appeared to be, I'd better finish my training in the craft, and soon.

"I can't come back home, though," I said. "You know that."

"We could make it so. We could alter things."

"I'm not willing to do that, or have you do that. It would be wrong. It's dangerous."

Silence on the other end of the line.

"Would you be willing to come here? You could have the bedroom—it's a really nice place," I asked, hope in my voice but not in my heart. I knew she'd refuse. Like many powerful women, she was connected to the land, to her patch of dirt. She had worked her garden for decades, as had her mother before her. There was magick in the red earth.

"I don't fly on airplanes."

"I could meet you outside of Jarod and drive you from there to San Francisco."

"I don't ride that far."

"You could. For me."

There was shuffling on the other side of the line. After a moment, I heard her say, "Find a man named Aidan Rhodes."

"I already know him. How do *you* know him?"

There was a pause. *"Era amigo de tu papa."* He was a friend of your father's.

Graciela always reverted to Spanish when she was being discreet, as though her phone were tapped, and as if half the world didn't already speak Spanish.

"Yes, he told me that himself," I replied. "Is he ... Can he be trusted?"

"Only as far as you trust your father. *Con poca confianza.*"

Not really. Super.

"But he's very skilled," Graciela continued. "Very powerful. Very well trained, by *tu papa.*"

"Aidan was trained by my father?"

"Basta ya. That's all I will say on the subject."

"Okay. Thank you."

"One more thing: Never forget, *m'hija*, the difference between evocation and invocation."

And with that she hung up. Graciela didn't like the phone any better than I did.

I continued to grasp the receiver, as though still connected to Graciela, and pondered her final words. When we invoke energy or spirits, we create a personal connection to them, which, in the case of destructive energy, can be terribly dangerous. Invocations invite energy to build up within one's soul. The energy is discharged through one's aura, creating a strong link to the target— in this case, the demon. This is what had happened with Ginny, Luc, and Walker. Each had invoked Sitri simply by not knowing how to avoid him. Demons are tricky that way.

I sighed, wishing Graciela were here. I wanted to sit at her feet and place my head on her knees. I loved California and was happy to make my life here. I had found a home in San Francisco, in the Haight; a like-mindedness, if not with regard to witchcraft or magick per se, at least in terms of openness and respect for others and for beliefs that differed from one's own.

But there was a place in my heart for the hard-packed red dirt of my hometown, from which I had coaxed my first plants as a young child; for the hot, humid air that wrapped around my arms and legs like a damp blanket, caressing my skin; for the stern voices of my grandmother, and even my mother.

Time to cook Cajun again—just as soon as I brewed up a little exorcism tonic, packed a few haunted dresses into the van, and trapped me a nasty demon.

Eleanor Roosevelt once said, *Women are like tea bags. We don't know how strong we are until we're in hot water.*

I saw that quote as I flipped through my Book of Shadows. I had copied it down years ago when I read her biography. It seemed like the perfect sentiment for the night ahead of us.

After all, the water of my life was boiling, without a doubt.

I didn't question my abilities. I had found out not too long ago that I was made of stronger stuff than I would have imagined. Especially with the coven, and Graciela, and Oscar all on my side, working as backup.

But Sitri knew my father. That gave me serious pause. Was it just a coincidence that I had become involved in this whole mess? Could Sitri have somehow orchestrated this, to bring me in, to tempt me? Had he known I would come? Those were his mares that had been harassing us at night, I was now convinced. Any of us mucking around in the school's business seemed to be afflicted.

Oscar helped me load the van with the clothing from the closet, the music box, a shovel, and my cauldron.

Then I packed my special supplies: I decanted the brew I had prepared earlier into three jars, then pulled together various herbs, resins, salts, and sacred rope. Suddenly I realized I was out of cinnamon. Despite the urgency of the situation, I had to smile. Wouldn't it be something to blow an exorcism of this import because of a common baking supply?

I brought my backpack downstairs to the main shop floor and looked through Bronwyn's botanical stand, finding a whole jar of fragrant, curling cinnamon bark.

"Don't go."

I had been so absorbed in my task that I didn't even hear the bell tinkle on the door. I whirled around to see Max standing just inside the shop.

"*Max*. When did you get here?"

"I'm serious, Lily. We're not just talking your safety here, but your sanity."

"I take it someone filled you in on what's going on?"

"I got it out of Bronwyn."

I sighed. "Great."

"Don't blame her—I'm a trained journalist, remember?"

"Oh, I remember. Wait," I said, suddenly alarmed. "Where's Luc?"

"He's fine. He's with my dad in Mill Valley. I hid the car keys."

"I'd feel much better if you were actually there with him. Physically."

"I'm headed there now, while you're headed for, what, an *exorcism*? This whole thing is crazy, Lily; don't you see that? Don't do this, I beg you."

My heart sank. I had been dreading this conversation, hoping fate would cut me a break. Max Carmichael did not believe in—nor approve of—witches. If

I acted like a witch—if I was true to myself—I risked losing him.

"You seem to think I have a choice."

"Don't you?"

"This is what I am, Max. I've tried to explain that to you. There aren't many of us around, you know. If I abdicate my responsibilities . . . it's not as though there's anyone to step in and take my place."

Max started to say something but stopped when Sailor opened the front door and poked his head in. The men exchanged glares but said nothing.

"You ready?" Sailor asked me.

"I am." I nodded, not too surprised to see the reluctant psychic at my door. Aidan must have sent Sailor in his stead. Nice to have minions to do your bidding. I packed the last few items in my bag and slung it over my shoulder. "Sailor, would you wait for me outside for two seconds, please?"

Sailor gave me a curt nod and left, the door swinging shut behind him.

I turned to Max and tried to harden my heart. "I understand if you decide to walk away from this, Max. And away from me. I know this is a lot to ask of you. But . . . I hope you can accept it. Accept *me*."

Max's face softened. "Last night . . ."

"Last night was amazing. And it was. . . . I mean that sort of thing—it's rare for me."

He nodded. Our gazes held for a long moment.

I heard a tap on the window, and saw Sailor signaling "Come on already" with a hand gesture.

"I have to go now, Max. We'll talk later . . . or we won't."

As I turned to close the door behind me, I couldn't help myself. I looked back at Max.

He stood as still as a statue, desperate, miserable . . .

and cold. I couldn't shake the sensation that Lily Ivory, little old magical me, had made him that way.

"Maybe Max is right. Maybe I'm crazy to be doing this," I muttered as Sailor drove the van across town to the School of Fine Arts. Oscar, seemingly stricken by celebrity awe in the company of Sailor, rode in the back in his porcine guise, not making a peep.

"What's the alternative—to end up all bitter and twisted like me?" Sailor scoffed. "Of course you have to do it."

I smiled in spite of myself.

"Besides, you'll be okay," he said in a surprisingly sincere voice.

"I thought you couldn't tell the future."

"I'm making an exception in this case," he said as he pulled up to the school. "Now get in there and kick some demon butt."

That's me all right, the demon butt–kicker.

Wendy, Bronwyn, Starr, and a half-dozen other excited, black-clad coven members met us at the loading dock and helped to unload the tools, the trunk, the clothes, and the music box from the van.

"Hey, Lily," Sailor called out.

"Yes?"

"You'll be okay."

"You already said that."

His dark gaze held mine with a rare earnestness. "I'm serious."

"Thank you."

"I'll be out here in the van if you need me."

I nodded and turned to go.

"Do me a favor," Sailor grumbled. "Don't need me."

I smiled at him, then joined the coven members.

"It breaks my heart to think we have to burn all of

these beautiful Victorian items," Bronwyn said as we toted bags of clothes to the school's main courtyard. I noted with relief that the police, or fear, or . . . *something*, had finally managed to clear the building of its human denizens.

"I know," I said, "but it's necessary. It's the only direct connection we have. I don't want to risk going back into that closet. Not yet, anyway. Oh and by the way, it turns out I was wrong. The clothes aren't Victorian era— they're Edwardian. The Victorian era ended with Queen Victoria's death in 1901. I can't believe I made such a rookie mistake."

Bronwyn looked at me, puzzled, then started laughing. The rest of the coven joined in.

"What?" I asked. "What'd I say?"

"*You*," Bronwyn chuckled. "Worrying about vintage clothing at a time like this."

I smiled. "I'm just saying, is all. Can't very well go around calling myself a professional without knowing the basics, now can I?"

We piled the items in the center of the courtyard, atop the old stones that had kept the convent safe from the 1906 fire. On top of them Wendy placed pieces of old, dry lumber.

"That looks like a real pyre," I said, impressed.

"Girl Scouts. Four years. Fire-building badge."

"Awesome," said Starr.

"Shall we get started?" said Bronwyn, anxiety beginning to show on her face.

As she spoke, a thick layer of fog blanketed the moon, and the courtyard, lit only by a few sconces along the building, dimmed.

I nodded. It was time.

The coven gathered and cast their circle. The last time I had witnessed this ceremony, I had been part of it. But not now. I remained apart, Oscar sitting quietly at my side, watching, making sure that the demon would duel with me, not with the innocent Wiccans. The circle called on the powers of the moon, of the goddess Artemis, and shared a goblet of the brew I had prepared. Wendy, acting as high priestess, approached the pyre and lit the fire.

The beautiful old clothes ignited with a *whoosh*, as though soaked in gasoline. Flames popped and sparks flew, but they could not leave the circle created by the women. The fire burned so bright and hot that the coven members backed away, but still they did not break the circle. They continued to chant, to call upon the powers of the moon and the goddesses, until the fire began to slowly die out, finally extinguishing itself. It took less than half an hour for everything to be reduced to a pile of ashes.

At a nod from Wendy, the circle opened, and I used the shovel to transfer the smoldering ashes into the iron cauldron. Carrying the heavy cauldron by myself would be a strain, but I didn't want anyone else to risk going into the building.

"You all stay here," I said to the Wiccans. "Whatever happens, whatever you hear or see—do *not* come into the building. Promise me."

"Are you sure, Lily?" Bronwyn asked quietly, her large eyes worried.

I smiled to reassure her. "I'm not looking to be a martyr, believe me. But it has to be this way."

I looked down at Oscar. "That goes for you, too, pal."

I lugged the iron cauldron up the bell tower stairs, stone step by stone step, pausing occasionally to rest my burning muscles. The ghost of John Daniels was eerily silent tonight. I almost missed his breathy moans. When a ghost was spooked, it was time to worry.

At last, sweating and panting, and gasping for air as

I chanted, I made it to the third floor, and slowly set the cauldron down. The door at the landing shimmered, beckoning, warning. I reached for the handle, which was hot to the touch. I flinched, but grasped and turned it anyway, and stepped into the hallway.

A misty blue light poured through the hole in the closet door, bouncing off the walls of the empty third-floor hallway. I braced myself as I heard a soft voice from behind the door, calling to me.

Chapter 23

"*Lily . . .*"

Graciela?

"*Come, chica, come give your* abuela *a kiss. . . .*"

Not Graciela. Of course not. Demons like to play.

I burst through the door, flinging it open with my mind as much as with my foot.

The room was empty Or so it seemed. Lit in an odd blue light.

I hauled the cauldron inside, positioned it in the center of the tiny room, and scattered the ashes from the fire. As I dragged the mirror over to position it next to the cauldron, I noticed a letter on top of the bureau. Yellowed with age, it was written in French. And with it was a note written in collage materials, proclaiming neverending love, and declaring the anguish of betrayal. A suicide note. And candles and herbs and a drawing of Sitri's sigil. Someone had tried to call the demon with those papers.

I took the jar of potion I'd brewed at home and started to cast a circle, but before the first drop had touched the floor, a mass of flies swarmed around me, filling the room. Soon they were joined by wasps and hornets, buzzing around me angrily.

Ignore them, Lily, I told myself, and concentrated on chanting. *They're just cheap demonic parlor tricks.*

The brew turned to steam the instant it struck the floorboards, filling the room with mist. Just as I completed the circle, I heard the sound again: air rustling through reeds, morphing into a cry of human anguish.

Still chanting, I drew a triangle within the circle and sketched the demon's sigil, a crown topped with four crosses, in the ashes on the floor.

"With the strength of my ancestors, I am the power. I command you to show yourself," I called to Sitri, my *athame*, or ceremonial dagger, in my right hand. *"With the strength of my ancestors, I am the power. I command you to show yourself."*

The mirror shattered, sending pieces of glass bouncing off the invisible walls of the circle, peppering me with tiny, stinging shards. To confuse the evil and dispel the bad luck, I jumped up and spun around, thrice, in a counterclockwise direction. I thought I heard a far-off giggling, followed by crying.

"With the strength of my ancestors, I am the power. I command you to show yourself," I repeated. My helping spirit became the conduit of my ancestors, and I channeled all the witches who had gone before me. Their power became my power as I tapped into the stream of spirit that united us all.

I pointed my *athame* at the sigil. My arms and the palms of my hand were covered with tiny droplets of blood from the bits of glass, making the blade sticky. The blood shimmered with power.

The mist began to swirl, reeking of must and sulfur.

Wrong. It's wrong.

I felt my pulse speed up, my heart pound. I was doing it wrong, all wrong. It was a mistake to come here; I wasn't strong enough. I felt that now; I knew it. I should have stayed at the shop as Max asked me to. I should never have endangered the women of the coven, or my familiar. I should—

I heard them scream—Bronwyn, Wendy, Oscar. . . .

No! It was the demon at play.

A surge of fury and renewed determination coursed through me. Sitri was playing with my mind, making me doubt myself. But I refused to stop summoning him, and as I watched, the sigil shifted, starting to glow, becoming refined, beautiful, seductive.

And then, Sitri showed himself: *He appeareth at first with a leopard's head and the wings of a gryphon, but after he putteth on human shape, and that very beautiful.*

He was massive, and though restricted to the triangle, he seemed to fill the entire space. Rising over me, he flapped those terrible wings.

And smiled. A sly, mocking smile.

"Lily," a soft voice said from behind me, and I turned to confront this new menace.

It was my father. Not as he had been the last time I had seen him—badly scarred—but as he was when he left me and my mother. I shouldn't have been able to remember the day, for I was still a toddler. But I did remember. He had been handsome and younger than I am now, and I wanted to go with him. A wave of anger at Graciela and my mother for refusing to allow it swept over me. I should have gone with him, learned, and trained with him. Perhaps I would have been able to save him . . . if only . . .

My power flickered, beginning to seep from me.

"You're not real," I said, and mustering my strength, I turned my back on the chimera. I heard him cry out, begging me to save him. Telling me he loved me. It broke my heart.

"How sweet . . ." hissed the demon. I felt tears burning at the back of my eyes, and a wave of nausea and regret

enveloped me. The temptation to change the past swirled around me; all I had to do was reach out for it. . . .

I shook myself, angry. I knew I must not react in anger, but I could use it, use its power, to center myself. Pointing my *athame* at the sigil once more, I started to recite the lines of the exorcism.

"I do here license thee to depart unto thy proper place; without causing harm or danger unto man or beast . . . I compel thee."

"Lily!" Luc called to me from the door.

This was no magical creation, but the man.

"Luc, leave, now!" I yelled.

He did not move, concern and fear in his eyes. I realized I had never seen such a beautiful person; somehow I knew he would love me, care for me, and I yearned to go to him, to be with him—forever.

I continued to chant, fighting this new temptation.

Luc's eyes went dark; he did not blink, and he began speaking in tongues. His beauty transformed, sliding into seductiveness. "Liiiilllly . . ."

I turned my back on him, focusing on Sitri's sigil. I repeated the lines of the exorcism, pointed with my *athame*, channeled my helping spirit, subsumed myself to the power.

Max appeared in the doorway. He caught his brother just as Luc fell to the floor.

Without thinking, I grabbed Max's hand, cut a small X, and dropped his blood into the circle to mingle with mine.

There was an explosion of light and energy.

And Sitri was cast out.

But not gone. The demon was out of the school, but not silenced forever. I imagined it would find me one of these days, when it had regained strength and was bored.

But for now it was over.

I slumped to the ground, still in the circle, and tried to catch my breath. I was covered in glass shrapnel, fly bites, and wasp stings, and I smelled of sulfur and fear. I imagined I looked like three miles of bad road. Not a pretty picture.

"Lily! Are you all right?" Max demanded, his brother limp in his arms.

"What are you doing here?"

"My sister stopped by to check on Luc, and he took her car. How did you know he would come here?"

"Take him out of here, *now*."

"Only if you come with us."

"I'll be right there," I rasped. My throat felt tight and my body so weary I could barely speak. "The danger's passed for now. Please, take him outside. I'll meet you there."

Max wrapped Luc's arm around his neck and half carried, half dragged him out.

I breathed a shaky sigh of relief. The closet was nothing now but a tiny, musty room full of ashes, mirror shards, dead insects, and a drop or two of magical blood. But though Sitri was bound, he was not dead. We were still vulnerable until this room was sealed up, once and for all.

I left the closet, walking unsteadily down the hall and through the door that led to the bell tower stairs. Before descending two steps, I felt so dizzy that I slumped down to sit on the stone, closed my eyes, and put my head on my knees. Behind me, I heard footsteps on the stairs, then soft moaning.

I didn't have to turn around to guess that this was John Daniels, resident bell tower ghost.

"John," I croaked without bothering to open my eyes, "I swear on all that is holy, if you start moaning and screaming, I will throttle you. So to speak. Or the ghostly equivalent. I am so *not* in the mood."

The only sound that came to me was as soft as a gentle spring breeze through the leaves of a tree. I had the strangest sensation. It was cold, but ... comforting.

It felt as if I were being hugged.

After a few moments, the feeling went away. I sensed another, human presence. I looked behind me to see Todd Jacobs holding the antique ceremonial knife I had seen in Ginny's room.

I had been hoping to hold him off, to speak to him with Inspector Romero at my side. Todd had talked to Andromeda in the stairwell the night of Jerry Becker's death, even though he told Marlene he was out with the boys. He had convinced Landau to blackmail the Big Cheese. And he must have discovered what everyone else at the school seemed to know, that Becker had been seeing Marlene.

"I did think it was romantic, you know," Todd said quietly. "I really did."

"What are you talking about?"

"That night, I had planned to throw myself down the stairs for love, just like the legend of John Daniels. We both know he didn't really kill himself, but still ... it seemed, somehow, fitting for me to join him here. Let Marley think about *that* for the rest of her life." Todd's eyes filled with tears. "I wrote her a suicide note; even used her own collage materials. But then Jerry showed up, right in front of me, at the top of the stairs. He laughed at me. Told me I was too young to satisfy a real woman. He dared me to kill him; said I didn't have the guts. And I—I lost it."

"What did you do?"

"I don't know what came over me—it was like a blind rage. I shoved him as hard as I could. Who knew it would be that simple to rid the world of scum?"

"Todd, listen to me. I don't think you were entirely in control of yourself. I suspect an evil spirit caused you to do something you wouldn't normally have done. The inspector on this case, Carlos Romero, understands what's been going on here at the school. We can talk to him together. There's got to be some way—"

Todd laughed. The sound was seductive.

"Don't provide it a host," I said very quietly. I had just cast Sitri out. Could Todd somehow be calling him back? He had been mucking around with things in the closet, trying to use the French letter and his own suicide note. Was he still linked to the demon?

"You want to hear something ironic? Throughout this whole ordeal, Marley has turned to me, relied on *me*. Murder has done wonderful things for our relationship."

I heard the scrabble of hooves running up the stairs, and my miniature potbellied pig appeared . . . and then transformed into his natural goblin shape.

"What the *hell*?" Todd said, recoiling from Oscar. He glanced over at me. "Get that thing out of here. He creeps me out!"

I began to stroke my medicine bag and chant.

"Stop that, Lily," Todd said.

I ignored him.

"Stop it!" Todd continued, raising his voice. "Look, obviously I don't want to do this, but now that I've decided to live, you'll have to die."

Todd lunged at me, but Oscar intervened, ramming Todd in the shin with his big goblin head.

"*Ow!* I'm gonna gut you, you worthless pile of bacon," Todd said, and raised his arm to stab Oscar with the knife. Without thinking, I flung out my hand and hit Todd so he was left off balance.

A horrified look came over his handsome young face, and for a brief, heartbreaking second, time stopped as Todd teetered on the edge of the landing.

Then he fell backward down the steps, tumbling, his

body hitting the stone steps, one after another, with sickening thuds that echoed in the stairwell.

I sat down, stunned and shocked. Oscar crouched beside me.

"Thank you, mistress. You saved my life," he growled.

"Or *you* saved *mine*," I said, my voice shaking as much as my hands. Had Todd survived the fall? I had acted in self-defense, but . . . could the influence of the demon still be strong? I shook my head, wrenching my thoughts back to Oscar. I hugged him to my side. "I thought I told you to stay outside where you'd be safe. How come no one ever does what I tell them?"

"*Lily!* Are you all right?" I heard Max yell, and his footsteps sounded on stone as he raced up the stairs toward us.

I heard Bronwyn call out to me as well, and Wendy, and lots of other voices growing louder as they approached and attended to Todd.

My friends. My backup.

"I'm okay," I shouted, then turned to my familiar. "Least I'm fixin' to be. Oscar, have you ever heard the expression, 'Nothing goes over the devil's back that doesn't come under his belly'?"

"What's it mean?" Oscar asked right before transforming himself into a pig.

"What goes around, comes around."

Chapter 24

Kevin Marino was growing on me. I like a man who can swing a hammer.

The day after the exorcism, I was back at the school, sprinkling the inside of the closet with a powerful brew, hanging protective herbal sachets, and sweeping up the mirror shards, which I would bury in my garden. Kevin and I, with Oscar's dubious porcine assistance, removed the closet's door frame and filled the opening with cement block and mortar, permanently sealing the closet and its demonic inhabitant. I mixed a batch of plaster using brew instead of water, and applied the fortified plaster to the cement block. While the plaster was still wet, I drew symbols of protection and binding on the wall. The plan was to reposition the heavy cabinet in front of the new plaster wall. With luck, no one would ever know the closet existed.

Sitri was not gone for good, but at least this portal was sealed. No one connected to him—Ginny, Luc, Walker, or Todd—would be able to call him now without fully intending to do so.

To my great relief, Todd had survived his fall. He had a concussion and several broken bones, but the doctors believed he would recover. Formal charges against him were pending, but I was just as happy to leave those decisions to the SFPD and the district attorney's office.

"That should do 'er. I'll run and fetch a mop to clean up the rest of this mess," Kevin said, gesturing at the plaster dust on the tiled floor, which somebody's hooves had tracked up and down the length of the hallway. "C'mon, little guy," he said to Oscar. "Race ya."

"Thanks, Kevin."

I was admiring our handiwork when I sensed a presence behind me.

"Am I supposed to believe you trapped a demon in there?" Max asked.

"I don't guess you're 'supposed to' believe anything," I said. "And it's not trapped so much as exorcised, but that's just splitting hairs. How's Luc?"

"Seems okay. My brother tends to land on his feet. Still, he's a little confused."

"I'll bet."

"So am I."

I steeled myself against the impulse to throw myself into Max's arms and promise to be a good little non-practicing witch. "I can't keep explaining myself, Max."

"I know," he said with a nod. "I've got an assignment in Washington—I'll be back east for a couple of weeks. May I call you?"

"Of course."

He hugged me, kissed my head, and then cleared his throat.

"We still have a date, right?" he said, a note of forced jocularity in his voice. "Whose wedding is it, again?"

"Susan's niece."

"Right. I'll be there. And I'll wear a tux."

"Max, I can't—"

"I know. Give me a little time here, Lily." His light gray eyes were sad, his feelings guarded. "I've got to chew on this awhile. Get my head straight."

I nodded. We hugged one last time, and he left.

Oscar trotted back down the hall toward me.

"Scared him off, huh?" Oscar asked.

"Seems like."

"It's like a—whaddayacallit?—an occupational hazard, isn't it?"

I nodded and swallowed hard.

Good thing witches can't cry.

The night mares were gone. I surprised myself by sleeping about twelve hours a night for the next couple of days and for the first time had to open the store late.

But by Friday, things were returning to normal. Bronwyn and Maya arrived at the store early, bringing baked goods and hot drinks from Coffee to the People, and we sat around the counter, chatting and enjoying a lazy morning. Even Conrad came inside to sit with us, something he almost never did.

"Good morning, everyone," chimed Aidan as he swept through the door, Luc Carmichael by his side. "Look who I found lurking in the bushes."

"I wouldn't say lurking, exactly," Luc said with a crooked smile. "I just wasn't sure . . . after what happened, how I acted . . . I came to apologize."

"It wasn't your fault, Luc," I said, crossing over toward him so we could talk a little more privately. "We all know that."

"Max was furious with me."

"How *is* Matt?" Aidan butted in. I ignored him.

"Don't worry about it, Luc," I said. "It's all taken care of, anyway. It's done. All I want to think about now is which dress I'm going to wear to the Art Deco Preservation Ball."

"You're going to the ball?" Luc asked. "Need an escort?"

"I appreciate the offer, but I hear it's all the rage to go stag."

He raised his eyebrows.

"Besides, I think your brother might take it amiss."

"I thought you two were ... taking a break?"

"I'd like to wait and see. He's only gone for a couple of weeks."

"*I'll* take you," Aidan interrupted again. "I was planning on going, myself."

"Dude, *I'll* take you," echoed Conrad from his seat at the counter.

"Thanks, guys." I had to smile. This for the witch who was quite literally banned from any and all high school dances. "But, really, I sort of like the idea of going solo."

Just then we all looked around as the bell on the front door tinkled again, this time announcing the arrival of Inspector Carlos Romero.

"Blessed goddess!" Bronwyn exclaimed, throwing up her hands. "Don't tell us you're here to ask Lily out as well? I'm beginning to feel like a *dueña*."

"No," Carlos said, looking puzzled. "I'm afraid I'm in need of her expertise."

"I thought things were back to normal at the school," I said, my fingers crossed.

"Oh, they are. Unfortunately, there's another crime scene I might need your help with. Seems you're now the department's unofficial expert in the occult."

"Does that come with dental insurance?"

"I said '*un*official.'"

"What's up?"

"Have you ever heard of the Serpentarian Society?"

"I know Serpentarius is the thirteenth sign of the zodiac, but I've never heard of a society in his honor."

"I thought there were only twelve zodiac signs," Bronwyn said.

"Me, too," said Carlos. "But then I looked it up—and there used to be thirteen signs."

I nodded. "One for each month of the year."

"Of which there are . . ."

"Thirteen." Every face in the room—with the notable exception of Aidan's—looked at me as though I were crazy, reminding me of how odd my knowledge base was. "One month for each moon. There were thirteen until the Gregorian calendar added a few extra days to each month except February."

"Why would they do that?" asked Maya.

"To get rid of what they thought of as an unlucky number—thirteen."

"I figured you were the right one to talk to," Carlos said with a satisfied nod. "I need you to come take a look."

"At?"

"A posh apartment, set up with all the bad luck signs you can imagine. And at the moment they're all surrounding a dead guy."

"Duuuude," whispered Conrad, shaking his head.

"You want me to look at a murder scene?"

Carlos nodded.

Great. From demon butt-kicker to unofficial consultant to the SFPD—heady stuff for an outcast who had arrived in San Francisco a few scant months ago determined to fly under the radar. I looked around my fabulous store—at my friends, who had demonstrated repeatedly that I was no longer alone in this world; and at my familiar, who made me laugh every day. And I realized that Graciela was right: If I wanted to make a life for myself here in California—or anywhere, for that matter—it was high time I completed my training.

I glanced at Aidan, lounging smug and self-satisfied near the rack of vintage leather jackets as he took in the scene. *Don't look now*, I thought, *but here I come*.

I just hoped Aidan Rhodes, male witch, was the right man for the job.

Author's Note

The San Francisco School of Fine Arts does not actually exist, though the campus is loosely based on the graceful San Francisco Art Institute on Chestnut Street. The SF Art Institute is housed in a beautiful red-roofed, Spanish-style building . . . complete with a bell tower that is rumored to be haunted.

Most of the spells used throughout the book are based on information gathered in personal interviews from practicing witches, but none should be repeated.

Turn the page for a glimpse of
another of Lily's adventures in
the Witchcraft Mystery series

HEXES AND HEMLINES

Available now from Obsidian.

It didn't take a witch to figure out something was very, very wrong on the thirteenth floor of the Doppler Building.

It wasn't called the thirteenth floor, of course. It was called the Penthouse, and Malachi Zazi lived there. Or *used* to live there. At the moment his body was splayed atop a long banquet table, a jagged shard from a shattered mirror protruding from his chest. Deep red blood spatters created a gruesome Rorschach pattern on the snowy white Belgian lace tablecloth.

I took a deep breath and concentrated on not losing my lunch.

Most days I deal in vintage clothing, not corpses. I may be a natural-born witch, but I'm no more comfortable around violent death than any other mortal merchant on Haight Street. I was here only because SFPD inspector Carlos Romero had taken the unusual step of asking for my help. I now understood why.

"When was he found?" I asked.

"This morning," said Inspector Romero. "By his housekeeper."

"Time of death?"

"Medical examiner hasn't determined that, but the

victim had guests for a midnight supper. The last ones apparently left around two thirty in the morning."

"The body hasn't been moved? The legs were pointed toward the door like this?"

The inspector nodded. "Everything's just as it was found. Including the bird."

"What bird?"

As if on cue, a small brown sparrow swooped past me and landed on the table near the corpse. Looking about brightly, it chirped and hopped before flying away. I jumped when a black cat sprang onto the tabletop, then gave chase. Feathers and fur disappeared into the bedroom.

I clutched the medicine bag hanging on a braided string from my waist and whispered a quick protective chant.

Romero raised an eyebrow. "I didn't think witches were scared of black cats."

"We aren't. But a sparrow trapped in a house . . . is a sign of death."

"Did you happen to notice the dead guy on the table?"

"Death is still lurking. It's a bad sign."

"That's nothing." The inspector snorted. "We've got a ladder in front of the door that you have to walk under in order to enter the room, a broken mirror over the fireplace, an open umbrella in the corner, and a black cat. Even *I* recognize those as signs of bad luck."

"There are thirteen chairs around the table," I added. "And we're on the thirteenth floor. Not that there's anything unlucky about the number thirteen; quite the opposite. But a lot of people think it's cursed."

I decided not to point out that lying atop a table, and reclining with one's feet toward the door in what was traditionally considered to be "the corpse position" were also bad omens.

"Yeah, whatever. What else do you see?"

"I need a minute," I said, and the inspector gave me an "after you" gesture. I wasn't ready to take a close look at the body, in part because it was a corpse, but mostly because I sensed there was something not right with it.

How to describe it? It . . . shimmered. There was something *off* about the former Malachi Zazi.

I took a breath and wandered around the apartment, sidestepping the crime scene investigators who were dusting for prints and photographing possible evidence. Apart from the staccato camera flashes, the only light in the room was the dim amber glow of the hand-blown sconces. The apartment reeked of cigar smoke combined with aromas from the late-night supper. Tall windows were covered by tasseled red velvet drapes that blocked the afternoon sun; muted oriental rugs covered generous portions of the dark mahogany floor; vivid oil paintings in ornate frames lined the paneled walls; and plush leather armchairs invited visitors to linger by the carved stone fireplace. The whole apartment looked like a stage set for a Victorian play about a convoluted murder mystery.

"For the record, we're on the fourteenth floor," Romero said as he trailed after me. "Not the thirteenth."

"Only because the building doesn't have a thirteenth floor," I pointed out. "Otherwise-right-thinking architects pretend there's no thirteenth floor when they build buildings. It's a holdover from a less rational era. It's almost charming."

"Not for Mr. Zazi. Man was in here with all these bad luck signs, and now he's dead. Stabbed in the heart. Look, Lily," the inspector said with a half-embarrassed, half-weary expression, "you know it pains me to ask for your help, but I thought you might be able to offer certain . . . insights into this case. So give it to me straight. I can take it."

"Fair enough. You noticed the bad luck signs, but except for the mirror, the ladder, and the bird, those are mere superstitions. They wouldn't lead to murder. And even the real bad luck omens are subtle and tend to work on some sort of time delay."

"So he was just an eccentric guy who thought bad luck signs were amusing? You don't . . . *feel* anything?"

I took a deep breath and approached the body. "May I touch him?"

"Go ahead."

I laid the fingertips of my left hand on Zazi's cold, waxy forehead, closed my eyes, and concentrated, filtering out the static from the various people in the apartment whose nervous energy was bouncing off the walls. I focused my powers, subsumed my conscious self, and allowed myself to be a conduit.

Nothing.

Which was not good.

People—*normal* human people—give off sensations for hours after death.

Turning Malachi's hand palm up, I searched for his fingerprints. The tips of his fingers were slick—like a doll's.

I examined his palm: no creases, no lifeline. Nothing.

"Could you have someone roll him for prints?" I asked.

The inspector nodded. "What are you looking for?"

"Confirmation that he doesn't have any."

"Any what?"

"Fingerprints."

"What, you mean like you?"

"Like me."

Our eyes met.

Some humans—not many—are born without fingerprints due to a rare medical condition. Others, rarer still, are born without them even though they show no other signs of that condition. Like me. *I used* to think it was caused by something metaphysical, a cosmic *sign* that I was meant to go through life without leaving a trace. But then I decided I was just an oddity.

So, apparently, was Malachi Zazi.

"Probably also a good idea to check out his DNA."

"Why? What am I looking for?"

"Make sure he's human."

Romero glanced around at the crowd, took me gently by the upper arm, and hustled me into the bedroom. Our entrance startled the cat, who disappeared beneath the bed.

One hand on the door, as though holding it closed by force, Romero blew out a frustrated breath.

"What do you mean, make sure he's human? What else would he be?"

I shrugged.

He swore under his breath and rubbed the back of his neck. "*Please* tell me we're not talking about . . . a demon?"

I flinched. In my world, it's best not to throw around words like "demon." You just never knew who might take that as an invitation to drop in.

"Of course not," I said. The inspector relaxed until I added, "Well, probably not. Could be anything, really."

"Such as . . . ?"

"A doppelganger, a changeling . . . maybe just a freak." I looked at Romero pointedly. "Like me."

I wandered around the bedroom, checking it out. An ornate cherry armoire drew my attention, its open doors revealing a bonanza of silk and satin ladies' gowns and gentlemen's suits from another era. Late eighteen hundreds, I thought. They were stunning, and it was rare to find them in such good condition.

"What's all this?" I asked.

"Don't know and don't particularly care unless it has something to do with my murder investigation."

I reached into the closet, hugged several of the items to my chest, and concentrated.

Clothes were usually an easy read. They emitted a discernible hum, alive with the energy of the past, whispering traces of the mortals who had worn them. But not these. These were as soulless as the dead man on the dining room table.

I drew back, as unsettled by the clothing's lack of vibrations as a normal person would be to discover her T-shirt and cargo pants humming.

"What's wrong?" Romero asked.

I shook my head. I didn't know what to make of it all.

"Okay, this guy was supposedly the head of something called the Serpentarian Society—the thirteen members all had dinner here last night," Romero said, consulting his notebook. "What can you tell me about that?"

"Nothing, I'm afraid. I've never heard of the society. But Serpentarius is the thirteenth sign of the zodiac. There used to be thirteen months in a year, each with twenty-eight days, like February. Think about it: thirteen times twenty-eight is three hundred and sixty-four."

The corners of Romero's mouth tugged up in a reluctant smile. "You do that equation in your head? I'm impressed."

"Then you're also gullible." I returned his smile. "Math and I don't get along. Anyway, each month was associated with a sign: Serpentarius was the last one, following Sagittarius."

"You think this guy Serpentarius is somehow significant with respect to this murder?"

"The only thing I know about Serpentarius is that, unlike the other horoscope signs, he was a real man. A medical man, I believe. I'll find out more about him if you like, and let you know."

The sparrow appeared from wherever it had been hiding and fluttered around the room, the cat's eyes following its moves closely. I went to the window and pulled back the velvet curtains, a pair of dusty sheers, and a heavy-duty blackout shade until I finally reached a casement window that probably hadn't been opened for years. After a brief struggle it opened, and I stood back, hoping the bird would take note of the light and air and leave this unnatural place.

Instead it landed on my shoulder. The cat leapt onto the regal four-poster bed, its green-eyed gaze fixed on the sparrow, as though ready to pounce on it—and on me.

"Go on now, sugar," I turned my head and said to the bird. "Away with you."

The sparrow took me in with one bright eye, lifted its wings, and flew out the window. The cat bounded up to the window ledge and watched its quarry disappear.

"Did you just talk to that bird?" Carlos asked.

"Yes."

"You talk to animals now?"

I laughed. "A lot of people talk to animals, Inspector. It doesn't mean they understand. Watch: Come down from there, cat," I said to the feline preening on the window ledge. The cat ignored me. "See, the cat didn't obey."

"Cats never obey."

"True."

"The way the windows were covered up, maybe Zazi was afraid of the light. Like a vampire."

"Don't be ridiculous," I scoffed. "There's no such thing as vampires."

"Of course not. Changelings and ghosts and demons and doppel-whatzits? Sure—no problem. But no vampires."

"It's not the same at all," I protested, though I saw his

point. How does one separate superstition and folktale from nature and the supernatural? All sorts of supposedly imaginary creatures are, in fact, real: unicorns and elves and brownies and faeries. But others were inventions of the always fertile human imagination. Since I had never finished my witchcraft training, I was unclear on a lot of the finer points of supernatural genealogy. Looked as though I should check in with a higher authority: Aidan Rhodes, male witch and unrivaled leader of the Bay Area spooks. Speaking of whom . . .

I glanced at my vintage Tinker Bell watch, which I'd picked up for a song at a garage sale in Sunnyvale. I was late for my lesson with Rhodes, who had agreed to complete my training. I didn't trust him as far as I could throw him with a banishing spell, but I did need him. Among other things, he might be able to shed some light on the late Malachi Zazi, if not upon the identity of the murderer.

"I've got to get going, Inspector. I'll ask around, see what else I can find out," I said. "I'm sorry I wasn't more helpful; I don't feel much, and that worries me. Normally I would be on sensory overload."

"Okaaaay," Romero said, a cynical note in his voice. He had asked me here, which was no small thing, and I hadn't come through for him. It's not every day that a vintage clothing dealer and witch is called in to consult with the SFPD.

I had recently moved to San Francisco and opened a vintage clothing store, Aunt Cora's Closet, in the former hippie haven of Haight Street, near Ashbury. Though I had hoped to keep my witchcraft under wraps, Fate had other plans for me, as she so often did. Not only did I have a whole new group of friends who admired, rather than reviled, my talents; but now even the police had come to me for help. This was heady stuff for a woman who, a few short months before, had been friendless and adrift, afraid to embrace what she could not outrun: that she was a witch, through and through.

On my way out, Carlos Romero stopped me. "You want this?"

The black cat hung limply in Romero's hands, gazing at me with huge yellowish green headlamp eyes.

"I can't," I said. "I'm allergic to cats."

"I thought you witches loved cats."

"Even among witches I'm a freak."

The cat meowed. Sort of. It was more like a raspy squeak than a proper meow.

"Don't *you* need a pet?" I said. "I think it likes you."

Carlos gave me a look. "What would I do with a cat?"

"Same thing I would?"

"Listen, Lily, it's a black cat. You're a witch. Allergy or not, you two go together like white on rice. Tell you what: Take it home with you; give it a try. It'll keep your potbellied pig company."

"I am *not* taking a cat."

"All right," he said with a sigh. "Kind of a shame, though."

"Why? What are you going to do with it?"

He shrugged. "We'll call animal control. They'll take it to the pound."

"And the pound will find it a home?"

He shrugged. "They'll try, but they always have too many cats. Plus, black cats are the hardest to place. People get funny about them. Bad luck and all that . . ."

"But if they can't find a home, then . . ."

"It'll be euthanized. Don't worry—they'll make it quick." Romero stroked the cat's soft, thick fur. It purred. "Sure hate to see it happen to this li'l fella. Zazi wasn't the murderer's only victim."

I knew he was playing me. I knew it.

"You are an evil man, Inspector."

I took the cat.

ALSO AVAILABLE
FROM

Juliet Blackwell

Secondhand Spirits
A Witchcraft Mystery

Lily Ivory feels that she can finally fit in
somewhere and conceal her "witchiness" in San
Francisco. It's there that she opens her vintage
clothing shop, outfitting customers both
spiritually and stylistically.

Just when things seem normal, a client is
murdered and children start disappearing from the
Bay Area. Lily has a good idea that some bad
phantoms are behind it. Can she keep her
identity secret, or will her witchy ways be forced
out of the closet as she attempts to stop
the phantom?

**Available wherever books are sold or at
penguin.com**

S0056

FROM

VICTORIA LAURIE

The Psychic Eye Mysteries

Abby Cooper is a psychic intuitive.
And trying to help the police solve crimes
seems like a good enough idea—but it
could land her in more trouble than even
she could see coming.

<u>AVAILABLE IN THE SERIES</u>
Abby Cooper, Psychic Eye
Better Read Than Dead
A Vision of Murder
Killer Insight
Crime Seen
Death Perception
Doom with a View

Available wherever books are sold or at
penguin.com

OM0014

GET CLUED IN

Ever wonder how to find out about all the
latest Berkley Prime Crime and
Obsidian mysteries?

berkleyobsidianmysteries.com

- See what's new
- Find author appearances
- Win fantastic prizes
- Get reading recommendations
- Sign up for the mystery newsletter
- Chat with authors and other fans
- Read interviews with authors you love

Mystery Solved.

PO #: 0003242519